By Sue Grafton

Kinsey Millhone mysteries:

*Published by The Ballantine Publishing Group
**Published by Bantam Books

"P" IS FOR PERIL

Sue Grafton

BALLANTINE BOOKS • NEW YORK

A Ballantine Book
Published by The Ballantine Publishing Group
Copyright © 2001 by Sue Grafton

www.ballantinebooks.com

ISBN 0-345-44980-0

This edition published by arrangement with G. P. Putnam's Sons, a member of Penguin Putnam Inc.

Manufactured in the United States of America

First Ballantine Books International Edition: February 2002

10 9 8 7 6 5 4 3 2 1

THIS BOOK IS DEDICATED TO

The Santa Barbara Police Department and
the late Richard Breza, Santa Barbara Police Chief

The Santa Barbara County Sheriff's Department

The Santa Barbara County Coroner's Office

and

Harriet Miller, Mayor of Santa Barbara

With appreciation for your competence,
integrity, dedication, and generosity of spirit.

Acknowledgments

The author wishes to acknowledge the invaluable assistance of the following people: Steven Humphrey; Captain Ed Aasted (ret.) and Sergeant Brian Abbott, Santa Barbara Police Department; Melinda Johnson; Jamie Raney, attorney-at-law; Sam Eaton, attorney-at-law; Lynn McLaren, private investigator; E. Robert Jones, DDS; Hildy Hoffman, Santa Barbara's Mayor's Office; Robert Failing, M.D., forensic pathologist (ret.); Judy Crippen; Tracy Brown; Norm Arnold; Sheila Harker, Lynn Lazaro, R.N., and Joyce Tevenan, R.N.; Leslie Minschke, RHIA; Ron Shenkman of Ron Shenkman & Associates; Lorna Backus, Santa Barbara County Department of Vital Statistics; John Hunt, CompuVision; Jamie Clark; and Neville Blakemore.

With a special thank you to Alan Cates, Chief, Medi-Cal Fraud Prevention Bureau, State of California.

"P"
IS
FOR
PERIL

1

THE HOUSE ON Old Reservoir Road appeared to be in the final phases of construction. I spotted the site as I rounded the curve, recognizing the unfinished structure from Fiona Purcell's description. To my right, I could see a portion of the reservoir for which the road was named. Brunswick Lake fills the bottom of a geological bowl, a spring-fed body that supplied the town with drinking water for many years. In 1953 a second, larger catch basin was established, and now Brunswick is little more than an irregular blue splotchlet on maps of the area. Swimming and boating are forbidden, but seasonally the migrating water birds rest on the placid surface as they make their way south. The surrounding hills are austere, gentle swells rising to the mountains that mark the northernmost boundary of the Santa Teresa city limits.

I parked my VW on the gravel berm and crossed the two-lane road. The steeply pitched lot was still bare of landscaping and consisted entirely of raw dirt and boulders with a dusting of weeds taking hold. At street level, a big commercial Dumpster was piled high with debris. A small grove of signs planted in the yard announced the names of the

1

building contractor, the painting contractor, and the architect, though Mrs. Purcell had been quick to assure me by phone that she'd drawn up the plans herself. The design—if that's what you want to call it—would have been approved by the Department of Defense: an implacable series of concrete boxes, staunch and unadorned, stacked up against the hillside under a pale November sun. The facade was as blank as a bunker, a radical contrast to the sprawling Spanish-style homes on adjacent properties. Somewhere to the rear of the house, there must have been a driveway leading to garages and a parking pad, but I opted for the stairs built into the barren hillside. At six A.M., I'd done a three-mile jog, but I'd skipped my Friday-morning weight lifting to keep this early appointment. It was just now eight o'clock and I could feel my butt dragging as I mounted the steps.

Behind me, I could hear a dog bark. Its deep-throated yaps echoed through the canyon, conveying a message of excitement. A woman was calling, "Trudy! *Truuddy!*" while the dog barked on. She emitted a piercing whistle, and a young German shepherd came bounding over the hill, heading in my direction at full speed. I waited, bracing myself for the force of muddy feet, but at the last possible second, the whistle came again and the dog sprinted off. I continued climbing Fiona's wide concrete steps, tacking twice before I reached the upper terrace with its plain limestone portico that shaded the front entrance. By then, my thighs were burning, I was huffing and puffing, and my heart was *rat-a-tat-tatting* like machine-gun fire. I could have sworn there was less oxygen in the air up here, but I'd actually only climbed the equivalent of two stories and I knew it was probably no more than three- to four-hundred feet above sea level. I turned, pretending to admire the view while I recovered my breath.

From this aerie, I could see the broad, shimmering band of the Pacific Ocean stitched to the shoreline some five miles away. Before me, the day was so clear, I could almost count the mountain ridges on the islands twenty-six miles out. Behind me, the clouds were peering over the mountaintops, a fast-moving blanket of dark gray in advance of a storm. San Francisco, four hundred miles to the north of us, was already feeling its lash.

By the time I rang the bell, my breathing had slowed and I'd done a quick mental review of the subject I was here to discuss. Fiona Purcell's ex-husband, Dr. Dowan Purcell, had been missing for nine weeks. She'd had a messenger deliver a manila envelope filled with newspaper clippings that recapped events surrounding his disappearance. I'd sat in my office, tilted back in my swivel chair, my Sauconys propped on the edge of my desk while I studied the articles she'd sent. She'd arranged them chronologically but had otherwise presented them without editorial comment. I'd been following the story in the local papers, but I'd never anticipated my involvement in the case. I found it helpful to have the sequence laid out again in this truncated form.

I noticed that over the course of nine weeks, the character of the coverage had shifted from the first seventy-two hours of puzzlement, through days of feverish speculation, and into the holding pattern that represented the current state of the investigation. Nothing new had come to light—not that there was ever much to report. In the absence of fresh revelations, the public's fascination had begun to dwindle and the media's attention to the matter had become as chilly and abbreviated as the brief November days. It is a truth of human nature that we can ponder life's mysteries for only so long before we lose interest and move on to something else. Dr. Purcell had been gone since Friday, September 12, and the lengthy column inches initially devoted to his disappearance were now reduced to an occasional mention nearly ritual in its tone. The details were recounted, but the curiosity had shifted to more compelling events.

Dr. Purcell, sixty-nine years old, had practiced family medicine in Santa Teresa since 1944, specializing in geriatrics for the last fifteen years. He'd retired in 1981. Six months later, he'd been licensed as the administrator of a nursing care facility called Pacific Meadows, which was owned by two businessmen. On the Friday night in question, he'd worked late, remaining in his office to review paperwork related to the operation of the nursing home. According to witnesses, it was close to nine o'clock when he stopped at the front desk and said good-night to the nurses on duty. At that hour, the occupants had settled down for the night. The corridors were empty and the residents' doors were closed against the already dimmed hall lights. Dr. Purcell had paused to chat with an elderly woman sitting in the lobby in her wheelchair. After a cursory conversation, less than a minute by her report, the doctor passed through the front door and into the night. He retrieved his car from his reserved space at the north side of the complex, pulled out of the lot, and drove off into the Inky Void from which he'd never emerged. The Santa Teresa Police and the Santa Teresa County Sheriff's Departments had devoted endless hours to the case, and I couldn't think what avenues remained that hadn't already been explored by local law enforcement.

I rang the bell again. Fiona Purcell had told me she was on her way out of town, a five-day trip to San Francisco to purchase furniture and antiques for a client of her interior design firm. According to the papers, Fiona and the doctor had been divorced for years. Idly, I was wondering why she'd been the one who called me instead of his current wife, Crystal.

I saw a face appear in one of the two glass panels that flanked the entrance. When she opened the door, I saw that she was already dressed for travel in a double-breasted pin-striped suit with wide lapels. She held a hand out. "Ms. Millhone? Fiona Purcell. Sorry to make you wait. I was at the back of the house. Please come in."

"Thanks. You can call me Kinsey if you like. Nice meeting you," I said.

We shook hands and I moved into the entrance hall. Her handshake was limp, always startling in someone who, otherwise, seems brisk and businesslike. I placed her in her late sixties, close to Dr. Purcell's age. Her hair was dyed a dark brown, parted on one side, with puffy bangs and clusters of artificially constructed curls pulled away from her face and secured by rhinestone combs, a style affected by glamour-girl movie stars of the 1940s. I half-expected an appearance by John Agar or Fred MacMurray, some poor, feckless male who'd fallen prey to this vixen with her fierce shoulder pads. She was saying, "We can talk in the living room. You'll have to pardon the mess."

Scaffolding had been erected in the foyer, reaching to the lofty ceiling. Drop cloths lined the stairs and the wide corridor leading to the rear of the house. To one side of the stairs, there was a console table and a streamlined chrome lamp. Currently, we seemed to be the only two on the premises.

"Your flight's at ten?" I asked.

"Don't worry about it. I'm eight minutes from the airport. We have at least an hour. May I offer you coffee? I'm having mine in here."

"No, thanks. I've had two cups this morning and that's my limit most days."

Fiona moved to the right and I followed in her wake, crossing a broad expanse of bare cement. I said, "When do the floors go in?"

"These *are* the floors."

I said, "Ah," and made a mental note to quit asking about matters far beyond my ken.

The interior of the house had the cool, faintly damp smell of plaster and fresh paint. All the walls in range were a dazzling white, the windows tall and stark, unadorned by any curtains or drapes. A sly glance behind me revealed what was probably the dining room on the far side of the entry-way, empty of furniture, subdivided by rhomboids of clear morning light. The echo of our footsteps sounded like a small parade.

In the living room, Fiona gestured toward one of two matching armchairs, chunky and oversized, upholstered in a neutral-toned fabric that blended with the gray cement floor. A large area rug showed a densely woven grid of black lines on gray. I sat when she did, watching as she surveyed the space with the practiced eye of an aesthete. The furnishings were striking: light wood, tubular steel, stark geometric shapes. An enormous round mirror, resting in a crescent of chrome, hung above the fireplace. A tall silver and ivory coffeepot, with a matching creamer and sugar bowl, sat on a silver tray on the beveled-glass coffee table. She paused to refill her cup. "Are you a fan of art deco?"

"I don't know much about it."

"I've been collecting for years. The rug's a Da Silva Bruhns. This is Wolfgang Tumpel's work, if you're familiar with the name," she said, nodding at the coffee service.

"Beautiful," I murmured, clueless.

"Most of these pieces are one of a kind, created by craftsmen who were masters in their day. I'd go on rattling the names off, but I doubt they'd mean much if you're not ac-quainted with the period. I built this as a showcase for my col-lection, but as soon as the house is finished, I'll probably sell it and move on. I'm impatient by nature and far too restless to stay here long." She had strong features: thinly arched brows and dark, smudged eyes, with pronounced streaks of weari-ness descending from the inner corners. She took a sip of coffee and then paused to extract a cigarette from a pack sit-ting on the table. The lighter she used was one of those small gold items and made very little sound when she flipped the cover back and thumbed the striker wheel. She held the lighter in her palm and drew deeply on her cigarette, clearly savoring the relief. She tilted her head toward the ceiling and blew the smoke out in a stream. I figured I could always drop my blazer at the cleaners on the way home.

She said, "I don't think I mentioned this when we chatted the other day, but Dana Glazer suggested I get in touch with you. I believe she was Dana Jaffe when you were acquainted with her."

"Really. How do you know her?"

"I'm helping her redecorate her home. She's now married to one of Dow's associates, Joel Glazer, whose first wife died. Do you know Joel? He's a partner in a company called Century Comprehensive that owns a chain of nursing homes among other things."

"I know the name Glazer from the papers. I've never met him," I said. Her call was beginning to make sense, though I still wasn't sure how I could be of service. Dana Jaffe's first husband, Wendell, had disappeared in 1979, though the circumstances—on the surface—were very different from the current case. Wendell Jaffe was a self-made real estate tycoon who'd faked his own death, showing up in Mexico shortly after his "widow" had collected half a million dollars in life insurance benefits. Wendell was facing jail time after a Ponzi scheme he'd cooked up threatened to unravel, exposing his chicanery. The "pseudocide" was his attempt to avoid the inevitable felony conviction. He might have pulled it off, but he'd been spotted in Mexico by a former acquaintance, and I'd been dispatched by the insurance company, who wanted their money back. I wondered if Fiona suspected her ex-husband had pulled a fast one as well.

She set her coffee cup aside. "You received the articles?"

"A messenger dropped them off at the office yesterday. I read them last night and then again this morning. The police have been thorough. . . ."

"Or so they'd like us to think."

"You're not happy with their progress?"

"Progress! What progress? Dowan is still missing. I'll tell you what they've accomplished: zilch. I grant you, they're going through the motions—making public pronouncements, trumpeting their concerns—but it's all sound and fury, signifying nothing."

I objected to her attitude but decided not to protest just yet. I think the cops are terrific, but why argue the point? She wanted to hire me and I was here to determine what, if anything, I could contribute. "What's the latest?" I asked.

"No one's heard a peep from him—at least as far as I've been told." She took another drag on her cigarette and then tapped the ash into a heavy crystal ashtray. Her lipstick was dark and bled into the fine hairline crevices along her upper lip. She'd left a distinct half-moon on the coffee cup and a full ring around the filter of her cigarette. Her jewelry was clunky: big clip-on silver earrings and a matching bracelet. The effect was stylish, but everything about her suggested estate sales and vintage clothing shops. I fancied if I'd bent close, I'd have picked up the whiff of moth balls and cedar closets, mingled with scents from the '40s, Shalimar and Old Golds. In moments, her looks were striking, harsh flickers of beauty she seemed at pains to accentuate. She lowered her eyes. "Of course, you realize we're divorced."

"There was reference to that in one of the articles you sent. What about his current wife?"

"I've only spoken to Crystal once throughout this whole ordeal. She's gone to great lengths to keep me out of the loop. I receive updates through my daughters, who've made it a point to stay in close touch with her. Without them, I'd have even less information than I do, which God knows, isn't much."

"You have two girls?"

"Correct. My youngest, Blanche, and her husband are only four blocks away. Melanie, the older one, lives in San Francisco. I'll be staying with her 'til Tuesday afternoon of next week."

"Any grandchildren?"

"Mel's never been married. Blanche is expecting her fifth in about three weeks."

I said, "Wow."

Fiona's smile was sour. "Motherhood's just her way of avoiding a real job."

"A 'real' job sounds easier. I couldn't do what she does."

"She barely manages herself. Fortunately, the children have a nanny who's extremely competent."

"How do your daughters get along with Crystal?"

"Fine, I suppose. Then again, what choice do they have? If they don't dance to her tune, she'll make sure they never see their father or their half-brother again. You know Dow and Crystal have a son? His name is Griffith. He just turned two."

"I remember mention of the boy. May I call you Fiona?"

She took another drag of her cigarette and placed it on the lip of the ashtray in front of her. "I'd prefer Mrs. Purcell, if it's all the same to you." Smoke trailed from her mouth as she spoke and she seemed to study it, bemused.

"Yes, well. I'm wondering if you have a theory about your ex-husband's disappearance."

"You're one of the few who's even bothered to ask. Apparently, my opinion is of no concern. I suspect he's in Europe or South America, biding his time until he's ready to come home. Crystal thinks he's dead—or so I've heard."

"It's not so far-fetched. According to the papers, there's been no activity on his credit cards. There's been no sign of his car and no sign of him."

"Well, that's not quite true. There've been a number of reports. People claim to have spotted him as far away as New Orleans and Seattle. He was seen getting on a plane at JFK and again south of San Diego, heading for Mexico."

"There are still sightings of Elvis. That doesn't mean he's alive and well."

"True. On the other hand, someone fitting Dow's description tried to cross into Canada but walked away when the immigration officer asked to see his passport, which is missing, by the way."

"Really. That's interesting. The papers didn't mention it. I take it the police have followed up?"

"One can only hope," she remarked. There was something hollow in her tone. If she could only persuade *me*, then perhaps what she said would turn out to be true.

"You're convinced he's alive?"

"I can't imagine otherwise. The man has no enemies and I can't conceive of his being the victim of 'foul play,' " she said, forming the quote marks with her fingers. "The idea's absurd."

"Because?"

"Dow's perfectly capable of taking care of himself— physically, at any rate. What he's not capable of doing is facing the problems in life. He's passive. Instead of fight or flight, he lies down and plays dead—in a manner of speaking. He'd rather do anything than deal with conflict, especially involving women. This goes back to his mother, but that's another story altogether."

"Has he done anything like this before?"

"As a matter of fact, he has. I tried to explain this to the police detective. In vain, I might add. Dowan's done this twice. The first time, Melanie and Blanche were—what?—probably only six and three. Dowan disappeared for three weeks. He left without warning and returned much the same way."

"Where'd he go?"

"I have no idea. The second time was similar. This was years later, before we separated for good. One day he was here; the next, he was gone. He came back a few weeks later without a murmur of explanation or apology. Naturally, I've assumed this recent disappearance was a repeat performance."

"What prompted his departure on those earlier occasions?"

Her gesture was vague, smoke trailing from the tip of her cigarette. "I suppose we were having problems. We usually were. At any rate, Dow kept saying he needed time to clear his head—whatever that means. One day soon after that he simply didn't come home. He'd canceled his appointments, including social engagements, all without a word to me or to anyone else. The first I became aware was when he failed to arrive for dinner. The second time was the same except, I didn't go out of my mind with worry."

"So in both of those instances, he behaved much as he did this time?"

"Exactly. The first time, it took *hours* before I realized he was gone. The man's a doctor and, naturally, he was often delayed. By midnight, I was wild—close to hysterical. I thought I'd go mad."

"You called the police?"

"I called everyone I could think of. Then first thing the next morning, a note arrived in the mail. He said he'd come home eventually, which is exactly what he did. I was furious, of course, but he seemed totally unconcerned. Fool that I am, I forgave him and we went on as before. The marriage was good, or good enough from my perspective. I thought he was happy—until this business with Crystal. For all I know, he'd been fooling around with her for years."

"What made you stay?"

"I thought he was a good husband. That's how innocent I was. He tended to be distant, but I didn't fault him—at least, on a conscious level. I might have harbored resentments, but I wasn't aware of them. Looking back, I realize there are many ways a man can disappear."

"Such as?"

She shrugged, stubbing out her cigarette. "Television, sleep, alcohol, books, uppers, downers. I'm speaking in general terms, but you get my drift."

"And in his case?"

"Dow buried himself in his work. Went in early, stayed at the office until all hours of the night. What you have to understand about him is, he's someone who avoids disagreements. That's why he loves the elderly—because they make no real demands on him. Being a physician gives him status, which has always been better, in his mind, than having to be accountable like any ordinary mortal."

"How long were you married?"

"Close to forty years. We met at Syracuse. I was majoring in art history and he was pre-med. We married shortly after graduation. Dow went on to medical school at Penn State and did his internship and residency out here. By then, we had the girls. I stayed home with them until they were both in school and then I went back and got my master's in interior design. I designed the house we built soon afterward in Horton Ravine. Of course, we hired an architect to handle all the nuts and bolts."

"He still owns that house?"

"Yes, though Crystal doesn't care for it from what I've heard."

"You didn't ask for the house in the settlement?"

"I couldn't afford the mortgage and upkeep. To hear him tell it, he was fleeced. Strictly his point of view. Believe me, he got the better deal. He probably paid someone off—the judge, my lawyer. You know how men stick together when it comes to the almighty buck."

I noticed she was busy shading my perception, scoring points for her team. Divorced folk always seem to angle for your sympathy, casting themselves in the best possible light. It seemed odd, in this case, when the reason for my visit was to see if I could be of help in the search for him. Was she still in love with the man? "It must have been difficult when the marriage broke up," I murmured.

"Humiliating. Devastating. It was such a cliché. Doctor

goes through a midlife crisis, leaves his middle-aged wife to take up with some whore."

The papers had had a field day with the fact that Crystal had been a stripper. Still, I questioned Fiona's use of the word "whore." Stripping, as a way of earning money, doesn't necessarily translate into hookerdom. For all we knew, Crystal might have earned *her* master's in psychiatric social work. "How did he meet her?"

"You'd have to ask her that. The truth is, Dow developed an appetite for . . . mmm . . . unusual sexual practices. His hormones were off or his anxiety levels began to climb as he aged. Possibly his problems harked back to his mother. Everything else connects to his relationship with her. Whatever the reason, once Dowan turned sixty, he began to falter. He couldn't . . . let's say . . . 'perform' without stimulus. Pornography, marital aids . . ."

"Which didn't appeal to you."

"I thought it was *revolting*. I can't even tell you the practices he wanted to pursue—unspeakable acts that I refused even to discuss with him. He finally stopped pressing."

"Because he'd taken up with her?"

"Evidently. He's never admitted it, but I'm sure he went looking. It did cross my mind he'd go out and find someone willing to submit to his perverse requests. I certainly wouldn't do it and I knew I'd made myself entirely clear on that point."

I was secretly panting for an example, but I thought it was wiser (for once) to keep my big mouth shut. Sometimes you don't want to know what people do—or refuse to do—in private. If I had occasion to meet the doctor one day, I didn't want to be distracted by an image of him cavorting in the nude with an organic carrot up his butt. "Did you ask for the divorce or did he?"

"He did. I was completely taken off-guard. I presumed he'd get his needs met outside the marriage and keep his family intact. I never thought he'd stoop to divorce at this late stage in his life. I should have known. Dowan's weak. Not that any of us relish owning up to our mistakes, but Dow always abhorred even the *appearance* of failure."

"Meaning what?"

"Well," she said, lowering her eyes. I watched her gaze dance across the floor. "I suspect his relationship with Crystal is not the union of souls he'd like others to believe. Some months ago, he'd heard she was screwing around on him. Better to disappear than admit he'd been cuckolded."

"Did he have any idea who it was?"

"No, but he was looking into it. After he disappeared, my friend Dana finally confided that she'd known the whole time. The fellow is Crystal's personal trainer. His name is Clint Augustine."

I heard a little *ding-dong* going off in my head. I was sure I'd heard the name before, possibly in the gym where I work out.

"You believe he left because of that?"

"Yes. We had a conversation—a long talk—on September 10. This was two days before he vanished. He was dreadfully unhappy."

"He said that?"

Her hesitation was distinct as she debated with herself. "Not in so many words, but you don't go through forty years of marriage without learning to read between the lines."

"What occasioned the conversation?"

"He came over to the house."

"You were seeing him," I stated.

"Well, yes. At his request," she said, her tone faintly defensive. "Dow adores this place, just as he adores the house in Horton Ravine. He was always interested in my design work, even before our relationship underwent the shift. Lately, he'd been stopping by in the evenings to have a drink with me. That night, he was exhausted. His face was *gray* with worry, and when I asked what was wrong, he said the pressures at the office were driving him insane. And Crystal was no help. She's extremely narcissistic, as you'll discover when you meet her, which I assume you will."

"Were you surprised he'd confide in you after everything he'd put you through?"

"Who else does he have? Anyway, he didn't really talk about her, but I could see the tension in his eyes. He'd aged a good ten years in a matter of months."

"You're saying he had problems at home as well as problems at work?"

"That's right. He didn't talk specifics, but he mentioned in passing that he needed to get away. That's the first thing I thought of when I heard he was gone."

"Couldn't that have been wishful thinking?"

"I suppose it could," she said. "I mean, he didn't pull out airline tickets, but he did seem desperate."

"Do you remember a reference to any place in particular?"

She tilted her head. "I've racked my brain, but I really can't remember. It was an offhand remark and I didn't think much about it until this came up."

"I assume you told the police."

Again, she hesitated. "Not at first. I thought his absence was voluntary and he'd come home when he was ready. I didn't want him to be embarrassed. Leave it to Crystal to turn this ordeal into a media circus."

I could feel myself bristle. "Mrs. Purcell, he's a prominent physician, well known and loved in this community. His disappearance is bound to attract media attention. If you thought he'd gone AWOL, why didn't you speak up?"

"I felt he was entitled to his privacy," she said, her cheeks coloring slightly.

"What about all the time and money being spent on the investigation? Weren't you at all concerned about that?"

"Of course. That's why I spoke to the police," she said. "After six weeks, I began to worry. I guess I was expecting a call or a note, *some* indication he was all right, wherever he was. Now that nine weeks have passed, I thought it was time to take matters into my own hands."

"What made you think he'd be in touch with you instead of her?"

"Because Crystal's the one he's been trying to escape."

"And now you're worried something's happened to him."

"I suppose so. That's why I decided to meet with the detective last week. Odessa was polite. He took notes. But I got the impression he didn't take me seriously. He said he'd get back to me, but that's the last I've heard. The police must be working *dozens* of other cases, which means they don't have the time or resources to devote to Dow. I said as much to Dana and she agrees. That's why she recommended you."

"I don't know what to say. Even if we come to some agreement, I can't spend twenty-four hours a day on this any more than the police can. I have other clients, too."

"I didn't say you'd have to be exclusive."

"Even so, I'm just one person. You'd be better off with a big Los Angeles agency, one with lots of operatives who can fan out across the country and do this properly. You might end up having to search for him overseas."

She cut me off with a wave of her hand. "I don't want a big L.A. agency. I want someone local who's willing to report directly to me."

"But all I'd be doing is repeating what the police have already done."

"You might have ideas they haven't thought of yet. After all, you tracked down Wendell Jaffe *years* after everyone assumed he was dead."

"I did track him down, but I didn't start from scratch. Someone spotted him in Mexico and that's why the case finally broke."

Her expression became withdrawn. "You won't help."

"I'm not saying that. I'm talking about reality, which doesn't look that good."

"But what if there's an angle the police have overlooked?"

"What if there's not?"

"Then at least I'd be satisfied with the job they've done."

I was silent for a beat, staring at the floor. Inside, a little voice was yelling, *"No, no, no!"* while my mouth said, "I'll do what I can, but I make no promises."

"Good. That's wonderful. We'll talk on Tuesday. Just keep track of the time you put in and you can give me an invoice as soon as I get back." She glanced at her watch and then rose to her feet.

I stood when she did. "I'll need a retainer."

"A 'retainer'?" She made a show of startlement, but I wondered if she was repeating the words for effect. Surely she didn't do business without a written agreement and earnest money changing hands. "How much did you have in mind?"

"I charge fifty an hour or a flat four hundred a day, plus expenses, so fifteen hundred dollars should cover it for now. If you give me Melanie's address, I'll overnight you a contract for your signature." In truth, I could have brought one with me, but I hadn't been sure we'd end up coming to an agreement.

She blinked as though baffled. "I'm sorry. I didn't picture anything so *formal*. Is this standard procedure in your line of work?"

"Actually, it is," I said. I noticed she didn't call it a "profession," which meant she probably lumped me in with retail clerks, short-order cooks, and Roto-Rooter men.

"What if you fail to find him?"

"That's exactly the point. If I come up empty-handed, you might decide I wasn't worth the hourly wage. Once I take a case, I persevere. I'll follow the trial right out to the bitter end."

"I should hope so," she said. She thought about it briefly,

and then she crossed to an ebony-inlaid console. She removed her checkbook, returned to her chair, and sat down. "And I'm to make the check out to . . . ?"

"Millhone Investigations."

I watched while she dashed off a check and tore it out of the book, scarcely bothering to disguise her irritation as she handed it to me. I noticed we were bank mates, sharing the same branch of the Santa Teresa City Bank. I said, "You're upset."

"I operate on trust. Apparently, you don't."

"I've learned the hard way. It's nothing personal."

"I see."

I held out the check. "I can return this right now if you'd prefer."

"Just find him. I'll expect a full report the minute I get home."

2

BEFORE I LEFT Fiona's, she gave me Melanie's home address in San Francisco, along with her home and office numbers. I couldn't imagine the need to call Fiona up there. She also gave me Crystal's Horton Ravine address and phone number. I'd never met Detective Odessa, whom Fiona'd mentioned in passing, but a conversation with him was the first item on my list. Driving back into town, I noticed my stomach had begun to churn with anxiety. I tried to pinpoint my doubts, laying them out one by one, though not necessarily in the order of importance.

1. I didn't particularly like—or trust—Fiona. She hadn't been candid with the cops and I didn't think she was being entirely candid with me. Under the circumstances, I probably should have declined to take the job. Already I was regretting the haste with which I'd agreed.

2. I wasn't sure I could be effective. I'm often uneasy at the outset of an investigation, especially one like this. Nine weeks had passed since Dr. Purcell was last seen. Whatever the circumstances surrounding a disappearance, the

passage of time seldom works in your favor. Witnesses embellish. They invent. The memory grows foggy. The truth tends to blur with repetition, and details are altered to suit various personal interpretations. People want to be helpful, which means they embroider their stories, coloring events according to their biases as the situation drags on. Entering the game this late, I knew the likelihood of my making any critical discovery was almost out of the question. Fiona did have a point in that sometimes a fresh perspective can shift the focus of an investigation. All well and good, but intuition was telling me that any break in the case was going to be the result of serendipity, a term synonymous with unadulterated dumb luck.

3. I didn't like the bullshit about the retainer.

I stopped off at McDonald's and ordered coffee and a couple of Egg McMuffins. I needed the comfort of junk food as well as the nourishment, if that's what you want to call it. I munched while I drove, eating with such eagerness I bit my own index finger.

I might as well take a moment here to identify myself. My name is Kinsey Millhone. I'm a licensed private investigator in Santa Teresa, California, which is ninety-five miles north of Los Angeles. I'm female, thirty-six, twice divorced, childless, and otherwise unencumbered. Aside from my car, I don't own much in the way of material possessions. My business, Millhone Investigations, consists entirely of me. I was a cop for two years early in my twenties, and through personal machinations too tedious to explain, I realized law enforcement didn't suit me. I was way too crabby and uncooperative to adjust to department regulations, with all the ethics clauses thrown in: I have been known to bend the rules. Plus, the shoes were clunky and the uniform and the belt made my ass look too wide.

Having left gainful city employment, I apprenticed myself
to a two-man office of private investigators, where I put in the
hours necessary to apply for my license. I've been on my own
now for a good ten years, licensed, bonded, and heavily insured. A good portion of the last decade, I spent pursuing
arson and wrongful death claims for California Fidelity Insurance, first as a bona fide employee, later as an independent
contractor. We came to a parting of the ways three years ago
in October 1983. Since then, I've rented space from the law
firm of Kingman and Ives, an arrangement that I'd begun to
suspect was on the verge of change.

For the past year, Lonnie Kingman had been complaining
about the shortage of space. He'd already expanded once,
taking over the entire third floor of a building he owns free
and clear. He'd now purchased a second building, this one on
lower State Street, where he intended to relocate as soon as
escrow closed. He'd found a tenant for our current digs, and
the only question that remained was whether I'd go with him
or find an office of my own. I'm a loner at heart, and while
I'm fond of Lonnie, the whole idea of working in close contact with other people had begun to get on my nerves. I found
myself going into the office nights and weekends, spending
half my days working from home—anything to create the
sense of space and solitude. I'd talked to a real estate broker
about month-to-month rentals, and I'd responded to several
classified ads. So far I hadn't seen anything that really struck
my fancy. My requirements were modest: room for my desk,
swivel chair, file cabinets, and a few fake plants. In addition, I
pictured a small but tasteful executive potty. The problem was
that everything I liked was too large or too expensive, and
anything that fit my budget was too cramped, too shabby, or
too far from downtown. I spend a lot of time at the Hall of
Records and I like to be within walking distance of the courthouse, the police station, and the public library. Lonnie's office was a haven, and he doubles as my attorney if the shit hits

the fan—which it very often does. The choice was tough and I still wasn't sure what I wanted to do.

As soon as I reached the two-hundred block of east Capillo, where Lonnie's office was located, I began the usual search-and-seizure mission, hunting for a parking place. One drawback to the current building was the tiny lot attached, which held only twelve cars. Lonnie and his partner were each assigned a slot, as were their two secretaries, Ida Ruth Kenner and Jill Stahl. The remaining eight spots went to the building's other tenants, so the rest of us were forced to ferret out parking where we could. Today I nosed my way into a short length of curb between two commercial driveways, a spot I could have sworn was almost legal. It was only later I discovered I'd been wrong.

I walked the five blocks to the office, climbed the requisite two flights of stairs, and let myself into the suite through an unmarked side door. I crossed the interior hallway to my office, unlocked the door, and stepped in, carefully avoiding Ida Ruth and Jill, who were deep in conversation a short distance away. I knew the subject matter would be the same one they'd been debating for the past two months. Lonnie's partner, John Ives, had urged the firm to hire his niece as the receptionist when the position became open. Jeniffer was eighteen years old and a recent high school graduate. This was her first job and despite being given a lengthy written job description, she seemed thoroughly perplexed about what was expected of her. She showed up for work in T-shirts and miniskirts, her long blond hair hanging down to her waist, legs bare, feet shoved into wood-soled clogs. Her phone voice was chirpy, her spelling was atrocious, and she couldn't seem to get the hang of coming in on time. She also took frequent two- to four-day vacations whenever her unemployed friends headed off to play. Ida Ruth and Jill were constantly exasperated at having to pick up the slack. Both bellyached to me, apparently reluctant to complain to Lonnie or John. Petty office politics have never held much appeal, which was yet another reason I was leaning toward a change in venue. Where I'd once been attracted to the sense of family I felt at the firm, now all I saw were attendant psychodramas. Jeniffer was Cinderella with a diminutive IQ. Ida Ruth and Jill, like the spiteful stepsisters, were simperingly nice to her in person but talked about her behind her back every chance they could. I'm not sure what part I played, but I did my best to avoid participation by hiding in my room. Clearly, I was no more adept at resolving conflicts than anyone else.

In the interests of escape, I put a call through to the Santa Teresa Police Department and asked to speak to Detective Odessa He was in a meeting, but the woman who took my call said he'd be free in a bit. I made an appointment for 10:30. I filled in a boiler plate contract and slipped it in an Express Mail envelope that I addressed to Fiona in care of Melanie's home in San Francisco. I tucked the whole of it in my handbag and then sat at my desk, making deeply symbolic doodles on my blotter between rounds of solitaire. It's not as though I didn't have a ton of other work to do, but I found myself distracted by the information circulating through my brain. I finally pulled out a manila folder and a yellow legal pad and started taking notes.

At 10:20 I locked my door and walked over to the post office, then continued to the police station, which was four blocks away. The morning air was chilly and the earlier pale sunlight had faded as the sky clouded over with the first hint of rain. The Santa Teresa "rainy" season is unpredictable. Intermittent periods of precipitation once began in mid-January and extend willy-nilly into early March. Of late, weather extremes in other parts of the world have resulted in capricious deviations. From late May until October, rain levels can still be measured in fractions of an inch, but the winter months now vary, and this one was shaping up to be one of the wettest in years. A cold front was moving down from Alaska, pushing a raw wind ahead of it. The tree branches moved restlessly, bending and creaking, while dried palm fronds broke loose and swept along the sidewalks like brooms.

The lobby at the police station seemed cozy by comparison. On my left, a small boy sat waiting on the wooden bench while his father talked to the civilian clerk about copies of an accident report. I moved to the L-shaped counter, where a uniformed officer monitored the walk-in trade. I told him of my appointment and he relayed the information to Detective Odessa's desk by phone. "He'll be right out."

I waited where I was, glancing idly into Records across the counter to my right. My friend Emerald had taken early retirement, leaving me with no buddy to slip me information. She'd never actually violated department policy, but she'd come close a few times.

Detective Odessa opened the door and stuck his head around the frame. "Ms. Millhone?"

"That's me."

"Vince Odessa," he said, and we shook hands. "Come on back."

I said, "Thanks." He handed me a visitor's badge that I clipped to my lapel.

He wore a blue dress shirt, a dark tie, chinos, dark socks, and shiny black shoes. His hair was dark and the back of his head was flat, as though he'd slept on his back for his entire infancy. He was taller than I, probably five foot nine to my five foot six. He held the door, allowing me to pass into the corridor in front of him. I paused and he took the lead. He walked ahead of me and turned left, passing through a door marked INVESTIGATIONS. I followed him through a warren of small offices. Over his shoulder, he said, "Shelly mentioned this was in regard to Dr. Purcell."

"That's right. His ex-wife hired me to look into his disappearance."

Odessa kept his tone neutral. "I had a feeling that was coming. She was in here last week."

"What'd you make of her?"

"I'll have to take the Fifth. You on the clock?"

"I haven't deposited her check. I thought it'd be smart to talk to you first."

His "office" was tucked into a standard cubicle: shoulder-high gray walls carpeted in a tight synthetic loop. He took a seat at his desk, offering me the only other chair in the compact space. Framed photos of his family were arranged in front of him: wife, three daughters, and a son. A small metal bookcase behind him was neatly lined with department manuals, texts, and assorted law books. He was clean-shaven except for a line of whiskers he'd missed when his razor jumped over the cleft in his chin. His dark brows were fierce over dark blue eyes. "So what can I help you with?"

"I'm not sure. I'd love to hear what you have, if you're willing to share."

"I got no problem with that," he said. He leaned forward, checking through a stack of thick files on one side of his desk. He pulled a three-ring binder from the bottom of the pile and set it in front of him. "Place is a mess. They tell us we're switching over to computers in the next six, eight months. Paperless office. You believe that stuff?"

"It'd be nice, but I doubt it."

"So do I," he said. He leafed through numerous pages to the initial incident report. "I just got this promotion. I'm junior man on the team so this is a training exercise as far as they're concerned. Let's see what we got." His gaze zigzagged along the page. "Crystal Purcell filed a missing persons Tuesday morning, September 16, seventy-two hours after the doctor failed to arrive home as scheduled. Records took the information. We'd had some residential burglaries that same weekend so I didn't pick up the report until noon Thursday, September 18. As far as we could determine, Purcell wasn't *at risk*, and there was nothing suspicious about the circumstances of his disappearance." He paused to look at me. "Tell you the truth, we figured he'd gone off on his own. You know how it is. Half the time the guy shows up later with his tail between his legs. Turns out he's got a girlfriend or he's been off on a bender with the boys somewhere. Might be half a dozen explanations, all of them harmless. It's aggravating to the wife, but nothing sinister."

He leaned back in his chair. "Half a million to a million people run away each year. It's tough on family and friends. You've probably seen it yourself. At first, they get into denial. Can't believe someone'd do such a rotten thing to them. Later, they get mad. Anyway, I called the current Mrs. Purcell and made an appointment for Friday afternoon. This was September 19. Frankly, I stalled, assuming she'd hear from him."

"Which she didn't?"

"Not then and not since. From what she says, he wasn't suffering any physical condition that raised a flag on that score—no heart problems, diabetes, no history of mental illness. She said she'd called and talked to him at the office— this was September 12, shortly after lunch. Purcell told her he'd be late, but there was no mention of his not coming home at all. By Saturday morning, she was frantic, calling everyone she knew—friends, relatives, his colleagues. Hospitals, CHP, the morgue—you name it. There was no sign of him.

"I sat with her for an hour, this was at the house in Horton Ravine. She's got another place at the beach she stays most weekends. I went through the drill. Asked about habits, hobbies, job, country club memberships; had a look at his bedroom; went through his chest of drawers, phone bills, credit card receipts. I checked his credit card accounts for any recent activity, address book, calendar—covering all those bases."

"Nothing surfaced?"

He held up a finger. "I'll get to that in a minute. Over the next couple weeks, we went through the mail at his home and at the clinic, arranged a mail cover, talked to his associates, entered him in the DOJ missing persons system, and put a stop on his license plate. Meantime, you have to understand, we're not talking about a crime here, so this is strictly a public service. We're doing what we can, but there's no evidence to suggest we got a problem on our hands."

"Fiona tells me his passport's missing."

Odessa smiled ruefully. "So's mine for that matter. Just because his wife can't lay hands on it, doesn't mean it's gone. We did come across a recent statement for a savings account at Mid-City Bank. And this is what caught our attention. It looks like he made a series of cash withdrawals—thirty thousand dollars' worth—over the past two years. Balance drops from thirteen grand to three in the past ten months alone. The last activity on the account was August 29. His wife doesn't seem to know anything about it."

"You think he was prepping for departure?"

"Well, it sure looks that way. Granted, thirty thou won't get you far in this day and age, but it's a start. He might've milked other accounts we haven't come up with yet. It's always possible the guy's a gambler and this is his stake. She says he's not, but she might've been kept in the dark."

"Could we go back to the passport? If Purcell left the country, wouldn't Customs have a record of it?"

"You'd think so. Assuming his was the passport he used. He might have traded in his personal ID—driver's license, birth certificate, and passport—for a set of phony papers, which means he could have flown to Europe or South America under someone else's name. Or he might have driven into Canada, booked a flight, and left from there."

"Or he might be lying low," I said.

"Right."

"Wouldn't someone have spotted his car?"

"No guarantee of that. He could've run it off a cliff, or driven into Mexico and sold it to a chop shop. Park a car like that in South Central and see how fast it disappears."

"What kind of car?"

"Four-door Mercedes sedan. Silver. Vanity plate reads 'Doctor P.' "

I said, "You haven't mentioned foul play."

"No reason to. Or if there is, I don't see it. It's not like we found blood stains in the parking lot outside the nursing home. No signs of a struggle, no evidence of assault, and no reason to believe he was forcibly removed. We canvassed the neighborhood, hitting every house within range. Nobody saw or heard a thing that night."

"Fiona thinks he might have left on his own. What's your take on it?"

"Personally, I don't like the feel of it. Nine weeks with zip. You almost have to assume there's something else going on. We're beginning to backtrack, looking for anything we might have missed the first go-round."

"Did Fiona's story affect the investigation?"

"In what regard?"

"All this talk of his past disappearances," I said.

Odessa waved that aside. "Air and sunshine. She says he's gone off before. Maybe so, maybe not. I'm not entirely clear about her motive."

"According to her, she wants results."

"Sure, but who doesn't? We're cops, not magicians. We don't perform miracles."

"Did you believe the story she told?"

"I believe he left *her*. Whether he was having problems with the current Mrs. P. is anybody's guess." He paused. "Have you met Crystal yet?"

I shook my head.

Odessa lifted his brows and shook his hand as though he'd

burned it. "She's a beautiful woman. Hard to picture anyone walking out on her."

"You have a theory?"

"Not me. From our perspective—so far—this is not a criminal matter. You got no crime, then there's no Miranda and no need for search warrants, which makes our job a hell of a lot easier. We're just a bunch of good guys trying to do the family a favor. Personally, I think things look bad, but I ain't gonna say that to anyone else, including you," he said.

I indicated the file. "Mind if I take a look?"

"Wish I could, but this is Paglia's case and he's hell on confidentiality. He doesn't mind us passing on the gist of it when it seems appropriate. The point is to find the guy, which means we cooperate when we can."

"He won't care if I go back and talk to some of these people?"

"You're free to do anything you want."

When he walked me out to the front, he said, "If you find him, let us know. He can stay gone if he wants, but I'd hate to keep putting in the hours if he's off in Las Vegas with a snootful of coke."

"You don't believe that."

"No, I don't. Nor do you."

On the way back to the office, I did a two-block detour and made a stop at the bank. I filled out a deposit slip, endorsed Fiona's check, and waited my turn in line. When I reached the window, I pointed to the account number printed on the face. "Could you verify the balance in this account? I want to be sure the check's good before I make the deposit." Another lesson learned the hard way: I don't start work until a check has cleared.

The teller, Barbara, was one I'd been dealing with for years. I watched while she typed in the account number on her computer keyboard and then studied the screen. She hit the Enter key once. *Tap.* Again. *Tap.* I watched as her eyes traced the lines of print.

She looked back at my deposit slip and made a face. "This is covered, but it's close. Want the cash instead?"

"The deposit's fine, but let's do it before another check comes in and leaves her short."

3

I RETURNED TO the office to find that Jill and Ida Ruth had left a note on my door: "Kinsey—Below is an itemized record of Jeniffer's tardy days, screwups, and unexplained absences. Please add any other incidents you know of, sign this, and leave it on my desk. We think it's best if we present a unified front. We mean business! Ida Ruth."

I dropped the list in my trash and put a call through to Crystal Purcell at the house in Horton Ravine. The housekeeper informed me she'd left for the beach house, where she'd be spending the weekend. She gave me the number, which I dialed as soon as we'd hung up. I hoped the woman who answered would be Crystal, but when I asked for her by name, I was put on hold until a second woman picked up. "This is Crystal," she said.

I identified myself by name and occupation, hoping she wouldn't be annoyed by the idea of yet another detective. According to the newspapers, she'd already talked to investigators from the Santa Teresa Police Department. I told her I'd met with Fiona that morning and that she'd asked me to look into Dr. Purcell's disappearance. "I know you've gone over the subject repeatedly, but I'd appreciate hearing the story from you, if you can bear telling it again."

There was a momentary pause wherein I could have sworn she was practicing her Zen deep breathing. "This is very hard."

"I'm aware of that and I'm sorry."

"How soon?"

"That's entirely up to you. The sooner the better."

There was another pause. "How much are you charging?"

"Fiona? Fifty an hour, which is on the low end of the scale. A big-city private eye is paid twice that." Briefly I wondered why I sounded so apologetic. Maybe she'd prefer to chat with someone whose services were worth more.

"Stop by at five. I'm on Paloma Lane." She gave me the number. "Do you know where that is?"

"I can find it. I'll try not to take too much of your time."

"Take all you want. Fiona's the one paying."

I left the office at four o'clock, stopping by my apartment on my way to Crystal's beach house. The accumulating cloud cover had generated an artificial twilight, and the smell of gathering rain had infused the air. I'd left windows open in the loft and I wanted to get the place buttoned down properly against the coming storm. I parked the car out in front and pushed through the gate with its reassuring whine and squeak. I followed the narrow concrete walk around the side of the building to the backyard.

My apartment was formerly a single-car garage converted into living quarters. My studio consists of a small living room, with a sofa bed for guests tucked into a bay window, a built-in desk, a kitchenette, a stacking washer-dryer combination, and a bathroom downstairs. Above, accessible by a tiny spiral staircase, I have a sleeping loft with a platform bed and a second bathroom. The interior resembles a sturdy little seagoing vessel, complete with a porthole in the front door, teak-paneled walls, and sufficient nooks and crannies, cubbyholes, and niches to accommodate my small store of possessions. The best part of all is the good soul who makes this possible, my landlord, Henry Pitts. He's eighty-six years old, handsome, thrifty, energetic, and competent. He worked as a commercial baker for most of his professional life and even in retirement, can't quite give up his addiction to breads, pies, and cakes. He not only produces a steady stream of baked goods, but he caters luncheons and high teas for all the old ladies in the neighborhood. In addition, he trades his fresh breads and dinner rolls for meals at the corner tavern, where he eats three to four nights a week.

At the head of the driveway, I could see Henry's garage door standing open, though both vehicles were in place. As I turned left onto the patio, I spotted him on a ladder outside his bedroom, putting up the last of his storm windows. He wore shorts and a tank top, his long legs looking knotty, his tan all but faded now that "winter" was here. The Santa Teresa temperatures never drop much below fifty, but he's originally from Michigan, and despite the fact he's been in Southern California more than forty years, his lingering attachment to the seasons dictates the installation of window screens in late spring and storm windows in late fall. The weather itself is immaterial to him.

The patio was still littered with cleaning supplies: the garden hose, wads of crumpled newspaper, a wire brush, a bucket of water mixed with vinegar, and numerous sponges gray with soot. Henry waved from his perch and then eased carefully down the ladder, whistling tunelessly to himself. I paused to help him clean up, tossing dingy water in the bushes while he rewound the hose into a terra-cotta pot. "You're home early," he remarked.

"I thought I better close my windows before the rain,

assuming we'll actually have some," I said. Henry'd often complained that the rain in California lacked the bluster and theatrics of a good Midwestern storm. Many times the promised rain failed to materialize at all or arrived in a form barely sufficient to wet the pavement. We're seldom treated to the displays of thunder and lightning he remembers with such enthusiasm from his Michigan youth.

Henry said, "Why didn't you call? I could have saved you a trip. Stick the brush in that bucket. I'll take it in with me when I go."

"This was right on my way. I have an appointment at five o'clock down on Paloma Lane so I was heading in this direction. Any excuse to avoid the office. Too much nonsense for my taste."

"How's the search for new space?"

I waggled my hand back and forth, indicating not so good. "Something will come up. Meanwhile, I have a new client. At least I'm ninety-nine percent sure."

"Why the hesitation?"

"Might be the aggravation at the office, spilling over into this. I am interested in the case, but I'm not convinced I can be effective. This is the doctor who's been missing."

"I remember reading about that. Still no sign of him?"

"Nope. His ex-wife thinks the cops aren't showing the proper initiative. Frankly, she strikes me as the type who likes to make people jump through hoops."

"You'll do fine." With that, he returned to the ladder, which he collapsed and carried back across the patio to the garage. I watched him ease around his 1932 Chevy coup and hang the ladder on the wall. His garage is lined with pegboard, with the location for each item neatly silhouetted in paint. "You have time for some tea?" he asked, coming back across the yard.

I glanced at my watch. "Better not. I'll see you later up at Rosie's."

"I'll be there closer to seven than to six. She's actually on her way over so I better get washed up. She's asked me for help, but she won't say with what."

I said, "Uh-oh."

He waved dismissively. "It's probably something simple. I don't mind a bit. If she shows while I'm gone, tell her I'll be back in a flash, as soon as I've cleaned up."

Henry crossed to his backdoor and went into the kitchen, where I could see him through the window, scrubbing up at the sink. He smiled when he caught my eye and started whistling to himself again.

I turned when I heard the gate squeak. Rosie appeared moments later, toting a brown paper bag. She owns the Hungarian tavern where Henry's older brother, William, now functions as the manager. William and Rosie were married Thanksgiving Day the year before, and they live in an apartment above her restaurant, which is half a block away. William is eighty-seven years old, and where Rosie once swore she was in her sixties, she now admits to being in her seventies, though she won't specify where. She's short and top-heavy with a coquettish cap of red hair dyed the color of Florida oranges. As usual, she was wearing a muu-muu, this one a gaudy jungle of orange and gold, the skirt lifting, sail-like, against the rising wind. She brightened when she saw me. "Kinsey, is good. Here's for Henry," she said, opening the bag for me.

I peered at the contents, half-expecting to see kittens. "What *is* that? Is that trash?"

Rosie shifted her weight from one foot to the other, refusing to make eye contact, a strategy she employs when she's guilty, ill at ease, or maneuvering like crazy. "Is my sister Klotilde's medical bills for hospital and after she died. Henry's going to explain. I can't make into heads or tails with this." Rosie's perfectly capable of speaking grammatically.

She only butchers vocabulary and syntax when she's trying to seem helpless, thus conning you into doing her some outrageous favor. This is especially true when she's dealing with her state and federal taxes, which Henry's done without a murmur for the past six years. Now slyly, she said, "You gonna help I hope. He shouldn't do by himself. Is not fair."

"Why can't William pitch in?"

"Klotilde preferred Henry."

"But she's *deceased*," I said.

"Before she deceased herself, she preferred," she said, smiling coyly, as though that cinched it.

I dropped the argument. It was really up to Henry, though it irritated me intensely that she'd take advantage of him. The Klotilde in question was Rosie's cranky older sister. I'd never been able to pronounce her Hungarian surname, which abounded in consonants and strange punctuation marks. She'd suffered for years from an unspecified degenerative disease. She'd used a wheelchair since she was in her fifties, plagued by a variety of other ailments that necessitated copious medications and numerous hospital stays. Finally, in her seventies, she'd been advised to undergo hip-replacement surgery. This was in April, some seven months back. Though the surgery had been successful, Klotilde had been outraged by the rigors of convalescence. She'd resisted all attempts to get her on her feet, balked at nourishment, refused to use a bedpan, pulled out catheters and feeding tubes, flung her pills at the nurses, and sabotaged her physical therapy. After the customary five days in the hospital, she was moved to a nursing home where, over the course of the next several weeks, she began to decline. She'd finally succumbed to pneumonia, dysphagia, malnutrition, and kidney failure. Rosie had not been exactly stricken when she "passed." "She should have pessed along time ago," said she. "She's a pain in the patooty. That's what happens when you don't behave. She should have done what doctor say. She shouldn't never resist help when he know best. Now I got this and I don't know what to do with. Here you take."

Judging from the weight and heft of the bag, she'd gotten into some resistance of her own, letting all the paperwork pile up. It'd take Henry weeks to get everything sorted out. He emerged from the backdoor and crossed the patio to us. He'd changed out of his tank top and shorts into a flannel shirt and long pants.

"I gotta scoot," I said, and set the bag on the ground.

Henry peered in. "Is this trash?"

By the time I let myself into my apartment, he was already hauling the bag toward his kitchen door, nodding sympathetically while Rosie lurched through a tortured explanation of her plight.

I dropped my shoulder bag on a kitchen stool while I circled the apartment, closing windows and locking them. I turned on lamps as I went so the place would look cheerful when I got home. Upstairs, I pulled on a clean white turtleneck, which I wore with my jeans. I shrugged back into my gray tweed blazer, traded my Sauconys for black boots, and studied myself in the bathroom mirror. The effect was just what you'd expect: a tweed blazer with jeans. *Works for me,* I thought.

Paloma Lane is a shady two-lane road that runs between Highway 101 and the Pacific Ocean, sharing the irregular strip of land with the Southern Pacific Railroad. Despite the proximity to the freight and passenger trains thundering past twice daily, many houses along Paloma sell in the millions, depending on the number of linear feet of beachfront a property claims. The houses vary in style from Pseudo-Cape Cod to Mock Tudor to Faux Mediterranean to Contemporary. All are situated as far away from the railroad tracks as possible

and as close to the sand as county setbacks permit. Crystal
Purcell's lot was one of the few without electronic gates. The
house next door, to the left of hers, bore a discreet For Sale
sign with a PRICE REDUCED banner across the center.

Crystal's house filled the narrow lot. The glass-and-cedar
structure was probably forty feet wide and three stories high,
each floor angled strategically to keep the neighboring houses
out of sight. To the left, an open carport sheltered a silver Audi
convertible and a new white Volvo, with a vanity license plate
that read CRYSTAL. The end slot was free; probably where Dow
Purcell had parked his Mercedes. To the right, there was room
for an additional three cars on the gravel stretch where I
parked my slightly dinged 1974 VW.

The rear facade of the house was austere, a windowless
wall of weathering wood. On either side of the door, a row of
thirty-foot fan palms had been planted in enormous black
jars. I trudged across the gravel to the entrance and rang the
bell. The woman who answered the door carried a wide martini glass by the rim. She said, "You must be Kinsey. I'm
Anica Blackburn. Nica's the name most people use. Why
don't you come in? Crystal's just finished her run. She'll be
down in a bit. I told her I'd let you in before I headed home."
Her dark auburn hair was slicked back, strands looking wet as
though she was fresh from the shower. A faint, damp heat
seemed to rise from her skin, which smelled of French milled
soap. Her body was slim and straight. She wore a black silk
shirt, crisply pressed jeans, and no shoes. Her bare feet were
long and elegant.

I stepped into the foyer. The lower level widened from the
entry, expanding into a great room that utilized the entire
width of the house. Tall windows looked out onto a weathered wooden deck with worn canvas chairs bleached to a hue
somewhere between putty and dun. The floors were a pale
wood, covered with pale sisal carpeting, probably selected for
its ability to disguise sand tracked in from the beach. Every-

thing else within view, from the walls to woodwork to the plump upholstered furniture dressed in wrinkled linen slip-covers, was as white as whole milk.

Beyond the deck, there was an apron of scruffy grass about ten yards wide. Beyond the grass, the ocean looked cold and unforgiving in the late-afternoon light. The sea was a pearly gray, dark at the horizon where the water and cloud cover met and melded into one somber mass. The surf tumbled monotonously against the shoreline. Waves relaxed and fanned out, reached, hesitated, and then withdrew again. Inside, somewhere above, I could hear voices raised in heat.

"SHUT UP! That's bullshit. You are such a bitch. I HATE you! . . ."

The reply was low and firm, but apparently ineffective.

A shrieking invective was hurled in response. A door slammed once and then slammed again so hard it made the windows shake.

I glanced at Nica, who had her face upturned, regarding the ceiling with an air of bemusement. "Leila's home for the weekend—Crystal's only daughter, age fourteen. That's skirmish number one. Trust me, the fights will escalate as the hours wear on. By Sunday, it's all-out war, but then it's back to school for her. Next weekend they start in again, and so it goes." She gestured for me to follow and then moved into the great room and took a seat on the couch.

"She's in boarding school?" I asked.

"Fitch Academy. Malibu. I'm the school guidance counselor and I provide personal transportation to and from. Not part of my duties. As it happens, I rent a house two doors down." She had strong, arched brows over dark eyes, high cheekbones with a smattering of freckles, and a pale wide mouth, showing perfect white teeth. "This particular Donnybrook is about whether Leila's going to spend the night with her dad. Four months ago she was fanatical about him. If she couldn't spend the weekend with him, she'd regale everyone in ear range with loud, shrieking fits. Now they're on the outs and she refuses to go. Up to this point, she was winning the battle. Once she slams the door, it's over. She loses big points for that, giving Crystal a tactical advantage."

"I'd find it difficult."

"Who doesn't? Girls her age are melodramatic by nature and Leila's high-strung. She's one of the brightest kids we have, but she's a handful. They all are—except for a few Goody Two-shoes. You never know where you stand with them. Personally, I prefer this, though it does get tedious."

"Fitch is all girls?"

"Thank God. I'd hate to imagine having to deal with boys that age, too. Can I fix you a drink?"

"I better not, but thanks."

She finished the last of her martini and then leaned forward and set her empty glass with a click on the light wood coffee table. "I understand you're here about Dowan."

"Yes, and I'm sorry to intrude. I'm sure she's been through a lot since this ordeal began."

"It can't be helped."

"How's she doing?"

"I'd say fair. Of course, the strain's been enormous. The days drag on and on, some worse than others. She keeps waiting for the phone to ring, looking for his car. The rumors keep flying, but that's about all. No real sign of him yet."

"I'm sure it's hard."

"Impossible. It really gets to her. If it weren't for Griff, I don't know how she'd manage to keep sane."

"Where was she that night, this house or the other one, in Horton Ravine?"

Nica pointed at the floor. "They're usually here on weekends. Crystal's a Pisces—a water baby. This is more her style than that pretentious pile of shit Fiona built in town. Have you been there?"

"Not yet."

"No offense," she added mildly. "I know she's your client."
You poor thing went unsaid.

"What about you? When did you hear Dow was missing?"

"Well, I knew something was going on that first night. I'd driven Leila up from Malibu as usual—we arrived about five o'clock—and she went off to her dad's. He's her stepfather, really, but he's helped raise her from infancy. At any rate, Crystal had already talked to Dow when we pulled in from school. He knew he wasn't going to be free in time for supper, so it was just Crystal and Rand and me."

"Rand?"

"Griff's nanny. He's great. He's been with the baby ever since Griff was born. You'll meet both in a bit. Rand'll bring Griff in for his goodnight kiss right after his bath. By then he's had his supper and he's ready for bed. On the twelfth, we put together a cold picnic and ate it out on the deck. It was gorgeous—quite clear and very balmy for that time of year; warm enough to linger without sweaters, which is unusual out here. We chatted about nothing in particular while we worked our way through a couple bottles of red wine. At seven forty-five, Rand took Griff and went over to the other house. He's got a couple of TV shows he likes and he wanted to be there in time to settle in for those."

"Rand and the baby stay at the house in Horton Ravine?"

"Ordinarily, no. I think Crystal and Dow were looking forward to some time alone. I was probably here until ten o'clock. It wasn't late, but I was bushed, finally winding down for the week."

"What time did she expect Dow?"

"Any time after nine. That was usually his pattern when he had to work late. I guess if you're married to a doctor, you don't pay much attention to the clock. Crystal fell asleep on the couch. She called me at three in the morning after she woke and saw that he wasn't here. She thought he might've come in late and gone into the guest room to avoid disturbing her. She checked and when she realized he wasn't there, she came back down and flicked on the outside lights. His car wasn't there. She put a call through to the clinic and they said he'd been gone for *hours*. That's when she called me and I told her to call the cops. She couldn't file a report until at least seventy-two hours had passed."

"What was she thinking? Do you remember what she said?"

"The usual. Car accident, heart attack. She thought he might've been picked up by the cops."

"What for?"

"Driving under the influence."

"He drinks?"

"Some. Dow always has a couple glasses of whiskey at the clinic when he works late. It's his reward for putting in the hours above and beyond the call of duty. She's warned him about driving home afterward, but he always swears he's fine. She was worried he might've run off the road."

"Was he on medication?"

"Hey, at his age, who isn't? He's sixty-nine years old."

"What went through your mind?"

A brief smile flickered. "Odd you should ask. I thought about Fiona. I'd almost forgotten, but it's really what popped into my mind the moment I heard."

"What about Fiona?"

"That she'd finally won. That's all she's angled for since the day he left, maneuvering to get him back, using any means she could." I thought Nica might say more, but she reached for her glass and tilted it to her lips, realizing belatedly she'd finished her drink. She sat forward on the couch. "I should be on my way. Tell Crystal I'll be at my place whenever she's done with this."

She got up and padded as far as the wide French doors.

I watched her cross the deck and disappear, striding down

the path and into the sand. From the rear of the house, I could hear the sound of bathwater running, a man murmuring, and then a squeal of childish laughter rebounding against tile walls: two-year-old Griffith with his nanny, Rand.

4

DURING THE TIME I was alone, I took advantage of the lack of supervision to do a quick assessment of the place. Ordinarily, if left to my own devices, I'd have opened a few drawers, sorted through the mail, perhaps even scanned a letter or a credit card statement. There's ever so much information embedded in our correspondence, which is why those pesky federal mail-tampering penalties are so severe. Hunt as I might, however, I couldn't find anything of interest and I was reduced to gazing at home furnishings, trying to calculate the value—not a specialty of mine. In one corner, there was a round table draped with a floor-length cloth, surrounded by four chairs wearing those little matching dresses with the bows tied in back. I pulled up one skirt and discovered a common metal folding chair. The table itself was constructed of a round of raw plywood bolted to a cheap set of legs. This was a workaday metaphor for much that I observe during the course of my work: What looks good on the surface usually turns out to be crap underneath.

To my left, on the far wall were floor-to-ceiling bookcases, a sliding ladder affixed to a railing midway up. Closer inspection revealed shelves lined with romance novels by women writers with made-up-sounding names. A free-standing Swedish fireplace provided warmth on chilly nights without obstructing the ocean view. A long angled counter separated the high-tech kitchen from an eating area that looked out at the beach. To the right, there was a staircase that I surveyed with longing. The second and third floors probably contained the bedrooms, perhaps a study or home office where all the yummy paperwork was kept. Of course, it was likely her mail was sent to the main residence in Horton Ravine, which might explain the absence of letters sitting out in plain view.

I heard someone cross the room just above me, the muffled thump of bare feet on bare hardwood floors. I glanced up without thinking, following the sound. Belatedly, I realized there was a "window" in the ceiling, clear glass or Lucite maybe thirty-six inches square with a view into the bedroom directly above. Startled, I watched Crystal Purcell parade naked across my line of view. Thirty seconds later, she padded down the stairs, still barefoot, wearing wash-faded jeans cut so low her belly button showed. Her short-cropped T-shirt was gray, the neck of it pulled out of shape by years of wear. By my reckoning, she hadn't had enough time to pull on any underwear.

Her hair was an upscale-salon blond, a little longer than shoulder length, framing her face in a tangle of soft curls. A few strands along her neck were still damp from the shower. Holding out her hand, she said, "Hello, Kinsey. I'm sorry to keep you waiting. I just came back from a run and wanted to get rid of all the sweat and sand." Her grip was strong, her voice mild, her manner pleasant but subdued. "Where's Anica? Did she leave? I asked her to keep you company until I came down."

"She just left. She asked if you'd call her as soon as you're free."

Crystal moved into the kitchen, sailing her comments in

my direction while she crossed to the stainless steel refrigerator and removed a bottle of wine. "She's been a godsend, especially with Leila coming home on weekends. It's been hard enough without worrying about her on top of everything else. Anica's the counselor at Leila's private school."

"That's what she said. Must be nice having her so close."

"She's a good friend. One of the few, I might add. Dow's Horton Ravine pals view me as beneath contempt."

I couldn't think how to respond so I kept my mouth shut. I moved as far as the counter, keeping her in view. I could see evidence of Griff's dinner. The tray on his chrome-and-plastic high chair still bore a three-sectioned Beatrix Potter plate, with drying curds of scrambled egg, toast crusts, and a smear of applesauce. A bib had been laid over the back of the chair.

"How long have you known her?"

"Really, not that long. Sometime early last spring. I saw her out on the beach and then later at Fitch at one of those dreadful parent-teacher conferences. Did she offer you a drink?"

"She did. I thought I'd better not have anything just yet."

"Really. How come?" She took a corkscrew from the kitchen drawer and began opening the bottle as she moved to the kitchen cabinet and fetched herself a glass.

"I don't know. It doesn't seem professional, given that I'm here on business."

Bemused, she took out a second glass and held it up. "You sure? It won't count against you. We can sit out on the deck and sip wine while we watch the sun go down."

"Oh, all right. Why not? You talked me into it."

"Great. I hate to drink by myself." She held out the glasses and the bottle. "If you'll take these, I'll make us up a plate of nibbles. That way we won't get looped . . . or any more looped than we choose."

I took the glasses in one hand, the stems forming an *X*, and tucked the bottle of white wine in the crook of my arm. I crossed the great room and pushed open one of the French doors with my elbow. Once on the deck, I set the items on a weathered wooden table between two wood-and-canvas sling chairs. The wind gusting in from the ocean was damp and smelled pungent, like an oyster liqueur. I took a deep breath, picking up the faint taste of salt at the back of my throat.

Two palms near the house made tiny scratching noises as the fronds swept back and forth against the graying exterior. I moved to the edge of the deck, my gaze sweeping along the surf. The beach was deserted, while out on the ocean, white lights were showing on the oil rigs like diamonds on dark velvet. The weather bore the edgy feel of danger. I sat down, crossing my arms as I huddled against the chill. It was nearly twilight; a gradual, indiscriminate darkening, with no color visible through the heavy clouds. Far out on the horizon, I could see patches of silver where rays from the late sun pierced the marine layer. I heard the distant whine of a commuter plane approaching along the coast. Through the French doors, the living room looked clean and cozy. I was grateful for the protection afforded by the long-sleeved turtleneck under my blazer. Idly, I glanced at the Chardonnay bottle with its classy black-and-silver label. I leaned closer. The price tag, $65, was more than I'd paid for my telephone and electric bills combined that month.

Two ornamental lamps came on, and Crystal, still barefoot, emerged from the house, carrying a tray of cheese and crackers, arranged with grapes and apple wedges. She'd pulled on a heavy navy sweater that hung, fetchingly, almost as far as her knees. She left the door open behind her, glancing over at me. "You look cold. I'm used to the ocean, but you must be freezing. Why don't I fire up the outside heaters? It'll just take a sec. You can pour the wine, if you would."

I did as she suggested and then watched as she hunkered next to a fat propane cannister with a heater element affixed.

Her fingernails and toenails were both done in a French manicure, white defining the half-moon at the base of the nail and
under the rim. The look was clean, though—like her hair—
the effect probably cost her dearly and had to be redone every
other week. It wasn't hard to imagine her doing a bump-and-
grind routine. She turned a valve, using an electric match to
ignite the hissing gas as it escaped. Soon after, the reddening
coils glowed nearly white. She lit the second of the two
heaters, turning them to face us so that warmth poured out
across the space between us. "Is that better?"

"Much."

"Good. If you need something warmer, don't hesitate to
say so. I have a huge supply of sweaters in the downstairs
closet."

We sipped wine in silence while I tried to decide how
and where to begin. "I appreciate your taking the time to talk
to me."

She smiled faintly. "I considered hiring a detective myself
half a dozen times, but I didn't want to undermine the police.
I have every confidence in the job they're doing. Apparently,
Fiona doesn't."

"She likes the idea of someone devoted solely to the
family's interests. The police have other cases requiring their
more immediate attention." I paused. "I just want to be clear
that any comments you care to make will be safe with me. If
you have relevant information, I'll report it to her, but nothing
else gets passed on. You can be as candid as you like."

"Thank you. I was wondering about that."

"I'm assuming there's no love lost."

"Hardly. Fiona's done everything in her power to make my
life hell on earth." Her face was angular, mouth wide. Her
eyes were gray, her brows pale, her lashes thick and black.
Aside from mascara, she seemed to wear little or no makeup.
I could tell she'd had her eyes done and probably her nose as
well. In fact, just about everything I was looking at had been

augmented or improved by some merry band of surgeons working on her, piece by piece. Crystal's smile was brief. "Look. I know she's busy painting a picture of herself as the victim in all of this, betrayed and put-upon. The truth is, she never gave Dow a thing. It was all take, take, take. Dow reached a point where he had nothing left. Poor guy. When I think of the hours he worked, all the sacrifices he made for them, and in exchange for what? For years, the three of them have stood around with their hands out. Fiona in particular. She was always coming up with some new harebrained scheme, her current business venture being one. Interior design? Who's she trying to kid? She's a Horton Ravine matron spending someone else's money and suddenly, she's talking about her talent and her 'eye' for design. She only has one client—some friend of hers named Dana . . ."

"She's married to one of Dow's business associates?"

"Joel Glazer, that's right. How do you know him?"

"I don't. I know her, or I did back when she was married to someone else."

"She couldn't be too bright. Fiona's milking her for everything she's worth."

"What about Dow's daughters? What's your relationship to them?"

Crystal shrugged that one off. "They're all right. They don't know the half of what goes on. They probably hate me, but at least they're too polite to say so. They're usually busy sucking up to their dad. I'm sure they're worried he'll die and leave all his money to Griffith and me, which I can understand. I'd worry about the same thing if I were in their shoes."

She picked up a butter knife and cut into a wedge of Brie. She spread the soft cheese on a cracker, which she held out to me. I took it, watching while she made a second for herself, popped it in her mouth, and chewed. "Anyway, with Dow gone, it doesn't seem important. Whatever quarrel I have with Fiona is immaterial."

"You have any idea where he is?"

"I wish. That's all I've really thought about for the past nine weeks."

"Do you believe he's alive?"

"No, not really, but I can't be sure. If I knew he was dead, at least I could make my peace with it and get on with life."

"The police detective mentioned money missing. He says close to thirty thousand dollars had been pulled from his savings over a period of the past two years."

"So I heard. I didn't know anything about that until they brought it to my attention. I know he kept a large sum of money somewhere, but he never said anything else about it. Apparently, the statements for that account were being forwarded to a post office box that I used to keep. Dowan asked about it a couple of months ago and I told him it'd been canceled. Now it looks like he was paying to keep it open all this time."

"I wonder why he asked you when he already had the answer."

Crystal shrugged. "Maybe he was wondering how much I knew."

"Why would he need that kind of cash?"

"I have no idea. He used credit cards for everything."

"Could it be extortion?"

"For what?"

"That's what I'm asking. Any ideas about that?"

"You think he's being blackmailed? That's ridiculous. How so?"

"Isn't it possible?"

She stared at me briefly and then shook her head, apparently drawing a blank. "You'd think a blackmailer would be interested in a lump sum, not a piddling three bills a week."

"Maybe it seemed more acceptable that way. It's one thing to demand a large sum of cash. It's something else again if someone asks for help making ends meet."

"I'm sure he'd have told me if someone were extorting money. Dow told me everything."

"As far as you know."

She blinked. "Well, yes."

"Besides, it might have involved you."

"In what way?"

"He might have paid the hush money in your behalf, as protection."

"I don't think so." I could have sworn her cheeks tinted, but in the fading light it was difficult to tell. Her hand certainly didn't tremble as she raised the glass to her lips. She set her wineglass on the deck and pressed her flattened hands between her knees as though to warm them.

I changed tactics, not wanting her to disconnect from the conversation. "Would you be willing to go back and talk about what it's been like for you the past nine weeks?"

She let out a breath. "It's been awful. Horrendous. At this point I'm numb, but the first two or three days, I was running on pure adrenaline and it really wore me down. The house was teeming with people—my friends, Dow's daughters, his friends and colleagues. I didn't want to see anyone, but I couldn't refuse. I didn't have enough energy to resist, so they swarmed right over me. I was barely holding on. All I wanted to do was sit and stare at the phone, pace to the door and back, scream, or get drunk. For days I'd get in the car and drive between the clinic and home, checking every possible route. I'd find myself on the road and then I'd realize how dumb it was. Dow could be anywhere and the chances of my spotting him were astronomically low."

"Was there anything unusual about the day he disappeared? Any behavior—anything he said—that seems different in retrospect?"

Crystal shook her head. "It was like any other Friday. He was looking forward to the weekend. Saturday, he was playing in a tennis tournament at the country club. Nothing special, but he enjoyed it. Saturday we were going out to dinner with friends—this was a couple who'd recently moved here from Colorado, where they owned some restaurants."

"Can you give me those names?"

"Sure. I'll give you a list before you leave."

"No one else reported anything unusual?"

"Not as far as I know. You can talk to his colleagues and the nursing home staff. I've spoken to most of them myself and asked the same question. The police have done informal interviews as well. People have tried to be helpful, but no one seems to know anything, or if they do, they haven't said."

"Was he having problems at work?"

"There are always problems at work. Dow takes his job very seriously. He's involved with patients and staff, management issues. He also handles all the hiring and firing and the annual salary reviews. There's always something going on. It's just the nature of the beast. Recently, he's spent a lot of time going over the books. The fiscal year at the clinic ends November 30 and Dow likes to be on top of it."

"I take it most of his time is devoted to the clinic?"

"That's right. He retired from private practice about five years ago. Aside from a few charities still dear to his heart, he spends his time at Pacific Meadows, keeping that up and running."

"Were—are—his responsibilities medical or administrative?"

"I guess I'd say both. He's very involved with the residents—not treating them, of course, they have their own personal physicians for their medical needs, but Dow's there every day keeping an eye on things. I have to tell you, it's not always easy. When your specialty's geriatrics, you're going to lose the very people you've grown most attached to."

"Anyone in particular?"

"Well, no. I wasn't speaking of anyone specific," she said, "and I'm not saying he couldn't cope. Of course he could.

He's been working with the elderly for many years. I'm just saying it took a toll on him emotionally."

"Is it possible he walked off?"

"No."

"You're sure of that?"

"Absolutely. And you want to know why? Because of Griff. That boy is the light of Dowan's eyes. If Dow got home late, he went to Griff's room first. He'd lie down on the bed with him and just watch him breathe. Sometimes I'd find him fast asleep in there. He'd never leave Griffith voluntarily."

"I understand," I said.

"There's something else as well. Dow's writing a book. This is a project he's been wanting to do for years. He's seen so many changes in medicine. He really has wonderful stories to tell. He wouldn't abandon that."

"What about the two of you? Are you doing okay?"

"We're very close. In fact, we've been talking about another baby now that Griffith is two."

"So you're convinced something's wrong."

"Very wrong. I just can't think what. If he'd been injured or abducted, surely we'd have heard by now."

"What about his employers? What can you tell me about them?"

"I really don't know much. I've only met Joel Glazer twice and one of those occasions was the groundbreaking for the new Pacific Meadows annex, and we didn't have time to chat. As I understand it, Joel and Harvey Broadus made a fortune in construction, developing retirement communities in the Southwest. They also own a chain of board-and-care homes, plus a number of nursing facilities across the state. We used to see Harvey occasionally at social events, but he's apparently in the middle of a nasty divorce so he's keeping a low profile. He's a bit phony for my taste, but maybe that's just me. Anyway, after Dow retired in 1981, he found himself at loose ends. Everyone knows how highly regarded he is in the medical community. They approached him with regard to Pacific Meadows and asked him to take over the administrative work."

"And they all get along?"

"As far as I know. I mean, they hardly ever see each other. Joel and Harvey seem to be happy with Dow, so they tend to go their way and let him go his. An operating company does the billing. I know at first he was worried they'd interfere with the running of the place, but it hasn't turned out that way."

"How long have they owned the place?"

"I believe they bought it in 1980. It's over on Dave Levine Street right there at the corner of Nedra Lane. You've probably passed it a hundred times. Looks like Tara without the acreage—big white columns across the front."

"Oh, that. I see it on the right side any time I drive in from that end of town. There must be five or six nursing homes along that stretch."

"The staff people all refer to it as 'Formaldehyde Alley,' no disrespect intended. Dow hates when I repeat that."

"How did you two meet?"

"Mom . . ."

Crystal glanced into the great room through the open door. "We're out here." She must have caught sight of Leila because she turned back with an expression of annoyance and disbelief. "Oh, for heaven's sake."

I followed her gaze.

Leila was clumping down the stairs in a pair of black satin pumps with heels so high she could hardly stand erect. Now and then her ankles wobbled as though she were setting off across the ice for the first time on skates. Under her black leather jacket, her top was a see-through confection of chiffon and lace, worn with a long, narrow wool skirt. At fourteen, she was still in that coltish stage of development: no bust to speak of, narrow hips, and long, bony legs. The length of her skirt couldn't have been less flattering. She looked like the cardboard cylinder in a spent roll of paper towels. She'd also done something strange to her hair, which was cut short, dyed a white blond, sticking out in all directions. Some strands had been dreadlocked while the rest remained as wispy as cotton candy. She came to the open door and stood there staring at us.

Crystal snorted. "What's that getup supposed to be?"

"It's not a 'getup.' What's wrong with it?"

"You look ridiculous. That's what."

"You do, too. You look like a bag lady. That sweater's down to your knees."

"Fortunately, I'm not going out in public. Now please go upstairs and find something decent to wear."

"God, you are always so *worried* what other people think."

"Knock it off. I'm really tired of fighting with you."

"Then why don't you leave me alone? I can dress any way I want. It's no reflection on you."

"Leila, you're not leaving the house dressed like that."

"Great. I won't go then. Thanks a lot and fuck you."

"Where's your suitcase?" Crystal said patiently, declining Leila's invitation to escalate.

"I don't have one. I told you I'm not going. I'd rather stay here."

"You didn't see him last time and I swore you'd be there."

"I don't have to go if I don't want to. It's my decision."

"No, it's not, it's mine, so quit arguing."

"Why?"

"Leila, I'm irritated at all the lip you've been giving me. What's the matter with you?"

"I just don't want to go. It's boring. All we do is sit around and watch videos."

"That's what you do *here*!"

"You promised I could see Paulie."

"I never said any such thing. And don't change the subject. Paulie's got nothing to do with it. Lloyd's your father."

"He is *not*! We're not even related. He's one of your stupid old ex-husbands."

"One ex-husband. I've only been married once before," she said. "Why are you being so hostile and obnoxious? Lloyd adores you."

"So what?"

"Leila, I'm warning you."

"If he's so full of adoration why does he force me to spend time with him against my will?"

"He's not forcing you. *I* am and that's final. Now get."

"I will if I can see Paulie."

"Absolutely not."

"God, you're so mean. You don't give a shit about me."

"That's right. I'm just here to abuse and mistreat you. Call Children's Protective Services."

"You think Lloyd's so great, why don't you go see him yourself?"

Crystal closed her eyes, trying to control her temper. "We're not going to do this in front of company. He's got joint custody, okay? He's picking you up at seven, which means he's already on his way over. I'll come get you Sunday morning at ten. Now go back up and change. And you better pack a bag or I'll do it myself and you'll hate what I choose."

Leila's face shut down and I could see a patch of red form around her nose and mouth where she held back tears. "You are so unfair," she said, and clomped back up the stairs again. She slammed the door behind her after entering her room, then screamed the word "bitch" again from the far side of the door.

Crystal returned to our conversation, making no reference to Leila beyond a shake of her head and a rolling of her eyes. "Dow and I met in Vegas at the home of mutual friends. The first time I saw him, I knew I'd marry him one day."

"Wasn't he married?"

"Well, yes. I mean, technically speaking, but not *happily*," she said, as though Dow's marital angst justified her poaching on Fiona's turf. "You've met Fiona. She's only six months younger than him, but she looks like she's a hundred. She drinks. She smokes two packs a day. She's also hooked on Valium, which I doubt she mentioned when she was hiring you. Dow was sixty-nine last spring, but you'd never guess by looking. Have you seen a picture of him?"

"There was one in the paper."

"Oh, that was terrible. I have a better one. Hang on."

She left the deck and moved into the great room, returning moments later with a framed color photo. She sat down on her chair again and passed the photograph to me. I studied Dow Purcell's face. The picture, taken on the golf course, had been cropped so that the others in his foursome were scarcely visible. His hair was white, trimmed close, and his face was lean. He looked tanned and fit, wearing a white golf shirt, pale chinos, and a leather golf glove on his right hand. I couldn't see the head of the club he was holding upright in front of him. "Where was this taken?"

"Las Vegas. The same trip. That was in the fall of 1982. We were married a year later when his final divorce papers came through."

I handed the photo back. "Does he gamble?"

She held the framed photograph and studied it herself. "Not him. He was speaking at a symposium on geriatric medicine. He loved Vegas for the golf, which he played all year long. He was a five handicap, really very good."

I wondered at the sudden use of the past tense but decided not to call attention to the shift. "Do you play?"

"Some, but I'm terrible. I play to keep him company when he's got no one else. It's nice when we travel because it gives us something to do." She leaned forward and set the picture on the table, studying it briefly before she turned back to me. "What happens now?"

"I'll talk to anyone who seems relevant and try to figure out what's going on."

"There's your mommy," a man said. He stood just inside the door, holding Griffith, who was dressed for bed in flannel jammies with enclosed rubber-soled feet and a diaper tailgate in back. His face was a perfect oval, his cheeks fat, his mouth a small pink bud. His fair hair was still damp, sharply parted on one side and combed away from his face. Blond curls were already forming where a few strands had dried. Mutely, he held his arms out and Crystal reached for him. She fit him along her hip, looking at him closely while she spoke in a high-pitched voice, "Griffie, this is Kinsey. Can you say 'Hi'?"

This elicited no response from the child.

She took one of his hands and waved it in my direction, saying, "Hewwoh. I weady to doh feepy. I dotta doh beddy-bye now. Nightie-night."

"Night-night, Griffith," I said, voice high, trying to get into the spirit of the thing. This was worse than talking to a dog because at least there you really didn't anticipate a high-pitched voice in response. I wondered if we were going to conduct the rest of the conversation talking like Elmer Fudd.

I glanced at Rand. "Hi. You're Rand? Kinsey Millhone."

"Oh, I'm sorry. I should have introduced you."

Rand said, "Nice to meet you." He appeared to be in his early forties, dark-haired, very thin, jeans, white T-shirt. I could still see damp splotches on his front from the toddler's bath. Like Crystal, he was barefoot, apparently impervious to cold.

I said, "I better go and let you get the little one to bed."

Rand took Griffith from his mother and retreated, chatting to the child as he went. I waited while she jotted down the names and phone numbers of her husband's business associates and his best friend, Jacob Trigg. We exchanged parting remarks of no particular consequence, and I left with her assurance I could call if I needed to.

On the way out, I passed Leila's stepfather Lloyd, who'd just arrived. He drove an old white Chevy convertible with a shredded sun-faded top and patches of primer where various dents and dings were being prepped for repainting. His brush cut was boyish and he wore glasses with oversized lenses and tortoise-shell frames. He had the body of a runner or a cyclist—long, lean legs and no visible body fat. Even with a nip in the air, all he wore was a black tank top, shorts, and clunky running shoes without socks. I placed him in his late thirties, though it was hard to determine since I glanced at him only briefly as he passed. He nodded, murmuring a brief hello as he approached the front door. As I started my car, the first fat drops of rain were beginning to fall.

5

ASIDE FROM HENRY, Rosie's tavern was empty when I arrived shortly after seven o'clock. I closed my umbrella and leaned it up against the wall near the door. The Happy Hour crowd had apparently been there and gone and the neighborhood drinkers hadn't yet wandered in for their nightly quota. The cavernous room smelled of beef and wet wool. Several sections of newspaper formed a sodden door mat inside the entrance, and I could see where people had trampled their wet feet across the linoleum, tracking dirt and lines of newsprint. At one end of the bar the television set was on, but the sound had been muted. An old black-and-white movie flickered silently across the screen: a night scene, lashing rain. A 1940s coupe sped along a winding road. The woman's hands were tense on the wheel. A long shot through the windshield revealed a hitchhiker waiting around the next curve, which didn't bode well.

Henry was sitting alone at a chrome-and-Formica table to the left of the door, his raincoat draped over the chair directly across from him, his umbrella forming a puddle of rainwater where it leaned against the table leg. He'd brought the brown paper bag in which Rosie had presented her sister's medical bills. He had a glass of Jack Daniel's at his elbow and a pair of half-rimmed glasses sitting low on his nose. An oversized accordion file rested on the chair next to him, the sections divided and labeled by the month. I watched him open a bill, check the date and heading, and then tuck it in the proper pocket before he went on to the next. I pulled up a chair. "You need help?"

"Sure. Some of these go back two years if not more."

"Paid or unpaid?"

"Haven't figured that out yet. A little bit of both, I suspect. It's a mess."

"I can't believe you agreed to do this."

"It's not so bad."

I shook my head at him, smiling slightly. He's a dear and I knew he'd do the same for me if I needed help. We sat in companionable silence, opening and filing bills. I said, "Where's Rosie all this time?"

"In the kitchen making a calf's liver pudding with anchovy sauce."

"Sounds interesting."

Henry shot me a look.

"Well, it *might* be," I said. Rosie's cooking was madcap Hungarian, the dishes impossible to pronounce and sometimes too peculiar to eat, her fowl soup with white raisins being a case in point. Given her overbearing nature, we usually order what she tells us and try to be cheerful about it.

The kitchen door swung open and William emerged, dressed in a natty three-piece pin-striped suit, a copy of the evening paper tucked under his arm. Like Henry, he's tall and long-limbed, with the same blazing blue eyes and a full head of white hair. The two looked enough alike to be identical twins on whom the years had made a few minor modifications. Henry's face was narrower; William's chin and forehead, more pronounced. When William reached the table, he asked permission to join us, and Henry gestured him into the remaining chair.

"Evening, Kinsey. Hard at work, I see. Rosie'll be out momentarily to take your supper order. You're having calf's liver pudding and kohlrabi."

"You're really scaring me," I said.

William opened his paper, selected the second section, and flapped the first page over to the obituaries. Though his lifelong hypochondria had been mitigated by marriage, William still harbored a fascination for those people whose infirmities had ushered them out of the world. It annoyed him when an article gave no clue about the nature of the final illness. In moments of depression or insecurity, he reverted to his old ways, attending the funeral services of total strangers, inquiring discreetly of the other mourners as to cause of death. Key to his query was identifying early indications of the fatal illness—blurred vision, vertigo, shortness of breath—the very symptoms he was destined to experience within the coming week. He was never at ease until he'd solicited the true story. "Gastric disturbances," he'd report to us later with a significant stare. "If the fellow'd only consulted medical authorities at the first hint of trouble, he might be with us today. His brother said so."

"We all have to die of something," Henry invariably said.

William would turn peevish. "Well, you don't have to be such a pessimist. Vigilance is my point. Listening to the body's messages—"

"Mine says, *You are going to die one day regardless so wise up, you old fart.*"

Tonight, Henry glanced at William's paper politely. "Anyone we know?"

William shook his head. "Couple of kids in their seventies; only one with a photo. Couldn't have been taken much later than 1952." He squinted at the page. "I hope we didn't look that smarmy when we were young."

"You certainly did," Henry said. He took a sip of whiskey. "If you go first, I know exactly the picture I'm going to give the paper for your obit. You in those knickers the summer we toured Atlantic City. Your hair's parted down the center and it looks like you're wearing lipstick."

William leaned closer. "He's still jealous because I took Alice Vandermeer away from him. She could jitterbug like the dickens and had money to burn."

Henry said, "She had a wen on her cheek the size and color of a small Concord grape. I never knew where to look so I palmed her off on him."

William turned several pages to the classified ads, where he compared descriptions of "found" dogs and cats with those reported missing, often spotting a match. While Henry and I continued to open and file Klotilde's medical bills, William entertained us with all the livestock currently being offered for sale. He glanced up at me. "Well, here's something. Still need office space? You should check this one out. Five hundred square feet, newly renovated, downtown. Two fifty a month, available immediately."

I stopped what I was doing and tilted my head in his direction. "You're kidding. Let me see that."

William handed me the section, pointing to the item, which read:

For lease: 500 sq ft in newly renovated Victorian, heart of downtown near courthouse; private bath and separate entrance w/private deck. $250/mo. Call Richard after 6:00 pm.

The phone number was listed.

I read the lines twice but they didn't seem to change. "I'll bet it's a dump. They always embellish in these ads."

"It won't hurt to call."

"You really think so?"

"Of course."

"What if it's rented?"

"You won't be out anything. Maybe the guy has others." He reached into his watch pocket and removed a coin, which he placed on the table right in front of me. "Go on."

I took the coin and the paper and crossed the room. The pay phone was in the vestibule, the area dimly illuminated by a neon Budweiser sign. I dialed the number and read the ad again while I listened to four rings. Finally, the line was picked up on the other end and I asked to speak to Richard.

"This is he."

I placed him in his thirties, though phone voices can be deceptive. "I'm calling with regard to the office space listed in tonight's paper. Is the place still available?" I noticed a tinge of plaintiveness had crept into my voice.

"Sure, but we're asking for a year's lease, first and last month's rent, plus a cleaning deposit."

"Can I ask what street it's on?"

"Floresta. Across from the police station and about six doors down."

"And the price quoted is correct? The ad says two hundred and fifty bucks a month."

"It's only one room. It's got a closet and bathroom, but it's not large."

I pictured a phone booth. "Would it be possible to see it tonight?"

"As it happens, my brother's in there laying carpet and I'm on my way over. You want to take a look, I can meet you there in fifteen minutes."

My watch said 7:30. "Great. I can do that. What's the address?"

He gave me the information. "You can pull on down the driveway to the parking lot in back. You'll see lights on, first floor rear. My brother's name is Tommy. The last name's Hevener."

"I'm Kinsey Millhone. Thanks so much. I'll see you in fifteen minutes."

The building had clearly once been a single-family residence: a one-story white-frame cottage with gables in the roofline and a lot of gingerbread trim. At 7:42 I eased my VW down the driveway, my headlights cutting through the shadows. I slowed and peered out the driver's-side window. The white paint looked fresh and there were flower beds along the side. How had I missed this? The location was ideal—one block away from the office I was now in—and the price couldn't have been better. I counted ten parking spaces laid out along the narrow backyard, which was paved with asphalt and fenced on two sides. A black pickup truck was parked in one spot, but the rest were empty at this hour. There was a big trash bin just at the exit to the alleyway in back. Looking up, I could see Lonnie's office windows and the back wall that framed the tiny lot behind his building. I parked and got out, trying to curb the sudden surge of hope. For all I knew, the property was on the market, or the lot was the site of a former gas station, the soil still contaminated by benzene and other carcinogens.

A wide redwood deck had been constructed across the back of the building, complete with a long wooden ramp installed for easy wheelchair access. A market umbrella with a big pale canvas shade stood open above a glass-topped table surrounded by four chairs. Several large terra-cotta pots had been planted with herbs. I was about to hyperventilate. First-floor lights were ablaze. I entered a small foyer. A door stood open to my immediate right. The scent of fresh paint was strong, overlaid by the staunch, secondary odor of brand-new carpeting. I closed my eyes while I offered up a quick prayer, repudiating my wickedness and promising to mend my evil ways. I opened my eyes and stepped through the doorway, absorbing the room at a glance.

The room was twelve by twelve, with new hand-crank windows on two walls. There were two tiers of white-painted shutters in place of conventional drapes. On the far wall, two doors stood open, one leading to a small bathroom, the other into what was clearly a spacious walk-in closet. A red-headed fellow in jeans, an olive green T-shirt, and heavy work boots was sitting on the floor kicking a carpet stretcher, forcing the carpet taut along the baseboard. A phone line had been installed and the phone was currently resting on the surface of an empty cardboard box.

The carpet itself was an industrial-grade nylon, a pattern of beige flecks against a charcoal gray background. I could see his carpet knife with its fat, curved blade, and the mallet he used to pound the carpet backing onto tack strips. Carpet scraps were piled up in the center of the room. An insulated plastic cooler was positioned near the wall beside a wastebasket that was filled to the brim with more carpet trimmings. The room seemed stuffy from the glaring two-hundred-watt bulb overhead.

I said, "Hi, I'm Kinsey. Your brother said he'd meet me here at seven forty-five. Are you Tommy?"

"That's me. Richard's always late. Written guarantee. I'm the good boy, the one who shows up when I'm expected. Hang on a minute. I'm almost done here." He glanced over, flashing me a smile, all green eyes and white teeth. Deep creases formed a bracket around his mouth. With his red hair and his ruddy complexion, the effect was electric, like a black-and-white film with a wholly unexpected sequence in Technicolor. I felt myself averting my gaze with a little frisson that danced its way along my spine. I hoped I hadn't inadvertently whimpered aloud.

I watched him kick, pound, and cut, the muscles in his back and shoulders bunching as he worked. His arms were knotted with veins and matted with a fine red hair. A trickle of sweat angled down along his cheek. He shrugged, blotting the side of his face with the sleeve of his T-shirt. He tossed his mallet aside and sprung to his feet, wiping his palms on his back of his pants. He held a hand out, saying, "What's your name again?"

"It's Kinsey. The last name's Millhone with two *L*'s."

The sun had taken its toll on his fair complexion, leaving a series of lines in his forehead, additional lines at the outer corners of his eyes. I pegged him in his late twenties, five foot ten, a hundred and sixty pounds. Having been a cop, I still view men as suspects I might be called upon later to identify in a lineup. "Mind if I look around?"

He shrugged. "Help yourself. There's not much to see," he said. "What kind of business you in?"

I walked into the bathroom, my voice echoing against the tile. "I'm a private detective."

Toilet, pedestal sink with a built-in medicine cabinet above it. The shower stall was fiberglass with an aluminum-framed glass door. The floor was done in a white ceramic tile that ran halfway up the wall. Above, there was a floral-print vinyl paper in beige, white, and charcoal gray. The effect was both fresh and old-fashioned. Also, easy to keep clean.

I moved back into the main room and crossed to the closet, peering into the four-by-six space, which was fully carpeted, empty, and painted a pristine white. Sufficient room for filing cabinets and office supplies. Even had a hook where I could hang my jacket. I turned back to the main room and let my gaze travel the perimeter. If I placed my desk facing the window, I could look out at the deck. The shutters were perfect. If a client dropped in, I could close the lower set for privacy and leave the upper set folded back for light. I tried a window crank, which turned smoothly, without so much as a whine or a creak. I leaned against the windowsill. "No termites, no leaky roof?"

"No, ma'am. I can guarantee that because I did the work myself. This is real quiet back here. You ought to see it by day. Lot of light coming through these windows. Trouble walks in, you got cops right across the street." His accent was faintly Southern.

"Fortunately, my job's not that dangerous."

He tucked his hands into his front pockets. His face was dappled with sun damage like a fine patina of freckles. I couldn't think what to say next and the silence stretched. Tommy launched in again without a lot of help from yours truly. "Place was in pretty bad shape when we took possession. We upgraded plumbing and electrical, put on a new roof and aluminum siding. Stuff like that." His voice was so soft I found myself straining to hear.

"It looks nice. How long have you owned it?"

"About a year. We're new out here. We lost our parents a few years ago—both passed away. Richard hates talking about that almost more'n me. It's still a sore subject. So, now it's just the two of us, my brother and me." He crossed to the cooler and opened the lid, glancing over at me. "Offer you a beer?"

"Oh, no thanks. I was just about to have supper when someone showed me your ad. After I talk to Richard, I'll head on back and eat there."

"Don't like to drink and drive," he remarked, smiling ruefully.

"That's part of it," I said.

He rooted through the crushed ice, pulled out a Diet Pepsi, and popped the tab. I held up a hand, but not quick enough to stop him. "Seriously, I'm fine."

His frown was softened by a tone of mock disapproval. "No beer, no soda pop. Can's open now. Might as well have a sip. You don't want the whole thing to go to waste," he said. Again, he proffered the Pepsi, waggling the can coaxingly in my direction. I took it to avoid a fuss.

He reached into the cooler and extracted a bottle of Bass Ale. He flipped the cap off and held it by the neck while he seated himself on the floor. He leaned his back against the wall, his legs extended in front of him. His work boots looked enormous. He gestured at the empty expanse of carpet. "Pull up a seat. Might as well be comfortable."

"Thanks." I picked a spot across from him and sat down on the floor, taking a polite sip of Pepsi before I set the can aside.

Tommy took a long draw of beer. He looked like a guy accustomed to smoking while he worked. "I used to smoke," he said, as though reading my mind. "Tough to give up, but I think I got it licked. You smoke?"

"Once upon a time."

"Been six months for me. Now and then, I still get the itch, but I take in a couple of breaths just like this. . . ." He paused to demonstrate, his chest expanding as he sucked air audibly through his nose. He let out his breath. "Pretty soon the craving goes away. Where you from?"

"I'm local. Went to Santa Teresa High."

"Me and my brother come from Texas. Little town called Hatchet. Ever hear of it?"

I shook my head.

"Right outside Houston. Pop was in oil. Luckily he sold the company before the bottom dropped out. Poured all his money into real estate. Developed shopping malls, office buildings, all kinds of commercial properties. California's weird. People don't seem all that friendly like they do where we come from. Especially the women. Lot of them seem stuck-up."

The silence settled again.

He took another pull of beer and wiped his mouth on his palm. "Private detective. That's a new one on me. You carry a gun?"

"Occasionally. Not often." I dislike being "drawn out," though he was probably only being polite until his brother appeared.

He smiled lazily as if picking up on my innate crankiness. "So which do you prefer? Guys way too young for you or guys way too old."

"I never thought about it like that."

He wagged a finger. "Guys way too old."

I felt my cheeks grow warm. Dietz really wasn't that old.

"Me, I like women your age," he said, showing a flash of white teeth. "You got a boyfriend?"

"That's none of your business."

Tommy laughed. "Oh, come on. You seeing someone steady?"

"More or less," I said. I didn't want to piss this guy off when I was hoping against hope I'd end up renting the place.

" 'More or less.' I like that. So which is it?"

" 'More,' I guess."

"Can't be much of a romance if you have to guess." He narrowed his eyes as though consulting his intuition. "So here's what I think. I bet you're real schizy. Bet you blow hot and cold about other human beings, especially men. Am I right?"

"Not necessarily. I wouldn't say that."

"But you must've seen a lot of bad guys, the business you're in."

"I've seen some bad women, too."

"That's another thing I like. Bad girls, bad women, rene-gades, rebels . . ." He lifted his head, checking his watch as he did. "Here he comes. Fifteen minutes late. You can just about bank on it."

I glanced at the window as a pair of headlights swept across the parking area. I rose to my feet. Tommy finished his beer and set the bottle aside. A car door slammed and shortly afterward Richard Hevener walked in, tapping a clip-board restlessly against the side of his leg. He wore jeans and a black T-shirt, over which he wore a supple-looking black leather sportscoat. He was taller than Tommy and a lot stockier, his hair dark. He was the somber brother and seemed to take himself very seriously. This was going to be a chore.

"Richard Hevener," he said as he offered me his hand. We shook hands and then he turned to Tommy. "Looks good."

"Thanks. Finish picking up and I'm out of here. You need anything else?"

I tuned out briefly while the two conferred. I gathered there was another property undergoing renovations and Tommy was starting work on that the following week. His manner had shifted in his brother's presence, his flirtatiousness gone. Their discussion finished, Tommy picked up the wastebasket full of carpet scraps and carried them outside, heading for the trash bin at the rear of the lot.

"So what do you think of the place?" Richard said, turning to me. "You want to fill out an application?" His accent and his manner of speaking were much less "Texas" than Tommy's. Consequently, he seemed older and more businesslike.

"Sure, I could do that," I said, trying not to sound like I was sucking up.

He passed me the clipboard and a pen. "We pay water and trash. You pay your own electric and phone. Heating's prorated and it varies, depending on the season. There's only one other tenant and he's a CPA."

"I can't believe the space hasn't been snapped up."

"Ad just went in. We've already had a lot of calls. Three, right after yours. I'm meeting another guy tonight."

I could feel anxiety begin to mount. I leaned on a windowsill and began to fill in the information. Applications are tedious, requiring tidbits of information that are actually nobody's business. I filled in my Social Security number and my California driver's license number, circled DIVORCED in the section that asked if I were single, married, or divorced. Previous addresses, how long, and reasons for leaving. Personal references I listed, along with the bank where I had my checking account. I made a few things up. I drew a dotted line where it asked for credit card numbers and the balance on those accounts. By the time I finished, Tommy had left. I heard his truck in the driveway and then it was gone. I handed Richard the clipboard, watching while he scanned the information.

"If you want a deposit, I can give you one tonight."

"No need. I'll call your references and run a credit check. We have a couple more people coming by on Monday."

"Do you have any idea how soon you'll be making a decision?"

"Middle of the week. Make sure we have a way to reach you in case I have a question."

I pointed to the application. "That's my home phone and my work phone. I've got a message machine on both."

"This your current business address?"

"That's right. I'm renting space from an attorney named Lonnie Kingman. He and my landlord will both tell you I pay on time."

"Sounds good. Something comes up, I'll call. Otherwise, I'll be in touch once I've processed all the applications."

"Fine. That sounds great. If you like, I can pay the first six months in advance." I was starting to sound ridiculous, fawning and insecure.

Richard said, "Really." He studied me, his eyes a dark, brooding brown. "Fifteen hundred dollars, plus the additional one seventy-five for the cleaning deposit," he said, making sure I knew the full extent of my folly.

I thought about Fiona's check for fifteen hundred bucks. "Sure, no problem. I could give you that right now."

"I'll take that into consideration," he said.

6

SATURDAY, I OPENED my eyes automatically at 5:59 A.M. I stared up at the skylight, which was beaded with rain, the entire Plexiglas dome scattered with tiny pearls of light. The breeze coming in the bedroom window smelled of leaf mold, wet sidewalks, and the dripping eucalyptus trees that lined the street beyond. Actually, the scent of eucalyptus is almost indistinguishable from the odor of cat spray, but I didn't want to think about that. I bunched the pillow under my head, secure in the knowledge that I didn't have to crawl out of bed for my run. As dutiful as I am about exercise, there's still nothing more delicious than the opportunity to sleep in. I burrowed under the covers, ignoring the world until 8:30, when I finally came up for air.

Once I'd showered and dressed, I made myself a pot of coffee and downed a bowl of cereal while I read the morning paper. I changed my sheets, started a load of laundry, and generally picked up around the place. When I was a child, my aunt Gin insisted I clean my room on Saturdays before I went out to play. Since we lived in a trailer, the task didn't amount to much, but the habit remains. I dusted, vacuumed, scrubbed

73

toilet bowls—mindless activities that left me free to rumi-
nate. I alternated fantasies, mentally rearranging furniture in
my new office space and thinking about who to query next in
my search for Purcell. With Fiona's fifteen-hundred-dollar retainer now safely in my account, I felt obligated to work
through the weekend. I resisted the temptation to theorize
after only one day's work, but if I'd been forced to place bets,
I would have plunked down my money on the notion that Purcell was dead. From what I'd learned of him, I couldn't see
him taking off without a word to his wife and small son. That
didn't explain the missing passport and the missing thirty
grand, but both might surface in due course. At this point,
there was no reason to believe they were germane.

At eleven o'clock, I hauled out the phone book and turned
to the yellow pages, checking out the section that listed
nursing homes. There were close to twenty by my count.
Many boasted large boxed ads detailing the amenities:

**COMPREHENSIVE RECUPERATIVE & LONG-TERM CARE . . .
SPACIOUS ROOMS IN A TRANQUIL SETTING . . . ELEGANT
DESIGN OF BUILDING AND INTERIOR . . . BEAUTIFUL NEW
FACILITY WITH SECURE GARDEN COURTYARD.**

Some included cartoon maps with arrows pointing out their
superior locales, as though it was preferable to decline in one
of Santa Teresa's better neighborhoods. Most facilities had
names suggesting that the occupants pictured themselves
any place but where they were: Cedar Creek Estates, Green
Briar Villa, Horizon View, Rolling Hills, The Gardens.
Surely, no one envisioned being frail and fearful, abandoned,
incapacitated, lonely, ill, and incontinent in such poetic-
sounding accommodations.

Pacific Meadows, the nursing home that Dow Purcell managed, touted twenty-four-hour RN care and on-site chapel

and pastoral services, which were bound to come in handy. It was also certified by Medicare and Medicaid, giving it a decided advantage over some of its private-pay competitors. I decided to make a visit to see the place myself. The regular staff probably wouldn't be there on weekends, which might prove advantageous. Maybe all the prissy, officious sorts were home doing laundry just like I was.

I tucked a fresh pack of index cards in my handbag, pulled on my boots, and found my yellow slicker and umbrella. I locked the door behind me and scurried through the puddles to my car parked at the curb. I slid in on the driver's side, shivering involuntarily at the chill in the air. The rain had picked up from the early morning lull and now pounded on my car roof with the staccato rattle of falling nails. I fired up the engine and then hunched over the steering wheel, driving in slow motion while the windshield wipers gave the royal wave.

When I pulled into the parking lot at Pacific Meadows, the sky was dark with clouds, and the lights in the windows made the place look cozy and warm. I chose a spot near the entrance, assigned to an employee whose name had been painted out; black on black and impossible to read. I shut down the engine and waited until the squall had passed before I emerged. Even then, I had to pick my way across the half-flooded tarmac to the relative dryness of the sheltered front entrance. I shook off my umbrella and gave my slicker a quick brush before I stepped through the door. Dripping raincoats and wide-brimmed water-repellent hats were hung on a row of pegs. I added my slicker to the mix and propped my umbrella in the corner while I took my bearings.

Along the wide hallway ahead, I could see a row of six elderly people in wheelchairs arranged against the wall like drooping houseplants. Some were sound asleep and some simply stared at the floor in a sensory-deprivation daze. Two were strapped in, their posture eroded by osteoporosis, bones melting from within. One woman, very thin, with long, white limbs, swung a bony leg fretfully over the arm of the wheelchair, moving with agitation as though prompted by pain. I felt myself recoil as if I were at the scene of a four-car pileup.

At the far end of the corridor, two women in green uniforms piled sheets on a laundry cart already heaped with soiled linens. The air smelled odd—not *bad*, but somehow alien—a blend of disassociated odors: canned green beans, adhesive tape, hot metal, rubbing alcohol, laundry soap. There was nothing offensive in any single element, but the combination seemed off, life's perfume gone sour.

To my right, aluminum walkers were bunched together like grocery carts outside a supermarket. The day's menu was posted on the wall, behind glass, like a painting on exhibit. Saturday lunch consisted of a ground chicken patty, creamed corn, lettuce, tomato, fruit cup, and an oatmeal cookie. In my world, the lettuce and tomato might appear as a restaurant garnish, a decorative element to be ignored by the diner, left behind on the plate to be thrown in the trash. Here, the lettuce and tomato were given equal billing, as though part of a lavish nutritional feast. I thought about fries and a QP with Cheese and nearly fled the premises.

French doors opened into the dining room, where I could see the residents at lunch. Even at a glance, I noted three times more women than men in evidence. Some wore street clothes, but the majority were still dressed in their robes and slippers, not bedridden but confined by their convalescent status. Many turned to stare at me, not rudely, but with a touching air of expectation. Had I come for a visit? Was I there to take them home? Was I someone's long-overdue daughter or niece proposing an outing in the clean, fresh air? I found myself glancing away, embarrassed I was offering nothing in the way of personal contact. Sheepishly, I looked back, raised my hand, and waved. A tentative chorus of hands rose in response as my greeting was returned. Their smiles were so sweet and forgiving I felt pricked with gratitude.

I backed away from the dining room and crossed the hall. A second set of doors stood open, revealing a day room, currently empty, furnished with mismatched couches, upholstered chairs, a piano, two television sets, and a cluster of game tables. The floors were done in a glossy beige linoleum, the walls painted a restful shade of robin's egg blue. The ready-made drapes were a blend of yellow, blue, and green in a vaguely floral pattern. Countless throw pillows had been needle-pointed, cross-stitched, quilted, and crocheted. Perhaps a clutch of church ladies had been afflicted by a fit of stitchery. One pillow had a saying embroidered across the face—YOU'RE ONLY AS OLD AS YOU FEEL—a disheartening thought, given some of the residents I'd seen. Metal folding chairs were stacked against the near wall for quick assembling. Everything was clean, but the "decorating" was generic, budget-driven, falling somehow short of good taste.

I walked past the front desk, which was located in a small alcove, and cruised down the corridor, guided by signs indicating the services of a dietary supervisor, a nursing supervisor, and a clutch of occupational, speech, and physical therapists. All three doors were open, but the offices were empty and the lights had been doused. Across the hallway I saw a sign for Admissions. That door was closed and a casual try of the knob told me it was locked. Next door was Medical Records, which apparently shared space with Administration. I thought I'd start there.

The overhead lights were on and I moved through the door. There was no one in evidence. I waited at the counter, idly staring at the wire basket filled with incoming mail. Casually, I surveyed my surroundings. Two desks back-to-back, one with a computer, the other with an electric typewriter humming faintly. There were numerous rolling file carts, a copy machine, and metal file cabinets on the far wall. There was also a big clock with a clicking second hand I could hear from fifteen feet away. Still no one. I rested my elbow on the counter, dangling my fingers near the basket full of mail. By fanning the corners and tilting my head, I could read most of the return addresses. Bills, the usual gas and electric, a lawn and gardening service, two manila envelopes from Santa Teresa Hospital, better known as St. Terry's.

"Can I help you?"

Startled, I straightened up and said, "Hi. How're you?"

The young woman had emerged from the door connecting Administration to Medical Records. She wore glasses with red plastic frames. Her complexion was clear, but she looked like she'd suffer a contagion of zits at the least provocation. Her hair was a medium brown in several irregular lengths; a layered cut grown out now and badly in need of a trim. Under her green smock, she wore brown polyester pants. The name MERRY and PACIFIC MEADOWS were machine-embroidered on the breast pocket above her heart.

She crossed to the counter, passing through a hinged door, and took her place on the far side. At first glance, I'd thought she was in her early thirties, but I quickly revised that downward by a good ten years. She wore metal braces on her teeth and whatever she'd eaten for lunch was still embedded in the wires. Her breath smelled of tension and discontent. Her expression remained quizzical, but her tone had an edge. "Can I ask what you were doing?"

I blinked one eye in her direction. "I lost my contact lens. It might have popped out in the car. I only noticed it just now. I thought it might have fallen in the basket, but there's no sign of it."

"Want me to help you look?"

"Don't worry about it. I have a whole box of 'em at home."

"Are you here to see someone?"

"I'm here on business," I said. I removed my wallet from my

shoulder bag and flipped it open. I pointed at my P.I. license. "I've been hired to look into Dr. Purcell's disappearance."

Merry squinted at my license, holding up the postage stamp–sized photo for comparison with my face-sized face.

I said, "Are you the office manager?"

She shook her head. "I'm temping here on weekends while the other girl's out on maternity leave. Monday through Fridays, I'm Mrs. Stegler's assistant."

"Really. That's great. And what does that entail?"

"You know, typing, filing. I answer phones and distribute mail to all the residents, whatever needs doing."

"Is Mrs. Stegler the one I should be talking to?"

"I guess. She's Acting Associate Administrator. Unfortunately, she won't be back until Monday. Can you stop by then?"

"What about Mr. Glazer or Mr. Broadus?"

"They have an office downtown."

"Gee, that's too bad. I was driving through the neighborhood and took a chance. Well. I guess it can't be helped."

I saw her gaze stray to her computer. "Could you excuse me a minute?"

"Go right ahead."

She moved around to her twelve-inch monitor with its amber print on black. She was probably using office hours to do her personal correspondence. She pressed keys until she'd backed out of the document. She returned to the counter, smiling self-consciously. "You have a business card? I can have Mrs. Stegler call you as soon as she gets in."

"That'd be great." I took my time fumbling through my handbag to find a business card. "How long have you been here?"

"Three months December 1. I'm still on probation."

I put my card on the counter. "You like the work?"

"Sort of, but not really. You know, it's boring, but okay. Mrs. S. has been here forever and she started out just like me.

Not that I'll stick around as long as she has. I'm two semesters short of my college degree."

"What field?"

"Elementary ed. My dad says you shouldn't job-hop because it looks really bad on your résumé. Like you're shiftless or something, which I've never been."

"Well yeah, but on the other hand, if you're interested in teaching, there's no point hanging on to a job that doesn't suit."

"That's what I said. Besides, Mrs. S. is real moody and gets on my nerves. One day she's sweet, like butter wouldn't melt in her mouth, and then she turns around and acts all crabby. I mean, what is her *problem*?"

"What's your guess?"

"Beats me. They're still looking for someone to fill the position, which gritches her but good. She thinks she should be promoted instead of just being used is how she put it."

"If she did get promoted, who would she replace?"

"Mrs. Delacorte. She's the one who got canned."

I kept my expression neutral. Not only was she bored, but she hadn't learned the basic rules, the most compelling of which is never, never, never confide company secrets in the likes of me. I said, "Golly, that's too bad. Why was she fired, has anybody said?" My lies and fake behavior are usually heralded by "Gollys" and "Gees."

"She wasn't fired exactly. It's more like she was laid off."

"Oh, right. And when was that?"

"The same time as Mrs. Bart. She's the bookkeeper since way back when. They were interviewing for her position the same time I applied for this one."

"How come?"

"How come what?"

"I wonder how the bookkeeper and the administrator got laid off at the same time. Was that coincidence?"

"Not at all," she said. "Mrs. Bart was let go and Mrs. Dela-corte got upset and raised a stink. Mr. Harrington suggested she might be happier finding work somewhere else, so that's what she did. This is all stuff I heard." She stopped what she was saying and her eyes seemed to widen behind the red plastic frames. "You're not taking notes. I'm not supposed to gossip. Mrs. S. is hell on that."

I held up my hands. "I'm just making conversation 'til the rain lets up."

She patted her chest. "Whew! For a minute, I got nervous. I wouldn't want you to get the wrong impression. I mean, it's like I told her, I'd never blab anybody's private business. It's not in my nature."

"You and me both," I said. "So who's Mr. Harrington? I never heard of him."

"He works for the billing company in Santa Maria."

"And he's the one who hired you?"

"Kind of. He interviewed me by phone, but only after Mrs. S. had already approved my application. That's the way it works around here. Make the guys think they're in charge when we're really the ones who do everything."

"I thought Dr. Purcell did all the hiring and firing."

"I don't know anything about that. I was here less than two weeks when he, you know, ran off or whatever. I think that's why Mr. Harrington was forced to step in."

"Where's Mrs. Delacorte work now? Has anybody said?"

"She's over at St. Terry's. I know because last week she stopped by to visit with Mrs. S. Turns out she found a great job so it's worked out fine. Getting laid off can be a blessing, though it didn't seem like it at the time is what she says."

"What about Mrs. Bart?"

"I don't know where she went."

"Did you know Dr. Purcell?"

"I knew who he was, but that's about it. That's his office in there. He just like, you know, vanished. It really gives me the creeps."

"Weird. I wonder what went on."

"No telling. The whole staff's upset. All the residents adored him. He made sure everybody got a card on their birthday and stuff like that. He paid out of his own pocket just so all these pitiful old people would feel special."

"Has anyone made a guess about what happened to him?"

"It's all they talked about at first. I mean, not me so much because I hardly knew him."

"What kind of thing . . ."

I could see Merry wrestle with her conscience, deliberating a good seven seconds before She-Who-Never-Blabs leaned toward me. "Promise you won't repeat this. . . ."

"I won't even say it *once*."

She lowered her voice. "Mrs. S. thinks he left the country."

I lowered my voice, too. "Because of . . ."

"Medicare."

"Oh, that's right. Someone mentioned that before, but I didn't have a chance to ask. Meaning what?"

She said, "*F-R-A-U-D*. Last winter, the OIG—"

"OIG?"

"Oh, that's the Office of Inspector General. They're part of the Department of Health and Human Services. Anyway, OIG faxed us this list of charts and billing records they wanted to see. Mrs. S. said at first Dr. Purcell didn't think anything of it. They do that sometimes just to keep you on your toes. But then they came back and he figured out how serious it was. He kept going over the information to see how it'd look to them. Not good. Up to his lower lip in poop, to coin her phrase."

"Is that why he'd been working late the last couple of months?"

"Well, yeah."

"So the place is under investigation?"

"Big time. It started as a desk audit. They wanted a bunch of stuff covering the past two years. That's when Dr. P. came in as the medical director. I mean, he's that and administrator with a hyphen in between. The way Mrs. S. tells it, if Pacific Meadows loses its funding, the place'll be shut down. Not to mention all the penalties—you know, fines and restitution. She says maybe even jail time, plus the public embarrass-ment. The Purcells are like this big-time la-di-dah social couple so you can imagine the disgrace. Dr. P. was the one lined up to take the brunt of it. Like his butt's in a sling. Those are her words, not mine."

"What about his employers?"

"Oh, the other two don't have anything to do with the hands-on stuff. They're all over the state, taking care of other business."

"Well, that sounds scary for Dr. Purcell," I said.

"I'd've died if it'd been me."

"I'll bet," I said. "When did this first come up?"

"I think last January, way before my time. Then in March, these two guys from MFCU swooped in unannounced—that's the Medicaid Fraud Control Unit. They came loaded with questions and a list of all the charts they wanted pulled. Everybody scrambled around, practically wetting their pants. Dr. P. was notified of this big list of violations and a lot of questionable claims, meaning P-H-O-N-Y. We're talking *thousands* of dollars. Half a million at least and that's just scratching the surface. He could turn out to be a major big-time crook."

"I'm surprised it didn't hit the papers."

"Mrs. S. says they'll keep a lid on it 'til they see what they've got. Meantime, they're breathing down his neck and they mean business."

"So she thinks he bolted to avoid punishment?"

"Well, I sure would if I was in his place."

"How do you know it was him? Other people must've had access to billing records. Maybe that's why the bookkeeper was laid off," I said.

She leaned forward and lowered her gaze. "You won't mention this, you swear? Cross your heart."

I crossed my heart and held up my hand.

"Mrs. Dorner—she's director of Staff Development? She thinks Dr. P. could've been kidnapped. Snatched in the parking lot to keep him quiet."

I said, "Wow," and made a skeptical face. "Unfortunately, the cops say there's no real evidence of that."

"It wouldn't take much. Slap tape on his mouth, throw him in the trunk, and take off," she said. "They could have used his own car, which is why it hasn't been found."

I saw Merry's look as she began to busy herself, fussing with the mail. "That's a very good point."

I glanced over my shoulder. A nurse in a white uniform was standing in the doorway. She had fixed us with a look that was both shrewd and intimidating. I cleared my throat and said, "Well. Merry. I better scoot and let you get back to work. I'll stop back on Monday and chat with Mrs. Stegler."

"I'll tell her you were here."

The nurse turned and looked at me as I passed through the doorway within inches of her. I repressed the urge to shudder once my back was turned, wondering exactly how much she'd heard.

At the entrance, I retrieved my slicker and took a moment to reassemble myself in rain garb. When I emerged from the nursing home, the rain had slowed to a drizzle and a mist seemed to float on the tarmac like smoke. The eaves still dripped water at irregular intervals. I bypassed a puddle and crossed the parking lot to the slot I'd taken. I could see now, with fresh eyes, that the name newly painted out at the foot of the parking space was P. DELACORTE.

Once in my car, I opened the pack of index cards and

started taking notes—one fact per card—until I'd emptied my brain. I couldn't help wondering why Crystal and/or the cops hadn't mentioned this fraud business when I'd talked to them.

7

AFTER I LEFT Pacific Meadows, I stopped by Kingman and Ives and let myself in the side door. I went into my office and peeled off my slicker, which I hung on my coat tree. Happily for me, the place felt deserted despite the fact there were lights on in most of the offices. The Saturday-morning cleaning crew had come and gone. Wastebaskets had been emptied. The air was scented with Pledge, and I could see rows of fresh vacuum cleaner tracks on the burnt-orange carpeting. The quiet was divine. Briefly, I conjured up an image of the new one-person office on Floresta Street. I was already feeling competitive with the other prospective tenants.

I pulled out my portable Smith-Corona and placed it on my desk. I sat down in my swivel chair and took out the file I'd opened. I sorted through the notes I'd assembled, adding the information on the index cards. Looming large in my mind was Fiona's return on Tuesday. I could already see her, arms crossed, one foot tapping with impatience while I brought her up to date. She'd have dollar signs dancing like sugarplums above her head, thinking, *Fifty bucks an hour for this?* My strategy was to outfox the woman by presenting a beautifully

constructed, typewritten report that would make it look like
I'd done a lot more than drive around chatting with folks.
What I labored under was the burdensome sense of Fiona's
disapproval, knowing she begrudged me every nickel I spent.
Even if her original display of irritation had been pure manipulation, I could feel the sting of her whip on my neck. I
tried not to dwell on the notion that I should have declined the
job when I had the chance.

I focused my attention on the business at hand. It took me
an hour to sketch out a rough draft. I typed it and did some
editing, revising it twice. I kept my language neutral, being
careful to avoid drawing conclusions from what I'd learned so
far. I also omitted much of what Crystal had said. I was being
paid to find Dow, not to tattle to Fiona on his second wife.
When I was satisfied the document was as polished as I could
make it, I typed the new draft. Then I got out my calculator
and added up my hours. How long had I spent with Detective
Odessa? I tapped with my pencil on my front teeth. Really it
was twenty minutes max, which I rounded out to half an hour.
Didn't want Fiona thinking I'd short-changed her with the
cops. Let's see. I'd spent almost two hours with Crystal and I
added another hour to cover my morning visit to Pacific
Meadows. I eyeballed the numbers. So far, I'd only earned
$175 out of the $1,500 she'd paid me up front, which meant I
still owed her $1,325 worth of my life. At this rate, I'd never
be out from under. Oh well. I typed the invoice and attached it
to the original of my report, then placed the copies in the
folder.

I stood up and stretched, working the kinks out of my neck
with a head roll or two. Feeling restless, I wandered down the
inner corridor, peering into offices along the way. As I passed
Lonnie's office, I was startled to catch sight of him. He sat
tilted back in his swivel chair, his feet propped up on the edge
of his desk, a transcript in his lap, apparently catching up on

work while the office was quiet and the phones were silent. In lieu of the usual dress shirt and suit, he wore a plaid flannel shirt and a pair of stone-washed jeans. His concentration was complete, a focus that caused his whole body to become still. I watched him reach for his pencil and underline a phrase, soft scratching in the quiet.

Lonnie looks like a boxer, his body dense and muscular, his nose thickened by scars. His hair is dark and unruly, growing in all directions. I've seen newborns like that, with a head of hair so thick and unexpected it seems comical. He's a man of high energy, generally souped up on vitamins, coffee, nutritional supplements, and competitive drive. This was probably as relaxed as I'd ever seen him.

"Lonnie?"

He glanced up and smiled, tossing his pencil aside. "Kinsey. Come on in. I've been wondering what you were up to. I haven't seen you for weeks."

"Not much. I didn't even know you were here. The place has been so quiet, I thought I was alone. Catching up on work?"

"Sure, but it's just an excuse. Marie's out of town. Some convention of butt-kickers down in San Diego. Tell you the truth, I'd rather be here than stuck by myself at home. Have a seat," he said. "What about you? What brings you in on a Saturday afternoon?"

"I was typing up some notes while things were fresh on my mind. Oh hey, before I forget. A guy named Richard Hevener may be calling to check my references."

"What's the deal?"

"I think I found office space, but I'm waiting to see." I filled him in on the situation, describing the newly renovated cottage with its redwood deck. "It's great. Small and quiet and the location's perfect."

"If he calls, I promise I'll sing your praises. I won't say a word about the tiny bit of time you spent incarcerated. Meantime, the door's always open if it doesn't work out."

"I appreciate that. Cross your fingers for me."

"Not a problem," he said. "Ida Ruth tells me you're working on Dr. Purcell's disappearance."

"How'd she hear *that*? I only took the job yesterday."

Lonnie waved a hand in the air. "Ida Ruth knows everything. She makes a point of it. Actually, she has a friend who used to work for him. Current speculation has it he's run away from home. Days when I think about doing that myself."

"Oh, please. Marie would come after you and hunt you down like a dog." His wife was a martial arts instructor, an expert in ways to cripple people with her size-five bare feet.

"There is that. Of course, the problem with disappearing is you can't do it on impulse. Not if you're serious. Takes long-term planning if you want to stay gone for good."

"So you'd think. Personally, I suspect he's dead, but his passport and thirty thousand dollars disappeared at about the same time."

"Thirty thousand dollars would evaporate in six months. Purcell's accustomed to living well. He's not going to pinch pennies. At his age? He'd have to be nuts."

"That was my reaction. On the other hand, if he settled in a Third World country, he could live pretty well on it, and if he ran short of funds, he could probably set up a small practice with no questions asked."

"Why not just stay where he is?"

"Ah. I forgot to tell you the wrinkle I came across today." I filled him in on my visit to Pacific Meadows and the chat I'd had with Merry, the Patron Saint of Loose Lips. "According to her, the federal fraud busters are hot on his trail. Half a million dollars in bogus claims. Guilty or innocent, he might have taken off once he realized they were closing in."

Lonnie winced with impatience. "Get serious. No way.

The feds aren't gonna put a guy like him in jail. The prosecutor has to prove criminal intent and how's he going to do that? Believe me, Medicare regulations would drive any honest man insane. So you weasel the deal; claim coding errors and incompetent clerical help. They might fine him and wag a finger, but any good attorney could get him off. Hell, I could do it myself and I don't know beans about that stuff. First thing you do is bore the hell out of the jury. Put up a bunch of charts and graphs, citing statistics 'til nine out of the twelve start nodding off. Suggest the old doc's gone senile or he's a poor businessman." He paused with a snort of amusement. "You hear about that case? Some guy up in Fresno got acquitted because a jury decided he was too dumb to be guilty of embezzlement. His own attorney painted him as such a buffoon, the jury took pity and cut the poor dunce loose. Purcell's in no danger."

"Yeah, but did he know that? And what about the public disgrace?"

"Nobody cares about those things in this day and age." Lonnie picked up his pencil and drew a box on his legal pad. "One thing you're forgetting. If the guy's smart . . . say he's ripped off the system to the tune of half a million bucks, which is probably conservative. All they know about so far. Call it two million dollars just to make it worth the risk. A smart guy makes two, maybe three trips abroad. Picks a country where he knows he can count on extradition laws if the feds track him down. He sets up a bank account and feeds money in, transferring funds until he has what he needs. Then he can go on merrily cheating 'til someone's onto him. Situation heats up, he's on the first plane out. In that case, the thirty thousand dollars is just his travel fund."

I thought about Fiona's story of Dowan's vanishing twice without explanation. "Good point." I was also thinking about the bookkeeper, who got fired, and the assistant administrator, who quit her job in protest. Maybe that was Dow's attempt to point a finger elsewhere. The phone rang and Lonnie picked up the handset. From the nature of his comments, it was Marie checking in. I waved at him and eased out of his office, leaving him to finish his conversation in private.

I returned to my office and reread my report. It seemed okay, but I thought I'd let it sit for a day. I'd be adding interviews once I figured out who I'd be talking to next. I drew up a list from the possibilities I'd gleaned. Purcell's business associates were among the top five names, along with Dow's best friend. I made sure I had the necessary phone numbers and then decided I'd done enough and it was time to go home.

At two o'clock, I made myself some milk of tomato soup and a gooey grilled cheese sandwich that I dipped in my bowl and lifted dripping to my lips. The liquid red of the soup against the crunchy golden surface of the bread was a culinary portrait of early childhood consolation. Aunt Gin first served me this confection when I was five years old, mourning my parents who'd been killed in a car wreck the previous May. The ooze of melted Velveeta will always prompt the curious sensation of sorrow and satisfaction commingling on the surface of my tongue. This sandwich, I confess, was the highlight of my weekend, which is what life boils down to when you're celibate.

Afterward, I did what any other trained professional investigator would do: I walked the six steps into the living room, flipped off my shoes, and settled on the sofa, where I covered myself in a big puffy comforter and started reading a book. Within minutes, I'd been sucked through a wormhole into a fictional world, traveling faster than the speed of words into a realm without sound and without gravity.

The phone rang, the sound annoyingly shrill. I'd sunk like a stone into a river of dreams and I was disoriented by the need to surface. I reached back, fumbling for the phone, which was resting on the end table above my head. I hadn't even realized

I'd fallen asleep, except for the drooling, which I don't ordinarily do when awake.

"Ms. Millhone?"

"Yes." If this was someone selling something I was going to say a very bad word.

"This is Blanche McKee."

Three seconds passed. The name meant nothing. I rubbed my face and said, "Who?"

"Fiona Purcell's daughter. I understand Mother's hired you. I just wanted you to know how relieved we all are. We've been urging her to do this ever since Daddy disappeared."

"Oh, right. Sorry. I couldn't place the name. How're you?" Groggily, I sat up, pulling the quilt around me like a tribal robe.

"Fine, thanks. I hope I'm not calling at a bad time. I didn't wake you, did I?"

"Not at all," I said. The truth is, everyone knows you've been sleeping regardless of how earnestly you might lie to them.

Blanche must have decided to take me at my word. "I'm not sure how much Mother's told you—quite a lot, I'm sure—but if there's anything I can do, I'll be happy to help. Did she mention my friend Nancy?"

"I don't believe so. The name doesn't sound familiar."

"I was afraid of that. Mother tends to be a cynic, which you might have guessed. Nancy's recently moved to Chico, but she's available for consultation anytime by phone."

"Nancy. Good news. I'm making a note." Whoever Nancy was.

"I'm assuming you'll want my personal impressions as well."

"Sure. I mean, eventually. That'd be great."

"I'm so happy you said that because I was thinking—if you have a minute this afternoon, you might want us to get together so I can share my concerns."

I hesitated. "Ah. Well. You know, at the moment, I'm more interested in facts than impressions and concerns. No offense."

"None taken. I didn't mean to imply that I don't have facts."

"Uh-huh." I hadn't forgotten Fiona's barely disguised contempt for her younger daughter, mother of four, soon to be mother of five. On the other hand, maybe Fiona'd told Blanche about me in order to test my perseverance, since I'd made such a point of it during our meeting.

Blanche said, "What time would suit?"

I went ahead and mouthed the bad word, adding another choice expletive from my extensive collection. "Hang on a second. I'll check my schedule." I held the receiver to my chest while I looked at my watch. 4:06. I allowed time to pass while I pretended to scan my day planner with its numerous Saturday-afternoon appointments. I had no particular desire to meet Blanche, especially at the cost of a first-class nap. I hated the idea of abandoning my lair and I certainly didn't want to traipse all over town on such a cold, damp day. My living room windows were already gray with the premature November twilight and I could see the drizzle slant against the bare branches that were tapping at the panes. I glanced at my watch again. 4:07.

I could hear Blanche breathing and when she spoke, her tone was sharp. "Kinsey, are you there?"

"I'm here. Gee, it looks like I'm booked up today. Tomorrow might be possible. I could be there by ten o'clock."

"That won't work for me and Monday's out of the question. Isn't there *any* way you could stop by? I feel it's terribly important."

What I personally felt was a surge of irritation. I could just see Fiona returning from San Francisco, carping because I hadn't taken time to interview Blanche. *Fifteen hundred dollars and you couldn't even bother to see my daughter?* I said,

"I could be there by five-thirty, but only for half an hour. That's the best I can do."

"Perfect. That's fine. We're up on Edenside at the corner of Monterey Terrace. The number's 1236. It's a two-story Spanish. You'll see a dark blue station wagon parked in the drive."

Edenside Road was part of a small housing development cunningly tucked into the foothills; five winding streets, each of which ended in a wide cul-de-sac. The builder had followed the terrain, taking the path of least resistance, the five streets built into the contours of the hill like rivulets of asphalt flowing from the highest point. My progress was halting, an exasperating ten miles an hour, as I slowed for a speed bump every fifteen yards or so. The neighborhood was ideal for children, whose presence was announced by the number of strollers, playhouses, swing sets, bicycles, tricycles, Big Wheels, and skateboards littering the yards. It looked like a Toys "R" Us had exploded close by.

The house at the corner of Edenside and Monterey Terrace was indeed a two-story Spanish hacienda with a courtyard in front. Even in the gathering dark, I couldn't miss the three-car garage that jutted forward aggressively like a pugnacious jaw. As I watched, the low-voltage landscape lights came on, illuminating the front of the house. The exterior stucco was tinted a gaudy pink and the roof tiles, while clay, were a series of interlocking orange *S*'s, clearly mass produced. The original clay tiles still gracing many older structures in town are now a dark faded red, mottled with lichen and shaped like a *C* where the worker once laid the soft clay across his thigh in forming it.

As promised, there was a dark blue station wagon parked in the drive. I pulled in at the curb, got out, locked my car, and approached the house along a crushed granite walk. The surrounding landscape was drought-proofed; all gravel and concrete, scattered with assorted cacti and oversized succulents. I let myself in through a small iron gate and crossed the tile-paved courtyard. A mock Spanish fountain splashed water by way of a circulating pump.

I rang the bell. I could hear shrieks, barking dogs, and the clattering of small feet as a pack of short folk battled for the honor of playing butler to me. As the door opened, a girl of perhaps five turned to sock the four-year-old boy-child behind her. Within seconds, fists were flailing, the children red-faced and tearful as they struggled for possession of the knob between shoves and kicks with brown hard-soled shoes. Meanwhile, two hyperactive Jack Russell terriers leaped up and down as though spring-loaded. The toddler bringing up the rear got knocked on his diaper and set up a howl. Another girl, her back turned, was walking down the hallway toward the rear of the house, bellowing, "Mom!! Mooommy! Heather's socking Josh and the dogs just knocked Quentin on his bee-hind."

"Amanda, what did I tell you about whining? Josh can take care of himself. Now please mind your own business and quit tattling or you will drive me insane."

Sway-backed, Blanche lumbered into sight, the sphere of her belly so large it looked a rogue moon, held in orbit by unseen gravitational forces. Her maternity outfit was a pale gray washable silk, palazzo pants, a long tunic, with tricky buttons and flaps. I was guessing that when the babe came, she'd be able to plop a boob out and feed the little tyke on demand. She had long blond hair, the strands fine and glossy, reaching almost to her waist. Her porcelain complexion was tinted a pale peach. Blue eyes, high forehead, finely arched brows. She looked like a storyland princess from a book of Grimm's fairy tales—except, great with child.

She swooped down and gathered up the howling baby, whom she settled on her hip. She grabbed Heather by the arm, hauling her away from her brother and then giving her a push along the corridor. "You kids go out in the backyard. Amanda's going to make you some peanut butter crackers. You can have a snack out there. Just don't eat too many. We're having supper in a bit. Now scoot. I mean it. Everybody go on outside."

"Mo-om, it's *dark*."

"Well, turn the porch light on."

"But we want to watch cartoons!"

"Too bad. You do what I say. And no running," Blanche warned. Heather and Josh were already pounding down the hall, but they slowed to a power walk, knocking and bumping each other. The dogs followed, barking, while Amanda veered off into the kitchen to make peanut butter crackers without an audible complaint. Amanda, who couldn't have been much more than seven years old, was already being cast in the role of secondary mom.

While Blanche was issuing orders, she'd managed to jiggle the crying baby and his howls had subsided. She turned and labored toward the family room with me tagging along behind her as well as I could. There were toys everywhere. In order to avoid crushing plastic underfoot, I had to shuffle, making a path through the Legos strewn on the floor in front of me. A wooden gate had been secured across the stairs to the second floor and what I assumed was the basement door had a hook-and-eye closure to prevent kidlets from tumbling headlong into the yawning abyss. Ever the optimist, I said, "Your mother mentioned a nanny."

"She isn't here on weekends and Andrew's currently out of town."

"What sort of work does he do?"

"He's an attorney. Mergers and acquisitions. He's in Chicago until Wednesday."

"When's the new baby due?"

"Technically, not for three weeks yet, but he'll probably come early. All the other ones have."

In the family room, a toy chest stood open, its contents flung in every direction: dolls, teddy bears, a bright yellow school bus filled with brightly painted spool kids with round painted heads. There was a wooden bench and mallet for pounding wooden pegs, crayons, picture books, Tinkertoys, small metal cars, a wooden train. A playpen had been erected in the center of the room. I spotted a mechanical swing, a circular walker with surrounding rubber bumpers, a high chair, an infant seat, and a portable crib. Every wall socket in view had been blanked out by plastic inserts. There was nothing on any surface below see-level, every breakable object removed to a high shelf as though in preparation for a coming flood.

From outside, I could hear a piercing shriek go up, this at a higher decibel level than the earlier shrieking in the hall. Amanda started screaming, "Mommy! Mom!! Heather pushed Josh off the jungle gym and he has blood coming out of his nose. . . ."

Blanche said, "Oh, lord. Here, take him."

Without pausing, she handed off the baby like a forward pass and waddled into the kitchen. Quentin was surprisingly heavy, his bones dense as stone. He watched his mother depart and then his eyes moved to mine. Though Quentin was as yet incapable of speech, I could see the concept "Monster" forming in his underdeveloped brain. The enormity of his plight began to dawn on him, and he pursed his small mouth in advance of a round of howls.

I called, "Can I put him in his playpen?"

"No. He hates that," she yelled as she went out the backdoor. The screaming in the yard was taken up by a second child apparently vying for equal time. As if in response, Quentin's mouth came open in a cry so deep-seated he made no sound at first. He curled his body inward while he gathered his strength. Without warning, he flung himself outward like a diver in the midst of a back flip. He might have torn himself entirely out of my grasp if I hadn't grabbed him and swung him up from the floor. I said, "Whee!" as though the two of us were really having fun. The look on his face suggested otherwise.

I tried jiggling him as she had, but that only made matters worse. Now I was not only a monster, but a Monster Baby Jiggler, intent on shaking him to death. I walked around in a circle, saying, "There, there, there." The child was not soothed. Finally, in desperation, I lowered him into the playpen, forcing his stiff legs to bend until he was fully seated. I handed him two alphabet blocks and part of a half-eaten soda cracker. The howling ceased at once. He put the cracker in his mouth and banged the letter *P* against the plastic padding under him. I stood up, patting myself on the chest while I moved into the kitchen to see what was happening.

Blanche was just banging through the backdoor with four-year-old Josh on her hip, his legs hanging way past her knees. I could see a lump on his forehead the size of an egg and copious blood on his upper lip. One-handed, she dampened a kitchen towel, opened the freezer, and took out some ice cubes, which she wrapped in the towel and pressed against his head. She carried him into the family room and sank into a chair. The minute she sat down, he worked his way through a flap in her tunic and began to nurse. Taken aback, I averted my eyes. I thought kids his age had been twelve-stepped out of that. She indicated a nearby chair, paying him not the slightest attention as he suckled her right breast.

I glanced down at the chair and removed a half-consumed peanut-butter-and-jelly sandwich before I settled on the edge. Josh's medical emergency apparently entitled all of the children to escape the chill and dark outside. The next thing I knew, a cartoon show blasted from the TV set. Heather and Amanda sat cross-legged on the floor, and Josh joined them moments later holding the towel-wrapped ice cubes to his head.

I tried to concentrate on what Blanche was saying, but all I could think about was that even at my age, a tubal ligation probably wasn't out of the question.

8

I GLANCED AT my watch, a gesture that wasn't lost on her.

"I know you're in a hurry so I'll get to the point. Has Mother filled you in on Crystal's past?"

"I know she was a stripper before she married your dad."

"I'm not talking about that. Did she mentioned Crystal's fourteen-year-old daughter was born out of wedlock?"

I waited, wondering at the relevance. I leaned forward, not from avid interest, but because the whistles, bangs, and manic music from the television set were loud enough to cause permanent hearing loss. I watched Blanche's lips move, putting the sentences together belatedly like the subtitles on a foreign film.

"I'm not even sure Crystal knows who the father is. Then she married Lloyd *somebody* and had another child by him. That boy died when he was eighteen months old, an accidental drowning—this was four or five years ago."

I squinted. "And you think this is somehow connected to your father's disappearance?"

She seemed startled. "Well, no, but you said you wanted

all the facts. I wanted to fill in the picture so you could see what you're up against."

"Meaning what?" A commercial came on, the sound ratcheted up a notch so the little children who lived across the street wouldn't miss the pitch for a vitamin-rich cereal that was supposed to look and taste like licorice.

Blanche was saying, "Doesn't Crystal's behavior strike you as odd?"

I was largely lip-reading by now and her comment had gone completely over my head. "Blanche, could we turn down the sound on the television set?"

"Sorry." She reached for the remote control and muted the sound. The silence was heaven. The children continued to sit on the floor, arranged in front of the set as though gathered around a campfire. Frantic images danced across the screen in colors so vivid they left an afterimage if I glanced away.

Blanche returned to her commentary. "I don't know about you, but Crystal doesn't seem at all distraught about what's happened. She's cool as can be, which seems inappropriate to me."

"It *has* been nine weeks. I don't think anyone can be distraught for that long. Defenses kick in. You manage to adjust or you go insane."

"I just think it's interesting that Crystal's never made a public appeal for information about Daddy. She's never offered a reward. She's never sent out any flyers. No psychics have been consulted. . . ."

That caught me up short. "You think a psychic would help?"

"It wouldn't *hurt*," she said. "My friend Nancy's uncanny. She has this amazing, quite incredible gift."

"She's a psychic? Is that why she's offering to consult with me on the phone?"

"Of course. When I lost my diamond ring, she was able to pinpoint the exact location."

"How'd she do that? I'm really curious."

"It's hard to describe. She said she smelled something sweet. She saw glimpses of white, maybe something nautical. She did two separate . . . readings, for lack of a better word . . . and the images were the same. Then I realized the last time I remembered seeing the ring, I'd taken it off to wash my hands at the bathroom sink. I'd already searched that area half a dozen times. As it turned out, I'd set the ring in the soap dish and it was embedded on the underside of the soap, which is exactly what she smelled."

I said, "What was the white part? Was that the bathroom sink?"

"Not in that bathroom. The sink is hunter green in there, but the soap was white."

"Got it. What was the nautical part?"

Blanche's tone was defensive. "Not everything's *literal*. Some of the images she sees are metaphorical . . . you know, associative."

"Nautical . . . faucet water," I suggested gamely.

"The point is, Nancy's offered to consult with Crystal, but she refuses to cooperate."

"Maybe she doesn't believe in psychics."

"But Nancy's fabulous. I swear."

"How much does she charge?"

"Oh, she doesn't want money. Ordinarily, she does, but this is strictly out of friendship with me."

"Why does Crystal have to be involved? Can't Nancy do a reading and simply tell you what she sees?"

"She has to have access to the house so she can pick up on Daddy's vibes, his psychic energy. I took her over to his office and let her sit in his chair. She keeps getting this picture of him approaching a house and going through the front door. Then nothing. This has to be Crystal's beach property because she visualizes sand."

"Could be the desert."

Blanche blinked. "Well, I suppose it could."

"Anyway, go on. Sorry to interrupt."

"But that's it. She sees a door and then blank. Without Crystal's help, she can only go so far. We think he left the office and drove out to the beach house as usual, only something went terribly wrong. Of course, Crystal denies this. She claims he never arrived, but we only have her word for it."

"So you think she knows where he is and she's covering?"

"Well, yes," she said, as though surprised I'd ask. "Nancy can feel his presence. She gets the strong impression he's been hurt. He's definitely surrounded by darkness. She says he's trying to reach us, but something's holding him back."

"He's alive?"

"She's sure he's alive. She's very clear about that. However, she says there are some very negative forces at work. She says he's distressed because he doesn't know where he is. He's encompassed by this oppressive spiritual consciousness. She can feel his confusion, but that's as much as she gets. Nancy says Crystal's very connected to Daddy's plight. In fact, she probably caused it."

"How?"

"Well, she could have knocked him out and driven him away somewhere."

"And done what with his car? I don't mean to argue. I'm genuinely puzzled."

"There could have been two of 'em. She could have hired someone. How do I know? I'm just telling you . . . nothing would suit her better than to have him out of the way."

"Why? I mean, just for the sake of argument, let's say she had him kidnapped and he's being held against his will. What's her motive? Can't be money. There hasn't been a ransom note and no contact from anyone offering to make a deal."

Blanche leaned forward. "Listen. Before she married my father, she signed a prenuptial agreement, according to which she gets absolutely nothing if they divorce."

"Wait a minute. Back up. You still haven't told me how she intends to profit if she had him snatched."

"I didn't say she had him kidnapped. I said she knows where he is."

"What's that have to do with a pre-nup?"

"She's been having an affair."

"Your mother mentioned that as well. This is Clint Augustine?"

"Exactly. Now she wants her freedom, but she wants the money, too. If she tries to divorce him, she'll end up with nothing. The only way she benefits is if Daddy dies."

"Which, according to Nancy, he hasn't done yet."

"That's right."

"Why would she risk anything as blatant as an affair with her personal trainer? Wouldn't word get out?"

"He was her personal trainer; he's not now. Once she started screwing him, I guess they decided to discontinue the public aspects of their relationship. The rumors started flying in any event."

"How did you find out?"

"From Mother's friend, Dana Glazer. She and her husband have a house in Horton Ravine. Joel's one of Daddy's—"

"Employers. Yes, I heard about that."

"The Glazer property backs right up to Daddy's with just a little fence in between. They have a guest cottage back there, and Crystal asked if they'd consider renting it temporarily to a friend of hers. She claimed he'd bought a house he had to renovate and the work wouldn't be finished until early fall. This was back in January. Anyway, the Glazers don't use the cottage, so they decided, hey, why not? They asked eight hundred dollars a month, and the guy never batted an eye. Of course, once Dana realized what was going on, she was horrified. She found it thoroughly repulsive, which is why she hated having to tell my mom."

"Why'd she tell you?"

"She didn't. I heard it from another friend. Dana confirmed the story, but only because I pressed. Believe me, I don't gossip."

"A lot of people don't. It doesn't seem to stop them from passing stuff on. Why didn't Dana evict him if she found the situation so repellent?"

"Because he signed a six-month lease. He's gone now and good riddance. You're welcome to talk to her if you don't believe me. I mean, Dana ought to know. It happened right under her nose. Poor mother. She still thinks Daddy's coming back to her. Bad enough he left her for such a . . . *tart,* but the fact that Crystal's still *doing* it makes Daddy look like a fool."

"Which leads us to what conclusion?"

"Crystal wants him dead. She wants him out of the way," she said with the first flash of feeling I'd seen in her. Her mouth trembled and she began to blink rapidly. She looked off toward the hallway, taking a moment to compose herself. Under her maternity tunic, I saw a knot move across her lap, probably the baby's foot. I could see why people reached out impulsively to lay a hand on such a belly. Blanche directed her comments to the far side of the room. "Believe me, she married Daddy for his money. The pre-nup was just a ploy. She might have meant it at the time, but then she ran into Clint and got involved with him. Like I said, if Daddy dies, she inherits the bulk of his estate and then she's home free. If she divorces him, she gets nothing. It's as simple as that."

"Blanche, you don't know for a fact your father's dead. None of us know that. Even your friend Nancy claims he's still alive."

Blanche's gaze swung back to mine, her blue eyes ablaze. "Don't say '*even* Nancy' like she's a charlatan. I resent that."

"Not my intention. I withdraw the word. The point is, she has an image of him helpless, but alive, at least from what you say."

"But for how long? The man's nearly seventy years old. What if he's tied up, what if he's gagged and can't breathe?"

"All right, all right. Let me see what I can do to check it out. So far, this is pure theory, but I can appreciate the worry."

The minute I got home, I went to my desk and began taking notes, writing down the list of possibilities for Dowan Purcell's fate. I'd dismissed the notion that he'd been kidnapped, but maybe I was wrong. He might have been forcibly removed and carted off somewhere, in which case, he was either dead (sorry, Nance) or being held against his will. I detailed the other options, writing them down as quickly as they occurred to me. He could have left voluntarily, departing of his own accord, on the run or hiding out. He could have met with an accident while driving under the influence. If he were lying at the bottom of a canyon, it would certainly explain the fact that his Mercedes hadn't been spotted yet. He could have been subject to any one of a number of fatal incidents: aneurysm, heart attack, stroke. If so, it was puzzling that no one had stumbled across the body, but it sometimes happens that way.

Or what? He could have established a secret life, having slipped from one persona into the next. What else? Fearing disgrace, he could have killed himself. Or, as Blanche suggested, someone could have killed him for gain, or to cover something worse. I couldn't think of any other permutations. Well, two. Amnesia, though that felt like an old '30s movie plot. Or he might have been assaulted by a mugger who overplayed his hand and then disposed of the body. The only other possibility was his having been arrested and jailed, but according to Detective Odessa, Purcell hadn't shown up in any law enforcement computer system. From this, I surmised that he hadn't been identified as the perpetrator of his own crimes or the victim of anyone else's.

I studied the list. There were certain variations I had no way to pursue. For instance, if Dow had been taken ill, if he'd been injured or killed in a fatal accident, I had no way to know unless someone stepped forward with information. The cops had already canvassed hospitals in the area. This was one of those times when being a small-town private investigator (and a lone operator on top of that) made the job difficult. I had no access to airline, immigration, or customs records, so I couldn't determine if Purcell had boarded a plane (or a train or a boat) in his name or someone else's (using a fake driver's license and a fake passport). If he were still in this country, he might well evade notice as long as he didn't use his credit cards, didn't rent or buy property, didn't apply for a telephone or utilities, didn't drive with expired tags, or in any other way attract attention to himself or his vehicle. He couldn't vote, couldn't do work that required his true Social Security number, couldn't open a bank account. He certainly couldn't practice medicine, which is how he'd earned a living for the past forty years.

Of course, if he'd cooked up a false identity, he could do as he pleased as long as his story was plausible and his bona fides checked out. If this were the case, finding him would be next to impossible after only nine weeks. There simply hadn't been enough time for his name to surface in the records. My only hope was to plod my way systematically from friend to friend, colleague to associate, current wife to ex, daughter to daughter, in hopes of a lead. All I needed was one tiny snag in the fabric of his life, one loop or tear that I might use to unravel his current whereabouts. I decided to focus on the areas over which I had control.

*   *   *

Sunday went by in a blur. I gave myself the day off and spent the time puttering around my apartment, taking care of minor chores.

Monday morning, I got up as usual, pulled on my sweats and my Sauconys, and did a three-mile jog. The cloud cover was dense and the surf was a muddy brown. The rain had eased, but the sidewalks were still wet, and I splashed through shallow puddles as I ran the mile and a half to the bathhouse where I did the turnaround. The earthworms had emerged and lay strewn across the sidewalk like lengths of gray string from an old floor mop. The path was also littered with snails traversing the walk with all the optimism of the innocent. I had to watch where I stepped to keep from crushing them.

Back at my place, I picked up my gym bag and headed over to the gym. I parked my car in the only space available, tucked between a pickup truck and a late-model van. Even from the parking lot, I could hear the clank of machines, the grunts of a power lifter straining with a dead lift. Inside, the rock-and-roll music coming in through the speakers competed with a morning news show airing on the ceiling-mounted TV set. Two women on the stair machines climbed patiently while a third woman and two men trotted smartly on treadmills set at double speed. All five sets of eyes were focused on the screen.

I signed in, idly asking Keith, at the desk, if he knew Clint Augustine. Keith's in his twenties, with a busy brown mustache and a gleaming shaven head.

He said, "Sure, I know Clint. You've probably seen him in here. Big guy, white-blond hair. He usually works out at five o'clock when the place first opens up. Sometimes he comes in later with his clients, mostly married chicks. They're a specialty of his." Keith's intermittent use of steroids caused him to swell and shrink according to his consumption. He was currently in shrunken form, which I personally preferred. He was one of those guys with a great chest and biceps, but very little in the way of lower-body development. Maybe he figured because he stood behind a counter, he didn't need to buff out anything below his waist.

"I heard he's been working with Crystal Purcell."

"He did for a while. They'd come in late afternoon, Mondays, Wednesdays, and Fridays. Isn't she the wife of the guy who disappeared a while back? Man, that's a tough one. Something skanky going on there."

"Could be," I said. "Anyway, I gotta get a move on. Thanks for the info."

"Sure thing."

I pulled on my workout gloves and found a quiet spot. I stretched out on a gray mat and started with my ab routine, two sets of fifty sit-ups, hands behind my head, my bent legs resting on a free-weight bench. I could smell glue fumes wafting through the asphalt-gray carpeting. The Nautilus and Universal machines looked like elaborate constructions built from a full-size Erector set: metal verticals, bolts, pulleys, angled joints. Once I finished my sit-ups, I started with leg curls, the exercise I most despise. While I counted fifteen reps, I pictured my hamstrings popping loose and rolling up like window shades. I moved on to leg extensions, which burned like hell, but at least didn't threaten any crippling side effects. Back, chest, and shoulders. I finished my workout with preacher curls and dumbbell curls. I saved the best machine for last: triceps extensions, always a favorite of mine. I left the gym damp with perspiration.

Home again, I showered, pulled on a turtleneck, jeans, and my boots, grabbed a bite of breakfast, and packed myself a brown-bag lunch. I reached the office at nine o'clock and put a call through to the police department, where Detective Odessa assured me he'd do yet another computer check to see if there was any sign of Dow Purcell. He'd already sorted through numerous bulletins describing the unidentified dead throughout the state. There were no Caucasian males in Purcell's age range. Local police, sheriff's department, and CHP officers were being briefed weekly on the importance of keeping an eye out for him. Odessa had increased his coverage, papering most of the medical facilities in the surrounding counties in case Purcell showed up incoherent or comatose.

I briefed him on the people I'd spoken to so far. When I told him about the issue of Medicare fraud, he said, "Yeah, we know that."

"Well, why didn't you tell *me*?"

"Because it's Paglia's call and we're under orders from him."

By the end of the conversation, it was clear we were both still in the dark, though he did seem to appreciate my bringing him up to date. He was even moderately charitable about Blanche's consulting a psychic, which surprised me somehow. I forget that police detectives, in addition to being hard-assed, are also capable of entertaining doubts about such things.

I pulled out the phone number for Jacob Trigg, whose name Crystal had given me, saying he was Dow's best friend. I dialed and spoke briefly to him, explaining who I was, and we set up an appointment for ten o'clock Tuesday morning at his place. I made a note on my calendar and then called Joel Glazer at the office number Crystal had given me. His secretary told me he was working from home and gave me the phone number there so I could reach him. I called the number, briefly identified myself and the fact that Fiona'd hired me. He seemed pleasant and cooperative to the extent that he gave me his address and set up a meeting for one o'clock that afternoon. I then called Santa Teresa Hospital and learned that Penelope Delacorte was now Director of Nursing Services, in her office from nine to five weekdays. I made a note of the title and decided to try her later in the day, after my meeting with Glazer. Lastly, on my own behalf, I made a call to Richard Hevener, whose machine picked up. I left a message inquiring about the status of my rental application. I tried to sound especially winsome on the phone in hopes that might tip the odds in my favor.

At lunchtime, I sat at my desk and ate the peanut-butter-and-pickle sandwich I'd brought from home. At twelve-thirty, I left the building and started walking around the block, hoping I'd remember where I parked my car. I found the VW, unmolested, at the corner of Capillo and Olivio, much closer than I'd thought and in the opposite direction. For the fifth day straight, the sky was overcast, a brooding gray, roiling at the edges where a thick mass of clouds threatened rain.

Santa Teresa is constrained on the north by the mountains and on the south by the Pacific Ocean, limiting geographic growth. The westernmost neighborhoods feather out as far as Colgate; the easternmost sweeping into Montebello where the prices jump. Horton Ravine, where I was headed, is a moneyed enclave, carved out by land grant and deed, whereby successive California governors rewarded military leaders for killing people, really, really well. The resulting three thousand plus acres were passed from rich man to richer, until the last in line, a sheep rancher named Tobias Horton, had the good sense to subdivide the land into saleable lots, thus making a killing of another kind.

I took the 101 as far as the La Cuesta off-ramp, turned left, and followed the road around to the right, heading for the main entrance, which consisted of two massive stone pillars with HORTON RAVINE spelled out in curlicue wrought iron arching between them. The Ravine was lush, the trunks of sycamores and live oaks stained dark from the recent rains. Most of the roads are called "Via *something*"; *vía* being the Spanish word for "way" or "road." I drove past the Horton

Ravine Riding Club, continued a mile, and finally took a right turn and went up a hill.

The Glazers lived on Vía Bueno ("Road Good" . . . if I remember rightly from my brief matriculation in night-school Spanish). The house was 1960s modern, a dazzling white cluster of abstract forms superimposed on one another in what amounted to an architectural pig pile. Three soaring stories were variously angled and cantilevered with a steeply pitched tower driving straight up out of the center of the mass. There were wide decks on all sides and large expanses of glass, into which birds probably regularly propelled themselves and died. When I'd first met Dana Jaffe, she was living in a small housing tract in the town of Perdido, thirty miles to the south. I wondered if she was as conscious as I of how far she'd come.

I parked in a circular motor court and crossed to the low sweeping stairs that led up to the front door. A few minutes passed and then she answered the bell. I could have sworn she was wearing the same outfit I'd seen her in the first time we'd met—tight, faded jeans and a plain white T-shirt. Her hair was still the color of honey, with silver, as fine as silk threads, now appearing in the mix. She'd had it cut and layered, every strand falling into place as she moved her head. Her eyes were khaki or hazel, sometimes reflecting green, sometimes brown under softly feathered brows. Her most arresting feature was her mouth. Her teeth were slightly occluded and the overbite made her lips appear plump and pouty.

She said, "Hello, Kinsey. Joel said you'd be stopping by. Please come in. Let me take that."

"This is beautiful," I said as I stepped inside, slipping off my slicker, which I handed to her. While she hung it in the closet, I had time to gape. The interior was cathedral-like, a vast space crowned by a vaulted ceiling thirty feet above. Bridges and catwalks connected the irregular levels of the house and shafts of sunlight formed geometric patterns on the smooth stone floor.

Dana joined me, saying, "Fiona probably told you we're redoing the place."

"She mentioned that," I said. "She also said you suggested me for this job, which I appreciate."

"You're entirely welcome. I confess I didn't like you back then, but you did seem honest and persistent, a regular little terrier when it came to finding Wendell. Your friend, Mac Voorhies, at California Fidelity, gives you the credit for the fact I got to keep the money."

"I've wondered about that. Last I heard they were still debating the issue. I'm glad it worked out. How well did you know Dow?"

"I ran into him occasionally because of Joel, but we weren't friends. I met Fiona after they divorced, so I tend to side with her. I'm polite when I run into him, but that's about it. Joel's on the phone at the moment, but I'll take you up to the office as soon as he's done. Would you like a look around?"

"That'd be great."

"We're doing this piecemeal. Not my preference. Fiona and I wanted to do it all at once . . . a full installation, which is so much more dramatic and lots more fun, but Joel put his foot down, so we're doing the job in stages. This is the living room, obviously . . ."

She rattled off the rooms as I followed along behind. "Sun room, den, formal dining room. The kitchen's in there. Joel's office is in what we call the 'crows nest' upstairs."

The rooms were clearly in transition. The floors were covered with palace-sized Oriental carpets, probably quite old to judge by the softness of the colors and intricate designs. The furniture, which I assumed was chosen by the deceased Mrs. Glazer, appeared to be almost entirely antique, with massive armoires and occasional pieces in polished mahogany. The few upholstered pieces were done in white linen, the lines clean and clear. A variety of fabric swatches had been draped across the chairs and two-inch samples of paint colors had been taped in various places on the wall. Some of the upholstery fabrics I hadn't seen since my youth, when my aunt Gin would take me to visit her friends. Jungle prints, fakey-looking leopard skin, banana palms, bamboo, zigzags, and chevrons in shades of orange and yellow. The wall paint under consideration was that noxious shade of green that marked most 1930s bathrooms when they hadn't been done in an oh-so-modern mix of pink and black.

"She's found us a sharkskin-top Ruhlmann desk for this wall, with an André Groult mirror. We're thrilled about that."

"I can imagine," I murmured. I could see where Fiona's art deco taste wouldn't be completely out of place, but I couldn't for the life of me picture these cool, elegant rooms redone in black lacquer, plastic, leather, enamel, curly maple, and chrome.

Dana was saying, "Joel was widowed four years ago. He lived here with his wife for the past twenty-two years. The truth is, I'd love to level it, but he can't see the point."

Good for him, I thought. "How's Michael?" I was afraid to ask about her younger son, Brian, because the last time I'd seen him he was on his way back to jail.

"He and Brendon are fine. Juliet left. I guess she got tired of marriage and motherhood."

"Too bad."

"Well," she said, briskly, "let me check and see if Joel's off the phone."

I realized she was just as eager as I to avoid talk of Brian. She moved to an intercom in the dining room, pressing a button that apparently rang through to Joel's office. "Sweetie, are you free?" I heard his muffled reply.

She turned with a smile. "He says to come right on up. I'll walk you to the elevator. Maybe we can chat when you've finished your talk with him."

"I'd like that."

9

JOEL GLAZER'S OFFICE was located on the third floor, a spacious, airy tower room with windows on all four sides. There were no curtains or drapes, but I could see narrow blinds pulled up to the tops of the panes to permit maximum light. His views were spectacular: the ocean, the coastline, the mountains, and the western edges of Horton Ravine. The thickened cloud cover spread gloom across the landscape, at the same time making the deep blue of the mountains and the dark green of the vegetation seem more intense.

In place of a desk, he used a heavy refectory table. All the other pieces of furniture were antiques, except for the seven-foot sofa, done in a tailored rust-colored velvet with white piping along the seams. As in the rooms below, the area rug was an oversized Oriental carpet, probably seventeen feet by twenty-three. Because of the extended use of windows, there was no artwork to speak of. Bookcases and file drawers were built along the walls from the windowsills down. The office was not only immaculate but orderly—everything arranged just so. The edges of the papers and documents on his desk were squared, pencils and pens lined up parallel to the blotter.

Joel Glazer rose to greet me and the two of us shook hands. His looks surprised me. I was so enamored of Dana Jaffe's beauty that I'd imagined a mate for her equally good-looking. My reaction to Joel was much like mine when I first saw the photographs of Jackie Kennedy and Aristotle Onassis—the princess and the frog. Joel was in his sixties, with a high, balding forehead, his once fair hair turning a tawny shade of gray along his temples. Behind frameless glasses, his eyes were brown, with heavy creases near the outer corners. His mouth was bracketed with deep lines. When he stood up to greet me, I realized he was shorter than I, probably only five feet four. He was portly and his shoulders were hunched in a way that made me want to monitor my calcium intake. His smile revealed a gap between his two front teeth, which were discolored and slightly askew. He wore a fresh white dress shirt, with a pair of flashy cuff links, his suit jacket arranged neatly over the back of his chair. I picked up the faint citrus of his aftershave. "Nice to meet you, Miss Millhone. Have a seat. I understand you and my wife have a prior acquaintance."

I settled into a brown leather wing chair that blended perfectly with the cream, beige, rust, and brown of the carpeting. "Seems like a long time ago," I said. I wasn't sure how much Dana'd told him about her prior life and most of that story seemed too complicated to summarize in conversation.

He settled back in his chair, his right hand resting on the desk in front of him. He had a signet ring on the middle finger that glinted in the light. "No matter. You're actually here with regard to Dow. Fiona tells us she's hired you to track him down. I'll tell you what I can, but I'm not sure that's going to be much help."

"I understand," I said. "Could we start with Pacific Meadows? I gather there's been a problem with the Medicare billing."

"My fault entirely. I blame myself for that. I should have kept an unofficial eye on the day-to-day operations. Harvey Broadus and I—don't know if you've met him—my partner . . ."

I shook my head in the negative, allowing him to continue.

"We've had a host of projects in the works this past six months. We've been partners for years. My background's business and finance where his is real estate and construction—a match made in heaven. We met on the golf course fifteen years ago and decided to go into partnership building retirement communities, nursing homes, and board-and-care facilities. Both of us had parents who were deceased by then, but the need for attractive housing and skilled nursing care for the elderly was something we'd both struggled to find and not always with success. Anyway, long story short, we've now put together an impressive chain of residential health care and intermediate-care facilities. Pacific Meadows, we acquired in 1980. At the time, it was shabby and poorly run. We could see the potential, but the place was losing money hand over fist. We poured close to a million dollars into the renovation and improvements, which included the new annex. Soon after that, we made the lease arrangement with Genesis Financial Management Services. Somebody—I forget now who—suggested Dow's name to Genesis as a possible administrator. I'd known him socially and could certainly vouch for his reputation in the medical community. He'd just retired from private practice and was looking for a way to occupy his time. Seemed like a worthwhile arrangement for all the parties concerned."

"What happened?"

"I wish I knew. Harvey and I are often out of town, crisscrossing the state. We've probably taken on more than we should, but Harvey's like me—the two of us thrive on pressure." The phone on his desk began to ring. He glanced at it briefly.

"You need to get that?"

"Dana will pick up. I should go back and fill you in, at least superficially, on how this business works. What you have essentially are three separate entities. Harvey and I own the property through Century Comprehensive, which is a company we formed back in 1971. By property, I'm talking now about the land and the building occupied by Pacific Meadows. The nursing home is actually operated by Genesis, as I've mentioned before. They lease the physical plant from us. They also handle all the billing: accounts payable and receivable, Medicare and Medicaid billing, DME purchases—that's durable medical equipment, in case you're wondering. Genesis falls under the larger umbrella of a company called Millennium Health Care. Millennium is publicly held, and as such, they're required by law to submit financial information to Social Security, and by that, I mean lists of assets, liabilities, and the return on equity capital. A certified public accountant has to verify those figures. Ten, fifteen years ago, an owner and operator were often one in the same, but times have changed. By law, those functions now have to be separate and distinct. It's like a system of checks and balances, keeps everybody on the up and up."

"Where did Dr. Purcell fit in?"

"I'm just getting to him. Under the management company, you have Dow, or his equivalent. He's the medical administrator of the facility, responsible for the day-in, day-out nuts-and-bolts decisions, which is where he may have gotten into trouble."

"The three of you are partners?"

"Not really. That's how Dow refers to us, but it's not technically true. For the layperson, it's the easiest explanation of our relationship. We couldn't be in partnership with Dow or the management company that runs the business. Believe me, the government gets very testy about any agreement that isn't the result of an arm's-length negotiation: in other words, two unrelated parties not in collusion with one another. Dow could hardly make unbiased decisions about billing practices if he stood to profit. What you're probably referring to is the fact he bought stock in Millennium Health Care, which is a chain we also own stock in. I guess that makes us partners of a sort. We're all in the same business, which is service to the elderly in our community. Of course we had no real say in the matter, but Harvey and I both thought Pacific Meadows would be the perfect venue for a man with Dow's experience and reputation. I see now he may not have had quite the head for business I'd been led to believe. The first we heard about this Medicare business was last May. I thought then, and I'm still convinced, any discrepancies would turn out to be simple clerical mistakes, a compilation of coding errors as opposed to actual inflation of the figures with any intent to defraud. Dow Purcell is just too fine a man to stoop to cheating in that way. My guess is, he either didn't have a thorough understanding of how Medicare works or he got impatient with all the nit-picking nonsense the bureaucrats put you through. I can't fault him for that. As a physician, his first thought is always going to be for the well-being of the patient. He might have bridled at seeing all the ridiculous amounts of paperwork get in the way of first-class care, or worse still, he may have felt the government had no right to dictate to him."

"So you think he might have bent the rules a bit?"

"I prefer that explanation to the one the fraud control investigator seems to be taking. A better guess is he was careless, penciling approval on charges he should have examined more closely. The notion of Dowan actively debunking the government is incomprehensible."

"Suppose he did, though. I don't understand how he benefits. If Medicare or Medicaid is overbilled, aren't those monies paid to the operating company? Seems like it's really their responsibility, isn't it?"

"Absolutely. But outside providers, such as ambulance companies and medical supply businesses, can collect thousands of dollars for services never rendered, or goods not de-

livered, or goods billed out at inflated prices. If someone in
Dow's position were in league with them, the contracts could
mean thousands of dollars to the companies involved. For this,
he'd receive remuneration—a kickback—perhaps under the
heading of a professional discount or a referral fee. Now that
HCFA—excuse all these acronyms, that's the Health Care Fi-
nancing Administration, which regulates Medicare and Medicaid programs—"

"Gets complicated," I remarked.

"Very. At any rate, now that HCFA has stepped in, they're
insisting on documentation for every such transaction, including the lease agreement, which is where we come in."

"But you don't think he's really guilty."

"I don't. At the same time, it isn't looking good for him."

"You think he left to avoid disgrace?"

"Possibly," he said. "If he felt unable or unwilling to face
the charges. I'm not sure how he'll deal with the humiliation
if they decide to prosecute. I'm not sure how any of us would
deal with that. He's a man in big trouble. I don't like to think
of him as a coward as well."

"When did you see him last? Do you remember the
occasion?"

"Of course. September 12, the day he disappeared. I took
him out to lunch."

"I didn't realize that. Was this at his request or yours?"

"His. He called and asked to see me. Of course, I said yes.
By then, I knew about his difficulties. I had some other business in that part of town so we met at a little place in walking
distance of Pacific Meadows. Just a hole in the wall called
Dickens, a mock English pub. It's quiet and affords a measure
of privacy, which I knew he'd appreciate."

"Did he talk about the problems with Medicare?"

"Not directly. He did ramble on a bit about the ongoing investigation. He was clearly upset. He seemed to want reassur-
ances that Harvey and I would come to his defense. I did what

I could to put his mind at rest, but I told him I couldn't condone anything underhanded. I don't mean to sound pompous, but in truth, if the charges turn out to be provable, then Dow's actions are not just unethical, they're illegal. As much as I like and admire the man, there's no way I'd be willing to cover for him, even if I could."

"But why would he risk it? Especially at his age and station in life. He couldn't need the money."

"I'm not so sure about that. Dow always did well for himself financially, but Crystal is high maintenance. She costs him a bundle. He has two houses to maintain—you know he bought Crystal that beach house at her insistence. Nothing would do, but she had to have that place. Plus he has Fiona's alimony, which is burdensome to say the least. Crystal likes to travel and she does it in style, including first-class airfare and accommodations for Griffith's nanny along with everyone else. She's the kind of gal who insists on being gifted—birthdays, anniversaries, Christmas, Valentine's Day—she expects to receive jewelry and nothing cheap. She makes sure of that. Dana's theory is she's busy accruing personal assets in case the bottom drops out."

The phone rang again. This time his eyes didn't even flicker, so I went right on. "You think she married him for his money?"

He considered the question briefly and then shook his head. "I wouldn't say that. I think she genuinely loves the guy, but she's been poor all her life. She wants to make sure she's safe just in case something happens to him."

"What about the rumors of an extramarital affair on her part?"

"You'd have to ask Dana. She's the one who spotted that piece of shenanigans. I prefer to steer clear."

"Did Dr. Purcell say anything to suggest he might flee?"

Joel shook his head. "I don't remember anything of the kind. Is that the direction the police are leaning in?"

"Well, they can't rule it out. Apparently, his passport and a substantial sum of money are missing."

Joel stared at me as though trying to take that in. "If he ran, he'd have to continue running for the rest of his life."

"Maybe that's not as bad as the alternative. From what you say, he was feeling desperate."

"Exactly. He was horrified at the prospect of facing criminal penalties."

"I talked to an attorney who thinks it wouldn't be that bad. He might have to pay restitution, but he wouldn't go to jail."

"That wasn't his perception. He was deeply depressed. The government's getting tough. He knew they might well decide to make an example of him. More than anything we're talking about the loss of face, something I'm not sure he could handle." He paused, moving four pencils from one side of his table to the other.

I saw his gaze shift. "What's going through your mind?"

He shook his head. "Something I haven't dared say to anyone else. It crossed my mind—after seeing him that day—he might have been thinking of doing himself in. He was trying to cover his distress, but it might've been too much. He wasn't sure Crystal would stick with him once the scandal came to light. You have to ask yourself just how despondent he was and how far he'd go to get relief. I should have asked how he felt. I should have done what I could to reassure him, but I didn't."

"Joel?"

We both turned to find Dana standing in the doorway.

"Harvey's on line two. This is the second time he's called."

"Sorry. I better get this."

"Sure, go ahead. I appreciate your time. It's possible I'll want to talk to you again at a later date."

"Any time," he said. He stood up when I did and the two of us shook hands across his desk. By the time I reached the door, he'd picked up the phone.

Dana walked me to the elevator with its two-person capacity, the interior about the size of the average telephone booth. I could have run down the stairs in the time it took. During its slow, whirring descent, I said, "What's the story on Clint Augustine?"

"Simple. For the six months Augustine rented from us, Dow would go off to work and the next thing you know, Crystal would come sneaking out her backdoor, through the trees, and into the cottage. She'd be there an hour or so and then slip back home. Meanwhile, Rand minded the baby, taking him for endless walks around Horton Ravine. It got to be the talk of the neighborhood." We reached the first-floor foyer.

"Couldn't there be another explanation?"

Dana's smile was jaded. "Maybe they were having tea."

Santa Teresa Hospital—St. Terry's—is located on the upper west side, a neighborhood once devoted to open farmland, working vineyards, dairies, and stables, all with sweeping views to the mountains on the northern edge of town. Early black-and-white photographs of the area show wide, dusty roads, shanties flanked by groves of citrus and walnut trees, all leveled long ago. It's a world that appears curiously bald and flat: rural expanses planted with pampas grass and star pines that look like mere sprigs. A few unpretentious structures from that era remain, tucked like vintage treasures among modern-day buildings. The rest—churches, the original county courthouse, the wooden boarding houses, the dry goods establishment, the early mission, the trolley car barn, and numerous snazzy three-story hotels—were razed by intermittent earthquakes and fires, Nature's demolition crews.

It was not quite two o'clock when I parked on a side street and walked a block and a half to St. Terry's front entrance. The wind had picked up and the trees seemed restless, stirring uneasily. Occasionally a miniature rain shower would shake loose from the upper branches. The very air seemed gray and I was happy to pass into the hospital lobby through the sliding glass doors that parted at my approach. On my left, the coffee shop was sparsely occupied by hospital employees and visitors. I inquired at the information desk and was given directions to the office of the Director of Nursing Services. I passed a ladies' restroom and made a brief detour before I continued my quest.

I found Penelope Delacorte in a small private office with a window looking out onto the street. Overhead fluorescent lights contrasted sharply with the gloom outside. She was seated at her desk, using her pencil point to trace the lines of print on a photocopied memorandum. When I knocked on the doorframe, she peered at me above a pair of half-glasses with tortoise-shell frames. She was in her early fifties, at that stage where she hadn't quite decided whether to dye her graying hair. I pictured her in arguments with her hairdresser, unsure of herself when it came to permanent versus temporary rinses. They likely also argued about the cut; Penelope clinging to the shoulder-length page boy she'd probably been wearing for years. Her bangs were too short and I wondered if she chopped them off herself between appointments. She removed her glasses and set them aside. "Yes?"

"You're Ms. Delacorte?"

"Yes." Her attitude was cautious, as though I might be on the verge of serving her with papers.

"Kinsey Millhone," I said. "I'm a private investigator here in town and I've been hired to look into Dr. Purcell's disappearance. May I have a few minutes?"

Without much in the way of encouragement, I'd entered her office, slipped off my rain garb, and eased myself into the chair near her desk. My shoulder bag and the slicker I left in a pile at my feet.

Penelope Delacorte got up and closed her office door. She didn't seem happy with my presence. She was close to six

feet tall, slim, conservatively dressed—a navy blue coat dress
with small brass buttons up the front. Her low-heeled navy
blue pumps were plain and looked vaguely orthotic, as though
prescribed for fallen arches or excessive pronation.

She sat down and put her hands in her lap. "I'm not sure
what I can tell you. I was gone by the time he . . . went
missing."

"How long did you work for Pacific Meadows?"

"I was the administrator there for the past eight years, until
August 23. I worked with Dr. Purcell for the last forty-seven
months of that." Her voice, like her manner, was carefully
modulated, as though she'd set her internal dial to "Pleasant."

"I thought he was the administrator."

"His title was Medical Director slash Administrator. I was
the Associate Administrator, so I suppose you're correct."

"Can you tell me why you left?"

"Genesis, the management company that oversees the operation of Pacific Meadows, received notification that Medicare was conducting a rigorous audit of our records."

I raised my hand. "What prompted them to do that? Do you
have any idea?"

"Probably a complaint."

"From?"

"One of the patients, a guardian, a disgruntled employee.
I'm not sure what it was, but they seemed to know what
they were doing. Apparently, the clinic was suspected of any
number of violations, from overpaying our suppliers to sub-
mitting false or inflated claims for services. Dr. Purcell was
in a panic and blamed the bookkeeper, Tina Bart, which was
absurd and unfair. Ms. Bart was working for Pacific Meadows
before I arrived and she was faultless in her performance. I
went to bat for her. I wasn't going to let them push it all off on
her. She didn't make the decisions. She didn't even pay the
bills; Genesis did that. She processed purchase orders and prepared the room-and-board bills for each resident, including

central supply, therapy, anything other than medication. This was Medicare, Medicaid, HMOs, private insurance, and private pay. The same information crossed my desk as well. She didn't *generate* the paperwork. She forwarded what she was given."

"Why isn't Genesis considered responsible for the problem if they pay the bills?"

"We supply them the information. As a rule, they don't stop to verify the data, nor did Ms. Bart."

"But she was fired, anyway."

"Yes, she was, and I turned in my notice the very same day. I was determined to file a complaint with the Labor Relations Board."

"What was their response?"

"I never got that far. I had second thoughts and decided not to go through with it. Tina Bart didn't want to make a fuss. She was as reluctant as I was to call attention to Dr. Purcell's situation."

"His situation?"

"Well, yes. We're all fond of him. He's a darling human being and a wonderful doctor. If he didn't have a head for business, that wasn't an actionable offense as far as we were concerned. I'm being candid in this. He just had no clue when it came to the Medicare rules and regulations—which items were billable and which would automatically be disallowed, co-payments, deductibles, claims for fee-based services. I grant you, it's enormously complicated. Make one mistake— god forbid you put a code in the wrong place or leave even one window blank—and the form comes right back at you, usually without a hint about where you've erred."

"But Dr. Purcell didn't do the billing."

"Of course not, but it was his job to review the TARs—"

"The TARs?"

"The Treatment Authorization Requests. He was also responsible for reviewing CPT codes and approving the cost of any ancillary services or DME's. I have to emphasize, he was always genuinely concerned and very innovative when it came to patient care and well-being—"

"You don't have to work so hard to defend the man," I said. "I'll take your word for it. What I hear you saying is when it came to the day-to-day management, he was incompetent."

"I suppose, though it seems too strong a word."

"Didn't Glazer and Broadus realize what was going on?"

"It wasn't their place. They purchased the property from the previous owner, did extensive improvements, financed and built the annex. The rest was up to Genesis and Dr. Purcell. Please understand, this is just my personal opinion, but I've worked with a number of doctors over the course of my career. It almost seems that the better a man is at the practice of medicine, the worse he is at business. Most of the doctors I know have a hard time admitting this about themselves. They're used to being gods. Their judgment is seldom questioned. They have no awareness of the limits they face, so they're easily duped. They may have medical knowledge, but often not an ounce of common sense when it comes to money management. At any rate, I didn't mean to digress. I'm just trying to explain how Dr. Purcell could have gotten himself into such a mess."

"Didn't you explain it to him?"

"On numerous occasions. He seemed to listen and agree, but the errors continued to accrue."

"But if you suspected he was screwing up, couldn't you have gone to the operating company yourself?"

"Over his head? Not if I wanted to keep my job."

"Which you lost, anyway."

Mrs. Delacorte pressed her lips together, color warming her cheeks. "I felt compelled to resign when Ms. Bart was fired."

I said, "Do you think Dr. Purcell was intentionally cheating the government?"

"I doubt it. I can't see how he'd benefit unless he had some covert arrangement with Genesis or the various providers. The point is, Dr. Purcell was on the premises. Genesis wasn't, and neither were Mr. Glazer or Mr. Broadus. It was his responsibility and ultimately, he's the one who'll be held to answer."

"What do you think happened to him?"

"I can't answer that. I was gone by then."

"I'm still not clear why you didn't file a complaint. If Tina Bart was unlawfully terminated, wouldn't that constitute a legitimate grievance?"

She was silent and I could see her struggle with her reply. "I suppose we were both reluctant to get into a public battle."

"With whom?"

"With anyone," she said. "Employment opportunities are limited in Santa Teresa. Talk travels fast, especially in medical circles. Despite the number of doctors, there are only three hospitals. Jobs at my level aren't easy to find. My roots here go deep. I've been in town close to thirty years. I can't afford to be labeled a troublemaker or a malcontent. You might consider that fainthearted, but I'm a widow with an aging mother to support. Now I think I've given you all the information at my disposal so if you'll excuse me . . ." She began to fuss with papers on her desk, lifting a stack and tamping the edges to even them up. Red patches, like moral hives, had begun to appear on her neck.

"Just one more thing. Where did Tina Bart end up?"

"You're the detective. You figure it out."

10

WHEN I GOT back to the office, I picked up a message slip on which Jeniffer had written, "Richard Heaven called. Pleas return his call." I could actually feel my heart begin to thump as I moved down the corridor to my office and unlocked the door. I hadn't expected to hear from him until Wednesday at the earliest. I dumped my shoulder bag on the desk and snatched up the telephone. I got a wrong number twice before I realized that Jeniffer had inverted the last two digits in the number she'd so laboriously copied. I reached Richard on the third try, saying, "Richard. Kinsey Millhone returning your call."

"Oh sure. Thanks for calling me back. How're you?"

"Fine. What can I do for you?"

"Uh, well, listen, I've been through the rest of these applicants and none of them panned out. Bunch of bums out there. The place is yours if you want it."

"Really? That's great. I'm really happy about that. When can I take possession?"

"I'm heading over there now. If you have a few minutes,

maybe you could give me a check. That's $1,675 with the cleaning deposit, made out to Hevener Properties."

"Sure, I could do that. I'm just across the alley. The building I'm in now looks right down on yours."

"I didn't realize that. Why don't you join me in a bit and as soon as the lease is signed, I'll give you the key." Like many people, he seemed to be uncomfortable discussing money, and I wondered how much experience he had in landlord-tenant relationships.

"What time?"

"Ten, fifteen minutes?"

"I'll see you shortly. And thanks."

As soon as I hung up I did a little dance of joy, my attention already darting forward to the practicalities of moving. Fortunately, I'd never completely unpacked in the three years since I'd landed at Kingman and Ives, so that would save time. Desk, chair, daybed, phony ficus plant. This was going to be a snap. I could park in my own spot a mere fifteen steps from my office door. I could eat lunches at the table on the redwood deck . . .

I opened my closet door and hauled out the top two boxes, looking for my tape measure, which I found at the bottom of the second box. The tape was one of those heavy-duty metal suckers with a reel-back so fast it would slice off your little finger if you didn't watch yourself. I tucked it in my shoulder bag, grabbed a yellow legal pad and pencil, made sure my message machine was on, then shrugged into my slicker and walked to my brand-new digs. I felt like skipping and then I wondered if kids ever did that these days.

I was already feeling extraordinarily possessive as I trotted along the driveway from the rear of the lot. While I could see the bungalow from Lonnie's office, I had to go halfway around the block and cut down the alleyway to reach the place. There were lights on throughout the bungalow and by hopping up just once, I caught a glimpse of the CPA who occupied the front office. I'd have to take a moment to introduce myself when time allowed. I rounded the corner, noting a sedate-looking dark blue sedan that I assumed belonged to the CPA. Tommy's black pickup was parked two slots down.

Once inside the backdoor, I was careful to wipe my feet on the shaggy cotton door mat provided for that purpose. The door to the back office was standing open and I could smell fresh paint. I peered in and found Tommy on his hands and knees, touching up the baseboards with a brush and a can of white latex paint. He flashed me a quick smile and continued with his work. He was wearing a khaki green coverall, and I was struck again by the vibrancy of the picture he presented. By day, his red hair carried glints of copper and a sheen of pale freckles seemed to make his skin ruddy.

I said, "Hi. How are you?"

"Doing good. Thought I'd get this finished while I had the chance. I hear you're the new tenant."

"Well, it looks that way. Richard said he'd meet me over here to do the paperwork." There was something nice about the fact that his attention was fixed on the job in front of him. It allowed me to study his shoulders and the soft reddish hair on his forearms where his sleeves were rolled up. I could see the lines in his knuckles where a fine bleed of white paint still clung to his skin. The hair along the back of his neck was in need of cutting and curled haphazardly.

He glanced over his shoulder at me. "Thought maybe you left, you're so quiet back there."

"I'm here." I moved over to the window just to have some-thing to do. "The deck's great." Really, I was wondering if he had a girlfriend.

"I built that myself. I was thinking to add some trellising, but it seemed like overkill."

"Looks nice as it is. Is that redwood?"

"Yes ma'am. Clear heart. I don't like cheap materials.

Richard bitches about that, but I figure in the end it'll save us money. Anything cheap, you end up doing twice."

I couldn't think of anything to add to that. I cranked the window open and cranked it shut again. Idly, I lifted the telephone handset. I could hear a dial tone.

"You got a call to make?"

"I just wondered if it worked. I guess I'll have to talk to the phone company and have the service switched."

"How's the boyfriend?"

"He's fine."

Another pause while Tommy dipped the brush in the can. "Hope he's treating you good."

"Actually, he's out of town." I winced when I said it because it sounded like a come-on.

"What's he do for a living? He some fancy-pants attorney?"

"He's a P.I. like me. Semiretired. He was laid up for a while with a knee replacement." Mentally, I crossed my eyes. The way I was describing Dietz made him sound like some old geezer who could barely walk. In truth, Dietz had been gone so long that my claiming him as a boyfriend was patently ridiculous.

"Sounds old."

"He's not. He's only fifty-three."

Tommy smiled to himself. "Now see? I knew you'd be the type to go for somebody old. What are you, thirty-five?"

"Thirty-six."

"I'm twenty-eight myself, which I figure is prime for a guy," he remarked. He lifted his head slightly. "Here comes Richard."

"How do you do that? I didn't hear him pull in."

"Radar," he said. He got to his feet and stood there for a moment, running a critical eye along the baseboard. "I miss any spots?"

"Not as far as I can see."

Tommy found the lid for the can of paint and tapped along the edges to effect a seal.

Richard appeared in the doorway wearing a long black raincoat with the ends of the belt tied together in the back. He wasn't nearly as appealing as his brother and certainly not as friendly, meeting my gaze with only an occasional flicker of his eyes. "I thought you had something else to do today," he said to Tommy.

"Yeah, well I wanted to finish this. I don't like leaving a job until I know it's done right." Tommy delivered his lines without looking at his brother.

There was something edgy going on between them, but I couldn't figure out what it was. They seemed chilly with each other, as though their current conversation were part of an ongoing argument. Tommy went into the bathroom where I could hear him running water to clean his paintbrush. He came out moments later and began to gather up his tools. It felt like a replay of the night I'd first seen the place, except that neither of them spoke.

"Let me write you that check," I said, trying to inject a warmer note. I reached for my bag and took out the checkbook and a pen, leaning against the wall while I filled in the date. "Hevener Properties, Inc.?"

"That's right." Richard stood with his hands in his raincoat pockets, watching me idly as I wrote in the amount. Meanwhile, as Tommy headed for the door, I saw the two exchange a glance. His gaze moved to mine and he smiled at me fleetingly before he disappeared through the door.

I ripped the check from the book and handed it to Richard, who removed the lease from the inner pocket of his raincoat. He'd already filled in the relevant blanks. I began to read through the lines of minuscule print while Richard studied me.

"I hope he's not bothering you."

"Who, Tommy? Not at all. We were chatting about the

deck. I stopped by to take some measurements. I'd like to put in some shelves."

"Of course. Everything look okay to you?"

"Fine. He did a great job."

"When are you moving?"

"I'm hoping the early part of next week."

"Good. Here's my card. I'm the one you should call if you need anything."

I turned my attention to the lease agreement, reading it line by line. Seemed like standard fare; no tricks, no hidden clauses, no unusual restrictions.

Richard was watching me read. "What kind of cases do you handle?"

"Just about anything. It varies. Right now, I'm looking into the disappearance of a doctor who's been gone for nearly ten weeks. January, I did a search for a missing heir."

"Mostly local?"

"For the most part, yes. Occasionally I go out of state, but it's usually cheaper for a client to hire a P.I. in their own geographic area. That way they don't have to pay travel, which can really add up." I scribbled my name at the bottom of the lease, handed him one copy, and kept the other for my files. "I'm always saying this, but the job's a lot duller than it sounds. Background checks and paper searches at the Hall of Records. I used to be associated with an insurance company, handling arson and wrongful death claims, but I prefer being out on my own." I didn't want to appear shiftless so I omitted the fact that CF had fired my sorry butt. I hoped he wouldn't press the point because I didn't want to lie to him this early in the game.

He said, "Well. I better give you a key." He dug in his raincoat pocket and pulled out a ring, sorting through ten to fifteen keys until he found the one he wanted. He freed it and dropped it in the palm of my hand. "You might want to get a second one made in case you lose this."

"I'll do that. Thanks." I took out my key ring and added it to my modest collection.

After he departed, I pulled out my tape measure and began to lay out the dimensions of the room: the spaces between windows, depth of the closet, distance to the door. I made a crude drawing on my legal pad and then I sat in the middle of the carpet, tapping on my lip with my pencil while I studied the room. Between the smell of new carpet and the scent of fresh paint, the office seemed as clean and as slick as a brand-new car. Outside the window, the day was dreary, but inside, where I was, there was a sense of new beginnings.

I was just about to pack up when the phone rang. I must have jumped a foot and then I stared at the instrument. Someone looking for Richard or Tommy; couldn't be for me. I picked up on the fifth ring, feeling hesitant. "Hello?"

The drawl again. "Hey, it's me. My brother still there?"

"He just left."

"I thought maybe the two of us might go out for a drink." His voice on the phone was low and flirtatious. I could tell he was smiling, holding the handset close to his lips.

"Why?"

"Why?" His laugh bubbled up. "Why do you think?"

"Is there a problem between you and Richard?"

"Such as what?"

"I don't know. I got the feeling he didn't like the fact that you were talking to me. So, you know, you ask me out for a drink and I'm not sure it's wise."

"You're a tenant. He's strict. That still doesn't make it any of his damn business."

"I don't want to get you in trouble."

He laughed. "Don't worry about it. I can take care of myself."

"I didn't mean it that way. I don't want to cause problems."

"I told you. It's not a problem. Quit trying to duck the question and let me buy you a glass of wine."

"It's only four o'clock."

"So?"

"I have work to do yet."

"When will you finish?"

"Probably closer to six."

"Good. We'll make it dinner instead."

"Not dinner. A drink. And only one," I said.

"You're callin' the shots. Name the place and I'll be there."

I thought for a moment, tempted by the idea of Rosie's, which was off the beaten path. This all felt faintly sneaky, like it wouldn't be good for Richard to see us together. Still, I couldn't see the harm in having one drink. "There's a place near the beach," I said, and gave him Rosie's address. "You know where that is?"

"I'll find it."

"I may be late."

"I'll wait."

After I hung up, I wondered if I'd made a mistake. It's not a smart move to mix the professional with the personal. He was my landlord now and if anything went wrong, I'd be looking for new digs. On the other hand, I was friendly with Lonnie Kingman and that hadn't presented any problems. It did cheer me up, the notion of seeing him again. With luck, he'd turn out to be a jerk and I'd politely decline any further contact.

In the meantime, I knew I had to get down to the business of Dow Purcell. I'd go back to square one, starting at Pacific Meadows and the night he vanished from the face of the earth.

This time the parking lot at Pacific Meadows was full. I tucked my VW in the very last slot on the left, squeezing up against the hedge. I locked my car and slopped through shallow puddles to the front door. The wind was blowing at my back and my leather boots were water-stained by the time I reached shelter. I leaned my umbrella against the wall and hung my slicker on a peg. Today the air smelled of tomato sauce, carnations, damp wool socks, potting soil, baby powder. I checked the dinner menu posted on the wall near the double dining room doors. Barbecued riblet, baked beans, broccoli-and-cauliflower medley (now there was a winner), and for dessert, gelatin with fruit cocktail. I hoped it was cherry, clearly the superior flavor for any age group. As this was a weekday, there seemed to be more residents moving about in the hall.

The dayroom was nearly full. The drapes had been closed and the room felt cozier. One group watched a television news show, while another group watched a black-and-white movie with Ida Lupino and George Raft. In the far corner, a middle-aged woman was leading six elderly female residents in an exercise program, which consisted of lifting their arms and marching their feet while they remained seated in folding chairs. The human body was meant for motion, and this small group of women was still doing what they could to keep fit. Hooray for them.

I nodded at the woman at the front desk, behaving as though I were an old hand at this. Unchallenged, I proceeded to Administration, where I found Merry laying out a hand of solitaire. She looked up with guilt, pulled the cards together, and quickly slid them into her pencil drawer. She said, "Hi. How are you?" I could tell she'd recognized my face but was drawing a blank on the name.

"Kinsey Millhone," I said. "I thought I'd stop by and see if Mrs. Stegler was here. I hope she hasn't left for the day."

Merry pointed to her right just as a woman emerged from the inner office with a pair of gardening clippers and a cluster of bald and brownish ivy vines. She was saying, "That looks much better. Dr. P. would never allow me to tend to his plants when he was here." She was slightly disconcerted to see me, but she continued on to the wastebasket, where she deposited her prunings.

Her hair was bushy on top and cut quite short around the ears. She wore an oversized brown blazer, a shirt, a tie, and a pair of mannish pants. She had a gold silk cravat bunched in the breast pocket of her jacket. The toes of her brown oxfords peered from beneath her shapeless trouser legs. She could have used another two inches in the length.

"Mrs. Stegler? My name's Kinsey Millhone. I'm hoping you can give me some information about Dr. Purcell."

She plucked a tissue from the box on Merry's desk and wiped her hands carefully before she finally offered to shake hands. "Merry said you stopped by on Saturday. I'm not certain I can be of help. I make it a policy not to discuss my employer without his express permission."

"I understand that," I said. "I'm not asking you to violate a confidence. You know Fiona Purcell?"

"Of course. Dr. Purcell's first wife."

"She hired me in hopes I could get a line on him. I'm actually here at her suggestion. She felt a conversation with you was the logical place to begin."

Mrs. Stegler shook her head. "I'm sorry, but I was gone by the time the doctor left the building that night," she said, almost stubbornly. I could tell she was happy she had nothing to contribute on the subject.

"Did you talk to him that day?"

Mrs. Stegler gave me a significant look and signaled with her eyes that Merry was listening to every word we said. "Perhaps you'd like to step into his office. We can talk in there."

She held open the hinged section of the counter and I passed inside. Her eyes were as small and as round as a parakeet's, a pale watery blue with a ring of black around the iris. As we entered the inner office, she turned to Merry. "Please see that we're not disturbed."

Merry said, "Yes ma'am," rolling her eyes at no one in particular.

For my part, I was intrigued by the opportunity to see Dr. Purcell's office, which was small and neat. Desk, swivel chair, two upholstered guest chairs, and a bookcase filled with medical textbooks and assorted health care manuals. On the edge of his desk sat the newly shorn ivy, looking like a cocker spaniel with a summer clip. I'd have given a lot for the chance to go through his desk drawers, but the chances of that looked dim.

It was clear Mrs. Stegler thought it inappropriate to sit at his desk. She perched on one of his guest chairs and I took the other, which put us nearly knee to knee. She scooted her chair back and crossed her legs, exposing a band of narrow, white hairless shin above the rim of her wool sock.

I said, "I hope this doesn't seem out of line, but I have to tell you I can't stand gossip. Even in my line of work, I never encourage anyone to talk out of turn or breach a trust, especially in a matter like this."

She looked at me with a hint of suspicion, perhaps sensing the bullshit, perhaps not. "We're in accord on that."

"I'd appreciate your telling me about his last day at work."

"I explained all that to the police. More than once, I might add."

"I'm hoping you'll explain it again to me. Detective Odessa told me you were very helpful."

She peered uneasily at my shoulder bag resting on the floor by my chair. "You're not recording this."

I leaned over, grabbed the bag, and held it open so she could inspect the contents. The only thing that looked even vaguely like a recorder was my government-issue, secret, plastic tampon container with its high-powered directional mike.

"And you won't quote me out of context?"

"I won't quote you at all."

She was silent, staring down at her lap. Finally, she said, "I've been divorced for years."

She was silent again and I allowed the subject to sit there

between us without comment on my part or elucidation on hers. I could see that she was struggling to speak. Her face twisted suddenly, her lips pulling together as though controlled by invisible strings. She spoke, but her voice was so tight and so raspy I could hardly understand what she said. "Dr. Purcell . . . was the closest . . . thing to a . . . friend I had. I can't believe he's gone. I came into work the following Monday morning and by then everyone was whispering that he was . . . missing. I was shocked. He was . . . such a sweet man . . . I so adored him. . . . If I'd known that was the last time I was going to see him, I would have expressed . . . my heartfelt thanks . . . for all his many, many . . . kindnesses to me." She took another deep breath, humming with the kind of sorrow that didn't lend itself to words. After half a minute, she seemed to regain her composure, though her grip was clearly fragile. She removed the cravat from her breast pocket and blew her nose noisily. The silk didn't seem absorbent. She folded her hands together in her lap, the wadded cloth between her fingers where she twisted it. I could see a tear plop into her lap and then a second, like a slow drip from a shower handle that hasn't been properly turned off.

I realized she was the first person, aside from Blanche, who'd shown any real emotional reaction to his vanishing. I leaned forward and clutched her cold hands. "I know this is hard. Take your time."

She took a deep breath. "Forgive me. I'm sorry. I shouldn't burden you this way. I just hope he's safe. I don't care what he's done." She paused, pressing the cravat against her lips. She took another deep breath. "I'm fine now. I'm fine. I don't know what came over me. My apologies."

"I understand. From everything I've heard, he was a wonderful man. My only purpose here is to help. You have to trust me on that. I'm not here to make trouble."

"What do you want?"

"Just tell me what you know."

She hesitated, her no-gossip policy too deeply ingrained to give up all at once. She must have decided to trust me because she took a deep breath and opened up. "That last day, he seemed preoccupied. I think he was worried . . . I mean, why wouldn't he be? Mrs. Purcell . . . excuse me, the first one, Fiona . . . stopped by to see him, but he'd gone out to lunch. She waited for a while, thinking he might return, and then she left him a note. When he came back, he worked in his office for the rest of the day. I remember he had a glass of whiskey sitting at his desk. This was late in the day."

"Did he go out for dinner?"

"I don't believe so. He usually ate quite late or skipped supper altogether. Many evenings, he had a little something at his desk . . . crackers or fruit . . . this was if his wife was going out and wouldn't be cooking. When I tapped on his door to say good-night, he was just sitting there."

"Did he have papers in front of him? Files or charts?"

"He must have. I didn't pay attention. It wasn't in his nature to be idle. I do know that."

"You had a conversation?"

"The usual pleasantries. Nothing significant."

"Any phone calls or visitors that you know of?"

She shook her head. "Not that I remember. When I came in the following Monday, his office was empty, highly unusual for him. He was always here at seven o'clock, before anyone else. By then, the rumors were beginning to circulate. Someone . . . I forget who . . . said he'd never gone home at all on Friday night. At first we didn't attach much to it. Then, people got worried he'd been in an accident or taken ill. When the police came, we were frightened, but we still expected him to be found within a day or two. I've thought and thought about this, but there's absolutely nothing else."

"Didn't I read in the paper he had a brief chat that night with an elderly woman sitting in the lobby?"

"That would be Mrs. Curtsinger. Ruby. She's been a resident here since 1975. I'll have Merry take you over to her room. I don't want you upsetting her."

"I promise I won't."

11

MERRY WALKED ME down the hall. I could see the meal carts being rolled out, the vertical shelves stacked with dinner trays for those who preferred eating in their rooms. It was not even five o'clock and I suspected the early supper hour was designed to condense all three of the day's meals to one long shift.

Merry was saying, " 'Member the nurse who was standing there when you left on Saturday? Her name's Pepper Gray. Anyway, she started asking all these questions about you. I never let on a thing, just said you'd be back to talk to Mrs. S. today. She read me out good, saying I shouldn't be talking to anyone about the clinic. I was so P.O.'d. She doesn't have any right to talk to me that way. She doesn't even work in my department."

"What do you think she heard?"

"Doesn't matter. It's none of her business. I just thought you should be aware of it in case we run into her."

We took a left, passing the staff lounge, central supply, and then a series of residential rooms. Many doors were closed, the exteriors decorated with greeting cards or wreaths of dried flowers. Sometimes the names of the occupants were spelled out in foil letters hanging jauntily from a miniclothesline of ribbon or string. Through the doors that remained open, I caught glimpses of twin-sized beds with floral spreads, photographs of family members lined up on the chests of drawers. Each room had a different color scheme and each looked out onto a narrow garden where flowering shrubs trembled with the first drops of a pattering rain. We passed an old woman, stumping down the hall with her walker. Her pace was rapid and when she reached the corner, she turned with such vigor she threatened to topple sideways. Merry reached out a hand and steadied her. The woman banked, swerving wide, and then tottered on.

Ruby Curtsinger was sitting in an upholstered chair beside a set of sliding glass doors, one of which was pushed back to admit a breath of damp, fresh air. Her feet were propped on a stool. Just outside, a bird feeder was suspended from the eaves. Small brown birds were perched on the feeder's edge. A line of birds, like clothespins, extended from the hanging support. Ruby was a tiny, shrunken woman with a small bony face and arms as thin as sticks. Her white hair was sparse, but it looked as if she'd recently had it washed and set. She turned a pair of bright blue eyes toward us and smiled, showing the many gaps in her lower teeth. Merry introduced us and explained what I wanted before she withdrew.

Ruby said, "You should talk to Charles. He saw Dr. Purcell after I said good-night to him."

"I don't think I've heard of Charles."

"He's an orderly on the night staff. He's probably here somewhere. He likes to come into work early so he can visit with Mrs. Thornton and some of the other girls. They play gin rummy for pennies and you should hear them hoot. When I have trouble sleeping, I ring for him and he'll put me in my chair and push me up and down the halls. Sometimes I sit in the staff lounge and play euchre with him. The man does love to play cards. I take my meals here in my room. There are folks in the dining room I don't much care for. One woman chews with her mouth open. I don't want to look at that when I'm eating. It's disgusting.

"The night you're asking about—when I last saw the doctor—I took my usual pills, but nothing seemed to help. I rang for Charles, and he said he'd take me on Toad's Wild Ride. That's what he calls it. In truth, he wanted to smoke so he parked me in the lobby and went outside. That's why I was sitting there, so Charles could sneak a cigarette. He's trying to quit and I guess he thinks if no one knows what he's doing, it won't count. Dr. Purcell doesn't allow anyone to smoke in here. He says too many people have problems breathing as it is. That's one thing we talked about that night."

"What time was this?"

"Five minutes to nine or so. We didn't chat long."

"Can you remember anything else?"

"He told me I was beautiful. He always says that to me, though I sometimes think he's fibbing just a tiny bit. I asked about his boy. I forget what his name is."

"Griffith."

"That's it. Doctor used to have his wife bring the little boy in to see us every week or so. Of course, she hasn't brought him even once since his daddy disappeared. I notice the child's feet scarcely ever touched the floor. They carried him everyplace and anything he wanted, he pointed to and grunted. I told the doctor, 'He's never going to learn to talk as long as you treat him that way,' and he heartily agreed. And then we talked about the weather. It was a lovely night out-side. Felt just like spring and I believe the moon was almost full. He went through the door and that's the last I saw of him."

"Could you tell what kind of mood he was in? Mad? Sad?"

She put an index finger against her cheek and gave that some thought. Arthritis had bent the thumb on that hand until it formed a painful-looking angle perpendicular to her hand. "Absentminded, I'd say. I had to ask him twice if he could arrange an outing for us. The food here is good. I don't mean to complain, but eating out is fun and gives us all a lift. Any little change makes such a difference."

A Hispanic woman in scrubs appeared at the door. "I have your dinner tray, Miss Curtsinger. You want to eat in front of the TV so you can watch your show? It's coming on in five minutes and you don't want to miss the opening. That's the best part you said." She crossed to Ruby's chair and set the dinner tray on a small rolling table that she pulled in close. She removed the aluminum lid, revealing the barbecued riblet laid out with all its accompaniments. The Jell-O was green with a smattering of fruit cocktail submerged in its glowing depths.

"Thank you," Ruby said, and then she smiled at me. "Will you come back and see me, dear? I like talking to you."

"I'll do what I can. Tell you what—next time, I'll bring you a Quarter Pounder with Cheese."

"And a Big Mac. I see those ads on television and they always look so good."

"Believe me, they are. I'll bring you one of those, too."

I walked down the hall as far as the staff lounge, where I stuck my head in and said, "I'm looking for Charles."

The man I saw sitting at the table with the evening paper was in his fifties and was dressed in scrubs, like the woman bringing out the trays. He was a mild nut brown, and narrow through the shoulders, his arms hairless and scrawny. He set his paper aside and got to his feet politely to identify himself. "Charles Biedler," he said. "How may I help you, Miss?"

I explained who I was and what I wanted, repeating the gist of what Ruby Curtsinger had told me. "I know you've answered these questions before, but it would really be a help if you'd tell me what you remember."

"I could show you where he was parked and where I stood that night."

"I'd love that," I said. He picked up a folded section of the paper and carried it with him as we moved toward the entrance. I paused to retrieve my umbrella and my slicker, which I held over my head like a yellow plastic tent. Charles used his newspaper as a rain hat and we hurried outside, hunched against the rain, which was blowing against us in gusts. Charles paused at the end of the walkway, pointing toward the cars. "See where that little blue VW's parked? Doctor's space was right there. I saw him crossing the lot and then he got in his car and pulled out right around to here."

"You didn't see anyone else?"

"No, but now that corner of the parking lot was darker at nine o'clock than it is right now. Warm that night. I was in my shirt sleeves like this only without the gooseflesh. I spoke to him like always, you know, calling out a word and he said something back, kind of bantering like."

"There was nothing unusual?"

"Not as I recall."

"I'm trying to see this as you did. Ruby says he had his suit jacket over his arm. Did he carry anything else?"

"I don't think so. I can't picture it if he did."

"What about his car keys?"

"I guess he must have had those in hand. I don't remember him reaching in his pocket."

"So he unlocked the car door and then what?"

"I don't remember nothing about that."

"Did the interior light go on?"

"Might have. After he got in, he sat a while and then he started up the engine and swung around this way so he could drive out the front."

"Was that his pattern?"

Charles blinked, shaking his head. "Most times."

His newspaper was getting soaked and I knew it was time to retreat to the overhang.

"Let's get out of this rain," I said.

We headed back to the entrance, pausing again just outside the front door.

I said, "Was there anything else? Anything at all, even if it seems trivial."

"He didn't call out good-night like he usually did when he drove past. Last thing he'd do, he used to wave and shake a finger, kind of teasing me like, because I told him I quit smoking."

"Was the car window down?"

"I couldn't say for sure."

"You didn't see anyone in the car with him?"

Charles shook his head.

"Are you sure?"

"Pretty sure. And truthfully, that's as much as I know."

"Well, I appreciate your time. If you should think of anything else, would you give me a call?" I took a business card from my bag and handed it to him. "I can be reached at this number. There's a machine if I'm gone."

As I left the porch and started out across the parking lot, I turned and waved. Charles was still there, staring after me.

I sat in my car for a while, thinking about the fact that I was parked right where Dow Purcell had been on the night of September 12. I did a 180 survey, turning my head. What had happened to him? The rain kept tapping on my car roof like the restless drumming of fingers on a tabletop. He hadn't been assaulted. He'd gotten in his car and he'd sat there a while . . . doing what? I started the car and backed out of the space, heading, as Purcell had, toward Dave Levine Street. I glanced back at the building. Charles was gone by then. The walk was empty and the rain slanting against the light made the entrance seem bleak.

I turned right, scanning the street on either side of me. The area was residential. St. Terry's Hospital was only four blocks away. There were medical buildings in the surrounding area, apartment buildings, and a few private homes, but not much else. No bars or restaurants along this stretch where he might have stopped for a drink. Once I reached the next intersection, it was impossible to guess which way he might have gone.

I circled back to the office, and by 5:30, I was typing up a rough draft of the next installment of my report. It helped to be forced to lay it all out again in narrative form. I'd done an additional four hours of work, which I deducted from the balance of the retainer, leaving me $1,125 of indentured servitude. I could feel anxiety whispering through my bones. I was no wiser now than I'd been when I first started and probably no closer to finding Dr. Purcell. I didn't even have a *scheme*, no clever strategy about how to proceed. What more could I do? Fiona wanted results. I was moving, but getting nowhere. I checked my watch. 6:02. I leaped to my feet. I was already late for Rosie's, but it couldn't be helped. I shoved the report in my handbag, thinking I could work on it later if I needed to.

Traffic was heavy on the rain-slick streets. While stuck at a stoplight, I turned the rearview mirror to check my appearance. I seldom wear makeup so I looked much the same; sallow by the light of streetlamps, my hair a dense thatch of brown. I felt less than glamorous in my jeans and turtleneck, but it couldn't be helped. I didn't have time to go home and change. Into what? I don't have anything else. This is what I wear.

I parked my car in front of my apartment and dog-trotted the half block to Rosie's. I pushed open the door, dumped my umbrella, and left my slicker on a peg. Where Friday night the place had been emptied by the weather, tonight it was jammed. Both the jukebox and the television were going full-blast, *Monday Night Football* having captured a rowdy cluster of sports enthusiasts at the bar. The cigarette smoke was dense and all the tables were taken. I saw William emerge from the kitchen with a tray at shoulder height while Rosie was uncapping beer bottles as fast as she could. I searched the crowd, wondering if I'd managed to arrive before Tommy Hevener. I felt a plucking at my sleeve and looked down to find him looking up at me from the first booth on the right.

Oh, my.

He was freshly shaved and he'd changed into a white dress shirt with a sky-blue wool crew neck pulled over it. He said something I missed. I leaned closer to him, taking in the scent of Aqua Velva. When he repeated himself, his voice in my ear set up a tickling chill that went down to my feet. "Let's get out of here," he said. He got up and grabbed his raincoat off the seat across from him.

I nodded and began to inch my way toward the door again. I could feel him following, one hand against my back. The gesture assumed a familiarity I should have objected to, but didn't. We paused at the entrance while I collected my slicker and my umbrella. He shrugged into his raincoat and turned the collar up. "Where to?" he asked.

"There's a place one block over. Emile's-at-the-Beach. We can walk."

His umbrella was the larger so he raised it and held it over my head as we emerged into the pelting rain. I kept my hand on the stem a fraction of an inch from his and we moved forward with the odd gait one assumes when walking in tandem. The rain was coming down so hard, the water was propelled through the umbrella fabric like a mist. A car passed, throwing up a plume that landed in front of us with a splat.

Tommy stopped. "This is nuts. I've got a car right here." He took his keys out and unlocked the passenger-side door on a new Porsche, painted candy-apple red with a license plate that read HEVNER 2. I stepped from the curb to the interior, not a dainty maneuver given the low-slung chassis and the torrents of rainwater coursing through the gutter. He closed me in on my side and then circled in front of the car to his. The interior was done in caramel-colored leather, the whole of it smelling as earthy and rich as a tack room.

"Where's your pickup?" I said.

"That's business. This is play. You look great. I've missed you."

We chatted about nothing in particular on the short drive over to Emile's. Tommy let me off at the door. I went inside and staked out a claim for us while he found a place to park. We were seated at a table for two, next to the window in the narrow side room. The air smelled of sautéed garlic and onion, roasting chicken, and marinara sauce. The atmosphere was intimate with only half the tables occupied because of the rain. There was a quiet buzz of conversation and the occasional clatter of silverware. Votive candles provided circles of light in the darkened space. The waiter brought us two menus, and after a quick consultation, Tommy ordered a bottle of California Chardonnay. While we waited for that, he sat and played with a fork, making plow lines along the edges of a paper napkin. His watch was white gold and he wore a gold ID bracelet, heavy links glimmering against his ruddy skin. "I went back and read your rental application. You're divorced."

I held up two fingers.

He said, "I've never been married. Too much of a rolling stone."

"I tend to appeal to guys on the move," I said.

"Maybe I'll surprise you. Where's your family?"

"My parents died in a car accident when I was five years old. I was raised by my mother's sister, my aunt Gin. She's dead now, too."

"No siblings?"

I shook my head.

"What about the husbands? Who were they?"

"The first was a cop . . . I met him when I was a rookie . . ."

"You were a cop?"

"For two years."

"And the second?"

"He was a musician. Very talented. Not so good at being faithful, but he was nice in other ways. He cooked and played piano."

"Skills I admire. And where is he now?"

"I haven't any idea. You said your parents were gone?"

"It's weird being an adult orphan, though not as bad as you'd think. What'd your father do for a living?"

"Mail carrier. My folks were married fifteen years before I came along."

"So you only had five years together as a family."

"I guess that's right. I hadn't thought of it that way."

"Poor babe."

"Poor everyone. Such is life," I said.

The waiter returned with our Chardonnay and we watched him politely as he went through the ritual of extracting the cork, presenting a sample of wine, and then pouring two glasses. We hadn't even looked at the menus so we were accorded a few minutes to decide what we wanted. I ended up ordering the roast chicken and Tommy ordered the pasta puttanesca. We shared a salad up front. Once the entrées arrived, Tommy said, "Tell me about the boyfriend. What's the deal on him?"

I lowered my fork, feeling defensive on Dietz's behalf. "Why should I talk to you about him?"

"Don't be so prickly. I'd like to know what's going on here. Between us."

"Nothing's going on. We're having dinner."

"I think there's more to it than that."

"Really. As in what?"

"I have no idea. That's why I'm asking you."

"What are we doing here, defining our relationship? I've known you an hour."

His smile was slow. He seemed unaffected by my churlishness, which I couldn't seem to control. "Actually, I think it's closer to two hours than one. I saw you at the rental property twice before and now this." He finished the wine in his glass and poured himself more, adding wine to my glass first. His eyes were really the most extraordinary shade of green.

I said, "Well, I haven't known you long enough. Besides, you're too young."

He lifted his brows and I found myself blushing.

I said, "How'd you decide to move to Santa Teresa?"

"You're changing the subject."

"I don't like to be pushed," I said.

"Let's talk about sex. Tell me what you like in bed in case it ever comes up."

I laughed. "Let's talk about grade school. I hated mine. How'd you feel about yours?"

"Good. It was fun. I was captain of the Safety Council two years in a row. I went to four different colleges, but didn't graduate. I may try it again some day. I'd like to finish my degree."

"I did two semesters of junior college and didn't like it at all. I took Spanish in adult education, but I've forgotten everything except 'ola' and 'buenos dios.'"

"You cook?"

"No, but I'm a tidy little thing."

"Me, too. My brother's a pig. You'd never guess it by looking. He dresses okay, but his car's a mess."

"I carry cans of motor oil in my backseat."

"Part of your work," he said, forgivingly.

We chattered on in this fashion and I found myself liking his face. Also, I was not exactly unaware of his body, lean and muscular. I wondered where Dietz was tonight. Not anywhere in range, so what difference did it make? Few men ap-

peal to me, not so much because I'm picky about *them*. I'm
protective of myself, which means I disqualify all but the
most—what . . . ? I couldn't think what it was that allowed
some men to get through my defenses. Chemistry, I guess. I
focused on cutting my chicken, trying a sample of mashed
potatoes, which rank right up there with peanut butter, in my
opinion.

Tommy touched my hand. "Where'd you disappear to?"

I looked up to find him staring at me. I moved my fingers
away from his. "Is this a date?"

"Yes."

"Because I don't date."

"I can tell."

"I'm serious," I said. "I'm not good at this boy-girl stuff."

"You must be. You were married twice and now you have
this other boyfriend on the string."

"I've had guys in between. That doesn't mean I handle it
well."

"You do fine. I like you. You don't have to be a jerk.
Lighten up."

Humbled, I said, "Okay."

When we left the restaurant at nine o'clock, the streets
were still glistening with the rain, which had passed. I saw his
Porsche parked across the street. The children's playground
was dark and the boats in the marina beyond were bobbing
dots of light. I waited while he unlocked the car and let me in.
Once he fired up the engine, he said, "Something I want to
show you. It's early yet. Okay?"

He pulled away from the curb and did a U-turn on Cabana
Boulevard. We drove west, passing the yacht harbor on our
left and Santa Teresa City College on our right. Up the hill on
Sea Shore. Left at the next big intersection. Without being
told, I knew we were on our way to Horton Ravine. He smiled
over at me. "I want to show you the house."

"What about Richard? Won't he object?"

"He drove down to Bell Garden to play poker tonight."

"What if he loses and comes home?"

"He won't come back until morning whatever happens."

We drove through the stone pillars that marked the rear entrance to Horton Ravine. The road was wide and dark. Many properties on either side were unfenced and had the look of rural countryside: pastures and stables, house lights twinkling through the trees. The route he took was circuitous, and I suspected his intention was to demonstrate the power and handling of the Porsche. At length, he turned right and up a short driveway to a half-moon motorcourt. I caught a sweeping glimpse of the house: stucco walls, massive lines, red-tile roof. All the arches and balconies were washed with dramatic exterior lights. He reached for the remote garage-door opener, pressed a button, and then swung into the open bay of a four-car garage. The cavernous space was pristine; new white drywall that smelled of the plaster overcoating. Three spaces were empty. I imagined Richard driving a sports car as new and as flashy as Tommy's. I opened the car door on my side and let myself out while Tommy got out and fished for his house key. There were no shelves, no tools, and no junk piled up; no lawn chairs, no cardboard boxes marked XMAS ETC. He let us into the utility area off the kitchen. The indicator on the alarm panel by the door was dark. There was a half bath and maid's quarters to the left, a laundry room on the right. There were stacks of junk mail on the kitchen counters, catalogs and flyers. In a separate pile there were instruction manuals for the answering machine, the microwave oven, and the Cuisinart, which had clearly never been used. The floors were done in dull red Mexican pavers, sealed and polished to a high gloss. Tommy tossed his keys on the glossy white-tile counter. "So what do you think?"

"No alarm system? That seems odd in a house this size."

"Spoken like a cop. There's actually one installed, but it isn't hooked up. When we first moved in Richard set it off so often, the company started charging us fifty bucks a pop and the cops refused to show. We figured, what's the point?"

"Let's hope the burglars haven't heard."

"We're insured. Come on and I'll give you the ten-cent tour."

He walked me through the house, pausing to fill me in on their decorating plans. On the first level, wide-plank oak floors stretched through the living room, dining room, family room, paneled den, and two guest rooms. The upstairs was fully carpeted in cream-colored wool; two master suites, a workout room, and enough closet space for ten. The place had the feel of a model home in a brand-new subdivision, minus all the furniture and foo-foo. Many rooms were empty, and those that had furniture seemed empty, nonetheless. I realized Tommy traveled light, like me—no kids, no pets, and no houseplants. In the family room, there was a fully stocked wet bar, too much black leather, and a big-screen television for sporting events. I didn't see any art or books, but maybe those were still packed away.

In the bedrooms, it was clear they'd purchased entire suites of furniture off the showroom floor. All the pieces matched; light wood in Tommy's room—the style, "Moderne." In Richard's bedroom, the headboard, chest of drawers, armoire, and two bed tables were heavy and dark, the design faintly Spanish with wrought-iron pulls. Everything was spotlessly clean, which probably meant a crew of three coming in once a week.

We made the complete circuit and ended up back in the kitchen. Both of us were conscious of the passage of time. Despite his earlier nonchalance, he seemed as aware as I was that Richard might roll in at any moment. He wasn't due for hours, but I could feel his presence like a ghost in every room. Tommy had made no further comment about his brother's chilly attitude and I didn't want to ask. For all I knew, the tension between them had nothing to do with me.

Finally, in a show of bravado, Tommy said, "Would you like a drink?"

"I think not, but thanks. I have work to do. I appreciate the tour. This is really great."

"It needs work yet, but we like it. You'll have to see it by day. The landscaping's beautiful." He checked his watch. "I better get you home."

I picked up my shoulder bag and followed him, waiting in the car while he locked the house again. In the confines of the Porsche, I was conscious of the charge in the air between us. We chatted on the drive, but it was make-work in the face of my attraction to him. He found a parking space near Rosie's, half a block from my place. He parallel parked and then came around the car again to let me out. He offered me his hand in support and I extracted myself with as much grace as I could manage. Sports cars should come equipped with quick-ejection seats.

The crowd noise from Rosie's was muffled, but I was aware of the contrast between the raucous din in there and the quiet where we were. Residual rain dripped from the nearby trees and water gurgled along the gutters like a urban brook. We stood there for a moment, neither of us sure how to say good-night. He reached over idly and adjusted the metal clasp on the front of my slicker. "Don't want you wet. Can I walk you home?"

"I'm just down there. You can almost see the place from here."

He smiled. "I know. I got the address from your application and checked it out earlier. Looks nice."

"You're nosy."

"Where you're concerned," he said.

He smiled again and I found myself glancing away. We both said "Well" at the same time and laughed. I walked backward a few steps, watching while he opened the door and folded himself under the steering wheel. He slammed the car door and moments later the engine rumbled to life. The headlights flicked on and he took off with a roar. I turned, proceeding to the corner while the sound of his car faded at the end of the block. I confess my underwear felt warm and ever so faintly damp.

12

TUESDAY MORNING DAWNED in a haze of damp and fog. I went through my usual morning routine, including a jog so vigorous it left me rosy-cheeked and sweating. After breakfast, I spent some time working at home, finishing revisions on my report for Fiona. Maybe all these neatly typed pages would pass for progress in her eyes. This was one of the few times in my life when I could see that I might fail, and I was scared. I anticipated her return with the same enthusiasm I'd felt any time I had to have a shot as a kid.

I left my apartment at 9:35. With the temporary break in the storm, large bands of blue sky had appeared between the clouds. The grass had turned emerald green and the leaves on all the trees were looking glossy and fresh. My appointment with Dow Purcell's best friend, Jacob Trigg, was scheduled for 10:00. I'd studied a city map, pinpointing his street address in the heart of Horton Ravine. I drove east along Cabana Boulevard and ascended the hill as it swept up from the beach. I turned left on Promontory Drive and followed the road along the bluffs that paralleled the beach. I turned left again and drove through the back entrance to Horton Ravine.

Tommy crossed my mind and I smiled in a goofy glow I found embarrassing.

A mile down the road, I saw the street I was looking for. I turned right through a warren of winding lanes and drove up the hill. Water rushed in a torrent along the berm and what looked like entire gravel driveways had washed out into the road. A tree with shallow roots had toppled backward, pulling up a half-moon of soil. Despite the numerous houses in the area, Mother Nature was busy reclaiming her own.

I peered to my right, checking mailboxes as I crept along. I finally spotted the house number Jacob Trigg had given me. Enormous black wrought-iron gates stood open and I drove up a long curving lane between low stone walls. At the top of the slow rise, the parcel became flat and I could see gently undulating acreage sweeping out in all directions. The two-story house was Italianate in feel, elegant and plain with a symmetrical window placement and a small porch in front with a circular balustrade.

I parked and got out. All the ground-floor windows were disconcertingly dark. There was no doorbell and no one answered my repeated knocks. I circled the house, checking for lights or other signs of the inhabitants. The air was still except for the occasional water dripping from the eaves. Had Trigg stood me up? I took a moment to check my bearings. Formal gardens stretched out on either side of the house, but there was not a gardener in sight. Probably too wet to do much work.

I started down the sloping lawn, hoping to come across someone who'd tell me if Trigg was home. For the next five minutes, I wandered across the property, grass squishing underfoot where underground springs had suddenly resurfaced. At the end of a row of ornamental pears, I spotted a greenhouse with a small potting shed attached. An electric golf cart was parked nearby. I picked my way forward, mindful of the mud sucking at the soles of my boots.

I could see a man working at a high bench just inside the shed. Despite the cold, he wore khaki shorts and muddy running shoes. There were braces on both legs, secured by what looked like screws driven in on either side of his knees. I could see signs of atrophy in the muscles of his calves. Propped up against the counter beside him was a pair of forearm crutches. The billed cap he wore covered a thatch of gray hair. On the redwood surface in front of him, there were five or six ratty-looking potted plants in various stages of decline.

I paused in the doorway, waiting for acknowledgment before I went in. Beyond the far doorway, the greenhouse opened up, but the angled glass ceiling wasn't visible from where I stood. Most of the side panes were an opaque white, but in places the glass was clear, admitting brighter squares of light. The air was warm and smelled of loam and peat moss. "Hi. Sorry to interrupt, but are you Mr. Trigg?"

He scarcely looked up. "That's me. What can I do for you?"

"I'm Kinsey Millhone."

He turned and looked at me blankly, a knot forming between his eyes. His mustache was iron gray and his brows were an untidy mix of black and gray hairs. I guessed he was in his early sixties; red-nosed, jowly, and heavy through his chest, which sloped forward and down into a sizeable belly.

"I was hoping you could answer some questions about Dr. Purcell," I prompted.

His confusion seemed to clear. "Oh, sorry. I forgot you were coming or I'd have waited at the house."

"I should have called to remind you. I appreciate your taking the time to talk to me."

"Hope I can be of help," he said. "Folks call me 'Trigg' so you can skip all the 'mister' stuff. Doesn't seem to fit." He leaned against the crude redwood counter and stirred a quick squirt of detergent into one of two buckets of water sitting side-by-side. He reached for a twig of miniature rosebush festooned with cobwebs. He placed his hand on the soil at the base of the plant, turned it upside down, and dunked it in the water. "I'm surprised you found me. My daughter lives with me, but she's out this morning."

"Well, I did wander quite a bit. I'm glad you don't have a roving pack of attack-trained dogs."

"That bunch is put away for the moment," he said without pause.

I really hoped this was a sample of his dry wit. Hard to tell as his tone of voice and his facial expression didn't change.

"In case you're wondering what I'm up to, I'm not a horticulturist by trade. My daughter has a business taking care of houseplants for folks here in Horton Ravine. She does a bit of hotel work, too—the Edgewater, Montebello Inn, places like that. All live plants; no fresh flowers. I guess they hire someone else to do the big fancy arrangements. She brings me the sickly kids and I nurse 'em back to health." He righted the dripping rosebush and then swished it in the bucket of clear water. He pulled it out, shook it off, and studied the effect. "This little guy's suffering from an infestation of spider mites. Suckers are only a fiftieth of an inch long and look at the damage. Used to have healthy foliage and now it's no more than a twig. I'll keep it in quarantine. We see a lot of root rot, too. People overwater, trying to be helpful between Susan's visits. You a plant person?"

"Not much. Used to have an air fern, but I finally threw it out."

"Smell like feet," he said, with a shake of his head. He set the rosebush aside and reached for a corn plant in a terracotta pot. I watched while he sponged a dark gray powdery coating from the leaves. "Sooty mold," he said, as though I'd inquired. "Plain old soapy water's good for a lot of these things. I'm not opposed to a systemic poison, but something like aphids, I prefer to try a contact pesticide first. Malathion or nicotine sulfate, which is basically your Black Flag-40. I'm conservative, I guess. Susan sometimes disagrees, but she can't argue with my success."

I said, "I take it you're an old friend of Dr. Purcell?"

"A good twenty years. I was a patient of his. He testified in my behalf in the lawsuit following my auto accident."

"This was before he got into geriatrics?"

"I certainly hope so," he said.

I smiled. "What kind of work did you do?"

"I was a detail man; drug sales. I covered the tri-counties, calling on doctors in private practice. I met Dow when he still had his office over near St. Terry's."

"You must have done well. This property's impressive."

"So was the settlement. Not that it's any compensation. I used to jog and play tennis. Take your body for granted until it goes out on you. Hell of a thing, but I'm luckier than some." He paused, peering over at me. "I take it you talked to Crystal. She called to say you'd probably be getting in touch. How's it going so far?"

"It's frustrating. I've met with a lot of people, but all I've picked up are theories when what I need are facts."

His tangled eyebrows met in the middle, forming a crimp. "I suspect I'm only going to add to the general confusion. I've been thinking about him, going back over things in my mind. Police talked to me the first week he was gone and I was as baffled as anyone."

"How often did you see him?"

"Once or twice a week. He'd stop by for coffee in the mornings on his way to Pacific Meadows. I know you gals think men don't talk about personal matters . . . more like sports, cars, and politics is your sense of it. Dow and I, we were different, maybe because he'd seen me go through so much pain and suffering. Without complaint, I might add. He was a man tended to keep his own counsel and I think he valued that in others. He was only eight years my senior, but I looked on him as a father. I felt comfortable telling him just about anything. We built us a lot of trust and in time, he confided in me as well."

"People admire him."

"As well they should. He's a good man . . . or was. I'm not at all sure how we should speak of him. Present tense, I hope, but that remains to be seen. Crystal tells me Fiona hired you."

"That's right. She's in San Francisco on business, but she's coming back this afternoon. I'm scrambling around, talking to as many people as I can, hoping to persuade her the money's well spent."

"I wouldn't be concerned. Fiona's hard to please," he said. "Who's on your list aside from me?"

"Well, I've talked to one of his two business associates . . ."

"Which one?"

"Joel Glazer. I haven't talked to Harvey Broadus. I talked to people at the clinic, and his daughter Blanche, but not Melanie."

His eyebrows went up at the mention of her name, but he made no comment. "What about Lloyd Muscoe, Crystal's ex-husband? Have you spoken to him?"

"I hadn't thought to, but I could. I saw him at Crystal's on Friday afternoon when he came to get Leila. How does he fit in?"

"He might or might not. About four months back, Dow mentioned that he went to see Lloyd. I assumed it had something to do with Leila, but maybe not. You know, Leila lived with Lloyd briefly. She'd been busy telling everyone she was old enough to decide. Crystal got tired of fighting her, so Leila went to Lloyd's. She started eighth grade in the public schools up here. Wasn't here two months and she was out of control. Grades fell, she was truant, into alcohol and drugs. Dow put his foot down and that's when they stepped in and enrolled her in Fitch. Now she's strictly regulated and she blames Dow for that. Sees him as a tyrant—a tyrant being anyone who won't let her have her way."

"I think she's mad at Lloyd, too. When I was over there, she was refusing to see him, but Crystal insisted."

"I don't doubt she's mad at him. She thinks it's his job to get her out of there. Doesn't want to look at her own behavior. Her age, you always think it's someone else's fault."

"What happened when Dow went to see Lloyd? Did they quarrel?"

"Not that I know, but if Lloyd intended to do Dow harm, he'd be way too wily to tip his hand with any public display."

I reached in my bag and found a stray envelope so I could make a note. "Can you give me his address?"

"I don't remember offhand. I can tell you where it is, though. Big house, yellow shingles, pitch roof. Right there at the corner of Missile and Olivio. Lloyd rents the little studio in back."

"I think I know the place," I said. "I gather he and Crystal get along okay."

"More or less. She still tends to lick his boots. Crystal was always under Lloyd's thumb."

"How so?"

"He lived off her earnings when she worked as a stripper in Las Vegas. They had one of those hotheaded relationships full of drinking and fights. One or the other would end up calling the police, screaming bloody murder. Crystal would have Lloyd arrested and then next thing you know she'd change her mind and refuse to press charges. He'd accuse her of assault and battery, then they'd kiss and make up. Oldest story in the book. After she met Dow, she dropped everything and moved to Santa Teresa with the girl. I guess she saw Dow as her ticket out, which in a way he was. Problem was, Lloyd followed her and he was furious—couldn't believe she'd leave him after all they'd been through. Couldn't believe he'd lost control is more like it."

"How do you know all this?"

"I heard it from Dow," he said. "I think he was worried Lloyd would find a way to reassert his dominance. Crystal looks strong, but where Lloyd's concerned she's motivated by guilt. He claims she owes him big time for turning his life upside down."

"Doesn't he work?"

"Not so's you'd notice. He did construction for a while, but then he claimed he'd injured his back. He'll live on worker's comp until the money runs out. That's how his mind works. Why put out the effort if he can get what he wants by manipulating someone else?"

"But surely Crystal's out from under him."

"A woman like her is never out from under a man."

I tucked the envelope away, trying to think what other ground I might cover. "What about the book Dow was writing? That's one reason Crystal's convinced something's happened to him. She says he wouldn't just walk out: first of all because of Griffith and, secondly, because of the book he was working on."

A pained expression seemed to cross Trigg's face. "Started out, he was excited about the project, but the task turned out to be a lot harder than he thought. I'd say he was more discouraged than enthusiastic. He was also upset about Fiona. She kept pressing him for money. He knew she was convinced he was going back to her and that distressed him no end. That's why he was on his way up there."

"What do you mean 'up there'?"

"He was going to see Fiona to clarify the situation."

"The night he disappeared?"

"That's what he told me. We had breakfast together that Friday morning and he said she'd insisted on a meeting. She was always insisting on something. She's a pain in the ass, if you'll forgive my being blunt. I told Dow then what I'd been saying all along: She was always going to demand a pound of flesh from him. She couldn't stop him leaving her, but she could surely make him pay."

"What in the world made her think he'd leave Crystal and go back to her?"

"Oh, she had it all worked out, according to him. Said she was the only one understood him, for better or worse. I guess she was big on 'worse.' "

"Fiona tells me Dow disappeared on two previous occasions. Any idea where?"

"Rehab. He told me he went to a 'dry out' farm."

"Alcohol?"

"That's right. He didn't want it known, felt his patients would lose confidence if they knew his drinking was out of control."

"I've heard from a couple of different sources he was drinking again."

"Probably Fiona's influence. She'd drive any man to drink."

"Couldn't he have checked into another rehab facility?"

"I hope so. I surely do, but then again, you'd think he'd have let someone know by now."

"Fiona says he didn't say a word to anyone before."

"That's not quite true. He told me."

"What do you know about the business at Pacific Meadows?"

Trigg shook his head. "Not much. I know it wasn't looking good. I told him to hire an attorney, but he said he didn't want to do that yet. He had his suspicions about what was going on, but he wanted to check it out himself before he did anything else."

"Someone told me he was worried Crystal would jump ship if the uproar became public."

Trigg tossed his sponge in a bucket. "Maybe that's what Fiona was counting on," he said.

*   *   *

I walked into the office at 11:25 to find Jeniffer, bending over a file drawer, in a skirt so short the two crescent-shaped bulges of her hiney were hanging out the back. Her legs were long and bare, tanned from all the days she took off to go to the beach with her pals. I said, "Jeniffer, you're really going to have to wear longer skirts. Don't you remember 'I see London, I see France, I see someone's underpants'?"

She jerked upright and tugged self-consciously at the hem of her skirt. At least she had the good grace to look embarrassed. She clopped back to her desk in her wooden-soled clogs. She sat down, exposing so much bare thigh I felt compelled to avert my eyes.

"Any messages?" I asked.

"Just one. Mrs. Purcell said she's back and she's expecting you at two o'clock."

"When? Today or tomorrow?"

"Oh."

"Don't worry about it. I can figure it out. Anything else?"

"This came," she said, and handed me an Express Mail envelope. I opened the flap. Inside was the contract Fiona'd signed and returned. Shit. I already hated feeling bound to her.

"Also, someone's here to see you. I showed her into your office and took her a cup of coffee."

That got my attention. "You left her in my office by her*self*?"

"I have work to do. I couldn't *stay*."

"How do you know she's not back there going through my desk?" I said, knowing that's what I'd be doing if I were in her place.

"I don't think she'd do that. She seems nice."

I could feel my heat gauge rising into the red zone. "I seem nice, too. That doesn't count for much. How long's she been there?" To be fair, I was probably displacing my feelings about Fiona onto her, but I was pissed, anyway.

Jeniffer made a face to show she was thinking real hard. "Not long. Twenty minutes. Maybe a little more."

"Is she at least someone I know?"

"I *think* so," she said, faintly. "Her name's Mariah *something*. I just figured she'd be more comfortable back there than if she waited for you out here."

"Jeniffer, in that length of time, she could have ripped me off for everything I own."

"You said that. I'm sorry."

"Forget about 'sorry.' Don't ever do it again." I headed down the inner corridor. I looked back at her. "And get some pantyhose," I snapped. As I passed Ida Ruth's desk, she was studiously avoiding my gaze, no doubt thrilled I was being subjected to a sample of Jeniffer's continuing ineptitude.

My office door was closed. I barged in to find a woman sitting in the guest chair. She'd placed her empty coffee mug on the edge of the desk in front of her. Scanning the surface, I could've sworn my files were ever so slightly disarranged. I looked at her quizzically and she returned my gaze with eyes as blank and blue as a Siamese cat's.

She couldn't have been more than twenty-six, but her hair was a startling silver-gray, as polished as pewter. She wore very little makeup, but her skin tones looked warm against the frosty hair, which was combed back and anchored behind her ears. She had a finely sculpted jaw, a strong nose and chin, lightly feathered brows. The skirt of her gray wool business suit was cut short and sheer black hose emphasized her shapely knees, one of which carried the vestiges of an old scar. There was a black briefcase resting near the left side of her chair. She looked like an expensive lawyer with a high-powered firm. Maybe I was being sued.

Warily, I moved around my desk and sat down. She shed her jacket with ease and arranged it across the back of the chair to avoid wrinkling it. From the shape of her shoulders and upper arms, I knew she worked out a lot harder than I did.

"I'm Mariah Talbot," she said. The black silk tank top rustled faintly as she reached across the desk to shake hands. She had long oval nails painted a neutral shade. The effect was sophisticated; nothing gaudy about this one. The most riveting feature was a gnarly white scar, probably a burn, on the outer aspect of her right forearm.

"Do we have an appointment?" I asked, unable to keep the testiness out of my voice.

"We don't, but I'm here on a matter I think will interest you," she said, unruffled. Whatever my disposition, it wasn't going to bother *her*. The image she projected was one of composure, competence, efficiency, and determination. Her smile, when it appeared, scarcely softened her face.

"What's the deal?"

She leaned forward, placing her business card on the desk in front of me. The face of it read, MARIAH TALBOT, SPECIAL INVESTIGATIONS UNIT, GUARDIAN CASUALTY INSURANCE, with an address and phone number I scarcely stopped to read. The logo was a four-leaf clover with *Home*, *Auto*, *Life*, and *Health* written in each of the four loops. "We need to have a chat about your landlord."

"Henry?"

"Richard Hevener."

I don't know what I expected, but it wasn't that. "What about him?"

"You may not be aware of this, but Richard and Tommy are fraternal twins."

"Really?" I said, thinking, *Who gives a shit?*

"Here's something else you may not be aware of. Richard and Tommy murdered their parents back in Texas in 1983."

I could feel my lips parting slightly, as though in preparation for the punch line to a joke.

The combination of the blue eyes and the silver hair was arresting, and I could hardly keep from staring. She went on, her manner completely matter-of-fact: "They hired someone to break into the house. As nearly as we can tell, the plan was for the burglar to drill the safe and walk off with a substantial amount of cash, plus jewelry valued at close to a million dollars. The boys' mother, Brenda, was the older of two girls who came from an incredibly wealthy Texas family named Atcheson. Brenda inherited a stunning jewelry collection that she left, by will, to her only sister, Karen. These are pieces that have been passed down through the family for years."

She reached into her briefcase and pulled out a fat brown accordion file. She removed a manila folder and passed it over to me. "These are the newspaper clippings. Plus, one copy each of the two wills."

I opened the file and glanced at the first few clippings, dated January 15, 22, and 29 of 1983. In all three articles, Richard and Tommy were pictured, looking solemn and withdrawn, flanked by their attorney in a three-piece business suit. Headlines indicated the two were being questioned in the ongoing investigation of the homicides of Jared and Brenda Hevener. Additional articles covered the investigation over the balance of the year. I didn't stop to read the wills.

Mariah Talbot went on. "You'll notice their aunt Karen's name cropping up in some of the articles. The burglar was a punk named Casey Stonehart, who'd already been jailed six times for a variety of crimes ranging from petty theft to arson, a minor specialty of his. We believe he opened the safe using the combination they'd given him. Then he dismantled the smoke detectors and set a blaze meant to cover up the crime. Apparently—and this is only a guess—the deal was he'd take the bulk of the jewelry, which he was in a position to fence. The boys would take the cash and maybe a few choice pieces, then submit a claim to the insurance company for the house, its contents, the jewelry, and anything else they could get away with. Oh yes, the cars. Two Mercedes-Benz were destroyed in the blaze. Mr. and Mrs. Hevener were found bound and gagged in the master bedroom closet. They died of smoke inhalation, which is not as bad as being burned alive—lucky them. Neither boy was anywhere in the area. In fact, both by some miracle were out of town and had iron-clad alibis," she said. "Stonehart, the kid who did the dirty work, disappeared soon afterward; probably dead and buried somewhere, though we have no proof. He's been missing ever since so it's a safe bet they got rid of him. An accomplice is always the weak link in these things."

"Couldn't he be in hiding?"

"If he were, he'd have been in touch with his family. They're all deadbeats and bums, but loyal to a fault. They wouldn't care what he'd done."

"How do you know their loyalty doesn't include keeping mum about where he is?"

"The sheriff's department put a mail check in place and there's a trace on the phone. Believe me, the silence has been absolute. This is a kid with big dependency issues. If he were alive, he couldn't tolerate the separation."

I cleared my throat. "When was this again?" I knew she'd told me, but I could hardly take it in.

"1983. Hatchet, Texas. It didn't take long for suspicion to fall on the two boys, but they'd been extremely clever. There was little to suggest the part they'd played . . . beyond the obvious, of course. Financially, they cleaned up. For them, it must have been better than the lottery. To all appearances, there was no bad blood between them and their parents, no public disagreements, no recent increases in insurance coverage. There was also very little linking them to Casey Stonehart. No phone records showing calls between the brothers and him. Bank accounts showed no unusual withdrawals to suggest a down payment on Casey's services. The kid was such a lowlife he didn't even have a bank account. He kept his money in his mattress; the Sealy Posturepedic Savings and Loan. The three of them did attend the same high school.

Casey was a year behind the Heveners, but there was no overt connection. It's not like they bowled in the same league or hung out together."

Anything I'd felt for Tommy had evaporated. "What about the parents' wills? Anything of interest there?"

Mariah shook her head. "No changes in the terms since the document was drawn up when the boys were born. The attorney was a bit lax in that regard. The twins had reached their majority and adjustments should have been made. Their aunt Karen was still listed as their guardian if something happened to the parents."

"What made the cops fix on them?"

"For one thing, neither of them can act. They put on a good show, but the feelings were all phony, strictly crocodile tears. At the time, both were still living at home. Tommy was one of those perpetual college students; his way of refusing to grow up and go out on his own. Richard fancied himself an 'entrepreneur,' which meant he borrowed and squandered money as fast as it came into his hands. Jared was thoroughly disgusted with them. He considered them moochers and he was sick of it. Brenda, too. This we heard about later from close friends of theirs."

"I'm assuming the brothers were charged?"

Mariah shook her head. "Police investigators couldn't cobble together sufficient evidence to satisfy the D.A. Of course, the insurance company balked at paying, but the boys filed suit and forced them to perform. Since they'd hadn't been arrested, charged with, or convicted of any crime, Guardian Casualty had no choice but to pay up."

"How much?"

"Two hundred and fifty thousand each in life insurance. The homeowner's and auto claims came to a little over three quarters of a million dollars. This is Texas, don't forget. Not like real estate values you're used to dealing with out here. Also, despite his business acumen, Jared never managed to amass much in the way of wealth. Lot of what he did was probably under the table, which is neither here nor there. Anyway, along with the insurance, you add the cash in the safe—which probably amounted to another hundred grand—and the jewelry on top of that, and you can see they did well. Guardian Casualty and Karen Atcheson, the boys' aunt, are preparing to file a civil suit to recover their losses. We're convinced the boys still have the jewelry if we can find a way to prevail. I've been assigned to handle the preliminary investigation."

"Why now when the murders were three years ago? I know proof in a civil case is easier, but you still have to have all your ducks in a row."

"Someone's come forward . . . an informant . . . very hush-hush. This is the arsonist, a professional, who talked to Casey twice—once before the fire and then again right afterward. It was his expertise Casey was relying on, because the job was much bigger than anything he'd done in his piddling career."

"What was the arsonist getting in return?"

"A piece of Casey's action. Once the arsonist found out about the killings, he wasn't willing to 'fess up to any part in it. He was nervous about a felony murder charge, or worse—that the brothers would kill him. Now he's decided to do what's right and that's why we think we have a shot at this."

"Why doesn't he go to the cops and let them handle it?"

"He will if Guardian Casualty comes up with the evidence."

I pushed the file aside. "And you're here to do what?"

Mariah smiled to herself as though privately amused. "I've been nosing around. It looks like funds are low and the boys are getting on each other's nerves. We're counting on the fact they're having cashflow problems. That's why Richard agreed to lease the place to you, if you haven't figured that out. You offered him six months' rent in advance and he needed the bucks."

"How'd you find out about that?"

"We gimmicked up another applicant, a writer looking for an office away from his home. The cash is the explanation Richard gave when he turned him down. At any rate, the friction between the brothers could really work for us. I'm always hoping one will break down and rat the other one out. We've been after them for three years and this is as close as we've come."

"What's this got to do with me?"

"We'd like to hire you to do some work for us."

"Such as?"

"We want you to pass along the name of a fence in Los Angeles. He's a jeweler by trade. The business looks legitimate on the surface, but he's actually a fence. He deals in stolen property when the quality or quantity is sufficient to make it worth the risk. With money getting scarce, the boys might be tempted to dip into the stash, which we don't think they've touched."

"But they can't get anywhere close to true value through a fence."

"What choice do they have?"

"Wouldn't they be better off trying to auction some of the pieces through Christie's or Sotheby's?"

"Christie's or Sotheby's would insist on a provenance . . . proof the jewelry was theirs . . . which they can't provide. They may try selling to a private party, which is yet another reason we're stepping up the pace."

"So I pass along the information about the jeweler and then what?"

"We wait to see if they take the bait and then we nail them. The Houston D.A.'s already talked to the D.A.'s office here and they're ready to roll. Once we know the jewelry's in the house, we'll ask for a warrant and go in."

"Based on what?"

"We'll have the fence and the fence will have at least a portion of the jewelry. The boys are going to have a hell of a time explaining that."

"What if they don't make contact with him?"

"We have another scheme in mind that I'd rather not go into. In the meantime, you might want to see the jewelry." Again, she reached into her briefcase, this time removing a manila folder with what looked like appraisals and a series of Polaroids. She sorted through the stack, laying picture after picture on the rim of my desk, rattling off the contents. "Diamond rivière necklace valued at $120,000. An art deco diamond-and-sapphire bracelet—that one's $24,000. Diamond ring with a stone weighing in at 7.63 carats, worth $64,000. And check this one: a necklace with 86 graduated diamonds. That's somewhere between $43- and $51,000. Sorry about the pics. These are preliminary Polaroids. All the good appraisal photos are being circulated through Southern California." She finished dealing out the pictures, reciting prices like a pitchman for a company selling door to door.

"What makes you so sure they still have them?"

"An educated guess," she said. "We know they bought a safe from a local locksmith. We figure they installed it at the house so each of them could keep an eye on the other. The problem is, we have no legitimate means of getting in."

"Funny you should say that. I was there last night."

"How'd you manage that?"

"Richard was gone. Tommy took me over and showed me around."

"I don't suppose you spotted the safe."

"I'm afraid not. There's barely any furniture and no wall art. I can tell you this—the entire alarm system's down. Tommy told me Richard set it off so many times they finally discontinued service. Now it's strictly window dressing."

"Interesting. I'll have to think about that. When will you see him again?"

"I'm not going to see him again! After what you've told me?"

"Too bad. We could really use your help. He's taken an interest in a woman more than once and Richard always puts a stop to it. He doesn't trust his little brother's tendency to blab. I don't think Richard realizes what a threat you are."

"*I'm* a threat?"

"Of course. Tommy's hustling you and that gives you power—not a lot, but enough. You have access, for one thing."

"I'm not going to go sneaking around in there. I'd have no reason whatever to tour the house again. Besides, even if I found the safe, I wouldn't have the faintest idea how to open it."

"We wouldn't want you to do that. All we need is the location, which couldn't be that hard. Once we have the warrant, we don't want the boys disposing of the evidence."

I thought about it briefly. "I won't do anything illegal."

Mariah smiled. "Oh, come now. From what we've heard, you're willing to cut corners when it suits you."

I stared at her. "You ran a background on me?"

"We had to know who we were dealing with. All we're asking you to do is pass along the information about the fence."

"I don't like it. It's too risky."

"Without risk, where's the fun? Isn't that the point?"

"Maybe for you."

"I told you, we intend to pay you for your time."

"It's not about money. I don't want to be pimped."

"Meaning what?"

"I won't peddle my ass so you can nail these guys. I'm a big fan of justice, but I'm not going to offer up my body to get the goods on them."

"We're not asking you to go to bed with him. What you do in private is strictly your concern." She closed her mouth, a move I've often employed myself, giving the other person the opportunity to work it out.

I picked up a pencil and tapped it on the desk, letting my fingers slide the length as I flipped it end over end. "I'll think about it some and let you know."

"Don't take too long." She placed a slip of paper on the desk with a name and address written across the face of it. "This is the name of the jeweler. I'll leave it up to you how you play out the information. You can bill us for your time and gas mileage. If you decide you can't help, then so be it. Either way, we'll trust you to keep your mouth shut."

I took the paper and looked at the name. "You have a number where I can reach you?"

"I've been moving around. In an emergency, you can use the number on my card, but I think it'd be better if I called you. I'll touch base in a day or so and see how things stand. Meanwhile, I don't want the boys to know I'm here. I've been dogging them for years and with this gray hair, I'm not exactly inconspicuous. If they find out we've spoken, you're in the soup, so take care."

13

BY 1:45, HAVING confirmed my appointment with Fiona, I found myself driving once more along Old Reservoir Road. The sky was a steel gray, the earlier patches of blue covered over with thick clouds again. I flicked a look to my right, taking in the sight of Brunswick Lake. Gusts of wind skipped like stones along the surface of the water, and trees at the shoreline tossed their shaggy heads. I parked, as I had before, on the side of the two-lane road. I reached for my shoulder bag and the brown manila envelope containing my report. I looked up at the house, which was dug into the hillside as though meant to withstand attack. Four days had passed, but with the surfeit of rain, fresh weeds were sprouting across the property.

I wasn't looking forward to the meeting, but it was better than having to think about Richard and Tommy Hevener. That problem was stuck in my throat like a bone. My first impulse was to bail on the new office space, thus severing all ties, but (cheap as I am) I hated to say bye-bye to more than sixteen hundred dollars. The conflict was thorny. Morality aside, it *can't* be socially correct to consort with a couple of stone-

cold killers. But how could I get out of my deal with them?
Even in California, the etiquette was baffling. Was one polite? Did one confess the reasons for refusing to do business?
I thought about the soft light in Tommy's eyes, then pictured
him patiently tying up his mother's hands before the house
was set on fire. If he called me again, should I *mention* his
parents' murders or simply make some excuse? I wanted to
act swiftly. Then again, by breaking off all contact, I was, in
effect, refusing to help Mariah Talbot. I seldom shy away
from risk and—as she had so rudely observed—I was willing
to cut corners when it suited me.

As I locked my car door, I saw Trudy, the German shepherd
I'd encountered on my last visit. She came racing up the road,
a spirited pup, probably less than a year old and thrilled to be
out in the chill November air. The dog squatted to take a whiz,
then placed her nose to the ground, tracing the erratic trail of
a critter that had passed that way earlier—rabbit or possum,
possibly a waddling raccoon. The dog's owner, coming up behind, was keeping an eye on her progress in case she stumbled
across something much bigger than she. By the time I'd clam-
bered up the stairs to Fiona's front entrance, the woman and
the dog were already out of sight. Henry and Rosie were always after me to get a mutt of my own, but I couldn't see the
point. Why take responsibility for a creature who can't even
use a flush toilet?

Fiona must have been waiting because I'd barely touched
the bell before she opened the door. Her latest outfit consisted
of a long-sleeved crepe blouse modeled on a postwar Eisen-
hower jacket belted at the waist. Her black wool skirt was
tubular and ended mid-shin, thus exposing the least attractive
portion of any woman's leg. Her high heels were chunky,
with multiple ankle straps. Perched on her dyed brown curls
was a version of the U.S. Women's Army Corps cap done in
sequined velvet. I could smell cigarettes and Shalimar and I
was suddenly reminded of my aunt's jar of Mum cream

deodorant, which she'd rub into her armpits with the tips of her fingers.

"You could have parked out back in the driveway instead of climbing all those stairs," Fiona remarked. The content was harmless, but her tone was resentful, as if she'd like nothing better than to pick a fight with me.

"I need the exercise," I said, refusing to take the bait.

As she stepped away from the door, she adjusted her watch, glancing down surreptitiously to see if I was late. As usual, I was bang on time and I thought *Ha-ha-on-you* as I followed her in.

In the foyer, the painter's scaffolding was still in place, drop cloths blanketing the floor like a thin canvas snow. Nothing had been touched since our meeting on Friday, and I assumed she didn't trust the workmen to continue without her. Or maybe it was they who knew better than to go on laboring in her absence. She was the type who'd make them redo all the work as soon as she walked in the door. I could see that the wall still bore patches of three different shades of white.

When I held out the brown manila envelope, you'd have thought I was offering her a bug on a tray.

"What's this?" she asked, suspiciously.

"You said you wanted a report."

She opened the envelope and peered at the pages. "Well, thank you. I appreciate that," she said, dismissing my labors with a glance. "I hope you won't object to talking in the bedroom. I'd like to unpack."

"Fine with me." In truth I was curious to see the rest of the place.

"The flight home was murder, one of those thirty-seat orange crates blowing all over the place. I didn't mind the up-and-down so much as the side-to-side. I thought I'd never get home."

"Probably wind from the storm."

"I'll never fly on one of those small planes again. I'd rather go by rail even if it takes half a day."

She picked up a makeup case she'd stashed in the hall. She barely glanced at the larger suitcase. "Grab that for me."

I picked up the hard-sided suitcase, feeling like a pack mule as I followed her up the stairs. That sucker was heavy. I watched her legs flashing in front of me as she mounted the steps. She wore stockings with seams. With her affinity for the '40s, I was surprised she didn't draw a line down the back of each bare leg the way women did during World War II rationing. We turned right at the landing and went into a white-on-white master suite, which featured a large wall of glass overlooking the road. I set her suitcase on the floor. While Fiona moved into the bathroom with her makeup case, I crossed to the windows to absorb the view.

The coastline was completely enveloped in fog, thunder heads rising like ominous mountains in the distance. The hills were saturated with green, plant life responding to the rain with a sudden burst of new growth. In the overcast, Brunswick Lake had turned silver, its surface as flat and as mottled as an antique mirror. I turned. Fiona's four-poster bed was situated so that she saw much of this: sun rising to her left, going down on her right. I tried to imagine what it would be like to sleep in a room this big. At one end of the room, double doors stood open to reveal a large walk-in closet the size of my loft. At the opposite end, there was a fireplace with easy chairs and a low glass coffee table arranged in front of it. I pictured Fiona and Dow having drinks up here on the nights when he stopped by. I wondered if they'd ever gone to bed together just for old time's sake.

Fiona emerged from the bathroom and moved to the bed, where a second hard-sided suitcase was already laid open on the pristine spread. She began to remove the articles of clothing she'd packed with such care. "Why don't you start from the beginning and fill me in."

I opened my verbal recital with an improvisational medley of interviews, going back over my report in a series of beautifully articulated summations of events. I began with Detective Odessa, segued into my visit with Crystal Purcell, and then moved on to Pacific Meadows, at which point I delineated the nature of the difficulties Dow Purcell was facing. I wasn't even fully warmed up when I hit a sour note that undercut my confidence. Fiona had been moving back and forth from the bed to the walk-in closet, carrying blouses and skirts, which she hung on matching white satin-padded hangers. She said, "You might as well follow me. Otherwise, I won't hear you and you'll have to repeat. My ears are still stopped up; just one more reason for taking the train."

I moved to the closet and stood in the doorway to continue the program. "At any rate, Saturday afternoon I went up to Blanche's shortly after she phoned . . ."

Fiona turned to me. "You went over to see Blanche? Why in the world did you do that?"

"She called me at home. I got the impression you'd already spoken to her."

"I did no such thing and I can't believe you'd take such a step without consulting me. No one's to be brought into this unless I say so. I'm paying for your time. If I'd wanted you to see Blanche, I'd have given you her number."

"I thought you did."

"I gave you Melanie's, not hers. How much did you tell her?"

"I really don't remember. Honestly, I'm sorry, but she acted as if she knew all about me, so I assumed she'd talked to you or to Melanie. She said the two of them were so relieved because they'd been urging you to hire someone ever since their father disappeared."

"That's immaterial. I'll pass on information to the girls if it seems relevant, but I think it's inappropriate coming from you. Is that clear?"

"Of course," I said, stung. Having paid Richard Hevener the entire $1,500 Fiona'd given me, I no longer had the means to refund her original retainer. Deducting $50 for the time I'd spent with Trigg, I now owed her $1,075 worth of services and realized if I quit, there was no way to pay her back, short of pulling the money from my savings account.

"Please go on," she murmured, resuming her chores.

My temper emerged hard on the heels of injury and I had to bite my tongue bloody to keep from telling her where to stick it. This resolution lasted until I opened my mouth. "You know what? Fun as this is, I'm already tired of taking crap from you. I've worked my butt off this weekend and if my methods don't suit you, I'm out of here."

For the second time within minutes, I'd managed to surprise and amaze. She seemed genuinely flustered, backing down as fast as she could manage it. "That's not what I meant. I apologize if I offended you. That wasn't my intent."

There's nothing more effective than an apology for knocking me off my high horse. I backed down as fast as she had and we spent the next few minutes smoothing one another's ruffled feathers before moving on.

Then Fiona asked me about the game plan. Like I had one.

"How do you intend to go about finding him?"

"Ah," said I. "Well. I have some other people I want to talk to first and then we'll see where we stand." In truth, I was at a loss.

Her eyes glittered briefly and I thought she might challenge me, but she seemed to think better of it.

"Couple of questions," I said. "Someone thought Dow might have gone into an alcohol rehab facility on the two occasions when he disappeared in the past. Any chance he might have left the country instead?"

She hesitated. "What difference would that make?"

"Lonnie Kingman questioned it. He's the attorney I rent

space from. He suggested Dowan might have been moving currency into foreign bank accounts in preparation for flight."

"It never occurred to me."

"I didn't occur to me, either, but the first time we met, you did seem to think he might be in Europe or South America."

"Well, yes, but I can't believe he'd plan such a thing all those years in advance."

"Did you ever look at his passport?"

"Of course not. What reason would I have?"

"Just an idea," I said. "Maybe that's why the passport's missing—he took it so no one could go back and see where he'd been on those earlier trips."

"You mentioned two questions."

I waited until she made eye contact with me. "Why didn't you tell me he was on his way over here that night?"

Casually, she placed a hand against her throat. The gesture was self-protective, as though she were warding off a slash at her carotid artery. "He never arrived. I thought it was a miscommunication. I tried calling his office the next day, but he was already gone by then."

"Why was he coming?"

"I don't see why it matters since he never showed."

"Was anyone else in the house with you that night?" I asked.

"To support my story?"

"That'd be nice, don't you think?"

"I'm afraid I can't help. This is a small town. Tongues wag. I wouldn't even let him leave his car on the parking pad. I had him pull into the empty garage. No one knew about his visits."

"At least no one you told." I felt badly as soon as I said it because the look in her eyes was one of betrayal.

"He swore he wouldn't tell Crystal. He said it would only hurt her and neither of us wanted that."

"I didn't say he told Crystal. This was someone else."

"Trigg."

I said, "Yes." After all, it was her money. She was entitled to the information. My scruples, though few, are somewhat spotty as well. "What about Lloyd Muscoe? Did Dow ever talk to you about him?"

"A bit. They disliked each other and avoided contact whenever possible. At first, it was territorial—they were like rival apes—which Crystal must have enjoyed. Later, the friction between them was more about Leila's relationship with Lloyd."

"I heard that Dow considered Lloyd a bad influence on the girl."

"I don't really know Lloyd so I'm reluctant to discuss the subject."

"Oh, give it a try. I'm sure you can manage something."

"He's common, for one thing."

"Happily, that isn't a crime in this state or I'd be under arrest myself."

"You know perfectly well what I'm talking about. They're paying a great deal of money to send her to that private school. I don't see the point when she spends half her weekends with someone like him."

"But Lloyd's the only father she's known. Crystal must feel it's important for Leila to maintain a relationship with him."

"*If* that's her motive. Perhaps she prefers to have the time to herself. Leila's behavior goes way beyond the norm for her age. It's obvious the girl is seriously disturbed. I'm sure Lloyd resented Dow's interference. Instead of taking time with Blanche, you should have been talking to him."

Trigg had told me Lloyd lived in the little studio behind the big yellow shingle house at the corner of Missile and Olivio. I parked out in front and made my way down the narrow driveway on foot. Shaggy hedges encroached on either side, forming walls of wet foliage that showered drops as I passed.

There was a 1952 Chevrolet parked on the grass at the end of the drive. The occasional wet leaf was plastered to the hood, but aside from that it seemed clean and well cared for. The backyard was overgrown and the small wood-frame studio might have been a gardener's shed at one time. I went up two shallow wooden porch steps and rapped on the frame of the screen door.

No one answered my knock. I took a few minutes to circle the studio, moving from window to window, peering in at the place. I could see four small rooms—living room, kitchen, two tiny bedrooms, with a bath between—all empty. I went back to the front door and opened the screen. I tried the knob. The door swung open at my touch. I turned and stared at the main residence, but no one seemed to be staring back at me. I entered the studio, my footsteps echoing against bare plaster walls.

The rooms smelled of mildew. The floors were covered in scuffed linoleum, the pattern worn. In the first bedroom, there were coat hangers strewn about. Nothing in the closet. In the second bedroom, there was a bare twin-sized mattress on the floor, and when I opened the closet door, I spotted two bedrolls tucked out of sight to the right. The window in that bedroom had been left open a crack, a detail I hadn't noticed when I circled the place. Maybe Lloyd crept in here to sleep now and then. Anyone could ease in along the hedges to the rear of the place, gaining access to the cottage without being seen. There was nothing in the bathroom, with its claw-footed bathtub and its toilet stained with rust. In the kitchen, cabinets stood open. On the counter, I could see a take-out cup holding the dregs of some drink. Smelled like bourbon and Coke, or something equally gross. I opened all the kitchen drawers. Optimist that I am, I'm always hoping for a clue, preferably a torn scrap of paper with a forwarding address.

I did another quick tour, which turned out to be as unenlightening as the first. I pulled the door shut behind me and struck out across the yard to the wide rear porch. The back-door was half glass and I could see an old woman in a house-dress fussing with a coven of cats. There were seven by my count: two calicoes, a black, two gray tabbies, an orange tabby, and a white long-haired Persian the size of a pug. I tapped on the window. The old woman looked up, giving me a scowl to indicate she was aware of my presence.

She was tall and gaunt, her white hair arranged in thin braids wrapped around her head. She was apparently in the process of feeding her brood because they circled her atten-tively, rubbing against her legs, their mouths opening in cries I couldn't hear through the glass. I could see her talking back, probably some long-winded comment about how spoiled they were. She put their bowls on the floor. All of the cats set to work, seven heads bowing as though in prayer. The woman crossed to the backdoor and opened it. The odor of cat litter wafted out through the gap.

"Not for rent," she said, loudly. "I saw you go through the place, but it's not available. Next time you might ask first be-fore you intrude." Her dentures were loose and she settled them in place with a kind of chewing motion between sentences.

"I'm sorry. I didn't realize anyone was here."

"That's clear enough," she said. "Past sixteen years I rented it out for two hundred dollars a month. Nothing but riffraff moved in. Turnover was constant and some of 'em was no better than bums. It was Paulie pointed out that's all I'd get at those prices. Now I'm asking eight fifty and the place stays empty. Big improvement."

"I'm looking for Lloyd Muscoe. Wasn't he living out there?"

"Did at one time. Twice he was late on his rent and once he didn't pay at all, so I kicked him out."

"Good for you." Where had I heard the name *Paulie* be-fore? Crystal's battle with Leila at the beach house the first time we met. "Paul's your grandson?"

"Granddaughter and the name's *Pauline*. I raised her since the day her drunken mother dropped her on my doorstep when she was six years old."

"Isn't she a friend of Leila's?"

"Who?"

"Lloyd's daughter, Leila."

"Not anymore. Leila's mother put a stop to it. Said Paulie was too wild. Ask me, that Lloyd's the wild one. Thought he'd get around me because I'm old and deaf, but I surprised him. Evicted him proper and had a marshall show up, and make sure he went without a fuss. Fellow like that might decide to trash the place if he doesn't get his way."

"Any idea where he went?"

"No, and I don't care. You a bill collector?"

"I'm a private detective."

"What kind of trouble is he in?"

"None as far as I know. I need to talk to him."

"Can't help. I think he's somewhere in town, but that's as much as I know. Can't even forward his bills, so I have to throw 'em in the trash. Nice-looking man, but shiftless as they come."

"So I've heard. Thanks, anyway."

"You're entirely welcome," she said, and closed the door.

I sat in the car and considered my options. The simplest course of action would be to ask Crystal where Lloyd had gone. Since the two shared custody, I assumed she'd know. I fired up the engine and headed for Horton Ravine again.

Dr. Purcell's house was built on a lush, wooded knoll with a narrow view of the ocean if you raised up on tiptoe. The residence itself wasn't impressive, despite Fiona's boasting about her talent for design. In typical fashion, she'd piled box on box in tiers up to a flat concrete roof. A reflecting pool extended from the front, providing a mirror image of the house in case you happened to miss it the first time around. The

style, though futuristic, was oddly dated, imitative of archi-
tects more talented than she. It was clearly not Crystal's taste
and I could see where she'd chafe at having to live there. Given
her love of the glass-and-frame Cape Cod beach house, this
must have felt like a prison. The white Volvo and the Audi convertible were parked in the drive, along with a snappy little
black Jaguar I hadn't seen before.

When I rang the bell, I heard nothing, but within a minute,
Crystal appeared at the door. She was wearing boots, black
wool slacks, and a heavy black wool sweater. Her hair was
feathered away from her face, the layered blond strands carelessly disarranged. "Good. Thank God. Maybe you can help.
Nica, it's Kinsey! Come on in," she said to me, harried.

I stepped through the door. "What's going on?"

"Anica's just driven up from Fitch," she said. "Leila left
campus without permission and we're trying to track her
down before she blows it. She'll be kicked out of school as
soon as they realize she's gone. Don't worry about me. I'm
only going out of my mind. Rand took Griff to the zoo."

Anica appeared from the kitchen, wearing navy blue slacks
and a red blazer with a gold-stitched Fitch Academy patch on
the breast pocket. Her shirt was tailored, crisp white, and she
wore a pair of low-heeled navy blue pumps. Her manner was
straightforward, and she managed a wide smile despite Crystal's distress. "Always walking into uproar. Hello, Kinsey. Nice
to see you again. How are you?" She reached forward and we
shook hands.

"Fine. I'm sorry about Leila. You think she's heading this
way?"

"Let's hope," Crystal said. She passed us on her way into
the kitchen, talking over her shoulder. "I'm making coffee
while we try to decide what to do. She knows she's not allowed to hitchhike. I've expressly forbidden it. . . ."

"That's probably why she's done it," Anica said.

"I'd be sick with worry if I wasn't so mad at her. How do you take yours, Kinsey?"

"Black's fine with me."

While Anica and I followed her into the kitchen, I made a quick eyeball assessment of the living room to my right. The interior of the house was curious: stone floors, stark white walls, no window covering, all angles and cold light—clearly Fiona's imprint. Over it Crystal had asserted her own taste: assorted shabby Oriental carpets laid together like pieces of a puzzle, sagging upholstered furniture slipcovered with faded chintz. The wood tables and padded chairs were an antique white with green-and-white checkered seats. Some of the stray pieces were made of bentwood; big rounded chairs that had been woven from twigs. There was a white-painted wrought-iron daybed piled with oversized pillows in mismatched fabrics. Books were stacked on the coffee table and there were vases of flowers carelessly arranged. The effect was comfortable and slouchy, a place where kids could roam without ruining much since everything looked ruined to begin with.

The kitchen showed the same sort of changes. I could see Fiona's bare-bones approach: cold, streamlined surfaces and the rounded art deco corners. Crystal had introduced glass-fronted cabinets and a hutch where her collection of assorted china plates was displayed. The room looked old-fashioned, a place grandma would have loved for putting up peaches and tomatoes. The appliances were obviously up-to-date. The stove was a six-burner Viking. I spotted two dishwashers, four ovens, and an island topped with speckled gray granite. Dried herbs hung from the rafters along with a rack for copper pots and pans. At the far end of the room, there was a red-brick fireplace that looked like it was added after Fiona's departure. Too folksy for her taste.

Nica perched on one of the stools lined up in a row along the length of the island while Crystal took cups and saucers from the nearest cabinet, saying, "She's going to get her butt kicked. I swear she's going to be grounded for months. What time did she take off?"

"Had to be nine-fifteen," Nica said. "She reported to PE at nine o'clock, but she claimed she had cramps and was going to the nurse's office. She had an appointment with me at ten. When she didn't show for that, I tracked down her roommate, Amy, who told me she'd seen Leila leaving campus with her backpack."

Crystal looked at her watch. "Where the hell could she be?"

"I just hope Amy has the good grace to keep quiet to the school authorities," Nica said, exempting herself.

"Mind if I look in Leila's room? Maybe I can pick up some clue about where she might be."

Crystal said, "Go right ahead. It's the second door to the right at the head of the stairs."

I went up. Leila's door was closed but unlocked, so I let myself in. I stood for a moment, surveying the space. The room was done in frilly pastels. Talk about wishful thinking. She was at that stage of maturity (or lack of it) where the half-nudie rock star posters ran neck and neck with the stuffed animals of her youth. Every surface was covered with knickknacks. Most looked like the sorts of items teenaged girls give each other: mugs with cute sayings, figurines, jewelry, bottles of cologne. Her bulletin board was a collage of ticket stubs, concert programs, and color snapshots: kids at pep rallies, girls acting goofy, guys engaged in drinking beer, smoking pot, and other wholesome pursuits. For someone who claimed to have no friends, she had an amazing collection of memorabilia. The floor was carpeted in discarded clothes, which were also draped over chairs, garments hanging on the closet door, the window seat, and two small upholstered chairs.

I did a quick but thorough search of her drawers. Most of her underwear was already out on the floor, which made my job simple. I went through her closet—jammed full of old board games, sporting equipment, and items from her summer wardrobe. I got down on my hands and knees and made a circuit of the room, checking under chairs, under the bed, under the chest of drawers. The only discovery of interest was the narrow metal lockbox hidden between the mattress and box spring. I shook it but heard only the softest of sounds in response. Probably her dope stash. I didn't have time enough to pick the lock. I returned the box to its hiding place. I felt better for having searched, though the foraging netted me nothing.

Returning to the kitchen, I paused at the planning center to study the family calendar for November, which sat open on the desk. The calendar showed one full month for each page, which was also illustrated with a series of photographs of dogs dressed in children's clothing. November was a cocker spaniel in a navy blue sailor suit. The dog had big brown eyes and appeared to be embarrassed half to death.

Each day was given its own block, an inch-and-a-half square. I could see that three different people had added notes about social events and other activities. Judging from handwriting and the nature of the events posted, I was guessing that Leila's was the oversized printing—angled *T*'s, puffy *I*'s. Crystal's was the elegant cursive in red ink. And Rand's was the scrawl written with a blue ballpoint pen. The personal reminders ranged from meetings to tennis lessons, dental and doctor appointments, to a weekly play group for Griff. The Audi was serviced early in the month. Various telephone numbers had been written in the margins. Notes on alternate weekends indicated Leila's return from school. She apparently wasn't scheduled for this weekend, perhaps because she'd been with Crystal the previous one.

Behind me, Crystal and Nica were busy berating Leila in absentia. I leafed back three months to July and August, noting a fourth handwriting: bold block letters in black. This (I surmised) was Dr. Purcell, whose presence was visible up until Monday, September 8, four days before he vanished. He'd jotted in notes about two board meetings, a medical symposium at UCLA, and a golf date at the country club. None of the entries seemed significant and I assumed the police had followed up.

"I've had it with her," Crystal was saying. "I don't know why I even bother to get upset. That's exactly what she wants."

Nica said, "She's probably on her way to Lloyd's. It'd be like her to make a beeline straight for him."

"Great. Let him deal with her. I'm sick of it. If she doesn't show up soon, I'm calling the cops. All I have to do is declare her an out-of-control minor and she's screwed for sure."

"What good is that going to do?" Anica said. "I know you're mad, but you turn her over to the courts and you'll regret it."

"*She's* the one who'll have regrets. This is about Paulie. I'll bet you dollars to doughnuts."

Anica said, "Quit with the Paulie stuff. It's pointless."

I picked up the calendar and moved over to the island where I claimed my coffee cup. "Mind if I ask about this?"

Crystal glanced over at me, distracted. "What do you need?"

I placed the calendar on the counter and tapped at the page. "I gather Leila doesn't come home every weekend."

"For the most part, she does. Lloyd and I usually alternate visits, but things do come up."

"Like what?"

Crystal glanced at the page, pointing to the second weekend in July. "This was the weekend she had an invitation to go home with her friend, Sherry, in Malibu Colony. Her father's in the movie business and he takes the girls to all the big premieres."

I pointed to the weekend of September 12, when Dow Purcell disappeared. "And this?"

"Same thing, different friend. Emily's family owns horses. They have a ranch at Point Dume. Leila loves to ride. Actually that weekend was canceled—I think Emily got sick— and Leila ended up over at Lloyd's. Why do you ask?"

I shrugged, checking back through the months. Leila's schedule seemed to vary, but it looked like she went off with her school friends on an average of once a month. "I'm thinking she might have left campus with one of her classmates from Fitch."

"I guess it's possible, but I doubt it. Most of her friends are college prep. They'd never risk expulsion." She turned to Nica. "What do you think?"

"It wouldn't hurt to check. It crossed my mind as well, so I brought along the school roster in case we needed to phone any of the other parents." She reached down into the large navy bag near her feet and removed a spiral-bound directory with the school logo on the front. "You want me to go through these and see what I come up with?"

Crystal said, "Hold on a second and let me try Lloyd again." She crossed to the planning center and picked up the phone. She punched in seven numbers and listened for a moment, and then replaced the handset. "He's still not answering. Leila's stepfather," she added by way of explanation.

"I know. I saw him at the beach house the day I met you."

"I've been calling him since Nica arrived. He's there, if I know him. He's always got collection agencies on his case so he refuses to pick up. I've left six messages so he knows this is serious. You'd think he could manage to call back."

I said, "Look, I need an excuse to talk to him, anyway. Why don't you let me go over to his place and see if Leila's there? If she's not, I can start scouring the roads."

"That's not a bad idea. Nica and I can stay here in case she decides to make an appearance." Crystal reached for a pen and scribbled down some numbers on a scratch pad, tearing off the sheet. "These are my numbers and Lloyd's address and phone."

"You have two lines?"

"That's right. This one's personal. The other's business."

I pointed to the first. "Why don't you leave this one free? You can use the other to check with some of Leila's friends."

"If you find Lloyd, you can tell him I'm tired of doing this alone. It's time he took his fair share of the load."

Walking out to my car, I had to wonder how kids of divorced parents survive all the bickering.

14

LLOYD LIVED ON a street called Gramercy Lane, which looped along the foothills, one of those roads that proceeded by fits and starts. I checked my street map of Santa Teresa, looking up the coordinates. I'd have to intercept Gramercy at some point and then check house numbers to see where I was in relation to Lloyd's address. I left the map open on the passenger seat while I turned the key in the ignition. The rain was picking up again, oversized drops that popped on my hood like gravel being flung up from a roadbed. I flipped on my windshield wipers and glanced at my watch. It was currently 3:15. Between the short November days and the gloom of the rain, twilight seemed to start gathering by 4:00 in the afternoon. At the moment, I felt more like heading for home than cruising the town in search of a runaway teen.

I sailed through the stone gate that marked the front entrance to Horton Ravine and followed the road as it curved around to the right. At the first red light, I glanced at the map again, tilting my head. Gramercy Lane, or parts of it at any rate, were within a two-mile radius of the Purcell house in the Ravine. If Leila had thumbed a ride from Malibu traveling north on the 101, she'd probably have asked to be let off at Little Pony Road, which was one off-ramp south. The light changed and I eased into the stream of southbound traffic, hugging the outside lane. Little Pony Road was less than a mile away.

The notion of Leila thumbing a ride made my stomach churn. Odds were some decent citizen would offer her a lift, but there was also that freakish chance that she'd miscalculate. Not every soul on the road had her best interests at heart. At fourteen, she still felt invincible. For her, assault, rape, mayhem, and murder were events she read about in the papers, if she read them at all. *Perversion* and *deviance* were words on a high school vocabulary list, not vicious behaviors with any relevance to her. I hoped her guardian angels were hovering.

I took the Little Pony off-ramp. At the top, I turned left and headed toward the mountains, scanning both sides of the four-lane road. My windshield wipers were thunking merrily, smearing a swipe of dirt back and forth across the glass. I passed a couple huddled under an umbrella. They were walking on my side of the road with their backs to me. I was looking for Leila on her own so I dismissed them at first. I could tell the two were young. It wasn't until I passed them, catching a second glimpse in my sideview mirror, that I identified Leila's cottony white-blond hair and her long, coltish legs. The boy at her side was tall and lean, toting a backpack with the straps arranged awkwardly across the shoulders of his black leather jacket. Both of them wore tight jeans and hiking boots, and their heads were bowed against the rain. I could have sworn the two were sharing a joint. I slowed and pulled in at the curb just ahead of them. In the sideview mirror, I saw Leila hesitate, then drop something on the ground and step on it. As they walked by my car, I leaned over and rolled down the window on the passenger side.

"Can I give you a ride?"

Leila leaned forward, looking across her companion. When she saw me, her expression registered a look of confusion that signaled recognition without context. She knew she knew me, but she didn't remember how. The kid with her leveled a gaze at me filled with hostility and disdain. I took in the smooth complexion, the rain-bedraggled lank brown hair, the plain white T-shirt visible under the open leather jacket. I was startled by the boobs, since I'd assumed the kid was a male. This had to be Paulie. I could see she was destined to be beautiful even though, at the moment, she was unkempt and had defiance written into every inch of her slender frame. She wasn't conventionally pretty, but she had a fierce, worldly air: big dark eyes, cheekbones sharpened by poor nutrition. A photographer with the right instincts could make a fortune from the image of belligerent sexuality she projected.

I focused on Leila. "Hi. I'm Kinsey Millhone. We met last Friday at the beach house. I just came from your mom's. She's worried about you. You should have let her know you were leaving school."

"I'm fine, but tell her thanks for her concern." Leila's tone was sarcastic. Her flippancy was intended to impress her friend, but the insolence was hard to sustain with rainwater dripping down her face. Two strands of hair were plastered to her cheek and the mascara on her lashes had turned to a watery ink.

"I think you should tell her yourself. She needs to know you're okay."

Leila and Paulie exchanged a look. Paulie said something to Leila under her breath; co-conspirators, trying to make the best of the fact they'd been caught. Paulie eased the backpack from her shoulders and passed it to Leila. After a few murmured words, Paulie took off toward the highway at a pace meant to convey nonchalance.

Leila leaned closer to the half-opened window. Her eyes were heavily lined, the lids shadowed with turquoise blue.

Her lipstick was dark brown, too harsh a shade for her fragile blond coloring. "You can't make me go home."

"I'm not here to *make* you do anything," I said. "You might consider getting out of the rain."

"I will if you promise not to tell Mom who was with me."

"I'm assuming that's Paulie."

Leila said nothing, which I took as assent.

"Come on. Get in. I'll drop you off at your dad's."

She thought about it briefly, then opened the car door and slid into the passenger seat, shoving her backpack into the cramped space at her feet. Her hair had been bleached so many times it looked synthetic, still arranged in the odd mix of dreadlocks and tufts that must have made the boarding school authorities wring their hands in dismay. Or maybe Fitch was progressive, a school where students were allowed to "express themselves" through outlandish appearances and oddball behaviors. In the body-heated confines of the car, I could smell eau-de-marijuana and the feminine musk of undergarments worn several days too long.

I glanced over my shoulder, checking the flow of traffic behind me, and pulled onto the road once the passing cars had cleared. In my rearview mirror, I could see Paulie's departing figure, reduced by now to the size of a toy soldier. "How old is Paulie?"

"Sixteen."

"I take it your mom's not that fond of her. What's the problem?"

"Mom doesn't like anything I do."

"Why'd you leave school without permission?"

"How'd you know where I was going?" she asked, bypassing the issue of truancy.

"Your mother figured it out. When we get to a phone, I want you to call and tell her where you are. She's been worried sick." I didn't mention royally pissed off as well.

"Why don't you do it? You'll turn around and talk to her, anyway."

"Of course I will. You're a minor. I'm not going to contribute to your bad behavior." We drove for a block in silence. Then I said, "I don't get what's bugging you."

"I hate Fitch. That's what's bugging me, if it's any of your business."

"I thought you got sent to Fitch because you screwed up in public school."

"I hated it up here, too. Bunch of goof-offs and retards. Everybody was so dumb—I was bored to death. Classes were a joke. I've got better things to do."

We crossed State at the intersection and headed into a residential area called South Rockingham. "What's wrong with Fitch?"

"The girls are such *snobs*. All they care about is how much money their fat-ass daddies make."

"I thought you had friends."

"Well, I don't."

"What about Sherry?"

Leila stole a look at me. "What about her?"

"I'm just wondering how you enjoyed yourself in Malibu."

"Fine. It was fun."

"What about Emily?"

"Why are you asking me all these questions?"

"Your mom said you liked riding horses at her place."

"Emily's okay. She's not as bad as some."

"What else did you do?"

"Nothing. We made grilled cheese sandwiches."

The arrow on my bullshit meter zinged up into the red zone. I was much better at lying when I was Leila's age. "Here's my best guess. I'll bet you skipped both those visits and spent the weekend with Paulie."

She said, "Ha ha ha."

"Come on. 'Fess up. What difference does it make?"

"I don't have to respond if I don't want to."

"Leila, you asked me to keep my mouth shut. The least you could do is tell me the truth."

"So what if I saw Paulie? What's the big deal about that?"

"What about all the other weekends you were supposed to be off visiting classmates?"

Another sullen silence. I tried another tack. "How'd you two meet?"

"In Juvie."

"You were in Juvenile Hall? When was this?"

"A year ago July. Bunch of us got picked up."

"Doing what?"

"The cops said loitering and trespass, which is crap. We weren't doing anything, just hanging around."

"Where was this?"

"I don't know," she said, crossly. "Just some boarded-up old house."

"What time of day?"

"What are you, a district attorney? It was late, like two o'clock in the morning. Half the kids ran. Cops were all bent out of shape and took the rest of us in. Mom and Dow came and picked me up and they were pissed."

"What about Paulie? Was she in trouble with the law?"

Leila said, "You just missed my dad's street."

I slowed and pulled into the next driveway, then backed out. I retraced the half block to Gramercy and turned left. This section was only a block and a half long, a jumble of cheap cottages that might have once served as housing for itinerant pickers in the nearby avocado groves. The road here was unpaved and there were no sidewalks. I spotted one streetlight along the entire block. Leila pointed at a weathered A-frame sitting on a small dirt rise. It was the only structure of its kind—a funky wooden chalet among shacks. I pulled into the driveway and killed the engine. "You want to see if he's there? I'd like to talk to him."

"What about?"

"Dr. Purcell, if it's all the same to you," I said.

Leila snatched open the door and reached for her backpack, which I snagged with one hand. "Leave that with me. I'll be happy to bring it in if he's home."

"Why can't I have it?"

"Insurance. I don't want to see you taking off on me. You're in enough trouble as it is."

She sighed, exasperated, but did as she was told. I decided to ignore the vigor with which she slammed the car door. I watched her hurry to the house along a gravel path. Rainwater streamed down the hillside, flattening the long strands of uncut grass. She reached the porch, which was protected by no more than a narrow inverted *V* of wood. She knocked on the door and then huddled with folded arms, staring back at me while she waited for him to respond. The place looked dark to me. She knocked again. She moved over to a front window, cupped her hands, and peered in. She knocked one more time and then splashed her way back to the car and let herself in. "He's probably coming right back. I know where he keeps the key so I can wait for him here."

"Good. I'll wait with you. The two of us can visit here in the car until he gets home."

The suggestion didn't seem to fill the child with joy. She kicked at the backpack with her muddy hiking boots. "I want to go in. I have to pee."

"Good suggestion. Me, too."

We got out of the car. I locked the car doors and followed her along the path. Once we reached the house, Leila shifted a pot of dead geraniums and removed the house key from its terribly original hiding place. I waited while she unlocked the door and let us in.

"Does he rent this?"

"Nuhn-uhn. He's house-sitting for a friend. Some guy went off to Florida, but he's coming back next week."

The interior was basically one big room. The ceiling soared to a peak. To the right, a narrow staircase led to a sleeping loft. In the living area below, the wood furniture was clumsily constructed, covered with imitation Indian rugs. The wood floors were bare. I could hear grit popping under the soles of my shoes. There was an old black pot-bellied stove exuding the scent of cold ash. At the rear, a counter separated the kitchen, which looked dirty even at this distance.

I spotted the phone sitting on a small side table. "You want to call your mom or should I?"

"You do it. I'm going to the bathroom and don't worry— I'm not going to run away."

While she availed herself of the facilities, I put in the requisite call to Crystal. Temporarily honor-bound, I omitted any mention of Paulie. "I'm going to stay here until Lloyd gets home. If it gets too late, I'll try to talk Leila into coming back to your place."

"Honestly, I'm so mad at her I really don't want to see her. I'll be better in a bit, as soon as I have a drink. Anica's calling the school. I have no idea what she'll tell them. It would serve Leila right if she were suspended or expelled."

"I hear you," I said. "I'll keep you posted on our progress. Wish me luck."

I heard the toilet flush and Leila emerged from the tiny bathroom located under the stairs.

"What'd she say?"

"Nothing much. She's not real happy with you."

Leila moved over to the lumpy sofa. Ignoring me, she opened her backpack and removed a zippered pouch filled with her makeup. She took out a compact and opened it so she could study her face. She cleaned up the smeared mascara and then peered closer at herself. "Crap. A fuckin' zit," she said. She put the compact away. She picked up the remote control and turned on the television set, muting the sound with a glance at me.

I said, "I used to be just like you when I was your age."

"Great. Can I smoke?"

"No."

"Why? They're only clove cigarettes."

"Don't push me, Leila. The place smells bad enough without throwing in clove smoke. Tell me about Dow. And don't get all huffy. I'm bored with that shit."

"Like what do you want to know?"

"When did you see him last?"

"I don't remember stuff like that."

"Here, I'll help. September 12 was a Friday. Emily was sick and she canceled so you must have been home. Were you at the beach house?"

"Nuhn-uhn. I was here."

"Do you remember what you did that night?"

"Probably watched a video. That's what I usually do. Why?"

"I'm wondering when you last talked to Dow."

"How should I know? I try not to talk to him at all if I can help it."

"You must talk occasionally. After all, he's your stepdad."

"I know who he is," she said. "I thought you weren't allowed to question a kid without a parent present."

"That's only true if you're detained by the police."

"What are you?"

"A private eye. Phillip Marlowe in drag." From her expression, I could tell she thought Phillip Marlowe was a rock band, but she was smart enough not to commit herself on that score. I said, "How old were you when Dow and your mom got married?"

"Eleven."

"You like him?"

"He's all right."

"You two get along?"

"About as well as you'd expect. He's old. He wears dentures. His breath smells all moldy and he has a bunch of really stupid rules: 'I want you home and in bed by ten. I don't want you sleeping late. Help your mother with your brother,' " she said, mimicking him. "I told him, 'Hey, that's what Rand's for. I'm not her fucking maid.' My grades have to be perfect or I'm grounded for weeks. He won't even let me have my own phone."

"The bastard," I said. "Where do you think he is?"

"In Canada."

"Interesting. What makes you say that?"

She stared at the television screen, flipping from channel to channel.

"Leila?"

"What!"

"I asked why you thought he was in Canada?"

"Because he's a shit," she said. "All he ever cared about was looking good. I heard him talking to some woman on the phone. I guess six months ago these people came into the clinic and picked up financial records and a lot of patient files. He was shitting bricks. Whatever it was, I guess he could have gone to jail for it, so I think he skipped."

"Who was he talking to?"

"I don't know. He never said her name and I didn't recognize her voice. Just about then, he figured out I was on the line so he waited 'til I got off before he said anything else."

"You were listening in?"

"I was up in my room. I wanted to make a phone call. How was I supposed to know he was on the line?"

"When was this?"

"Couple weeks before he went."

"Did you tell the police?"

"Nobody asked and besides, it's just a guess. Can I watch this now?"

"Sure."

She hit the mute button again and the sound came blasting back. MTV.

I went into the bathroom, which wasn't as tacky as I thought it'd be. I closed the door. It looked like Lloyd had made a modest effort to keep the sink and the bathtub clean. The toilet water was rendered a permanent blue from a pungent smelling cake of something hung in the tank. Once I peed and flushed, I checked the medicine cabinet and sorted through his dirty clothes basket.

When I got back to the main room, Leila had sunk into that hypnotic state television generates. The A-frame was getting dark. I turned on some lights. Since she was paying absolutely no attention, I took advantage of the moment to search the desktop and the contents of the drawers. Most seemed to be filled with the other fellow's junk. I wasn't looking for anything in particular. I simply couldn't resist the urge to stick my nose in where it didn't belong. I sifted through a handful of Lloyd's bills, all overdue. Restlessly, I moved into the kitchen. The refrigerator didn't yield much, but the pantry turned out to be better stocked than mine. Dried pasta, jars of sauce, canned soups, condiments, peanut butter, the strange orange macaroni and cheese in a box that only kids and dogs will eat. I was bored and getting hungry.

I moved across the great room and climbed the stairs to the loft, peering over the rail. Below I could see Leila, still engrossed in the flickering images on the screen. I couldn't believe she was leaving me to snoop at will. Lloyd's bed was unmade. On the bed table there was a framed eight-by-ten photograph of Lloyd and Leila. I picked it up and studied it. The picture must have been taken at a birthday celebration. The two were sitting at a kitchen table, a wobbly-looking chocolate cake festooned with candles in front of them. Lloyd and Leila had leaned their heads close together, grinning and clowning for the photographer. Lloyd's right ear was pierced. A newly opened package was visible and Lloyd was holding one of a pair of earrings to his ear—a tiny dangling gold skull and crossbones—apparently a gift from her. Hard to tell how long ago this was; sometime within the past year, judging from her hair.

A check of the dresser drawers revealed nothing except a wide array of flashy-looking boxer shorts. I turned and surveyed the area. There was a telescope on a tripod standing by the window and that interested me. I crossed and studied the view with my naked eye at first, orienting myself to my surroundings. This was not a neighborhood I knew and I had no idea what Lloyd could see from here. Startled, I realized his current digs were located just across the reservoir from Fiona Purcell. Through the haze of mist and rain, I could see the barren outline of her house, jutting out from the far hill like a fortress. Lloyd's view was toward the mountains while Fiona's view stretched in the opposite direction taking in the ocean and the islands twenty-six miles out. I bent to the eyepiece on the telescope and squinted through the lens. Everything was black. I removed the lens cap, which improved the visibility, though at first, all I saw was the surface of my own eye. The landscape was reduced to a big yawning blur: objects distorted by the magnification.

I lifted my face and found the focus mechanism, then peered through the lens again and adjusted the knob. Abruptly, the far shore came into sharp relief. I could see the scarring on a boulder standing out in such sharp contrast it looked as if it rested just a foot away from me. The water in the reservoir was ragged where the raindrops hit. The sky was reflected in hammered silver on its surface. I caught movement to the right and shifted my view a hair.

There was Trudy, the German shepherd, barking at a stick—one of those brainless behaviors dogs seem to thrive on. I could see her mouth open and shut like a doggie hand puppet. The enthusiasm of her barking caused her whole body to shake, but the sound was reduced by the window glass to the faintest report. Her legs and feet were muddy and I could clearly see the raindrops beading on her coat. Behind her, a wide path through the undergrowth had been flattened and I could see white where a line of saplings had been snapped off at ground level. Maybe a boat trailer had been backed down close to the water's edge to launch an outboard. Faintly, I heard Trudy's owner whistle and then her barely audible call. "Trudy! *Truuudy!*"

Trudy looked over her shoulder with regret, torn between her current obsession and her need to obey. Obedience won out. She went bounding up the hillside and disappeared over the crest. I lifted my sights to Fiona's house, where the lights were winking on in sequence, probably on timers. I zoomed in on her bedroom window, but there was no sign of movement. Odd that she appeared to be living so close that I nearly reached a hand out to touch a windowpane. Traveling by car, her place was actually a mile and a half away, the long way around. Her side of the reservoir was peppered with expensive homes, where this side was shabby: board-and-batten rentals without much market value. I wondered if Lloyd realized whose house he had in his sights. I wondered if he stared in her bedroom window, watching her undress at night.

I shifted my view again, feeling like a bird skimming across the surface of the lake. I let my gaze come to rest on the narrow end of the reservoir where the vegetation grew densely all the way to the point at which the water met the hill. A sign was posted on a fence post and I could read the larger of the lines. Swimming and boating were forbidden. The light was fading rapidly and I could feel myself strain. I lifted my eyes and stared at the gathering dark. What had I seen?

I closed my eyes and when I opened them again, I felt my perception shift. The alteration was abrupt, like the test to determine which eye is dominant. Cover your left eye with your palm and stare at your right index finger, held out at arm's length. Then remove your palm from your left eye and cover your right eye instead. Looking through the dominant eye, the alignment of your finger against the background remains constant. Using the nondominant eye, the finger will appear to jump to one side. In reality, nothing changes. The finger remains where it is, but the brain registers a difference. I felt a spurt of anxiety and my heart began to thump.

I turned and trotted down the stairs. Leila emerged from her trance long enough to look up at me. She was stretched out full-length, her sock feet resting on the arm of the sofa, her hiking boots on the floor.

I said, "I have to go out for a few minutes. Will you be all right by yourself?"

"I'm here alone all the time," she said, insulted.

"Great. I shouldn't be long, but I'd appreciate your staying put until I get back. Okay?"

"Yeah." She turned her attention to the set again and switched through several channels, finally settling on an old *Tom and Jerry* cartoon.

I closed the front door behind me and picked my way down the muddy path to my car. The light was draining from the sky and the air temperature was dropping. The rain wasn't falling hard, but it was annoying, nonetheless. I unlocked my car and slid under the wheel. I reached over and popped open the glove compartment. I took out my flashlight and I pushed the button, gratified to see that the battery was still strong. I turned off the flashlight, laid it on the passenger seat while I started the car, and backed out of Lloyd's short drive. I swung around and headed back to the main road. At the intersection, I turned right, drove half a mile, turned right again on Old Reservoir Road, and began the winding ascent. The curves were familiar and I drove with a thumping heart, wishing I had stopped to pee again before I left. Fear is a powerful diuretic.

Ahead, Fiona's house came into view and I pulled over on

the berm. I grabbed my flashlight, got out, and set off on foot. Out here, there was still enough ambient light that I could see my way. I climbed the wet grassy hill, my feet slipping out from under me when I least expected it. I paused at the crest of the hill, looking out across the reservoir to the A-frame where Lloyd was living. The lights glowing in the house made it look like a chapel perched on the opposite hill. I hoped Leila wouldn't disappear while I was scrambling through the dark.

Traversing the downside of the hill was even trickier, and I found myself losing purchase, half-slipping, half-sliding as I maneuvered my way along. At the bottom, I turned on my flashlight. The area was cold and silent and the air smelled dank. The water was black near the shoreline and showed no evidence of a current. In places, I could see Trudy's paw prints. I shone the beam of my flashlight along the hill behind me, locating the boulder I'd seen and the path of broken saplings. I stood where I was, following the line of the hill to the top. From where I stood the road wasn't visible. I turned my beam on the silty water, tracing the shallows. The lake bottom apparently dropped off abruptly, but I could see the curve of a chrome bumper glowing dully, like buried treasure. I couldn't read the name on the vanity plate, but I knew I was looking at the trunk of Dow Purcell's silver Mercedes submerged in the depths.

15

AN ACCIDENT SCENE at night is as bleak and gaudy as a carnival. It was now fully dark, close to eight P.M. The coroner's car, the mobile crime lab, and a Ford sedan were parked on the berm, along with two patrol cars with red-and-blue bar lights flashing, radios squawking insistently between spurts of static. Two uniformed officers stood together talking while the police dispatcher, like a barker, issued a monotonous, nonstop account of crimes and misdemeanors in progress: complaints about noise, a call reporting a domestic disturbance in another part of town, a prowler, a drunk urinating on a public street. Santa Teresa is a town of eighty-five thousand with more crimes against property than crimes against persons.

Five minutes after I'd spotted the submerged Mercedes, I'd scrambled up the hill and down the other side to the road. I'd crossed and climbed Fiona's stairs two at a time, not pausing for breath until I reached the top. I pounded on her front door and rang the bell simultaneously, willing her to respond. I'd been reluctant to leave the scene unattended, but I had to notify the cops. I rang the bell again. Having observed Fiona's house from Lloyd's loft across the lake, it didn't take much to persuade me she was still out somewhere. I trotted around the side of the house to the rear where the driveway entered the property from the roadway above. There were no cars on her parking pad and all three of her garage doors were down and locked.

Fiona's nearest neighbor was just across the road. I knew knocking on doors at random would be a pain in the ass. Though it wasn't late, it was dark out. Everyone had heard stories about intruders using a ruse to gain entrance to the victim's house. What choice did I have, short of hopping in my car and driving until I found a public phone? I rang the bell, talking to myself the whole time: *Come on, come on, be here, help me out here.* I peered through the glass side panels, which afforded me an abbreviated view of the foyer. I could see someone moving around in the kitchen, probably preparing supper. She appeared in the hall and approached the front door. I waved, trying to look like a law-abiding citizen instead of a cunning and devious crazed killer. She was middle-aged, in a sweater and slacks, with an apron tied around her waist. If she was apprehensive at the sudden summons, she gave no indication. She turned on the porch light and studied me with caution.

I spoke loudly, hoping she could hear me through the glass. "I'm a friend of Fiona's. She's out and I need to use your phone."

I saw her eyes stray toward Fiona's house while she assimilated the request. She made sure the burglar chain was secure, and then she opened the door a crack. I don't remember now how I explained the situation, but I must have been persuasive because she let me in without argument and showed me to the phone.

Seven minutes later, the first black-and-white patrol car had come careening up the road.

Nearly two hours had passed and neighbors from many of

the surrounding houses had straggled out to the road. They
stood in clusters under the meager shelter of their umbrellas,
conversing in subdued and fragmentary bursts while the rain
pattered on. Word had apparently spread that the doctor's car
had been found. Under ordinary circumstances, they probably
didn't have much occasion to meet. None of the houses up
here was built close together and with many residents holding
day jobs, my guess was their paths seldom crossed. A rag-tag
crew, they looked like they'd pulled on their coats and their
rain boots in haste. They waited with patience, their vigil ritu-
alistic, a community of the concerned conferring at this un-
precedented gathering. A temporary fence of plastic pylons
and tape prevented their approach. Not that there was much
to see from where they stood. Looking toward the city, the
roadway itself was cloaked in darkness, no streetlights within
range. In the opposite direction, the asphalt petered out. Beyond the last cul-de-sac, there were only black and looming
foothills, raw land knit together with sage and chaparral.

I sat in my car, feeling tense with the cold. At intervals, I
fired up the engine so I could keep the heater running and the
windshield wipers on, though the steady *thunk-thunk-thunk-
thunk* nearly put me to sleep. To my right, the hill rose at a
thirty-degree angle for a hundred yards or so before it crested
and curved down to the lake. From the water's edge, the
floodlights glowed eerily, silhouetting the few scrub trees
stretched out along the crest. At intervals, the light was
broken by shadows as the police went about their business.
I'd spoken briefly with Odessa when he'd first reached the
scene. He'd asked me to stay and said they were putting a
diver in the water to check the car's interior before they
hauled it out of the lake. He'd set off up the long slope and I
settled in for the wait.

At some point, Leila had appeared, accompanied by her
stepfather, Lloyd, who'd come home while I was in the
process of discovering Dow's car. They stood to one side

under a black umbrella, maintaining a distance from the neighbors. I was guessing the two had been attracted by the lights and had hopped in Lloyd's car. For once, Leila seemed to be experiencing an emotion other than boredom or contempt. With her thick black mascara and heavily shadowed lids, she looked like a waif, big-eyed and solemn, shivering uncontrollably. I knew I should go over and introduce myself to Lloyd, but I couldn't bring myself to do it. Down the road, I spotted two minicam crews, one from KWST-TV, the other from KEST-TV. The blond reporter from KEST was already picking up film clips and interviews for the eleven o'clock news. She stood under a big black umbrella, talking to one of the neighbors. I didn't see any other reporters, but they were doubtless around somewhere.

I adjusted my rearview mirror and watched as a pair of headlights swept into view around the curve in the road. I was hoping to see Fiona, but the vehicle turned out to be Crystal's white Volvo. She slowed as she approached. She waited while a smattering of people ambled out of the roadway and passed in front of her, and then pulled in and parked on the berm just ahead of me.

I grabbed my slicker from the backseat and held it over my head as I left the comfort of my VW and moved gingerly along the road to her car. She turned and caught sight of me and rolled down her window. Her face was drawn, her hair pulled back in an untidy knot at the nape of her neck. Gone were the black slacks and sweater she'd worn earlier. She looked like she'd dressed in haste, pulling on jeans and a gray utilitarian sweatshirt bearing the name of our gym. She said, "I was already in my robe and slippers when the officer came to the door. He wanted to bring me over in his patrol car, but I wanted my own wheels. What's happening?"

"Nothing much. This is worse than a movie set, with all the people standing around. Where's Anica?"

"She had to get back to school. Hop in."

I said, "Thanks." I opened the door and slid into the front seat. Behind me, Griffith's car seat was buckled into place, the surrounding area decorated with an assortment of cookie crumbs and broken pretzels. A plastic baby bottle filled with apple juice had left a sticky residue in the spot where I rested my hand. There was a pink plush squirrel on the floor by my feet. I pictured him flinging his binky, his bottle, his snacks, and stuffed animals, a hurricane of objects announcing his presence. The interior air smelled of flowers and spice, Crystal's cologne.

I said, "How are you?"

"Numb."

I said, apropos of nothing, "The car might have been abandoned."

"Let's hope that's all it is." She angled the rearview mirror in her direction and ran a knuckle under her lower lashes where her eyeliner had smeared. She pushed the mirror back and slouched down on her spine. She leaned her head back on the seat and closed her eyes. In profile, I could see the irregularities of her features. Her nose was too sharp, her lower jaw too narrow for the width of her brow. Properly done up, she seemed more intimidating than she was in the moment. "When did you get here?" she asked, as though talking in her sleep.

"Hours ago. At six."

"They said not to hurry. I was watching TV when the officer arrived at the door."

"You're lucky. I'm starving. I missed dinner. I'm about to eat my arm."

Crystal reached over to the glove compartment and flipped the door down. "Try this." She removed a battered Hershey's bar and passed it over to me. "How'd they find the car?"

"I was the one who spotted it and called 9-1-1. The cops

are over there now doing god knows what." I removed the outer wrapper and opened the white inner paper liner. The scent of chocolate rose like a vapor. I broke the candy bar into perfect sections and placed one on my tongue. I could almost read the engraved letter H as I pressed one softening chocolate square against the roof of my mouth.

"How'd you know the car was his?"

"The vanity license plate."

We were silent. Crystal turned on the radio and then thought better of it and turned it off again. The rain on the roof was a soft percussion, a drummer's brushes on cymbals. The atmosphere was oddly intimate. We were both out of our natural habitats, constrained by the unfamiliar setting, bound by the wait. "I take it they haven't pulled the car out of the water yet," she said at length.

"They're waiting for the tow truck. Odessa said he'd let us know as soon as there's something to report." I ate an E and stuck the rest of the Hershey's in my shoulder bag. I crossed my arms in a vain attempt to get warm.

Crystal made a sound that was half sigh and half something else: tension, impatience, simple weariness. "I knew he was dead. That's the only explanation that made any sense. I told you he wouldn't walk off and leave Griff."

"Crystal, they haven't even brought the car up. We don't know he's in there."

"He's there. Leila's going to freak."

"How so? She doesn't like him."

"Of course not. She treated him like dirt. How's she going to make her peace with that?"

I hesitated, wanting to press. She was more vulnerable than I'd seen her. This might be my only opportunity. "What's her anger about?"

"It's too complicated to go into."

"Nothing's too complicated if he's dead."

Crystal roused herself and turned. "Why should I tell you? You're not working for me."

"I'm not working against you, either. What's her problem?"

"Why is that any concern of yours?"

"It isn't, if you put it that way, but it's going to get worse."

"I don't doubt that," she said. And after a long pause, "There's been a certain amount of trauma in Leila's life. She needs help sorting it out."

"She's seeing a shrink?"

"She's been seeing one for years. At first, three times a week. Now it's down to twice a month on weekends when she's up from school."

"He has appointments on weekends?"

"It's a she."

"Sorry. I didn't think psychiatrists were that obliging."

"This one is. She's truly fabulous with kids. This is the fifth shrink Leila's seen and I was at my wit's end."

"How'd you find her?"

"We were lucky for once. Charlotte Friedman's a woman Anica went to school with. Her husband retired and they moved here from Boston."

"What sort of trauma? I'm still not getting it."

Crystal seem to debate with herself. She stared straight ahead and when she spoke her tone was as flat and distant as an old phonograph record. "I had a little boy who drowned. Of course, it affected us all. That was the beginning of the end where Lloyd and I were concerned. Some things you never recover from. A child's death is one."

"What happened?"

"That was Jordie. My sweet one. He was eighteen months old. I was working one night and left him with the woman next door. She was talking on the phone when Jordie toddled out the screen door and fell in the pool. By the time she found him and called the paramedics, he couldn't be revived."

"I'm sorry."

"I thought I'd die, but it was worse for Leila. Children aren't prepared for loss. They don't understand and it's hard to explain death in terms that they comprehend. I've never been religious. I didn't want to sell her a fairy tale, especially one I wasn't buying myself. Dr. Friedman says when faced with the death of a sibling, some children disconnect. They act like nothing's happened. Others, like Leila, start acting out. She's difficult. You've seen it yourself. Rebellious. Emotional. I've talked to Charlotte—with Leila's permission of course. Charlotte feels Leila's behavior is her way of distancing herself, creating a barrier between herself and a world that she finds treacherous. If she doesn't care about anyone, she can't be hurt. At any rate, I know I'm protective. I'm not even sure how I'm going to tell her about all this."

"She's here. Didn't you see her back there with Lloyd?"

Crystal sat up abruptly. "I had no idea. Where?"

"Far side of the road, about three cars back. At least they were a while ago."

"I better see how she's doing." Crystal reached around the seat for a big black umbrella that was stashed on the floor. She opened the car door a crack and stuck the umbrella out, popping the automatic latch that caused it to *thwop* into full sail.

"Thanks for the Hershey's. You saved my life."

"You're welcome."

The tow truck appeared, its headlights illuminating the roadway as far as the next curve. I opened the door on my side, tented my slicker over my head, and got out, closing the door behind me. I turned, watching as the tow truck driver's assistant hopped out of the cab. Crystal passed him, trekking back along the road while the driver did a three-point turn and started backing up the slope. The heavy tires slipped, chewing two channels in the grass. The driver craned a look over his shoulder, one hand on the wheel. His assistant whistled sharply and gave rolling-arm instructions about the angle of ascent. The blond reporter caught sight of Crystal and moved to intercept her. Crystal shook her head, waving her off.

I retreated to my car and turned the key in the ignition. The rain was reduced by now to an icy mist, soaking the unwary onlookers by slow degrees. The interior temperature had dropped while I was gone and the tepid breeze generated by the heater wasn't even as effective as my own breath. I watched the tow truck slip sideways and then lumber backward up the hill to the top. I couldn't imagine how they'd manage to haul the Mercedes out of the water and up the sodden hill.

I turned, looking over the backseat to check Crystal's progress. She'd reached Leila, who was standing by the side of the road with Lloyd. Lloyd had his arm around her, but the minute Leila saw Crystal she fled to her mother's embrace. Crystal held her and rocked her where they stood, resting her face in Leila's hair. After a moment, the three conferred; Leila looking miserable, Lloyd withdrawn. Whatever the debate, it was evident that Crystal prevailed. Mother and daughter passed my car in their return to the station wagon. Crystal was talking earnestly while Leila wept without sound. I watched as she settled her daughter in the front seat and then went around the rear of the car and slid in under the wheel.

I adjusted my rearview mirror, keeping a watchful eye on Lloyd, who'd started toward his car, his head bent, hands in his jacket pockets. Maybe the two were in competition, playing good parent. Leila was the prize and Lloyd had been forced to forfeit this round. In mirror-reverse, I saw him light up a cigarette and belatedly I smelled smoke drifting through the damp night air. Idly, I wondered how far out into dark I'd have to go so I could pee without being arrested for indecent exposure.

Detective Odessa, in a hooded water-repellent jacket, appeared at the crest of the hill and began his descent, his footing as tenuous as mine had been. He spotted my VW and began to tack in my direction. I leaned over and cranked down the window a couple of inches. He reached the car and peered in. Drizzle had collected on the shiny surface of his jacket and the water slid in runnels along the stitching in the seams. His nose was slightly too prominent and something in the shape of it left him just short of handsome. He gestured toward the work lights on the far side of the hill. "I want you to meet Detective Paglia."

I said, "Sure." I rolled up the window and killed the engine. I got out, taking a moment to shrug into my slicker before I followed him up the hill. The two of us struggled together, Odessa holding on to my arm as much for stability as for support.

I said, "How's it going?"

"It's a bitch," he said. "I see Crystal's here. I sent an officer to the house. I thought she should know what was happening."

"What about Fiona? Anybody heard from her?"

"Nope. We notified the daughter, but she can't make it over here until the nanny gets back from dinner."

"Does she know where her mother is?"

"Not offhand. She says she'll put in a few calls and see if she can track her down. Otherwise we wait and hope she comes home."

We scrambled the last few yards to the top of the hill and stood there together staring down at the lake. The light from the flood lamps had washed the color from the scene. Steam rose like smoke where the rain came in contact with the hot metal flanges. An assortment of people stood in clusters, apparently waiting for additional technicians or equipment. I could see an eerie green glow moving under the surface of the water as a search went on in the depths. With the angle of the floodlights, the butt end of the Mercedes glimmered incongruously. "Is he in there?"

"Don't know yet. We've got a diver in the water. The shelf drops off sharply to a depth of twenty feet . . . this is five or six yards out. Car got hung up against a boulder or it'd be down on the bottom and we'd be out of luck."

The diver surfaced in a dark blue wet suit and hood, a compressed-air cylinder strapped to his back. He removed his mouthpiece and let it dangle as he waded ashore, algae clinging to his fins. He lifted off his face mask and left it resting on the top of his head like a hat. Once on shore, he was intercepted by the coroner and another man, both in raincoats, who listened while he reported, complete with gestures.

Meanwhile, the tow truck had backed down within range of the shore. Two men in hip boots and yellow slickers had entered the water in preparation for the salvage operation. One was already attaching a chain to the Mercedes's axle. As I looked on, one of the two men miscalculated and slipped into deeper water, his slicker billowing out around him like a deflated life raft. He flailed, cursing, while his partner snorted with suppressed laughter and pushed forward through the water to lend him a hand.

Odessa nodded in the diver's direction. "That's Paglia with the coroner."

"I gathered as much."

As if on cue, the other detective turned and caught sight of Odessa and me. He excused himself and headed in our direction across soft ground already trampled with footprints. Days of rain had obliterated any trace of tread marks, but the projected path of the car had been secured and searched. Evidence was doubtless in very short supply after so much time had passed. When he reached us, Detective Paglia held out his hand. "Ms. Millhone. Jim Paglia. Con Dolan's spoken to me about you." His voice was deep and uninflected. I placed him in his fifties. His head was shaved, his freckled forehead etched with a trellis of vertical and horizontal lines.

We shook hands and said hi-how-are-you-type things. Lieutenant Dolan had been in charge of the homicide unit until a heart attack dictated his early retirement. "How's Dolan doing these days?"

"So-so. Good, but not great. He misses the job." Paglia's eyebrows were black twists that tipped up at the outer corners like a pair of wings. He wore small oval glasses with thin metal frames. If the raindrops falling on the lenses annoyed him, he gave no sign of it. He'd been smoking a cigarillo with a white plastic tip, dead by the look of it, extinguished by the rain. He removed it from his mouth and glanced at the tip. "We owe you a big one. How'd you happen to come down?"

Odessa touched my sleeve. "You two go ahead. I'll be right back."

I watched him cross to the diver, whom he engaged in conversation out of earshot of those nearby. I turned my attention to Detective Paglia, whose gaze had settled unrelentingly on mine. I pegged him as ex-military, a man who'd seen death and dying at close range, possibly administering a fair amount of it himself. His manner suggested friendliness without the irksome encumbrance of any underlying warmth. If he was personable, it was a trait he'd acquired by meticulous application of the "personable behavior" rules he'd observed in the world around him. If he was pleasant, it was because pleasantries usually got him what he wanted, which in this case was aid, information, cooperation, and respect. If I were a career criminal, I'd be wary of this man. As it was—given my past tendencies toward lying, breaking and entering, and petty theft—I made certain to frame my explanation with care. While I didn't imagine he suspected me of anything, I wanted to appear honest and artless—not difficult since (in this one rare instance) what I had to offer was the truth. "I'm not sure how to describe the process. I was up at Lloyd's. He's Crystal's ex-husband."

"Leila's stepdad."

"Right. This morning, she left boarding school without

permission and Crystal figured she was headed for his place. I told Crystal I'd see if I could track her down, so I began cruising the area there at Little Pony Road and the 101. She must have hitchhiked because I spotted her walking on the berm. I talked her into letting me drive her up to Lloyd's. He was gone when we got there, so she let us into the house. His is that A-frame," I said, and pointed to the far side of the lake. Under the weight of Paglia's gaze, my tone sounded false and I found myself adding a few extraneous details. "Well, it's actually not his. He's house-sitting for a friend who went to Florida. Anyway, I was just messing around while we waited for him to show. Leila was watching TV and I went up to the loft. I saw the telescope and thought it'd be interesting to take a peek. I was surprised to see where I was. I hadn't realized that section of Gramercy put him directly across the reservoir from Fiona."

"You think there's a connection?"

"Between Lloyd and Fiona? I don't know, but I doubt it. I've never heard anything to that effect."

He took out an Altoids box. He opened the lid and deposited the dead butt. I could see he'd filled the bottom of the tin with ash, his way of avoiding contamination at the scene. He returned the box to his raincoat pocket and his gray eyes met mine.

I said, "Do you consider this a crime scene?"

"Suicide's a crime," he said. "Go on with your story." His lower teeth were buckled together in the center and rimmed with stains. It was the only thing about him that seemed out of control.

"When I looked through the telescope I saw the dog—this is a German shepherd named Trudy. I'd seen her up here on my two visits to Fiona's house and she was always over in this area, barking her head off."

Paglia said, "Dogs can smell a body even under water." This was the first piece of information he'd offered me.

"Really. I didn't know that. I could see she was excited, but I had no idea why. Aside from Trudy, I could see some scarring on that boulder halfway up the slope." Again, I pointed like a fifth-grader giving an oral report. "There was also damage to the vegetation, saplings snapped off. At first I figured somebody must have backed a trailer down to launch a boat, but then I caught sight of the posted warning and I remembered that swimming and boating were forbidden."

He seemed to study me, his expression one of calculated kindness. "I still don't understand how you made the connection."

"The idea just suddenly made sense. Dr. Purcell was last seen at the clinic. I'd heard he was on his way up here to see Fiona so I—"

"Who told you that?"

"A friend of Purcell's, a fellow named Jacob Trigg. Dow told him he had a meeting scheduled with her that night."

"You talk to her about this?"

"Well, I *asked* her. Why not? I was pissed. I work for her. She should have given me the information the moment I hired on."

"What'd she say?"

"She claims he didn't show, called it a 'miscommunication.' I assumed he stood her up and she was too embarrassed to admit it."

"Too bad she didn't mention it to us. We could have canvassed up here. Somebody might've heard the car. Nine plus weeks later, who's going to remember?"

Behind him, I heard the high whine of the gear, the rumble as the cable was wound around the drum, dragging the Mercedes from the lake. Water gushed from the open windows, from the underside, from the wheel mounts. Nearby, the coroner's van was parked in the grass, its rear doors open. The coroner's assistant and a uniformed officer were removing a long metal trunk, which I recognized as the stainless steel tank in which a floater could be sealed.

Paglia said, "Kinsey."

I turned my gaze back to his. I felt cold.

"The diver says there's someone in the front seat."

The Mercedes was now suspended in a forward tilt, front end down, three of the four windows opened. Lake water poured from every crack and crevice, draining through the floorboards, splashing onto ground already soaked by days of rain. I watched, my responses suspended as the vehicle was hauled partway up the slope, gushing like a tank that had sprung a sudden leak. The window on the driver's side had been shattered, the bottom half still a maze of crazed glass, the upper portion gone. In the front seat, I caught a glimpse of a vaguely human shape, amorphous, all bloat and slime, face turned toward the window gap as if peeking at the view. After weeks in the water, the once-living flesh was bloodless, bleached a pearly white. He still wore his suit coat, but that was all I could see of him from where I stood. I turned my head abruptly and made an involuntary sound. The glue holding his bones together had loosened and given way so that he seemed flaccid, indifferent, his eye sockets swimming with a pale gelatin. His mouth was open, his jaw relaxed. His lips had widened in a final expression of joy or surprise—a howl of rage perhaps.

"I'll be in the car," I said.

Paglia didn't hear me. He was heading for the Mercedes. The morgue crew stood back. Peripherally, I saw flashes as the police photographer began to document her work. I couldn't watch any longer. I couldn't be in that place. These people were schooled in the sight of death, tutored by its odors, by its poses, by the peculiar posture of bodies caught in their final bow to life. Ordinarily at such a scene, after the first jolt of revulsion, I can become detached. Here, I couldn't manage it, couldn't shake off the feeling that I was in the presence of something evil. Purcell—assuming the body was his—had either killed himself or been killed. There was no way he could have driven up that hill and down into the lake by accident.

16

BY THE TIME I returned to my apartment, it was after ten o'clock. The crime scene technicians were still busy at the reservoir, though I couldn't imagine what remained to be done. I'd hung around for a while and then decided to head home. I'd never eaten dinner. In fact, as nearly as I remembered, I hadn't eaten lunch. Hunger had asserted itself and then faded at least twice during the evening, and now had dissipated altogether, leaving a nagging headache in its wake. I was both wired and exhausted, a curious mix.

Mercifully, the rain had moved on and the temperature had warmed. The streets seemed to smoke, vapor rising in drifts. The sidewalks were still wet, water dripping from the tree limbs as silently as snow. The gutters gurgled merrily, miniature rivers diverted by debris as the runoff traveled downstream into sewers to the sea. A fog began to accumulate, making the world seem hushed and dense. My neighborhood looked unfamiliar, a landscape made alien by mist. Depths were flattened to two dimensions, bare branches no more than ink lines bleeding onto a page. My apartment was dark. I'd left home at ten A.M., nearly twelve hours earlier, and it hadn't occurred to me to leave lights on for myself. I paused in the process of unlocking my door. Henry's kitchen window was aglow, a small square of yellow in the hovering mist. I tucked the keys in my pocket and crossed the flagstone patio.

I peered into the upper portion of his backdoor. He was seated at the table, which was littered with paperwork: stacks of medical statements, canceled checks, and receipts, all sorted into piles. He was wearing his bathrobe, a ratty blue-flannel number with blue-and-white striped pyjamas visible under it, cuffs drooping over his battered leather slippers. On the floor near his feet, he'd placed a wastebasket and the brown accordion file he was using to organize Klotilde's bills. The grocery bag of bills Rosie'd given him was sitting on a chair and still appeared to be half-full. As I looked on, he ran a hand through his hair, leaving strands sticking out in three directions. He reached for his glass of Jack Daniel's and took a swallow, then frowned when he realized the ice had long since melted. He got up and moved to the sink, where he tossed the watery contents.

I called, "Henry," and then tapped on the glass. He looked over, unperturbed by the interruption, and gestured for me to enter. I tried the knob and pointed. "Door's locked."

Henry let me in. While I doffed my slicker and hung it over the back of the chair, he opened the freezer door and removed a handful of ice cubes, which he plunked in his glass, pouring a fresh round of whiskey over them. I picked up the scent of his afternoon baking—something with cinnamon, almond extract, butter, and yeast.

The litter on the table looked even worse at close range. "This is cute. How's it coming? I'm almost afraid to ask."

"Terrible. Just awful. The codes are gibberish. I can't figure out who owes what or which of these is paid. I had 'em sorted by date, but that turned out to be pointless. Now I'm filing them by doctor, hospital, and procedure, and I seem to be getting somewhere. I don't know how people ever make sense of these things. It's ridiculous."

"I told you not to do it."

"I know, but I said I'd help and I hate to go back on my word."

"Oh, quit being such a wuss and give the damn things back to her."

"What's she going to do with them?"

"She'll figure it out or she can have Williams do it. Klotilde was *his* sister-in-law. Why should you get stuck?"

"I feel sorry for her. Klotilde was her only sister and it's bound to be tough."

"She didn't even *like* Klotilde. They barely spoke to each other and when they did, they fought."

"Don't be so hard on her. Rosie has a good heart," he said. Having bitched, he now felt guilty for complaining behind her back. I could see that arguing with the man was only going to make things worse.

Mentally, I rolled my eyes. "I'll let you off the hook temporarily, but I won't give up."

Henry took a seat at the table. "So what's up with you? You look beat."

"I am." I lifted a stack of medical statements from the seat of the chair and stood there, puzzled about what to do with them.

Henry jumped up. "Here, let me take care of those." He handed me his drink while he shoved the papers to one side and cleared a space at the table. He scooped up the grocery bag and the accordion file and put both on the floor, then took the papers from my hand and put them on the floor as well.

I said, "Thanks" and took a swallow of Jack Daniel's, which flamed through my system like a sudden case of heartburn. I could feel my tension ease and realized, belatedly, how very tired I was. My head had begun to pound in a rhythm with my pulse. *Ka-thong, ka-thong.* I passed the glass back to him and sank into the chair he'd just cleared.

"What's going on?"

"We found Dr. Purcell's car and his body—assuming it's him. I can't really talk about it yet. Give me a few minutes to collect myself."

"Can I fix you a drink?"

"Don't think so, but if you have any Tylenol, I could use about forty, preferably extra-strength."

"I have something better. You just stay where you are."

"No problem. I'm incapable of moving. I'll fill you in momentarily unless I pass out first."

I crossed my arms on the table in front of me and laid my head down, feeling my body go limp. This was the pre-nap posture we adopted in "kinneygarden" and it still represents the ultimate in personal relief. At the age of five, I learned to drop into a deep sleep the minute my head hit my arms. I'd wake ten minutes later, the nerve endings in my fingers all sparkly for lack of circulation, my cheek hot with dreams.

I heard Henry cross to the refrigerator and transfer containers to the counter. I listened to the restful clink of jars and cutlery. It was like being in a sickbed, hearing homely sounds emanating from a nearby room. I must have dozed for a moment, the same fleeting lapse of awareness that'll send you careening off the highway when it happens at the wheel. Sound faded and returned, a brief slip into unconsciousness. "What are you doing?" I murmured, without lifting my head.

"Making you a sandwich." His voice seemed to come from very far away. "Roast beef with red onion that I've sliced paper thin."

I propped my head on one fist and watched him place two thick slices of homemade bread side-by-side. He spread them liberally with mayonnaise, spicy brown mustard, and horseradish. "This is virulent, but you need something fierce. Pep you up." He cut the sandwich in half and laid it on a plate with a sprig of parsley; pickles, olives, and pepperoncini clustered to one side.

He set the plate in front of me and returned to the refrigerator, where he opened the freezer and removed a beer mug so cold that a white frost formed instantly on the glass when it hit the air. He opened a bottle of beer and poured it gently down the side of the mug to avoid the foam. He picked up his whiskey glass and sat down across from me.

I took a bite of the sandwich. The horseradish was so ferocious it brought tears to my eyes. Pungent fumes licked through my sinuses making my nose run as well. "Mph. This is great. I can't believe how good it is. You're a genius." I paused, using my paper napkin as a nostril mop. The roast beef was succulent, its chill tenderness the perfect foil to the heat, salt, and sour of the condiments. Now and then I'd suck down a mouthful of cold beer, all tingle and bubbles tasting of hops. Life was reduced to its four basic elements: air, food, drink, and a good friend. I shoved in the last bite of sandwich, licked the mustard from my fingers, and moaned in gratitude. I took a long, slow breath, noting the fact that my headache was gone. "Better."

"I thought that might help. Now tell me about the doctor."

I gave Henry a summary of events leading up to my discovery. He knows how my mind works so I didn't have to fill in all the nitty-gritty details. Most intuition is the sudden leap the mind makes when two elements fuse. Sometimes the connection is made through trial and error; sometimes the underlying question butts up against observation and the answer pops into view. "I didn't spot the car so much as I spotted the traces it left in its journey down the hill."

"So that is the end of that job."

"I'm assuming as much, though I haven't spoken with Fiona."

"What now?"

"The usual. Dr. Yee will do the autopsy in the morning.

Don't know how much they'll learn, given the shape the body's in. The vehicle's probably been submerged since the night he dropped from view. As soon as the post is done, I'm guessing they'll cremate the remains."

"I'm sorry to hear this. It's too bad."

"It has to be worse when the questions are unresolved. At least now his family knows and they can get on with life."

We chatted on in this vein, exploring our reactions and speculations until the subject petered out. Henry picked up my plate and took it to the sink.

"I can do that," I said.

"Stay where you are." He ran hot water in the sink and picked up a dish sponge with liquid detergent in the handle. He soaped the plate, rinsed it, and set it in the rack. "By the way, I saw a friend of yours tonight."

"Really. Who?"

He put the cutting board in the sink and began to put the condiments away. "Tommy Hevener came into Rosie's. He was looking for you, of course, but we ended up having quite a chat. He seems like a nice fellow and he's clearly smitten. He asked a lot of questions about you."

"I have a lot of questions about him, too. That's the part of my day I haven't told you about yet."

He paused with his hand on the refrigerator door. "I don't like the tone of this."

"You won't like the rest of it, either." I waited until he returned to the table and took a seat.

He said, "What?" with apprehension, like he really didn't want to hear.

"Turns out Tommy Hevener and his brother hired a punk down in Texas to break into the family home and steal the valuables, including close to a million in jewels. The burglar did as instructed and then set fire to the house to cover his tracks. What the boys failed to mention to him was that Mom and Dad were stashed in the closet, bound and gagged. They died of smoke inhalation while the place burned down around them."

Henry blinked. "No."

"Yes."

"But that can't be true."

"It is," I said. "The insurance investigator—this is a woman named Mariah Talbot—came to the office this morning and showed me the clippings from the *Hatchet Daily News Gazette* or whatever the hell it's called. I left the file at the office or you could see for yourself."

"But if that's the case, why aren't they in jail?"

"There was never enough evidence, and since the 'boys' were never charged, they managed to collect on the fire loss, life insurance, and the inheritance. All told, they walked off with a couple million bucks. Their aunt and the insurance company are preparing a civil suit, hoping to recover whatever assets remain."

"But how do they know the burglar wasn't the one responsible? He might have surprised the parents, thinking they were gone when he broke into the house. Maybe he was the one who tied them up and gagged them."

"Unfortunately, the burglar hasn't been heard from since. Speculation has it they killed him, too."

"But they can't be sure," he said.

"That's why they've reopened the investigation. Recently, an informant stepped forward and Guardian Casualty is prepared to go forward on the basis of this new information."

"I can't believe it."

"I had the same reaction until I saw the articles. I mean, here's what gets me. The first time I met Tommy? He *told* me his parents died in an accident. He didn't want me to mention it to Richard because he said his brother was still 'touchy' about the subject. I thought, well, those poor dear fellows. Here I am, thinking about my parents and feeling *sorry* for these guys. It really galls me to think how easily I got sucked in. Such bullshit. According to the paper, they even offered a big reward—a hundred thousand dollars—for 'information leading to the arrest and conviction of the killer or killers of Jared and Brenda Hevener.' Why not offer millions? They're in no danger of paying unless one rats the other out."

"How can you do business with them?"

"That's what I'm getting to. I signed a year's lease and paid six months in advance, plus a cleaning deposit. We don't want to forget that little item. Now I can't figure how to get out of it. I'm willing to forfeit the money, but it pisses me off."

"Let Lonnie handle it. He'll know what to do."

"Good thought," I said. "Not that it ends there."

"Why not?"

"Mariah thinks the jewelry's still somewhere in that big fancy house of theirs. She's hoping I can locate the safe so the cops can get a search warrant. She says the Heveners' funds are just about depleted. They've been traveling in the fast lane and now they're close to broke. She's hoping they'll try to sell at least a portion of the jewelry. Since they filed a claim for the loss and since they've steadfastly denied any knowledge of the stash, it's not going to look good. If she can get them to tip their hand, the cops will step in with a warrant for their arrest."

"Why would they risk selling? They're not dumb."

"Not so far, but they're getting desperate."

"How's she going to persuade them? I can't imagine such a thing."

"Ah. She's not. She wants me to do it." I fished the piece of paper from my handbag. "She gave me the name of a fence in Los Angeles and asked me to pass the information on to them."

Henry took the scrap of paper on which she'd written the jeweler's name. "Cyril Lambrou's a pawnbroker?"

"A jeweler. She says he runs a legitimate business, as far as it goes. He also deals in stolen property when the goods warrant it. In this case, no sweat. She showed me the Polaroids—rings, bracelets, necklaces. Gorgeous. Really beautiful."

"Why can't *she* give them the information?"

"Because they know who she is and they'd never fall for it."

"But why you?"

Henry's tone was becoming belligerent and I could feel my face heat. "Because Tommy's interested in me."

"So what?"

"Mariah's shrewd. She ran a background on me and she knows I'm not above bending the rules."

"Aren't you talking about entrapment?"

"Why would it be entrapment? I mention a guy who buys jewelry. If they're not guilty, they won't have anything to sell. Entrapment's where the cops entice someone to break the law. I'm not encouraging them to steal. They've already done that."

"But they're going to smell a rat. You mention a jeweler. They pawn the stuff and shortly afterwards they're arrested and thrown in jail? You can't be serious."

"By then it's too late. They're already behind bars."

"Suppose they post bail? The minute they hit the street, they're going to come looking for you."

"Come on, Henry. Give me credit here. I won't come right out and say, 'Gee, anybody have any stolen jewels to lay off on this guy?' I'll think of a story to tell, something plausible."

"Such as what?"

"I don't know. I haven't made that part up yet."

Exasperated, Henry leaned back in his chair and stared at me. "How many times have we had a conversation like this? You come up with some stupid scheme. I urge you not to do it, but you go right ahead and do it. You always find some way to rationalize your behavior."

"So does everyone else."

"More's the pity," he said. "I'll tell you this once and then I swear I won't mention it again. Don't do this. Don't get involved. It's none of your business."

"I didn't say I would."

"How're you going to find the safe? You'll have to get into the house."

"Tommy's taken me up there once. All I have to do is talk him into taking me again."

"Which he'd do in hopes of getting in your pants."

"I can handle that."

"But why take the risk? I don't think you should be alone with either one of them."

"Not to make light of it, but I've done a lot worse with a lot less justification."

"*I'll* say."

"Henry, I promise you I won't act in haste. I haven't even figured out what I'll say . . . you know, assuming I decide to take the job."

"Why do this to yourself? Surely, you don't need the money."

"Money isn't the issue here. I just don't think people should get away with murder."

"It isn't up to you. If the police had had sufficient evidence, the Heveners would've been arrested and convicted back then. There wasn't any proof. That's the way the law works. You stay out of it. Please."

"You know what? I'm tempted to do this for exactly the same reason you're tempted to help Rosie. Because you can't resist. So here's the deal. You want me to butt out of this? You butt out of Rosie's business and we'll call it a wash."

"It's not illegal or dangerous to help a little old lady pay her sister's medical bills."

He had a point, but I refused to acknowledge it. "Skip it. Enough. Let's quit arguing. You take care of your life and I'll take care of mine."

"You're right. It's not my concern. Do anything you want."

"Don't play injured. It's not that. I think you worry too much."

"And you don't worry enough!"

It was 11:03 when I left Henry's place and headed to my apartment. We'd made a superficial effort to patch up our differences, but nothing had been resolved. I was feeling anxious and out of sorts and so, I suspect, was he. I let myself in and set my bag aside. I turned on the television set and turned to KEST. I'd missed the lead-in to the story but caught the report in progress: ". . . the silver Mercedes-Benz recovered this evening from Brunswick Lake has been positively identified as the vehicle belonging to prominent local physician Dowan Purcell, missing since September 12. Detective Paglia of the Santa Teresa Police Department would not confirm . . ." Over her commentary there was a series of clips: a shot of the hillside near the reservoir, a shot of Crystal arriving by car, a photograph insert of Dr. Purcell, followed by a shot of the family home in Horton Ravine. The anchor moved on to a story about a cat stuck in a length of pipe. Nine and a half weeks of agony reduced to less than a minute. Folks would probably have more sympathy for the cat.

There was a tap at my door. I figured it was Henry coming over to apologize. Instead, I found Tommy Hevener standing on my porch. "Hey. Where you been? I called you earlier, but your machine was on. I thought I'd see you at Rosie's."

"Henry told me he saw you."

"Yeah, we had a nice chat. He's a great old guy."

"Look. I've had a hard day. Something's come up on a case I've been working."

"You want to talk about it? I'm a good listener."

"I don't think so. I appreciate the offer, but I'm bushed and I think I better go to bed."

"I hear you. No problem. Call me tomorrow. I want to see you again."

"Okay, I'll do that."

"You take care."

"Yeah, you, too," I said. As soon as I closed the door, my heart began knocking rapidly in my throat. I threw the dead-bolt home and leaned against the wall to wait until I heard his departing steps. Outside, a car started up and I listened as the sound of the engine diminished down the street.

I don't know how I managed to get to sleep that night. I had no emotional attachment to Dow Purcell, but the sight of that body in the front seat of the car had left me unsettled. I'd seen death many times, but I couldn't seem to block the image of that four-wheeled silver coffin and its hoary contents. I replayed the moment . . . floodlights hissing in the rain, the sound of water gushing from the underbelly of the car, the smell of mud and crushed grass, followed by the quick flash of the body in its formless repose, eyes turned toward the window, mouth open with amazement. I didn't think it would take long to identify the body . . . half a day at best. It would take longer to examine the car and come up with a theory about how it had ended up in the lake. There was also the question of whether Purcell was dead or alive when he went into the water. Again, I flashed on that face, the wide grin, the sightless eyes . . .

I made a conscious effort to divert my attention, fixing on the problem of Tommy and Richard Hevener. Despite my obstinate and disputatious stance, I *had* seen Henry's point, which I knew was correct. I'm forever sticking my nose in where it doesn't belong, often with consequences more serious (and potentially deadly) than I care to admit. I was under no obligation to assist Mariah Talbot or Guardian Casualty Insurance, so why put myself in the line of fire? The "boys" were not my problem. Mariah had even hinted she had an alternative if I decided not to help. I still had to find a way to break the lease and recover my deposit, but maybe Lonnie could write the brothers such a blistering letter they'd be begging to get me out. As for the murder of their parents, I had to believe the law would catch up with them eventually. As much as it grieved me to admit it, retribution wasn't mine. Oh, darn.

17

MUCH OF WEDNESDAY I was occupied tidying up odds and ends. At 6:00 that morning, I'd managed to squeeze in a three-mile jog between cloud bursts, after which I'd gone to the gym. I'd come home, cleaned up, eaten breakfast, and arrived at the office at 9:15. I spent the bulk of the day catching up on paperwork, including my personal bills, which I paid with the usual sense of triumph. I love keeping all the wolves at bay.

Twice, I sat down at the typewriter to frame my final report to Fiona, thinking I might as well go ahead and drop it in the mail to her. However, having delivered both a report and an invoice just the day before, I was a tiny bit short on bullshit and tiny bit short on cash. I thought it could be bad form to charge for the time I'd spent waiting for the cops to pull Dow out of the lake. Since I'd forked over her $1,500 to the infamous Hevener brothers, the $1,075 I owed her would have to come out of my checking account, which currently showed a balance of $422. I had plenty of money in savings, but I didn't much feel like dipping into it. Besides, I was still entertaining the fantasy that Fiona would write off the balance out of appreciation for the speed and efficiency with which I'd concluded her business. She'd hired me to find Dow and I'd found him sooner than either one of us expected, though not in quite the condition one would have wished. I couldn't help but hope for a $1,075 pat on the back. *Ha, ha, ha,* I thought.

I considered calling Crystal to offer my condolences but couldn't bring myself to do it. I wasn't a family friend, and I was afraid my motivation would be interpreted as ghoulish curiosity, which of course it was.

Just after lunch, I went back to the file Mariah Talbot had left. I glanced at both wills, picking my way through sufficient legalese to confirm that the Atcheson jewelry had been left to Brenda's sister, Karen. I then went back and reread the news clips. Hatchet, Texas, was located roughly sixty miles from Houston and had a population of twenty-eight hundred souls. There'd only been one other murder in the town's entire history, and that was back in 1906 when a woman took a piece of firewood to her husband's skull while he was sleeping. She'd killed him with six blows after he got drunk once too often, knocked her teeth out, blackened her eyes, and broke her nose. Satisfied he was dead, she'd tossed the log on the fire and brewed herself a pot of tea.

The death of Jared and Brenda Hevener made headlines as far away as Amarillo, where Brenda had been born and raised. According to the paper, the bodies were discovered in the rubble the day after the fire. The blaze had been fierce and fast, fueled by accelerants, fanned by dry winds. The volunteer fire department was called at 1:06 A.M., arriving on the scene within seventeen minutes. By then the house was completely engulfed in flames and their efforts were largely focused on preventing the fire's spread to adjacent properties. Neighbors quickly realized the Heveners were unaccounted for. At first, the fear was expressed that all four family members had been taken unawares and had perished in the conflagration. As it turned out, Tommy Hevener had been visiting friends in San Antonio. He managed to track down his brother, Richard, who was traveling in the south of France.

The initial newspaper accounts were filled with shock at the deaths and sympathy for the sons whose loss everyone assumed must be devastating. There were long biographical pieces about Brenda and Jared: her community service, his rise in the business world. The turnout for the funeral was impressive. Newspaper photos showed the cortege stretching out for blocks. Pictures at the cemetery showed the two coffins surrounded by flowers, Richard with his head bowed, while Tommy stared bleakly at the grave site with an expression of despair. Mariah hadn't been impressed with their acting skills, but I could see how easily their grief could have been interpreted as heartfelt.

Within days, the time-delay device and accelerants were identified and traced to Casey Stonehart, twenty-three years old and clearly not that bright, as he'd purchased the materials in a town only sixteen miles away. With his troubled criminal history and his questionable IQ, it wasn't hard to conclude he was acting in concert with somebody else. He clearly wasn't smart enough to plan and execute the job by himself. Over the next six months, the tone of the story changed as public skepticism grew and the ongoing investigation shifted to the possibility that the two sons had been involved. On their part, there were many outraged denials and vigorous protestations of their innocence. Law-enforcement authorities and the fire marshall responded with a number of carefully worded statements, hoping to avoid a lawsuit if their suspicions turned out to be groundless. The story played for weeks and then died away. There were periodic updates, but most of the later coverage seemed to be an endless rehash of the original account. Casey Stonehart warranted very little in the way of column space beyond the occasional query as to his whereabouts.

Reading between the lines, I could see the bureaucratic tensions begin to accumulate. The D.A. was accused of bungling.

Pressure was brought to bear and he was forced to resign. Despite the launching of a second, even more extensive investigation, no new evidence came to light. Formal charges were filed against Casey Stonehart in absentia, but Richard and Tommy Hevener managed to evade official blame. A year later, two short clippings referred to the lawsuit they'd filed against Guardian Casualty, trying to collect various insurance benefits. Six months after that, there was a brief mention of the close of probate and the settling of the estate. What a depressing chain of events. I shuffled through the articles again just to make sure I hadn't missed anything.

The story made me restless. I could feel the Masked Avenger aspect of my personality girding her loins, prepared to seek justice and to right old wrongs. At the same time, Henry's accusations had hit perilously close to home. I'll admit I'm (occasionally) foolhardy and impetuous, impatient with the system, vexed by the necessity for playing by the rules. It's not that I don't applaud law and order, because I do. I'm simply indignant that the bad guys are accorded so many rights when their victims have so few. Pursuing scoundrels through the courts not only costs a fortune, but it offers no guarantee of legal remedy. Even assuming success, a hard-won conviction doesn't bring the dead back to life. In this matter, though I hated to be practical, I'd come around to Henry's point of view. I intended to mind my own business for once.

I left the office just before three o'clock and walked over to the bank. Fortunately for me, the check I'd written to Hevener Properties hadn't yet cleared. Maybe he accumulated rent checks and made a deposit on a regular basis instead of one by one. I put a stop payment on it, returned to the office, and wrote Richard a brief, apologetic note, indicating that circumstances had changed and I wouldn't be renting space from him after all. Given my signature on the lease, he might well take me to small claims court. I didn't think he'd do it.

Surely, in his position, he'd prefer to avoid legal wrangles. At five-thirty I locked up. On my way home, I drove by the main post office and dropped the letter in the outside box. I reached my apartment twelve minutes later, feeling lighter than I had all day.

Before I unlocked my front door, I crossed the patio to Henry's place. I wanted to tell him I'd heeded his words. In declining involvement, I'd offer him full credit for motivating this rare evidence of common sense on my part. His kitchen light was on. I tapped on the glass, expecting to see him come into the kitchen from the hall. No sign of him, no sound of his piano, no hint of activity. I picked up the tantalizing scent of one of his oven-baked stews so I didn't think he'd gone far.

I returned to my apartment and let myself in. I turned on the desk lamp and set my shoulder bag on a kitchen stool. I gathered up the mail that had been pushed through the slot and was splayed out across the floor. All of it was junk and I tossed it in the trash. The message light on the answering machine was blinking merrily. I pushed the Play button.

Tommy Hevener.

"Hey. It's me. I've been thinking about you. Maybe I'll catch you later. Give me a call when you get in."

I pressed Erase, wishing I could do the same with him.

I went into the kitchen. Saturday's can of tomato soup was the last I had so I already knew there was nothing in the house to eat. Dutifully, I checked my cupboards and my refrigerator shelves. I've never actually seen a recipe that calls for two plastic packets of soy sauce, half a cup of olive oil, Cheerios, anchovy paste, maple syrup, and six rubber carrots asprout with something that looks like hair. A clever home economist could have whipped up a nourishing dish out of just such ingredients, but I confess I was stumped. I picked up my bag again and headed out the door. Dinner at Rosie's—what a pleasant change of pace.

The night air was misty and smelled of basements. It had

been raining, off and on now for six full days. The novelty had worn off and those who'd rejoiced in its arrival were now cursing the rain's persistence. The ground was saturated and the creek-beds ran high, a noisy rush of water pushing debris in its path. Unless we had a few dry days, the torrents would jump the banks and flood the low-lying areas. There were already county roads awash with mud and stones, covered with creeping sheets of water that made driving perilous.

Given the ebb and flow of business at Rosie's, the bar area was teeming. The Happy Hour crowd would be gone by seven P.M. as soon as the drink prices went up. The noise level had risen to a harsh, edgy pitch that seemed to reflect the mounting irritability levels. People were tired of raincoats, wet shoes, and mold spores that made their allergies flare up in a rush of sneezes and clogged sinuses.

I left my umbrella propped against the wall by the front door, shed my slicker, and shook off some of the accumulated water before I hung it up. I made a useless display of wiping my feet just to be polite. As I stepped through the inner door, I spotted Tommy Hevener sitting by himself at a table near the front. I felt a flash of irritation, feeling cornered. How was I going to get him out of my life? He was drinking a martini, the wide-rimmed glass at his lips when he caught sight of me. I halted in my tracks—a split second of indecision—because the second person I saw was Mariah Talbot sitting in a booth at the rear. Adrenaline blew through my system like a hit of speed. Her telltale silver hair had been concealed beneath a dark, shag-cut wig, her blue eyes masked by glasses with plastic and rhinestone frames. The raincoat she wore made her body appear bulky. Unless you saw past the facade to the elegant bones of her face, she appeared frumpy and drab, not someone you'd notice in a crowd of this size. Tommy *couldn't* be expecting to see her, but he might make the same leap of recognition if he glanced in her direction. Looks as classic as hers are nearly impossible to

hide. The minute Mariah and I made eye contact, she rose
from the booth and slipped into the seat on the opposite side
of the table with her back to us. I hoped the shock of discovery hadn't registered on my face, but I wasn't sure how
I'd manage to hide my astonishment. My gaze flicked to
Tommy's. His expression was quizzical, as though he'd
sensed my surprise. He turned in his chair and scanned the
rear of the bar. Abruptly, I crossed and sat down at his table. I
touched his hand. "I'm sorry I was such a bitch last night."

His gaze returned to mine and he smiled. "Don't worry
about it. The fault was mine." The mild Texas accent I'd found
so attractive a day or two before now seemed to be an affecta-
tion. He was wearing a cashmere sweater, a soft downy gray
that played up his florid hair color and the green of his eyes.
He was making intense eye contact, enclosing my hand in his.
He lifted my fingers and placed a kiss in my right palm. I
wanted to shiver—not from arousal, but from dread. What
had once seemed seductive was only cheap display. He knew
he was handsome and he affected the shy country boy to en-
hance his appeal. I knew too much about him, and the force
of his sexuality struck me as pure manipulation. In a quick
recap, I realized that from the moment we'd met, he'd worked
to dominate, beginning with my declining to drink a beer
with him. He'd proposed a Diet Pepsi instead, popping it open
before I could refuse. I'd taken the path of least resistance and
he'd established his control. After that the transitions were
smooth and well rehearsed. He'd enlisted my sympathies by
rolling out the reference to his parents' death and then he'd
offered up his comment about California women being so
stuck up. Immediately, I'd worked to prove him wrong. His
final move was adroit. *"Which do you prefer? Guys way too
young for you or guys way too old?"* I couldn't believe I'd
been so easily taken in.

Peripherally, I saw Mariah leave the booth and head for the
ladies' restroom. I rested my chin on my hand. "Are you free

for dinner? We could go back to Emile's or try somewhere else."

"Buy me a drink first and we can talk about that."

I pointed to his glass. "What are you having?"

"Vodka martini." He lifted his glass and tumbled the green olive onto his waiting tongue.

I took his glass and got up. "I'll be right back." As I moved by him, he reached out an arm to halt my passage. I stared down at his face, which he'd tilted up to mine. I could smell his aftershave. I could feel his hot, proprietary hand on my ass. I shifted out of his grasp and leaned closer, keeping my tone light. "Don't be a bad boy."

His voice was low and laced with confidence. "I am a bad boy. I thought you liked that about me."

"I wouldn't count on it," I said.

I crossed to the bar where William was at work, pulling beers and mixing drinks. I ordered two vodka martinis and we exchanged inane remarks while I watched him pour a stream of vodka into a silver shaker and add a stingy dash of vermouth. William set two chilled martini glasses on the bar.

"Could you do me a favor? When you're done, will you take those over to that guy in the gray sweater? Tell him I'm in the loo and I'll be there in a second. He can go ahead if he wants. I'll have mine when I get back."

"Happy to be of help," William said. He put two doilies on a tray, set a martini on each, and came out from behind the bar.

I proceeded to the ladies' room and pushed through the door. The room smelled of bleach and had only one stall. I knew from sad experience the wooden toilet seat was cracked and pinched when you sat. Mariah was standing at the basin making an adjustment to her wig. Aside from the sink, there was only a big plastic-lined waste bin and a grille-covered window that opened onto a narrow backyard. Up close, I could see that under the raincoat, she'd pulled on a bulky knit sweater and a pair of flabby blue print slacks with some form of waist-thickening padding underneath. The Birkenstocks and white socks were a nice touch. Very chic.

She said, "What do you think?"

"That disguise is lame. I've seen you once in my life and spotted you straight off the minute I walked in."

She took a hair fork from her purse and lifted the top layers to increase the height. "Shit. This cost me a fortune and it's not even real hair."

"What are you *doing* here? Do you know how close you've come to blowing it?"

"Tell me about it. Me and my big ideas," she said. "I tried to call, but all I got was your answering machine. I didn't want to leave a message. It's not cool. You never know who's going to be there when those things are played back. I didn't want to take the chance Tommy'd hear my voice. I figured it'd be easier to find you here. I walk in, thinking I'm safe, and there he sits. I nearly had heart failure."

"You and me both. How'd he miss seeing you?"

"Don't even ask. It was dumb luck, I guess. He was fussing with his raincoat so I pretended to spot a friend and headed for a back booth. I sat there for fifteen minutes, planning an exit through the kitchen. Then I happened to look up and saw you come in. What are the chances you can get him out of here?"

"I'm doing what I can, but I don't like it. Last night he stopped by my apartment. I managed to avoid a visit, but he's persistent. I'm trying to turn him off and now I have to turn around and suck up to him to cover for you."

"Life's tough." She rearranged a few strands of artificial hair and then smiled to herself. "Here's a piece of good news. All their credit cards are maxed out. Six to eight cards each, eighteen percent interest on the unpaid balance. They're making minimum payments, just trying to keep afloat. Fancy watches, fancy cars. The mortgage is fifteen grand a month on that monstrosity they call home. They've got their nuts in a vise and they're feeling the squeeze."

"They're completely broke?"

"They will be if they don't act fast." Her eyes met mine in the mirror. The combination of the wig and the outfit made her seem coarse, not the cool professional she'd been in my office when she'd laid out her credentials. Maybe she was more of a chameleon than I'd given her credit for. "I don't suppose you've had time to tell Tommy about the fence."

"I'm not going to do that. I really can't help you there. I'm sorry."

"Don't sweat it." She tucked the hair fork away and then turned and leaned against the sink so she could study me. "I'll get the fuckers with or without your help."

"How'd this become so personal?"

"Murder's always personal. I take offense when I see guys like them getting off scot-free. Aside from that, Guardian's promised me a big fat bonus if I can bring this one in." Behind the glasses, her eyes were a clear blue and very cold. She nodded at the door. "You better get out there. Prince Charming awaits."

I left the restroom and stepped into the blast of noise unleashed by all the alcohol. Smoke was adrift in the cavernous room. I felt as though I'd been gone an hour, but a glance at my watch showed less than ten minutes had passed. I pushed my way through the crowd, returning to the table where Tommy waited. Henry had joined him and he was sipping his usual glass of Black Jack over ice. His elbows rested on the surface of a manila envelope and I wondered if he was planning to do some work later on. I experienced a momentary surge of hope. His presence would at least spare me any intimacies.

I sat down. "Hi, Henry. I knocked on your door earlier, but I couldn't seem to rouse you." I was sounding way too perky, but I couldn't help myself.

"I popped over to the market. I needed some fresh parsley to finish off my stew."

"Henry's stews are legendary," I said in Tommy's direction, though I couldn't meet his eyes. I lifted the martini glass and took a sip, then steadied the wobbling glass as I set it down again. I licked at my hand where the vodka had slopped over the rim.

Henry glanced over at me and we exchanged a brief look. I knew what he was up to. He was feeling protective. He had no intention of letting me consort with the enemy unchaperoned. His gaze settled thoughtfully on his drink. He said, "By the way, I looked into that business you were asking me about."

I said, "Ah." Thinking, *Business*? What *business*?

"The guy you want to try is Cyril Lambrou in the Klinger Building, off Spring Street in downtown Los Angeles. The woman I talked to sold him an assortment of her mother's antique jewelry. This was stuff she hardly ever wore and she was tired of paying the exorbitant insurance premiums."

I felt myself separating from my body. I couldn't believe he was doing it. I'd backed away from Mariah's scheme and here he was laying out the bait. Henry had launched himself on his maiden lie, which he'd offered in my behalf. I knew why he was doing it. If the jeweler's name came from him, how could I be blamed for it later when the deal went sour? Henry and Tommy had spent the previous evening together. Tommy would trust him. Everybody trusted Henry because he told the truth and he was straight as an arrow.

I said, "I can sympathize. I pay a fortune for insurance and I could use the cash." My voice sounded hollow. I moved my hand out from under Tommy's with the intention of lifting my glass for another sip of my martini, but I realized I was shaking too much to get the glass to my lips. I tucked my fingers under my thigh. I could feel how cold they were even through my jeans.

Meanwhile, Henry went on as smoothly as a con artist with an easy mark. "I called the fellow myself and described the diamond to him. He wouldn't make a commitment on the phone, but he seemed interested. I know you don't want to *give* the ring away, but you're going to have to be realistic. You'll never recoup the actual value, but he sounds a lot more generous than some. I think this would be for his personal collection, so it might be worth a shot."

I tried to reconstruct from his comments the phony tale he must have had in mind. The implication was that I had my mother's pricey diamond ring and was in the market for some cash. Apparently, I'd consulted him about selling it and he'd asked around. So far so good, but the trick with a good lie is not to push. I thought we might go another round or two, but then we'd have to move on. String a lie out for too long and it can trip you up.

My mouth was dry. *How much?* I cleared my throat and tried it again. "How much? Did he give you any idea?"

"Between eight and ten thousand. He says it depends on the stone and whether he thinks there's any secondary market, but he swore he'd be fair."

"The ring's worth five times that," I said, indignantly. I knew the ring was imaginary, but it still had sentimental value. Under the circumstance, eight to ten thousand sounded like chickenshit to me.

Henry shrugged. "Check around if you want. There are other jewelers in the building, but as he says, better the devil you know."

"Maybe. We'll see about that."

Tommy's expression hadn't changed. He seemed to listen politely, no more and no less interested than any ordinary guy would be.

I felt a trickle of sweat inch down my spine to the small of my back. I pointed and said, "What's in the envelope?"

"Oh. I'm glad you reminded me. I have a present for you."

He passed me the envelope, watching expectantly as I undid
the clasp and folded back the flap. Inside, neatly secured with
a paper clip, was a handful of bills, presumably Klotilde's.

"Okay, I'll bite. What *is* this?"

"See for yourself. Go on and open one."

I slid off the paper clip and picked up the first bill, which
appeared to be a lengthy itemized list of charges, most of
them for medical supplies:

brush, hair	$1.00
Steri-strips, 3m ¼ × 3	$1.22
Steri-strips, 3m ¼ × 3	$1.22
underpads, polymer 23 × 36	$3.35
syringe, monoject ins.	$0.14
syringe, monoject ins.	$0.14
syringe, monoject ins.	$0.14
catheter, all-purp Davol	$1.59
baby lotion	$1.62
tray, bard irrigation	$2.69
cups, denture	$0.14

There were roughly thirty items in all. The total was $99.10.
None of the charges seemed out of line to me. I glanced at the
next statement, a record of therapeutic exercises and physical
therapy sessions, totaling 130 minutes over the last few days
of July. The box for each day bore the initials *pg*, the therapist
who rendered the treatment.

I looked at Henry with puzzlement.

He said, "That whole batch is hers. I came across them this
morning and thought you'd be interested. Take another look."

I picked up the next invoice. This was a claim for portable
X-ray equipment, the transport for the portable X-ray, and
two X-ray exams, one of the wrist and one of the hand. The
total was $108.50. I glanced at the top of the form and then
shuffled back through the first two. All three were generated

by Pacific Meadows. "I didn't realize she'd been a patient at
Pacific Meadows."

"Neither did I. I showed them to Rosie and she said
Klotilde was admitted last spring. Pacific Meadows was one
of several facilities where she'd been a patient in the last few
years. I don't know if you ever paid much attention, but she'd
be hospitalized for something—a fall, pneumonia, that staph
infection she picked up. With Medicare, she was only allowed X number of days—I think, a hundred per illness. She
was so cranky and disagreeable, a couple of places refused to
take her. They just claimed there wasn't room. Are you following this?"

"So far."

"Check the date services were rendered."

"July and August."

Henry leaned closer. "She passed away in April. She'd
been gone for months by then."

For a moment, I let the information sink in. This was the
first tangible evidence of financial shenanigans that I'd seen.
But how had they managed it? Klotilde must have died at just
about the same time the paper audit was being conducted at
Pacific Meadows. According to Merry, a substantial number
of charts had been ordered for review. Maybe hers wasn't
one. I tried to recall the sequence of events whereby deaths
were reported to Social Security. As nearly as I remembered,
the mortuary filled out the death certificate and sent it to
the local office of vital statistics, which in turn forwarded the
original to the county recorder's office. The death certificate
was then sent to Sacramento, where it was archived and the
information sent on to Social Security.

"Henry, this is great. I wonder if there's any way to check it
out?" I was of course pondering the notion of persuading
Merry to do some snooping for me. I'd have to wait until the
coming weekend, which was when she filled in. I didn't think
it'd be politic to approach her during regular weekday hours

with Mrs. Stegler standing by. Plan B was maybe doing a little search of my own if I could figure out what to look for. I glanced up to find both Tommy and Henry watching me. "Sorry. I was trying to figure out what to do with this."

Tommy must have decided he'd been polite long enough. His hand settled over mine. His grip was firm and prevented my pulling free without being conspicuous about it. "Hey, Henry. I hate to butt in here, but this lady's promised to buy me dinner. We're just having a quick drink before we walk over to Emile's."

Henry said, "Well, I better get back to my stew before it starts sticking to the pan." He flicked a look at me as he rose to his feet. I knew he didn't want to leave me, but he didn't dare persist. At the prospect of his departure, I felt the same desperation I'd felt when I was five and my aunt walked me over for my first day of elementary school. I'd been fine while she lingered, chatting with the other parents, but the minute she left I had a panic attack. Now, I could feel the same roar of anxiety that dulled everything but my longing for her. Henry and Tommy exchanged chitchat and next thing I knew, Henry was gone. I had to get out of there. I tried to withdraw my hand, but Tommy tightened his grip.

I tapped the manila envelope. "You know what? I really need to look into these. I'll have to take a rain check on dinner. I hope you don't mind."

Tommy minded. I watched his smile fade. "You're reneging on a promise."

"Maybe tomorrow night. I've got work to do." I knew it wasn't smart to go up against this man, but the notion of an evening alone with him was intolerable. Mariah had to be gone by now and if not, that was her problem.

He began to rub my fingers, the contact slightly rougher than was strictly necessary. The friction became uncomfortable, but he seemed unaware. "Why the sudden change of heart?"

"Please let go of my hand."

He was staring at me. "Has someone told you something about me?"

I could feel my jaw set. "What's there to tell, Tommy? You have something to hide?"

"No. Of course not, but people make things up."

"Well, I don't. If I say I've got work to do, you can take my word for it."

He gave my fingers a squeeze and then released my hand. "I guess I better let you go, then. Why don't I call you tomorrow? Or better yet, you call me."

"Right."

We stood at the same time. I waited while Tommy shrugged into his raincoat, picked up his umbrella, and adjusted the clasp. When we reached the entrance, I retrieved my slicker and umbrella. Tommy held the door. I made short work of the fare-thee-wells, trying to control my desire to flee. I turned toward my apartment while he walked off in the opposite direction on his way to his car. I forced myself to stroll though my impulse was to scurry, putting as much distance as possible between him and me.

18

I WENT BACK to my apartment and locked myself in. Tommy gave me the creeps. I went from window to window, closing the latches, pulling the shutters across the panes so that no one could look in. I didn't relax until every possible bolt and bar had been secured. I sat down at my desk and found Mariah Talbot's business card, which I'd tucked in my bag. I was nervous about my association with her. Tommy'd been uncanny in his suspicions about me. I pictured him rummaging in my purse the minute my back was turned, coming across her card. People like him, obsessed with control, need the constant reassurance that no small detail has eluded them. I committed the number to memory and cut the card into small pieces. I was uncomfortably aware that he still held my rental application, which spelled out more about me than I really wanted known. He'd never fully believe I was focused on matters related to Dow Purcell. In his mind, whatever I was up to must have something to do with him. Narcissism and paranoia are flip sides of the same distorted sense of self-importance. In the eerie way of all psychopaths, he'd picked up on my newly minted fear of him. He must be wondering who or what had caused my attitude to shift.

I sat down at my desk and dialed Mariah's Texas area code and the number on the card. I knew I wouldn't reach her, but at least I could leave her a message to get in touch with me. I thought about how deftly Henry had stepped in with the name of the fence. He'd lied as well as I did and with the same finesse. The question now was whether Tommy would act on the information.

Mariah's answering machine clicked in. "Hello, this is Mariah Talbot. You've reached the offices of Guardian Casualty Insurance in Houston, Texas. My usual work hours are eight-thirty to five-thirty, Monday through Friday. If you're calling at any other time, please leave a message giving me your name, the time, and a number where I can reach you. I check my machine frequently and I'll get back to you as soon as possible. Thank you."

I said, "Hi, Mariah. It's Kinsey. We need to talk. Please call me at my office number. If I'm unavailable, leave me ten seconds of silence. After that, just keep checking your messages. I'll call and suggest a time and a place to meet. Thanks." As I spoke, I found myself hunched over the phone, my hand cupping the mouthpiece. What did I imagine? Tommy Hevener pressed against the outside wall with a hand-held listening device? Well, yeah, sort of. Talk about paranoid.

Having placed the call to Mariah, I turned my attention to the bills Henry'd given me, sinking into the comfort and safety of the job before me. The first in the pile bore the heading "Medicare Summary Notice" and further down the page, a line that read "This is a summary of claims processed on 8/29/86." If I could lay my hands on her medical chart, I could find out what the doctors had been treating her for. I knew about some of her illnesses, but I wanted to see what medications and supplies had been ordered for her. I could then compare the actual orders to the items for which Medicare had been billed. Shuffling through, I found an Explanation of Medical Benefits form; account statements with codes, boxes for co-pays and deductibles; invoices; plus several records of daily treatment—physical therapy by my guess. No diagnosis was ever mentioned, but in the first half of August, the charges for medication alone totaled $410.95. Hundreds of additional items, many of them minor, had been billed to Medicare in the months since her death. Of course, this *could* be an error, a mix-up in accounts with goods and services being charged inadvertently to the wrong patient billing number. On the other hand, Klotilde's surname, with its odd, impossible Hungarian spelling, appeared throughout, so this was hardly a matter of someone misidentifying a "Smith" or "Jones," or switching one "Johnson" for another with the same first initial. Most helpful to me was the fact that while the claim number changed, Klotilde's Medicare number followed her from form to form. I made a note of the information on a scrap of paper, folded it, and slid it into my jeans pocket. I wondered whether her records were still available at Pacific Meadows. Almost had to be, I thought. She'd died in April and I assumed the facility would keep her records in their active files for at least a year before retiring them to storage.

I waited until 9:30, filling my time with various household chores. Cleaning out a toilet bowl can be wonderfully soothing when anxiety levels climb. I scrubbed the sink and the tub, and then crawled around on my bathroom floor, using the same damp sponge to wipe down the tiles. I vacuumed, dusted, and started a load of laundry. From time to time, I looked at my watch, calculating the hour at which the residents of Pacific Meadows would be bedded down for the night. Finally, I exchanged my Sauconys for black tennis shoes and then slipped into a black windbreaker, which was better for night work than my gaudy yellow rain gear. I separated the house key and the VW key from the larger collection on my key ring, transferred my driver's license and some cash from my wallet to my jeans, and then added a small leather case that contained my key picks. This particular kit had been designed by a felonious friend who'd spent his spare moments in prison fashioning an assortment of picks that looked like a manicure set. In between breaking-and-entering gigs, I could nip my cuticles and file my nails. The only other item I took with me was a flat flashlight the size of a playing card that fit neatly in my bra. On my way to the nursing home, I made a detour by the drive-through window at McDonald's, where I picked up a sack of burgers, two Cokes, and two large orders of french fries.

When I arrived at Pacific Meadows, the parking lot was close to empty. The day personnel had departed and the night shift operated with a considerably reduced staff. I parked my car in a darkened area, picked up the sack of fast food, and locked the door behind me. The rain had been held in abeyance, stalled over the mountain range just north of us. Meanwhile, we'd enjoyed a sufficient break between showers that the pavement was dry in patches. Crossing the tarmac, I reviewed the layout of the building, calculating the location of Ruby Curtsinger's room. I knew a bird feeder hung outside her sliding door, and I was hoping I could use that as a reference point. I had just reached the corner of the building when a car turned into the lot behind me.

In stealth mode, I stepped into the protective shadow of a juniper while the driver backed the vehicle into a slot midway down the row. The car was a classic, long and snub-nosed, fenders softly rounded, its make and model one I wasn't able to identify on sight. The body looked like something from the '40s: the paint color, cream; the front bumper, a chunky affair of highly polished chrome. Four doors, no running board, a set of dazzling whitewall tires, no hood ornament. The man who emerged was as smart looking as the car. He tossed a lighted cigarette aside and I watched it wink briefly on the asphalt before the damp extinguished it. He wore a pale raincoat over a dark three-piece suit, black wingtip shoes with heels that tapped sharply as he walked. As he approached the lighted entrance, I could see his thick mustache and a substantial head of silver hair. He disappeared from view. When I was certain he was gone, I continued around to the rear of the building on the walkway that paralleled the narrow gardens.

Most of the residents' rooms were dark, the drapes drawn securely across the sliding glass doors. I closed my eyes, trying to picture Ruby's room in relation to her neighbors; difficult to do since I'd only visited her once. I searched for the bird feeder that had graced her eaves, hoping the nursing home hadn't provided one per resident. Ahead of me, one of the sliding glass doors was partially opened and I could see the flickering gray light of a television set. Outside, an empty bird feeder was visible, hanging like a little lantern from a thin strand of wire. I leaned close to the screen. "Ruby? Is that you in there?"

Her wheelchair was parked no more than two feet away. She leaned forward and peered through the screen door at me. It seemed to take her a moment to figure out who I was. "You're Merry's friend. I'm sorry, I don't remember your name."

"Kinsey," I said, holding up the bag. "I brought you something."

She unlatched the screen door and motioned me in, her bony face brightening. I slid open the screen and stepped into her room. She pointed to the bag. "What's in there?"

I held it open to her and she peered in while I identified the contents. "Two Big Macs, two QP's with Cheese, two Cokes, two fries, and numerous packets of ketchup and salt. I figured you'd need that." I passed her the sack. "The stuff's probably cold and I apologize for that."

"I have a microwave."

"You do? Good job. I hope you're hungry."

"You bet." She set the bag in her lap and wheeled herself over to the low chest of drawers. On top, she had an electric tea kettle and a microwave oven the size of a bread box. She put the bag in and set the timer. Over her shoulder, she said, "Make sure the coast is clear."

I crossed to the hall door, which had been closed for the night. I turned the knob, opened the door a crack. The corridor was dim. At the far end, I could see the nurses' station in a hot oasis of light. Standing with his back to me was the gentleman I'd seen entering only moments before. Maybe a relative making an after-hours visit. The door across from Ruby's opened abruptly and a nurse came out wearing a snappy white uniform, with a starched white cap, white hose, and crepe-sole white shoes meant to stave off varicose veins. I didn't think nurses even dressed like that these days. The few I'd seen wore street clothes or nursey-looking pantsuits made of machine-washable synthetics. It was Pepper Gray, the bitchy nurse who'd eavesdropped on the conversation between Merry and me during my initial visit. She had a stethoscope hung around her neck and her expression was preoccupied as she checked her watch. She turned toward the nurses' station and padded briskly down the hall.

Behind me, Ruby's microwave oven pinged. I jumped and swiftly pushed the hall door shut. There wasn't a lock and I hoped the cheap, heady fumes of junk food wouldn't bring attendants running. Ruby retrieved the bag from the microwave and wheeled herself back to her place by the sliding glass doors. She pulled the rolling tray between us and pointed to a chair. I wasn't sure about sharing her food, but I'd really brought more than she could eat and I was starving to death. She seemed tickled at the company and wolfed down her Quarter Pounder almost as fast as I did. Both of us made little snuffling sounds as we moved on to the Big Macs and the cartons of fries.

"I hope your heart doesn't seize up," I said, taking a sip of my Coke.

"Who cares? I've got a no-code on my chart and I'd rest in peace." She held up her Big Mac, delighted at the sight of juices dripping out the bottom. She licked a dab of Special Sauce from the corner of her mouth. "Not as big as the ones on TV, but it's good."

"I'm a sucker for these things. So how've you been?"

She tilted her head, so-so. "I heard they found the doctor's car so I thought you might stop by. I was looking for you all day."

"Took me a while to get myself together. How are people dealing with the news?"

"Some are upset, but I don't think many of us are surprised. Was the body his?"

"Don't know yet. I'm assuming it was. The autopsy was done today." I filled her in on the story, adding a few of the grimmer details, which she appeared to enjoy. I said, "Tell me about the night staff. They do much prowling around at night?"

"Not often, no. When I'm wheeling myself up and down the hall, I see them sitting at the desk chatting or doing paperwork. Some have coffee or watch TV in the staff lounge. Most nights it's quiet unless someone dies."

"How many total?"

Ruby did a head count. "Seven, if you include the orderlies, the nurses, and the nurse's aides."

"Do they make regular rounds checking on the residents?"

"Half the time they don't even check on us if we ring for them. Why? Are you casing the joint?"

"Absolutely." I paused to wipe my mouth and wad up the paper napkin and the wrappers in my lap. "Actually, I need to check some files. Think they keep the records locked up?"

Ruby shook her head, tucking a bite of burger in her cheek so she could answer. "Hardly anybody wants to steal geriatric charts."

"How'd you like to be a lookout? I could use some help."

She hesitated, suddenly a lot less cocky. "Oh, dear. I don't know if I could do that. I'm not good at sneaking. Even as a child, I could never manage it well."

"Ruby, it takes practice. You can't expect to be good unless you're willing to apply yourself."

Her already diminutive body seemed to shrink. "I'll try, but I don't think I'll do a very good job of it."

"I'm sure you'll do fine."

Moments later, I watched through her partially opened door as she wheeled herself down the hall toward the nurses' station around the corner. Her single responsibility—aside from chatting with the staff—was to park her chair so she could keep an eye out, making sure no one headed for the office while I was mucking around in there. The layout of the corridor was such that I could get in without being seen, but I was worried one of the nurses would come looking for a chart that wasn't out on the floor. Seemed unlikely, but I'd have no way to explain myself if someone happened to barge in.

I allowed time enough for Ruby to reach the nurses' station, and then I slipped out of her room, pulled the door shut behind me, and turned right, walking down the hall as though I had legitimate business there. I passed the dayroom, the entrance, and the dining room. The doors to both the dayroom and the dining room stood open, but all the lights were out. I paused, leaning against the wall. Like an animal on the hunt, I closed my eyes, taking in the scents, deciphering the secrets that lingered in the air. This was the world of the elderly: cinnamon rolls, pine scent, freshly ironed cotton, and gardenias.

When I reached the administrative offices, I took a deep breath and tried the knob. Locked. I considered using my key picks, but I was uneasy at the prospect of loitering for fifteen minutes while I manipulated the tumblers with assorted snap picks, torquing tools, and bent wire. Surely, there was a better way to go about this. I retraced my steps, returning to the front desk, which was abandoned at this hour in the dimly lighted alcove. I slipped behind the counter and searched through drawer after drawer. I kept my ears tuned, alert to any warning sounds that might signal someone's approach. In the bottom drawer, I saw a metal file box that opened at a touch. Inside was a small compartmentalized tray with various keys, all neatly tagged and labeled. Yea for my team. This was really more exciting than a scavenger hunt. To be on the safe side, I took three; one for Administration, one for Admissions, and one for Medical Records. I closed the lid on the box, slid the drawer shut, and scurried down the hall again.

I started with Administration. My hands trembled slightly, 1.2 on the Richter scale, but otherwise I did all right. Once inside, I didn't dare risk a light, though the door itself was solid. My chief concern was that someone pulling into the side parking lot would wonder why the windows were alight at this hour. I reached down my shirt and removed the flat pinch flashlight from its hiding place in my bra. When I squeezed it, the plastic felt warm and the beam emitted was wee, but sufficient for my purposes. I took a moment to reorient myself. I'd seen this office previously by day and I had a fair sense of how the space was organized.

On the far side of the counter was Merry's desk, which was arranged back-to-back with an identical desk. In addition, there were several rolling file carts, the copy machine, and a row of metal file cabinets along the far wall. Merry's computer screen was dark, but a small dot of amber pulsed steadily like a heart. In the darkness, I couldn't see the big wall clock, but I was aware of its relentless *click, click, click* as the second hand measured the circumference of the face. To my right was the door to Dr. Purcell's office where I'd had

my chat with Mrs. Stegler. To the left was the door that connected this office with Medical Records. I flashed the light on
my watch. It was 10:22.

Cautiously, I tried the door to the Medical Records department, which I discovered was unlocked. Oh, happy day. I
swept my light across the space, yawning and dark, with four
desks, a worktable, assorted chairs, and a copy machine. File
cabinets were built along the periphery of the room with an
additional double bank down the middle. On the far wall, I
saw a second door. I crossed and tried that knob and was delighted to find that it was unlocked as well. I poked my head
in. From a quick survey of the space beyond, I realized I'd
gained access to Admissions; all three offices were connected
by a series of interior doors. I was sure the medical records
personnel, the secretaries, and front office clerks appreciated
the ease with which they could move from one department to
the next without resorting to the public corridor. I was getting
happier by the minute.

I went back into the Medical Records department. I focused on the job at hand, that being to find Klotilde's chart in
this warehouse of densely packed medical records. I toured
with my tiny handheld beam, scanning the drawer fronts for a
clue about the game plan here. I'd hoped for an organizing
principle as basic as *A, B, C*. No such luck. I opened the first
drawer and stared at the endless march of paperwork. The
charts seemed to be arranged according to a number system—
a row of six digits. I selected fifteen charts, which I chose
randomly, looking for the underlying principle that linked
that particular run of charts. None of the fifteen patients
shared age, sex, diagnosis, or attending physician. I stood
there and stared. I flipped pages back and forth. I couldn't see
the pattern. I opened the next drawer down. Still, not a patient
name in sight. I moved to the bottom drawer and tried ten
more charts. I couldn't spot the defining shared characteris-
tics. The patient identification numbers bounced all over the

place: 698727 ... 363427 ... 134627. I tried a file drawer two cabinets over. How could I hope to find Klotilde's chart when there had to be thousands more in these drawers? I looked for a common denominator: 500773 ... 509673 ... 604073. I'm embarrassed to say how long it took me to spot the element that linked each particular series of charts, but it did finally dawn on me that they were grouped according to the last two digits in the numerical sequence.

I pulled out the scrap of paper on which I'd jotted down her Medicare number. It seemed to bear no relationship to the numbers on the charts, which were apparently assigned to each patient on admission. I could feel my frustration mount. I really hate it when my illegal efforts turn out to be fruitless as well. Somewhere in this room there had to be a list of patients in alphabetical order. Nobody could keep track of all these charts otherwise. I closed the file drawers and made a circuit of the room. The beam from my flashlight had taken on that worrisome yellow tint that suggests the battery is about to peter out and die.

I checked the windows. No sign of movement in the parking lot. I crossed to the light switch and turned the damn thing on. I did a slow visual assessment, turning in a circle so that I could take in every aspect of the room. Near the door, I spotted an eleven-by-fourteen-inch book with a heavy cover, containing what looked like computer-generated pages to a height of three to four inches. I moved over to the book and opened the front cover. Oh, glory. This was the Master Patient Index, laid out, most blessedly, in alphabetical order. I found Klotilde's impossible last name, picked up her patient ID number, and went back to work. I left the lights on, thinking, *To hell with it*. I renewed my search, this time tracking her chart according to the last two digits in her patient ID number. I found her within minutes, removed her chart from the drawer, and stuffed it down the front of my underpants.

I flipped the lights out and moved back into Administration. I was just about to let myself out into the corridor when I had the following thought: *If anyone was ever going to succeed in uncovering the truth, the fraud investigators would need to find Klotilde's files on the premises. "Down my underpants" was not going to be admissible in a court of law. Once I removed the records from this facility, the evidence would be tainted and the proof of Dow's innocence or guilt would be irreparably compromised.*

Well, shit.

I flew back into the Medical Records department, where I laid the chart open on the nearest desk. The pages were filed in reverse chronology: the most recent entries first, going back page by page to the last in the chart, which was her admissions form. I lifted the prongs and removed the metal clasp. Heart pounding with panic and impatience, I lifted the cover of the copy machine and laid the first sheet facedown. I pressed the button. With a whirring, the copier began to warm up. At an agonizing pace, the bar of light traced its way across the data and then back. The finished copy slowly appeared in the tray to my left. I lifted the cover and replaced the first sheet with the second. At least there was plenty of light to see by. Many of the doctors' notes were cursory, and I could see where the cheaters might take advantage of the gaps. Aside from the items of a medical nature, who could possibly track back and determine if the patient received Steri-strips or a bottle of baby lotion? As each page emerged, the bar of light glowed brightly just long enough for me to insert the next page. What would I do if someone happened to walk in? In between worrying about that, I worried I was being permanently sterilized.

Sixteen minutes later, I'd completed the run. I straightened the stack of copies and slid those, still warm, back in my underpants. I reassembled the pages of the chart, put the prongs back in place, slid the clasp onto the prongs, folded them over, and secured them. Now what? I couldn't take the chart with me and I couldn't be sure someone wouldn't come along later and destroy the information. I went back to the drawer where I'd uncovered her medical chart. The last two digits in her six-digit patient ID number were 44. I moved over one bank of drawers and slid her chart among the ID numbers ending in 54, instead. That way I'd know where she was, and any medical records clerk would simply discover that her chart was gone. It was always possible someone would stumble across the chart in its new location, but I'd have to take that chance.

I left Medical Records, closed the door behind me, and returned to the main office, where the pulsing dot on Merry's screen provided surprising illumination. By now I was accustomed to the dark and I could see the clock face. 11:34. Time to scram. I pushed through the hinged gate in the counter and I'd just reached the hall door when I heard approaching footsteps. I froze, trying not to panic. The tapping sound of hard-sole shoes was soft but distinct. News must have traveled about the overhead light in the records room because someone was definitely heading in my direction to investigate. I didn't want to believe anyone would actually walk into the office, but in the interest of caution, I made a beeline through the hinged gate. I scanned the area for the easiest hiding place. I crossed to Merry's workstation, pulled out her rolling chair, and crawled into the kneehole space under her desk. I found myself sitting on a tangle of fat power cords, my head angled unnaturally to keep it from banging into the underside of Merry's pencil drawer. The corners of Klotilde's chart cut into my stomach and chest and made a strange crackling sound as I drew my feet up and hugged my knees.

The office door opened.

I expected the light to be turned on, but the room remained dark. I had no idea if any portion of my person was still visible, but I had to trust in providence that whoever had come in would soon go out again. A moment later, the door opened a second time and a second someone entered. I could hear a whispered consultation, a minor argument, and then the sound of the gate as first one and then the other pushed through into the area where I was (I hoped) concealed. Who were these two? Maybe we were on the verge of a burglar's jamboree, all three of us stealing files for differing but nefarious purposes. They had to be up to no good or why not turn the lights on?

Much shuffling of feet and suddenly the two of them were standing in front of Merry's desk. The dull glow of her computer screen shone softly. I closed my eyes like a kid. Maybe if I couldn't see them, the two of them couldn't see me. I heard rustling as someone removed a coat, settled it across the back of Merry's chair, and pushed it out of the way. When I opened my eyes again, I could make out a pair of men's trouser legs and the back of his heels. I could have sworn it was the fellow with the silver hair I'd spied in the parking lot. He now stood toe-to-toe with a woman whose ghostly white hosiery and sensible thick-soled shoes I'd seen earlier. Pepper Gray.

I heard a flurry of indistinct susurrations, a guttural moan, protests on his part, and intimate urgings on hers. I picked up the quiet but unmistakable rip of a zipper being lowered on its track. I nearly shrieked in alarm. They were about to play doctor and I was going to be stuck in the examining room! He leaned back against the desk—I could see his fingers grip the edge for support. Meanwhile, she dropped to her knees and started to work on him. His protests began to die down as his breathing increased. He clearly had a letch for nursie types, and she was probably turned on by the possibility of getting caught.

I did my best to distract myself. I tried to think worthy thoughts, elevating myself to a Zen-like plane. After all, I had only myself to blame for the predicament I was in. I decided to stop breaking and entering. I made up my mind that I'd repent my sins. Not that I wasn't already paying a stiff price, in a manner of speaking. For someone who gets as little sex as I do, this surely constituted punishment of a most cruel and unusual kind. Pepper was only three feet away from me, happily occupied with the guy's throbbing manhood, as it's euphemistically referred to in novels that abound in such scenes. I have to tell you, other people's sex lives are not that fascinating. For one thing, a guy moaning, "Pepper, oh Pep," didn't seem that romantic from my perspective. Besides, he was taking forever and I worried her jaw would unhinge like a snake's. She began to make little encouraging noises in her throat. I was tempted to chime in. From under the desk, even the surge protector made a small enthusiastic peep, which seemed to spur him on. His vocalizing was muffled, but the sounds accelerated and began to rise in pitch. Finally, he grunted as though his finger had been slammed in a door and he was trying not to scream.

All three of us fell back exhausted and I prayed we wouldn't have to pause for a postcoital smoke. Ten more minutes passed before they pulled themselves together. After a whispered discussion, it was decided that she would leave first and he would then follow at a suitable interval. By the time I crawled out of my hiding place, I was cranky and sore and had a crimp in my neck. This was the last time I'd ask Ruby to man the lookout post.

19

IT WAS 12:30 when I let myself into my apartment for the second time that night. I'd returned the keys to the front desk and walked straight out the front door, the stolen chart pages pressed against me like a paper truss. When I reached the parking lot, the vintage automobile was gone. I continued across the asphalt to the shadowy corner where I'd left my VW. Before I slid behind the wheel, I removed the stolen file copies and shoved them under the front seat. The pages looked battered, dog-eared by careless association with my thighs and ribs. I started the engine and put the car in reverse.

Once back in my apartment, I made a thorough tour of the place, assuring myself that all the doors and windows were locked as I'd left them. Tommy Hevener was never far from my thoughts. I was itching to work my way through Klotilde's medical chart, but for the moment I refrained. Instead, I sat at my desk and consigned a few new nuggets of information to my index cards. It was odd reviewing the assumptions about Purcell now that I knew the end of his sad tale. There wasn't any doubt in my mind that the body in the vehicle was his. In theory, I could imagine him substituting someone else's body. In reality, this was not so easily accomplished, especially in a drowning, where critical features remain. It wouldn't take long for the forensic pathologist to compare his dental records and his fingerprints and make a positive ID.

I laid the cards out in a line, arranging them first in chronological order, then in the sequence in which I'd actually done the interviews. I wasn't being paid for this, but then again, I hadn't been officially fired. Idly, I shuffled the cards together just to witness the effect. The story always came out the same. Whether by his own hand or another's, Dow Purcell was dead and the life he'd left behind was a mess. Three questions nagged. Where was his passport and where had the thirty thousand dollars gone? There was also the minor but troubling matter of the post-office box. If Dow had paid to keep it open for his personal use, why ask Crystal if she was still renting it?

At nine A.M., I put a call through to Fiona. Naturally, I didn't reach her. In the message I left, I told her I was hoping to track down the missing thirty thousand dollars and I implied, perhaps truthfully, that someone in Crystal's household might be responsible for the theft. I proposed putting in a couple more hours' work if she'd approve the expense. I was hoping she'd take advantage of the possibility of incriminating Crystal or someone dear to her. If not, I'd probably pursue it anyway just to satisfy myself. Not everything in this business is about the bucks.

It was not quite noon by the time I cleared my office calendar and dealt with phone messages from the day before. Jeniffer had called in sick, which meant she and her pals were off to Los Angeles to hear their favorite band in concert. She'd told Jill she'd dropped the outgoing mail at the post-office on her way home from work the day before. It's not that I doubted her. I was simply curious as I settled in her chair and began to go through her desk. I found what looked like a week's worth of letters piled together in the bottom drawer, among them my newly paid bills, all stamped and ready to go. I promptly ratted her out to Ida Ruth, who swore up and down she'd tell Lonnie and John and get her booted out the door.

Meanwhile, I put the batch of mail in a box and dumped it off at the post office myself. I wondered how soon Richard Hevener would get my letter and what he'd do when he figured out he couldn't cash my check. Too bad for him. He should have made the deposit the day I gave it to him. I walked from the post office to the police station hoping to catch Detective Odessa before he went out to lunch. Apparently, he and another detective had left on foot five or ten minutes before I arrived. I asked the desk officer if he had any idea where they'd gone. "Probably the Del Mar. They've been doing that a lot. If not, try the take-out window at the Arcade. Sometimes they bring back sandwiches and eat at their desks."

I put a business card on the desk. "Thanks. If I miss him, would you have him call me?"

"Sure thing."

I zipped up my windbreaker and trotted down the outside steps to the street. When I'd checked the weather report in the morning paper, the satellite photo showed a thick, white whirly-gig where yet another storm system spiraled toward the coast. The forecast was for morning low clouds and fog, with a 40 percent chance of rain in the afternoon. Temperatures were hovering in the mid-50s. Soon the local citizens would turn all cranky and mean-spirited, depressed by the bitter cold and the partly cloudy skies.

There was no sign of Odessa in the Del Mar so I hoofed it the half block to the Arcade, a sandwich shop with a pint-sized interior consisting of a counter, three marble-topped tables, and assorted bent-wire chairs. The take-out window was located around the side of the building, where two picnic tables and four wooden benches had been added in the shelter of a black-and-white striped awning. Detective Odessa was hunched over a red plastic basket that contained a massive paper-wrapped burger and a load of fries. The detective sitting across the table from him was Jonah Robb. This was better than I'd hoped.

I'd met Jonah initially about four years before when he was working Missing Persons and I was looking for one. He'd since been transferred to Homicide, promoted to lieutenant, and made unit supervisor—Paglia's boss, in effect. At the time we became acquainted, Jonah's on-again, off-again marriage was in one of its off-again phases, and we'd dallied for a season on my Wonder Woman sheets. Subsequently, his wife, Camilla, returned with their two girls in tow. The next time I ran into him, he told me she'd taken a job as a court clerk, a career move cut short when she left him again. This time, she'd returned pregnant with someone else's child. The purported father took off, leaving poor Camilla to fend for herself. Of course, Jonah'd taken her in and the last I heard he was busy parenting his patched-together brood. From the onset of our relationship, there'd been entirely too much melodrama to suit me. I'd finally bowed out, but I hadn't yet reached the point where I could see him without feeling a flicker of embarrassment.

Vince Odessa spotted me and waved.

I said, "Hi, guys."

Jonah turned on the bench and we both made a point of greeting each other with a pleasant distance in our voices, eyes not quite meeting. We shook hands as you would with the pastor of your church. He said, "How are you?"

"Fine. How's the baby?" I said. "He must be what, four months old by now?"

"He's great. He was born July 4, right on schedule; weighed in at eleven pounds, eight ounces. What a brute."

"Wow. What'd you call him?"

"Banner."

"Ah. As in 'star-spangled.'"

Jonah hesitated. "How'd you know? Camilla came up with the name, but you're the first to get it."

"Just a raggedy-ass guess."

Odessa gestured. "Sit down. Are you having lunch?"

Jonah promptly held out his plastic basket. "Here. You can have half of mine. Camilla's bugging me to diet. I bet I picked up fifteen pounds in the last few months of her pregnancy. Hers came right off, but I can't seem to get rid of mine." The hunk of flesh he pinched on his side formed a considerable sausage between his thumb and index finger.

I was standing closest to him and thought it'd be too conspicuous if I circled the table and settled beside Odessa, so I sat down on the bench beside him. I checked Jonah's sandwich, which was cut on the diagonal: bacon, lettuce, and tomato, with a gruel of guacamole in between the layers of mayonnaise. I added a snow flurry of salt to the mix. I hate to pass up a chance to give my kidneys a thrill.

"What are you up to?" Odessa asked. He'd caught me with a mouthful of sandwich, and while I struggled to clear my palate, he went back to their conversation. "We were just talking about Purcell. Jonah attended the post."

"Such as it was. Condition of the body, Dr. Yee says he can't run biochemical or biophysical tests. From the gross, it looks like he died from a single contact shot to the head. We found the gun on the front seat. A Colt Python .357 with one shot fired. The cartridge casing was still in the cylinder. Yee says there's a 99.9 percent probability he was dead when he went into the water."

"The gun was his?" I asked.

Jonah wiped his mouth and then crumpled the paper napkin in his hand. "He bought it before he and Fiona split. Crystal wouldn't let him keep it in the house on account of the kid. She thinks he either kept it in his desk drawer at work or in the glove compartment of his car."

Odessa said, "We're trying to figure out how he got up to the reservoir in the first place."

I raised my hand. "He was supposed to go see Fiona. She says he never showed, but she could be lying."

Odessa nodded happily, his mouth full. "Don't think it's escaped our attention that the guy turns up dead practically in her front yard."

"And catch this. She's the sole beneficiary on a life insurance policy. Part of the divorce settlement. We checked it out," Jonah said.

"How much?"

"A million."

"That would do it for me," Odessa said.

"Risky to kill the guy so close to home," I remarked.

"Maybe that's the beauty of it," Jonah said. "Could have been someone else. Lure him up there on some pretext and put a bullet in his head."

Odessa made a face. "How're you going to get him up there?"

Jonah said, "Ride in the same car. You call and arrange a meeting, say you want to go someplace quiet and talk about a situation, but you need a lift."

"What's the pretext?"

I said, "Who needs a pretext? You hide in the backseat and pull the gun on him."

"Then what? How do you get back down the road in the dark?"

Jonah said, "You hike. It's not that far."

I said, "What if you're seen? Now you've got someone who can place you at the scene."

Odessa said, "Could have been two of them. One meets him up there and does the job while the other one waits in a car parked somewhere down the road."

"But doesn't adding a coconspirator increase the risk?"

"Depends on who it is."

Jonah sipped his Coke. He offered me the cup and I took a sip as well. We were silent for a moment, contemplating the images before us.

I said, "On the other hand, Purcell was in trouble with the feds and facing social disgrace. He must have considered suicide. Wouldn't you in his shoes?"

Jonah said, "I guess." He sounded glum at the prospect. "The guys are still working on the Mercedes. He had this mohair blanket over his lap, empty whiskey bottle on the floor of the passenger side. Headlights off. Key in the ignition, which was turned to the On position. Radio's off. ID, his wallet, all of that was on the body, including his watch, which is still running by the way. Damn thing didn't lose a second after all those weeks."

Odessa perked up at that. "What make? Hell of an endorsement. We should get in touch with the company."

"Breitling, watertight down to four hundred feet."

Odessa said, "Remember that ad with the fountain pen?"

"That was a ballpoint."

"It was? I'm talking about the one that writes underwater. What was it called?"

"Who the hell cares?"

Odessa smiled sheepishly and said, "Sorry. What else?"

"Not much. The tempered glass in the driver's-side window was crazed—some glass missing, but most of it intact—where the bullet exited. I sent two guys back over there with a metal detector, hoping they can pick it up. The passenger-side window and the two in the backseat were opened, ostensibly to speed the water pouring in."

Odessa wadded up his paper napkin and made an overhead shot, aiming at the wastebin where it bounced on the rim and tumbled out. "I'm not sold on suicide. It makes no sense."

Jonah said, "I'm eighty-twenty against based on a couple of things."

"Like what?" I asked.

Jonah crossed his arms. "Let's assume he shot himself, just for the sake of argument. How did he manage to sink the car? But why even bother?"

"Maybe he was embarrassed," Odessa said. "Ashamed to kill himself so he hopes he can disappear."

"To spare his family the mess," Jonah said.

"Sure, why not?"

"Maybe the insurance policy has a suicide exclusion," Odessa said.

"So what? Fiona can't collect anyway until the body's been found. The minute that happens, the cause of death is going to be obvious. Bullet to the head and the gun's sitting there on the seat?"

"Might have a point there. Nobody's going to believe the guy shot himself in the temple by accident."

Jonah made a face. "Sorry to burst your bubble, but there isn't any suicide clause in the policy. I checked."

"Let's get back to the window on the driver's side. Why leave that up when all the others are open?"

"To muffle the sound of the shot," I said.

"Yeah, but why does he care? I mean, what's it to him if someone hears the gun go off? He's knows he's a dead man, so what difference does it make?"

"Wouldn't muffle much anyway if the other three windows were wide open," Odessa pointed out.

Jonah said, "Exactly. Something about it doesn't sit right. I don't like the redundancy. Shoot yourself before you drown? Seems like a bit much."

Odessa said, "Most suicides don't go in for drowning. It's too tough. Even if you want to die, your overwhelming impulse is to come up for air. Too hard to control."

"Virginia Woolf did it that way," I said. "She put stones in her pockets and walked into the water."

"But why double up the effort? That's what bugs me."

Odessa said, "People do it all the time. Take an overdose

of pills and put your head in a plastic bag. Mix vodka and Valium before you slit your wrists. One doesn't work, you have the other to fall back on."

Jonah shook his head. "I'm just trying to picture it. What's the order of business here? He opens three windows, puts a blanket over his lap, takes out his gun, puts it to his temple, and pulls the trigger. Meanwhile, the engine's running, he's got the car in gear, and his foot on the brake. Blam. Foot slides off the brake pedal, car rolls down the hill and into the lake. It's too elaborate. Seems like overkill."

"As it were," Odessa said.

"Another thing. I don't like the whiskey bottle. It's melodramatic. Guy wants to off himself, why's he need to take a drink?"

"To calm his nerves?" I suggested.

"Nah, you don't need an excuse to drink," Odessa said. "You drink because you love it and what better occasion? Toast yourself before you go. Bon voyage and all that."

"Yeah, but everything I heard about him, he's a straight-ahead kind of guy. Doesn't seem like his style, this whole complicated setup."

I said, "He did drink. A friend of his told me when he disappeared before, he was off at rehab getting dried out. I guess he fell off the wagon the last six months or so."

Odessa said, "I'd been him, I'd have put together a nice little cocktail of really fine drugs. He must've had access to anything he wanted. Vicodin, Codeine, Percocet, Halcion . . ."

"I'd be worried about constipation," I said to no one in particular.

Jonah was still feeling argumentative. "Drugs take too long. He knows enough about human anatomy to do the job right. Path the bullet took, I'm telling you that was the end of that."

"Pretty messy, though, for a guy that conservative," I said.

"The quick glimpse I got, he died in his suit, wearing a dress shirt and tie."

"And his seat belt," Jonah added.

"Nothing conservative about his marriage. A Las Vegas show tart? That's a walk on the wild side," Odessa said.

"Maybe that's not as much of a stretch as you think. Fiona claims he was having problems with impotency, getting into sex toys and pornography, that sort of thing. She thought it was disgusting. She says she refused to have anything to do with him and that's when he went out and found Crystal." I popped the rest of the sandwich in my mouth and reached for one of Odessa's fries.

Jonah said, "It bugs me there's no note. The guy might've been desperate, but he's not mean-spirited. Suppose the car's never found. Why leave everyone hanging? Guy wants to kill himself, all he has to say, 'Sorry, folks, but that's it. I can't take any more and I'm out of here.' And why put the car at the bottom of the lake? What's the point of that move?"

"Right," Jonah said. "What if we take the opposite tack. Let's say somebody did it for him. You shoot him with the windows up to muffle the sound. Then you open three of 'em to make sure the car sinks fast. You don't want an air bubble caught against the roof because the whole thing might float. The deal wouldn't be that hard to pull off. You do the guy, get out, release the emergency brake, give the car a quick shove, and send it on its merry way."

Odessa said, "Which brings us right back around to where we started. Look at it as murder, then the sinking of the car makes a lot more sense."

"The killer assumes the car's twenty feet down and won't be found," I said.

"Exactly. Now the scenario heats up. You find the car, and now he's forced to cope with something he never counted on."

I said, "If you're looking for a motive, I heard a rumor that Crystal was having an affair."

"Who with?"

"A personal trainer of hers. Some guy she worked with eight or ten months ago."

Odessa glanced at his watch. "Hey, I gotta get a move on. I promised Sherry I'd run an errand." He stood and picked up his plastic basket, picking up Jonah's as well. Jonah offered to help, but he was already at the take-out window. He left the baskets on the counter. "I'll see you back at the place."

"I better be going myself. You walking in that direction?"

I said, "Sure, if you don't mind." I picked up my shoulder bag and we walked for a beat in silence. "So how are things really?"

"Better than you'd think," he said.

"Good. I'm glad to hear it. I hope it works out for you."

"Something I never said. That time we spent together, I appreciate what you did. You helped me keep my head on straight or I'd have never made it through."

"I didn't see you as a charity," I said.

"That's how I feel, though; fucking grateful."

"Well, I am, too." I took his arm for a moment and then thought better of it. I moved my hand, pretending to adjust my bag higher on my shoulder. "You know, I'm still on Fiona's payroll and I owe her some hours."

"Meaning what?"

"I was going to clear this with Odessa, but it's probably better if I talk to you. I went through my notes last night and I'm curious about Dow's passport and the missing thirty thousand bucks. If I can get Fiona to underwrite it, do you care if I pursue that?"

"Depends. What are you proposing?"

"I'm not sure. For starters, Crystal mentioned a post-office box. It was hers at one time, but she claims she let the rental on it lapse. She assumed Dow kept it so he could divert bank statements, but I'm wondering if that's true."

He studied me for a moment. "I can't stop you."

"I know, but I don't want to step on any toes."

"Then don't fuck it up. You find out anything, I want you coming straight to me. And no tampering with evidence."

"I wouldn't tamper with evidence," I said, offended.

"Uh-hun. You wouldn't lie about it, either."

"Well, I wouldn't lie to you."

We paused at the corner, waiting for the light to change. I stole a glance at his face, which was looking weary in repose. "You really believe he was murdered?"

"I think we'll operate on that assumption until we hear otherwise."

I went back to the office. Fiona had left me a message, authorizing two hours, but no more. I sat in my swivel chair, feet on the desk, and swiveled for a bit while I stared at the phone. I was reluctant to call Crystal in the midst of the current crisis, but I had no alternative. If Crystal was upset about Dow, I'd just have to muddle through. I picked up the handset before I lost my nerve. I tried the number at the beach house, picturing her retreating to the place she loved best. Anica answered after two rings.

"Anica, it's Kinsey. I thought you went back to Fitch."

"I did, but then Detective Paglia called this morning to tell Crystal the body'd been identified as Dow's. She called me and I turned around and drove right up. I told them I'd take vacation days through the end of next week. This takes priority. We'll be here until Sunday and then we're going to the other house so we can sort through Dow's things."

"How's she doing?" I could hear murmuring in the background and I got the impression Crystal might have been nearby.

Anica lowered her voice. "She's a mess. I think it's the finality that's getting to her. Rand says she just lost it the minute she heard. She always swore something happened to him, but the whole time she must have been praying she was wrong."

"What about Leila? How's she taking it?"

"Oh, you know her. She was up in her room listening to music at top volume, driving everyone nuts. She and Crystal got into it, so I finally called Lloyd and asked him to pick her up and take her for the day. The quiet is heavenly."

"What about the funeral? Is she planning to have a service?"

"She's talking about Saturday if she can pull it together. She'll have to get the notice in the paper and an officiant lined up. Dow wasn't religious, so this is really more in the way of a memorial to him. I just called the mortuary and they said they'd make arrangements to pick him up. She's having him cremated . . . not that she has a lot of choice in the matter."

"I guess not."

"What happened? Detective Paglia never said, but I'm assuming he drowned."

I could feel my heart lurch. "Ah. I don't know. I haven't heard anything definitive. They're probably still working to determine that. In the meantime, is there anything I can do to help?" The question seemed false even to my lie-corrupted ear, but I had to get her off the subject.

"Not at the moment, but thanks, anyway. I should probably get back, but I'll tell Crystal you called."

"While I have you on the line, I wondered if I could get some information. Crystal mentioned a post-office box she used to keep here in town. I need the number and location."

"Hang on for a second." Anica placed a palm across the mouthpiece and I heard her muffled conversation with someone in the background. It reminded me of days spent at the public pool as a kid. I'd emerge from the water to find my hearing blocked, with much the same effect. It sometimes took hours before the tiny trickle of hot water cleared my ear canal.

Anica removed her hand. "P.O. Box 505. She says it's the Mail & More over in Laguna Plaza. Be sure and let her know what you find."

"I'll do that."

I'd no more put the phone down than it rang.

Mariah Talbot said, "Hi. Are you free to talk or do you want to meet somewhere?"

"This is fine. The phone's secure. All this cloak-and-dagger stuff feels dumb, but I can't help myself. Thanks for returning my call." I picked up a pen and began to doodle on a scratch pad . . . a dagger with blood dripping off the tip and a hangman's noose, one of my specialties. Sometimes, focusing on a doodle helps me articulate my thoughts.

"What's up?"

"Well, here's the situation." I went on to describe the conversation at Rosie's the previous night when Henry had laid out the bait about the jeweler in L.A.

"You think Tommy bought it?"

"I have no idea. I thought I'd report it because the last time we spoke I told you I wasn't going to help. Now the deed's been done, but only because Henry stepped in and did it."

"What a cool move on his part. If it's coming from him, it'll never occur to Tommy he's being conned."

"It's still a long shot."

"Not so. They're hard up for cash and their property is mortgaged to the hilt. The jewelry's their only asset. They have to sell to survive," she said. "By the way, where did you and Prince Charming end up? Not in the bedroom, I hope."

"Absolutely not," I said. "I canceled our dinner plans which he didn't like. He pretended it was okay, but he was pissed. I wish I knew how to dump the guy without setting him off."

"Oh, good luck. He's never going to let you get away with that. Tommy's an egomaniac. He dumps you. You don't dump him."

"He's like a spider. He lurks. Every time I go somewhere, he crawls out. He's really getting on my nerves."

"Well, what do you expect? These boys are both wacko. You ever want to see Richard lose it, ask him about Buddy and the bike."

"Why? What's that about?"

"This is a story I heard when I did the background work. This guy, Buddy, swears by the time those kids were ten, they were already competitive little shits, always at each other's throats. Jared thought it was time they learned to share, so he gave 'em a bike and said they had to take turns. Richard wasn't into taking turns so he stashed it somewhere and told his dad the bike got stolen. For weeks, he kept it hidden so he could ride it anytime he wanted."

"Didn't their father figure it out?"

"No, but Tommy did. They had a mutual friend—Buddy— who'd seen Richard do it. Buddy says Richard was always pounding on him, broke his nose once, so Buddy tattled to Tommy just to get even. Tommy waited until Richard was off somewhere. He stole the bike back and pushed it off the side of a bridge."

"He got away with that?"

"Richard guessed right away, but what could he do? It still pisses him off. The thing about those two is both would rather forfeit everything than see the other enjoy his half. Happened with a girl once and she ended up dead."

"You're really cheering me up here." I wrote THE END on the scratch pad and gave the letters a look of three-dimensions in the manner of gang graffiti. "Happily, I'm hanging up my spurs. I called to fill you in in case one of 'em makes a move."

"Come on. You can't leave me now with the job half done. What about the safe? You have to hang in until you locate that."

"Find it yourself. I'm bowing out of this."

"Just think how good it'll feel when we finally nail those guys."

"What's this 'we' shit? The problem isn't mine. It belongs to you."

Mariah laughed. "I know, but I keep hoping I can talk you into it."

"No, thanks. Nice doing business with you. It was fun," I said, and hung up. I lifted my eyes from my drawing to find Richard Hevener standing at my door, wearing a black raincoat and black cowboy boots.

I felt the icy-hot sensation of a bad sunburn, a stinging heat on my skin that chilled me to the bone. I had no idea how long he'd been there and I couldn't remember for the life of me if I'd mentioned his name or Tommy's in the final moments of my conversation. I didn't think I'd used hers.

I said, "Hello," trying to sound unconcerned.

"What's this?" He pulled an envelope from his pocket and tossed it toward the desk. My letter whicked through the air and landed in front of me.

I could feel my heart begin to thump. "I feel bad about that. I probably should have called, but it seemed so awkward somehow."

"What's going on?"

"Nothing. It's just not going to work."

" 'It's not going to work.' Just like that."

"I don't know what else to say. I don't want the space. I thought I did, but now I don't."

"You signed a lease."

"I know and I apologize for the inconvenience—"

"It's not a matter of inconvenience. We have an agreement." His tone was light but unrelenting.

"What do you want from me?"

"I want you to honor the terms of the lease you signed."

"You know what? Why don't you talk to my attorney about that. His name is Lonnie Kingman. He's right down the hall."

Ida Ruth appeared in the hall behind him. "Everything okay?"

Richard flicked a look at her and then looked back at me. He said, "Everything's fine. I'm sure we'll find the perfect solution to the little problem we have."

He backed out of the room. I watched him turn in her direction, careful not to touch her as he passed. He moved out of my line of sight, but Ida Ruth continued to stare. "What's with him? Is he nuts or what? He seems off."

"You don't know the half of it. If he shows up again, call the cops."

I locked my office door and placed a call to Mariah's Texas number, leaving another message on her answering machine. I wasn't sure how soon she'd check back, but I really didn't like the direction this was starting to take.

20

I HEADED NORTH on the 101 to the off-ramp at Little Pony Road, a distance of three to four miles in light traffic. I found myself reviewing that phone conversation with Mariah, the easy banter between us at the Hevener boys' expense. I was almost positive I hadn't tipped my hand. In the meantime, I had no idea what Richard had in mind for me, but I figured his "perfect solution" lay somewhere on a continuum between small claims court and death. I kept an eye on the rearview mirror, flicking a quick look at any car that pulled up even with mine.

Laguna Plaza is an aging *L*-shaped strip mall, much classier than some, but a far cry from the massive retail stadiums being built these days. No glass-enclosed atrium planted with full-sized trees, no food court, no second and third tiers with escalators running in between. I pulled my VW into a slot directly in front of Mail & More, a franchise that boasted private mailbox rentals, mail receiving and forwarding, copy machines, a notary public, custom business cards, rubber stamps, and twenty-four-hour access, seven days a week.

The interior was divided into two large areas, each with an entrance, and separated from each other by a glass wall and lockable glass door. The space on the right contained a counter, the copiers, office supplies, and a clerk to assist with the packaging and mailing services. Through a doorway in the rear wall, I could see banks of flat cardboard boxes in assorted sizes, continuous rolls of bubble wrap, wrapping paper, and bins of Styrofoam packing fill.

The clerk was gone, but she'd left a note on the counter: CLOSED FOR PERSONAL EMERGENCY. SORRY FOR THE INCONVENIENCE. BACK MONDAY. TIFFANY. If she was anything like Jeniffer, the personal emergency consisted of a tanning session and a pedicure. I said, "Yoo hoo" and "Hello" type things to cover my ass while I took the liberty of walking around the counter to inspect the backroom. Not a soul in sight. I returned to the front and stood for a moment, feeling thoroughly annoyed. Anyone could waltz in and steal the office supplies. What if I had a package to ship or a critical need for a notary public?

I crossed to the glass wall and peered into adjoining space: a veritable cellblock of mailboxes, numbered and glass-fronted, floor to head height, with a slot on the far wall for the mailing of letters and small packages. This was the section open twenty-four hours a day. I pushed through the glass door. I followed the numbers in sequence and found box 505—fifth tier over, five down from the top. I leaned over and looked through the tiny beveled glass window. No mail in evidence, but I was treated to a truncated view of the room beyond where I could see a guy moving down the line, distributing letters from a stack in his hand. When he reached my row, I knocked on the window of 505.

The fellow leaned down so his face was even with mine.

I said, "Can I talk to you? I need some help out here."

He pointed to my right. "Go down to the slot."

We both moved in that direction, he on his side of the

boxes, me on mine. The slot was at chest height. This time, I leaned close, catching a glimpse of mail piled in the bin beneath. The guy was much taller than I and the difference in our heights forced him not only to bend, but to tilt his head at an unnatural angle. He said, "What's the problem?"

I took out a business card and stuck it through the slot so he could see who I was. "I need information about the party renting box 505."

He took my card and studied it. "What for?"

"It's a murder investigation."

"You have a subpoena?"

"No, I don't have a subpoena. If I did, I wouldn't need to ask."

He pushed the card back at me. "Check with Tiffany. That's her department."

Her *department*? There were two of them. What was he talking about? "She's gone and the note says she won't be back until Monday."

"You'll have to come back then."

"Can't. I have a court appearance. It won't take half a second," I said. "Please, please, please?"

He seemed vexed. "What do you want?"

"I just need a peek at the rental form to see who's renting it."

"Why?"

"Because the man's widow thinks he might have been receiving pornographic material at this address and I don't think it's true. All I want to know is who filled out the form."

"I'm not supposed to do that."

"Couldn't you make an exception? It could make a really big difference. Think of all the grief she'd be spared."

I could see him staring at the floor. He appeared to be forty, way too old for this line of work. I could well imagine his debate. On one hand, the rules were the rules, though I personally doubted there was any kind of policy to cover my request. He wasn't a federal employee and his job didn't require a security clearance. Executive mail-sorter. He'd be lucky to earn fifty cents an hour over the minimum wage.

I said, "I just talked to the police and told them I'd be doing this and they said it was fine."

No response.

"I'll give you twenty bucks."

"Wait right there."

He disappeared for what felt like an interminable length of time. I pulled the twenty from my wallet, folded it lengthwise, bent it, and balanced it on the lip of the slot, thinking he might be morally dainty, shying away from a direct hand-to-hand bribe. While I waited, I kept my back to the wall, my attention fixed on the entrance. I entertained a brief fantasy of Richard Hevener crashing his sports car through the plate glass window, squashing me up against the wall like a dead person. In movies, people were always diving out of the path of runaway trains as they plowed into stations, flinging themselves sideways as jumbo jets smashed into airline terminals, or buses went berserk and jumped the curb. How, in real life, did one prepare for such a leap?

"Lady?"

I looked back. The guy had reappeared and the twenty I'd left in the slot was gone. He had the rental form with him, but he held it behind his back, apparently uneasy about letting go of it. I waited until his face was on a plane with mine and tried asking him some easy questions, just to get him in the mood. This is called private-eye foreplay. "How's this done? Someone comes in and pays the fee for the coming year?"

"Something like that. It can also be done by mail. We put a notice in the box when the annual fee comes up."

"They pay in cash?"

"Or personal check. Either way."

"So you might never actually see the person renting the box?"

"Most of them we don't see. We don't care who they are as long as they pay the money when it's due. I notice some renters have fancy stationery done up, acting like this is their corporate office with individual suites. It's a laugh, but it's really all the same to us."

"I'll bet. Can you push the form through the slot so I can see it better? This is a legitimate investigation. I'm really serious about that."

"Nope. I don't want you touching it. You can look for thirty seconds, but that's the best I can do."

"Great." What kind of world is this—you bribe a guy with twenty bucks and he still has *scruples*?

He held the card up on his side, angled so I could see it. He was checking his watch, counting off the seconds. Big deal. Little did this fellow know that as a kid my prime talent was the game played at birthday parties wherein the mother of the birthday girl put a number of articles on a tray, which she then covered with a towel. All the little partygoers clustered around. Mrs. Mom would lift the towel for thirty seconds, during which we were allowed to look, committing all the items to memory. I always won this game, primarily because it was always the same old stuff. A bobby pin, a spoon, a Q-tip, a cotton ball. I would use my thirty seconds to make note of any new or unexpected object. The only sad part of this contest was the prize itself, usually a plastic jar full of bubble syrup with the blower inside.

The rental form was a no-brainer and I assimilated the information in the first two seconds. The signature on the bottom line appeared to be Dow's, but he hadn't written in the data on the lines above. The printing was Leila's, complete with the angled *t*'s and puffy *i*'s. Well, well, well.

I said, "One more tiny thing. Would you spit on your finger and run it across the signature?"

"Why?"

This guy was worse than a four-year-old. "Because I'm wondering if it was done with a pen or a copier."

Frowning, he licked his index finger and rubbed the signature. No ink smear. He said, "Hnh."

"What's your name?"

"Ed."

"Well, Ed. I appreciate your help. Thanks so much."

I returned to my car and sat for a minute, considering the implications. Working backward, I had to conclude that Leila'd intercepted the rental renewal notice when it arrived with its request for the annual fee. Crystal had told me the Mid-City Bank statements were routed to the P.O. box. Very likely Leila had notified the bank, perhaps typing the request on a sheet of Pacific Meadows letterhead, forging Purcell's signature or affixing a photocopy, and asking that the statements for that account be mailed to 505. I let my gaze stray across the store front, thinking how easily she could have stopped by the Mail & More when she was up from school.

I started my car, backed out of the parking place, and headed for the exit. When I reached the street, I realized the Laguna Plaza branch of the Mid-City Bank was located on the opposite corner. Even from this distance, I could see the ATM she'd used to drain the account. All she really needed was the bank card and pin number for the account, which Dow probably left in his desk at home.

True to my word, when I got back to the office, I put a call through to Jonah.

"Lieutenant Robb."

"This is Kinsey. If you don't scrutinize my methods, I'll tell you what I found out. I swear I didn't mess with anything. I left it all in place."

"I'll bite."

I explained my trip to the Mail & More, leaning heavily on Leila's behavior while glossing over mine.

Jonah didn't say much, but I could tell he was taking notes. "You better give me the location of the P.O. box."

"The Mail & More at Laguna Plaza. The number's 505."

"I'll check it out," he said. "Devious."

I said, "Very," on the assumption he was talking about her. "Any idea where she is now?"

"I heard she was up at Lloyd's, but maybe I should check it out. Leila's got a friend named Paulie, some gal she met in Juvie . . . this was a year ago July, I think. Paulie's been in trouble before. It crossed my mind the two of them might be planning to take off. It might be interesting to track Paulie's history and see what she's done."

He told me he'd check into it, and I hung up. I was already feeling guilty. The last thing Crystal needed was to have her only daughter brought up on charges of grand theft.

I went out to my car again and made the trip up to Lloyd's. I had questions to ask him, anyway, and this would give me an excuse. If Leila decided to take off, there wasn't much I could do, but it wouldn't hurt to keep an eye on her.

Approaching his A-frame, I could see that lights were on. I pulled up to the driveway, parked the car, and got out. Lloyd was working in the small unattached garage. He'd raised the hood on his convertible and his hands were dark with grease. He looked over at me without reaction, as though my arrival at his doorstep was an everyday occurrence. I had no idea what he was doing to the guts of the engine—something manly no doubt. He wore cutoffs and a well-worn sweatshirt. Flip-flops on his feet. I could see a smudge on one lens of his glasses. He no longer wore the earring with the skull and crossbones.

"You're Millhone," he remarked as much to himself as to me.

"And you're Lloyd Muscoe."

"Glad we got that straight."

"I was in the neighborhood and thought I'd drop in. I hope you don't mind. Is Leila here?"

He smiled slightly to himself. "Depends on what you want."

I studied the exposed engine, which looked like it was made entirely of parts that would explode. I'd learned to pump my own gas. It was my big automotive triumph. "What's wrong with the car?"

"Nothing that I know of except that it's old and tired. I'm changing the oil, putting in new spark plugs, stuff like that."

"A tune-up."

"Of sorts. I'm taking off in a couple days." He reached in and removed a little knotty thing and wiped it clean with a rag before he put it back. He adjusted something down among the major organs.

"Where to?"

"Vegas. I thought I'd ask Crystal if I could take Leila with me. What d'you think?" He wasn't actually consulting me, just making conversation while he went about his business.

"I can't believe she'd say yes."

"Never know with her. She's tired of Leila's problems."

"That doesn't mean she'd kick her out," I said. I waited for a beat and when he said nothing, I went on. "You think it'd be good for Leila, moving her again?"

"At least over in Vegas she behaved herself. She hates that school she's in. Bunch of spoiled, rich debutantes. What a fuckin' waste."

"She seems to hate everything."

He shook his head. "She needs handling, that's all. Someone like me who won't let her get away with all the shit she pulls."

"Limits and boundaries."

"That's what I said."

"She gets that at Fitch and so far, it hasn't helped."

"Too much carrot. Not enough stick."

"How does Leila feel about it?"

He looked at me sharply. "Feeling doesn't have anything to do with it. She's headstrong and lazy. Leave it up to her and all she'd do is lie around watching TV. Crystal's too busy trying to be her best friend. Doesn't work that way. Kid needs a parent, not a pal."

I kept my mouth shut. Crystal wasn't going to let her go, but I wasn't there to argue with him.

His tone of voice turned wry. "You ever going to get around to telling me why you came?"

"Sure. I could do that," I said. "I understand Purcell came up here to talk to you about four months ago. I was wondering why."

"He'd heard a rumor Crystal was having an affair. He assumed it was me. Too bad I couldn't up and confess. I'd have taken a certain satisfaction shoving that in his face."

"It wasn't you."

"I'm afraid not."

"How long were you married to her?"

"Six years."

"Bad years? Good?"

"I thought they were good, but like they say, the husband's the last to know."

"I've heard your relationship was volatile."

He paused and leaned on the fender while he wiped his hands. "We had chemistry. Stone and flint. We'd come together and the sparks would fly. What's wrong with that?"

"She didn't have sparks with Purcell?"

"Are you kidding? The way I heard it, he liked the kinky stuff. That must have been the shock of her life. Here she marries the guy thinking he's the answer to her prayers. Turns out he drinks like a fish and can't get it up unless she wears high-heeled boots and beats his ass with a whip. It doesn't surprise me she'd cheat. I might have slapped her around, but I never did that stuff."

"Was she faithful to you?"

"Far as I know. I don't put up with any shit on that score."

"How'd you get along with Purcell?"

"Considering he walked off with my wife, we did fine."

"You remember where you were?"

He smiled, shaking his head. "The night he took a dive? I already went through that. The cops were here yesterday."

"What'd you tell them?"

"Same thing I'm telling you. I was working that Friday, the night of the twelfth. I had a gig driving cabs—it's on the company books. Leila was here with her friend Paulie, watching videos. Crystal picked her up Sunday morning as usual. You can ask her yourself if you don't believe me."

I watched him for a moment. "What happened to the earring?"

"Took it out for an interview I had a few months back. Didn't want the guy to think I was a fruit."

"You get the job?"

"No."

"Is that why you're going back to Vegas, to change your luck?"

"Here's my theory. Things get bad? Think about the last place you were happy and go there."

In a fit of guilt, I devoted all of Friday to other clients. Nothing exciting went down, but at least it paid the bills.

The memorial service for Dr. Dowan Purcell took place at 2:00 Saturday afternoon in the Presbyterian Chapel on West Glen Road in Montebello. I donned my black all-purpose dress and black flats and presented myself at 1:45. The sanctuary was narrow, with high stone walls, a beamed ceiling, and fifty pews divided into two sections of twenty-five. Outside, the day was damp and gray and the six stained-glass windows, done in tints of deep scarlet and indigo, reduced most of the available light to a somber gloom. I don't know much about the Presbyterian faith, but the atmosphere alone was enough to put me off predestination.

Despite the fact the mourners were assembled by invitation only, the crowd was sizeable and filled the chapel to capacity. Crystal's friends sat on one side, Fiona's on the other. For some, the decision seemed easy. Dana and Joel, for instance, took their seats without hesitation, studiously avoiding Dow's second wife out of loyalty to his first. Those I judged to be mutual acquaintances seemed torn, consulting one another surreptitiously before they slid into a pew. While the stragglers were being seated, an unseen organist worked her (or his) way through a selection of dolorous tunes, the funereal equivalent of Top Forty Dirges. I used the time to contemplate the brevity of life, wondering if Richard Hevener intended to shorten mine. Mariah, when she'd called back, didn't seem that alarmed. Her theory was the Hevener boys would never risk another murder so soon after the first. This was not a comfort.

Crystal had arranged things in haste and it felt about like that. I guess organizing a funeral is like planning any other social event. Some people have a flair for it, some people don't. What made this one odd was the absence of a casket, a crematory urn, or even floral sprays. The announcement in the paper had suggested that, in lieu of flowers, a charitable donation should be made in Dr. Purcell's name. There wasn't even a photograph of him.

In the matter of seating, I'd suffered a bit of conflict. Crystal had asked me to attend, but since I was still technically in Fiona's employ, I felt fiscally obliged to sit on her side of the church. I'd settled on the aisle in the last pew, affording myself a panoramic view. Fiona's older daughter, Melanie, had flown in from San Francisco and she walked her mother down the aisle as solemnly as a father giving away his daughter in marriage. Fiona was dressed, not surprisingly, in black; a two-piece wool suit with big rhinestone buttons on the jacket and the skirt cut midcalf. Her curls had been subdued under a black velvet cloche and she wore a veil suggestive of the Lone Ranger's mask. I saw her press a tissue to her mouth, but she might have been blotting her lipstick instead of holding back tears. Mel's hair, like her mother's, was dark, though the style was quite severe; hennaed and blunt cut with dense, unforgiving bangs. She was taller and more substantial, in an austere charcoal pantsuit and black ankle boots.

Blanche followed them down the aisle in a voluminous maternity tent. She moved slowly, both hands framing her belly as though holding it in place. She walked as carefully as someone whose soup is threatening to slop out of the bowl. Her husband, Andrew, accompanied her, his pace slowed to hers. She'd left the children at home, which was a mercy on us all.

Mrs. Stegler, from Pacific Meadows, sat just in front of me; brown suit, brown oxfords, and her mop of red curls. There were also numerous doctor types in dark suits and several elderly people I took to be Dr. Purcell's former geriatric patients.

On the other side of the aisle, Crystal and Leila were ushered to their seats in the first pew on the left. Crystal wore a simple black sheath, her tumble of blond hair giving her a look of elegant dishevelment. She looked tired, her face pinched, dark circles under her eyes. Leila had forsworn the outlandish in favor of the strange: a black latex tube top matched with a black sequined skirt. Her short white-blond hair stood out from her head as though charged with static electricity. Jacob Trigg, in a coat and tie, swung into the

church on his forearm crutches. He eased into a seat on
Fiona's side, near the rear. Anica Blackburn appeared and
smiled at me briefly before she took her seat in the pew across
from mine. There was the usual rustle and murmuring, an occasional cough. I checked my program, wondering how Crystal
managed to get it printed up so fast. Altogether, we were
looking at a scattering of hymns, a doxology, two prayers, a
soloist singing Ave Maria, followed by the eulogy, and two more
hymns.

A latecomer arrived, a woman with medium-blond hair
whom I recognized belatedly as Pepper Gray, my favorite
nurse. I watched her shrug out of her coat and tiptoe halfway
down the aisle, where she paused while a fellow rose to let her
into the pew. She walked as if she was still wearing crepe-
sole shoes.

The minister appeared in a robe like a judge, accompanied
by his spiritual bailiff, who intoned the corollary of a court-
room "All rise." We stood and sang. We sat and prayed. While
all heads were bowed, I occupied my thoughts by reflecting
on the state of my pantyhose and my unruly soul. I don't
know why pantyhose can't be designed to stay in place. As for
the state of my soul, my early religious training would have to
be considered spotty at best, consisting as it did of sequential
expulsions from a variety of church Sunday schools. My aunt
Gin had never married and had no offspring of her own. After
I was so rudely thrust into her care by the death of my parents, she fell headlong into parenting without any experience,
making up the rules as she went along. From the outset, she
labored under the misguided notion that children should be
told the truth, so I was regaled with lengthy and unvarnished
replies to the simplest of questions, the one about the origin
of babies being my earliest.

My most unfortunate Sunday-school experience came that
first Christmas in her care when I was five and a half years

old. She must have felt some obligation to expose me to religious doctrine so she dropped me off at the Baptist church down the block from our trailer park. The lesson that Sunday morning was about Mary and Joseph, of whom I instantly disapproved. As nearly as I could tell, poor baby Jesus had been born to a couple of deadbeats, with no more sense than to birth him in a shed. When my Sunday-school teacher, Mrs. Nevely, began to explain to my little classmates how Mary came to be "with child," I was apparently the only one present who knew how far off the mark she was. Up shot my hand. She called on me, pleased at my eagerness to make a contribution. I can still remember the change that came over her face as I launched into the doctrine of conception according to Aunt Gin.

By the time Aunt Gin came to fetch me, I'd been set out on the curb, a note pinned to my dress, forbidden to say a word until she arrived to take me home. Fortunately, no blame attached. She made me a "sammich" of white bread and butter, filled with halved Vienna sausages out of a can. I sat on the trailer porch step and ate my picnic lunch. While I played croquet by myself in her tiny side yard, Aunt Gin called all her friends, spoke in low tones, and laughed quite a lot. I knew I'd made her happy, but I wasn't quite sure how.

When the minister finally stepped up to the pulpit, he made the sort of generic remarks that were safe for any but the most depraved decedent. The service finally ended and people began to file out of the church. I lingered near the door, hoping to catch Fiona before she left the premises. I wanted to set up a time to chat with her so we could sort out the details of our relationship. I finally caught sight of her, leaning heavily against Mel, who walked in tandem with her. Melanie must have known who I was because she shot me a warning glance as she guided her mother down the steps and out to the parking lot.

Anica touched me on the arm. "Are you coming back to the house? Some people are stopping by."

"Are you sure it's okay? I don't want to intrude."

"It's fine. Crystal told me to ask. We're at the beach."

"I'd like that."

"Good. We'll see you there."

The parking lot emptied slowly. The crowd dispersed as though from a movie theater, people pausing to chat while departing vehicles inched by. I returned to my car and joined the thinning stream. The overcast had lightened and a pale hint of sun seemed to filter through the clouds.

The beach house was only two miles from the church on surface roads. I must have been one of the last to arrive because the gravel berm on Paloma Lane was completely lined with expensive cars. I grabbed the first spot I saw, locked my car, and walked the rest of the way to the house. I sensed the crotch of my pantyhose had slipped to midthigh. I hoisted the suckers back into place by giving a little jump. For ten cents, I'd peel 'em off and toss 'em in a bush.

As I turned into Crystal's driveway, I saw the same vintage auto I'd seen at Pacific Meadows. Cautiously, I paused and scrutinized the area, noting that I was protected from view. The entire rear facade of Crystal's beach house was windowless and the roadway behind me was momentarily empty. I circled the vehicle, checking the manufacturer's emblem affixed to the right front fender. A Kaiser Manhattan. Never heard of it. All four doors were locked and a quick look into the front and backseats revealed nothing of interest.

The front door had been left ajar and the sounds spilling out were not unlike an ordinary cocktail party. Death, by its nature, reshapes the connection between family members and friends. Survivors tend to gather, using food and drink as a balm to counteract the loss. There is usually laughter. I'm not quite sure why, but I suspect it's an integral part of the healing process, the mourner's talisman.

There were probably sixty people present, most of whom I'd seen at the church. The French doors stood open to the deck and I could hear the constant shushing of the surf beyond. A gentleman in a cropped white jacket walked by with a tray, pausing to offer me a glass of champagne. I thanked him and took one. I found a place near the stairs and sipped champagne while I searched for the man with the mustache and thick silver hair.

Jacob Trigg came up behind me, pausing as I had at the edge of the crowd. Many of the mourners were already engaged in animated conversations and the thought of breaking into any given threesome was daunting. Trigg said, "You know these people?"

"No, do you?"

"A few. I understand you were the one who found Dow."

"I did and I'm sorry he died. I was hoping he'd gone off to South America."

"Me, too." Trigg's smile was bleak.

"Did Dow ever mention money missing from his savings account?"

"I know he was aware of it. The bank manager became concerned and sent him a copy of the statement with a query attached. Dow thanked him, said he knew what it was and he'd take care of it. In truth, it was the first he'd heard. Initially, he figured it had to be Crystal since the statements were being routed to her P.O. box."

"Did he ask her?"

"Not about the money, but about the post-office box. She told him she'd dumped it about a year ago. He didn't want to press the issue until he'd looked into it. It almost had to be someone in the house because who else would have access to the bank card and the pin number for that account?"

"Who'd he suspect?"

"Crystal or Leila, though it could have been Rand. He'd

obviously narrowed it down, but he wouldn't say a word until he knew for sure. He and Crystal clashed over Leila so many times, she'd threatened to walk out. If he'd had a problem with Leila, he'd have handled it himself. Of course, when it came to Rand, Crystal was just as fierce. Why take that on? There'd have been hell to pay there, too."

"How so?"

"He's the only one she trusted with Griff. Without Rand, where's her freedom? Dow was in a bind any which way it went."

"Why not close the account?"

"I'm sure he did."

"Did he ever figure out who it was?"

"If so, he never told me."

"Too bad. With his passport missing, the cops figured he might have left of his own accord. I wonder why Crystal didn't fill them in."

"Maybe she didn't know. He might have decided pursuing it wasn't worth the risk."

"He'd let someone walk off with thirty thousand bucks?"

"Dad?"

Both of us turned. A woman with a thick blond braid halfway down her back stood behind us. She was in her forties, no makeup, in a long cotton sweater, a peasant skirt, and sandals. She looked like the sort who never shaved her legs, but I didn't want to check. She was too smart to wear pantyhose, so I gave her points for that. Mine were sinking again. Any moment, they'd slip down as far as my knees and I'd have to start hobbling, taking little mincing steps wherever I went.

"This is my daughter, Susan."

"Nice meeting you," I said. We shook hands and the three of us stood chatting for a while before she took his arm.

"I hope you don't mind if we go. This is all a bit rich for my blood," she said.

"She thinks I'm tired, which I am," Trigg confessed. "We'll talk again soon."

"I hope so."

21

As soon as they left, I set my glass down and found the nearest bathroom. The door was shut. I tried the handle and found it locked. I waited, leaning against the wall, making sure I was first in the one-person line. I heard the toilet flush, water running in the sink. Moments later, the door opened and the man with the mustache and silver hair emerged. He smiled at me politely and went into the den.

I shut myself in the bathroom and availed myself of the facilities. Having hoisted my pantyhose up the pole like a flag, I went out and found a perch on the stairs, three steps down from the top, the perfect vantage point from which to view the gathering. Rand was making the rounds with Griffith affixed to his hip. Griff was outfitted in a sky blue sailor suit, and Rand mouthed Griff's imaginary monologue as though the child were a ventriloquist's sidekick. I hadn't seen Leila but figured she was in the house somewhere. Crystal would never tolerate her boycotting the event.

The caterers had finished setting out a cold buffet of boneless chicken breasts, three kinds of salad, marinated asparagus, deviled eggs, and baskets of fresh rolls. People loitered near the table in clusters, everyone trying to avoid going first. Ordinarily, I'd have left Crystal's long before now, but I was curious about the man with the silver hair. I saw him return to the great room, this time in the company of a gaunt brunette, who had a wineglass in one hand, the other hand hooked through his arm. She wore a black long-sleeved leotard under skin-tight black leather pants, cinched by a wide silver belt. The stiletto heels on her boots looked like five-inch toothpicks. This was an outfit more appropriate to soliciting on street corners than attending a wake. Her body wasn't *quite* slick enough to bear up under such pitiless revelations. Her liposuctionist should have slurped another pint of fat from the top of each thigh.

She seemed watchful, her gaze flitting uneasily around the room. Her smile, when it appeared, was self-conscious and never quite reached her eyes. I'm not sure I buy into talk like this, but her "aura" was dark; I could almost see the magnetic force field surrounding her. She was bristling, battle-ready. What was the deal here? The guy seemed to know quite a few people. Relaxed and at ease, he chatted first with one group and then another while she clung to his arm. In contrast to her tartlike ensemble, his suit was well cut, a conservative dark blue that he wore with a pale blue shirt and a tone-on-tone pale blue tie. I pegged him in his late fifties, one of those men who'd aged well: trim and fit-looking. He had to be a doctor. I couldn't think what else he'd have been doing at Pacific Meadows at midnight, aside from the impromptu game with Pepper Gray.

He murmured to the woman and then took his place in the supper line, picking up his plate and a napkin-wrapped bundle of silverware. Though she moved into line behind him, they didn't speak to each other. I watched him fill his plate to capacity while she helped herself to a demitasse of salad and four asparagus spears. He settled on the couch in the only remaining space. He rested his wineglass and his plate on the pale wood coffee table and began to eat. When she tried to join him, there was no seat left. She stood there for a moment, clearly hoping he'd scoot over and make room for her. He seemed intent on his meal, and she was forced to take a chair by herself at a distance. She busied herself with her plate to cover her discomfiture, though no one else present seemed to notice. The server walked by with a bottle of Chardonnay. She looked up at him sharply and held out her glass, which he filled generously.

I sensed motion behind me and glanced up to find Anica coming down the stairs. She paused for a moment to peer over the rail. She was, as usual, dressed in understated good taste: a long-sleeved white silk shirt; wide-legged, pleated black wool slacks; and black leather loafers as soft as slippers. Her auburn hair had been moussed, a pompadour in front with the sides combed back into sweeping ducktails. "Good place to sit. Have you had something to eat?"

"I will in a minute when the line goes down. I've been doing some people watching. Who's that silver-haired fellow on the couch in the dark blue suit?"

She followed my gaze. "That's Harvey Broadus. He and Joel must be dividing the honors. Joel and Dana went off to the country club where Fiona's holding court. Harvey came here. That way, they can't be accused of playing favorites."

"Who's the woman in the leather pants?"

"Celine, Harvey's wife of twenty-ump years. He walked out on her eight months ago and now he's come crawling back."

"Oh, right. Crystal mentioned he was in the middle of a nasty divorce."

" 'Was' is correct. I guess the tab got too steep. He decided he was better off living with her than being stripped of his assets. He's a jerk, but I sometimes feel sorry for him. She drinks like a fish. Most of the year she's either checking into Betty Ford or checking herself out again. The rest of the time, she's goes off to some luxury spa—La Costa or the Golden Door. Nothing but the best for our girl."

"Aren't married people ever happy?"

"Oh sure. They're just not often happy with the person they're married to." I saw her gaze shift. "Uh-oh. I better go down. Talk to you later."

Anica slipped by me and headed down the stairs. I glanced over at the front door, where Pepper Gray had appeared. Anica spotted her and made her way over to the door. The two exchanged polite busses. Anica took her coat and then signaled the waiter, who veered in their direction with a tray of champagne glasses. Shorn of her white cap and white uniform, she seemed softer and prettier, less like a woman who'd perform extramarital first aid. I looked down at my silver-haired friend, wondering if he'd noticed her at the same time I had. Pepper moved into the great room. They had to be aware of each other, but neither paid the slightest attention—no nod of recognition, no greeting of any kind.

Celine looked up and her body grew still, a forkful of food poised over her plate. Anica took Pepper by the arm, guiding her through the French doors and out onto the deck. Celine's head seemed to swivel, her gaze glassy and fixed. She watched Pepper with all the caution of a rabbit when a fox is in range. Either she knew for a fact that her husband was philandering or her radar was superb, probably a little bit of both. It didn't take much to guess how the dynamic played out. He screwed around on her as compensation for the fact that she drank too much, and she drank too much to console herself for his screwing around. As I watched, she got up and left the room.

I waited on the stairs until the desserts had been arranged at one end of the table and then joined the buffet line, which had shrunk considerably. I wasn't particularly hungry, but a seat near Harvey Broadus had opened up and I wanted to take advantage. I filled my plate in haste and then crossed to the couch. He looked up as I approached. Nice blue eyes.

"Anybody sitting here?"

"No, go right ahead. I'm ready for dessert so you can save my place."

"Sure, no problem."

While he was gone, a woman in uniform came by picking up abandoned plates. I focused on the food, which turned out to be terrific. I ate with the usual animal enthusiasm, trying not to snuffle, belch, or spill down my front. Broadus returned with his dessert plate and a fresh glass of wine. "Thought you might need this," he said, setting the wineglass on the coffee table next to me.

"Thanks. I was about to go in search of the fellow with the Chardonnay."

Broadus held out his hand. "Harry Broadus."

"Kinsey Millhone," I said, shaking hands with him. I surveyed his dessert plate: a brownie, a wedge of fresh fruit tart, and a chunk of coconut sheet cake. "That looks good."

"My sweet tooth." He sat down again and balanced his plate on one knee. He chose the sheet cake first. "I caught sight of you earlier, sitting on the stairs."

"I'm not one for crowds and I don't know a soul. What about you? Are you a friend of Crystal's or Dow's?"

"Both. I was in business with Dow."

"Pacific Meadows?"

"That's right. What sort of work do you do?" He moved on to the brownie, making short work of it.

"Mostly research," I said. I took a big bite of roll so I wouldn't have to elucidate.

"Sad day," he said. "I feel terrible about Dow, though I wasn't surprised. He was unbelievably anxious and depressed in the weeks before he disappeared."

Oh good. Gossiping at a wake about the dead. How fun. I said, "The poor guy. About what?"

"I don't want to go into it . . . let's just say he left the clinic in a mess."

"Someone was telling me about that. Something to do with Medicare, wasn't it?" I took a bite of salad while he tackled the fruit tart.

"You heard about that?"

I nodded. "From a couple of different sources."

"I guess word must be out. That's too bad."

"What's the story?"

"We think it was probably an honest mistake, but we may never know."

"Doctors can sometimes be real dopes about business," I said, aping Penelope Delacorte.

"Tell me about it. We were shocked."

"I don't get what went on. I mean, as I understand it, the clinic doesn't actually do the billing. I thought there was an operating company to handle that."

He nodded. "Genesis Financial Management Services. They have offices downtown. Joel and I . . . you know Joel?"

"Met him once. I know his wife."

"Dana's great. I'm really crazy about her. Joel and I own the property through a company called Century Comprehensive, mostly real estate development, though we do other things as well. Genesis leases the physical plant from us. They also handle all the billing: accounts payable and receivable, Medicare, Medicaid—that sort of thing."

"So how'd Dow screw up?"

"That's what we're trying to figure out."

"Because I thought, you know . . . by law your company and the operating company had to be completely separate."

"True. But Genesis has to rely on the information they receive from Pacific Meadows. No one from the operating company's on site. If Dow reviewed and forwarded billing charges, Genesis took his word for it."

"So he could have told 'em anything he wanted."

"Could and did."

"How'd he get caught?"

"We're not sure. It might have been a guardian or relative of a patient who noticed the discrepancies and phoned in a complaint."

"What, to you guys?"

"To Medicare."

"A whistle-blower. Bad luck for him. So the fraud busters jumped in and followed up."

"That's our guess. At this point, we don't know what they have."

"What if it turns out it wasn't him?"

"His reputation's still ruined. A town this size, once you've been tainted by rumor, it's almost impossible to recover your good name. People will be polite, but it's the kiss of death."

"I guess from Dow's perspective, the whole thing looked hopeless no matter what."

"More or less."

"What if it turns out he's innocent?" I said.

"Either way, we're left holding the bag." He glanced at his watch, set his plate aside, and got up. "Well. I better go find my wife. Nice talking to you, Kinsey. I hope our paths cross again in happier times."

"I hope so, too," I said. I lifted my wineglass. "Thanks for this."

"Glad to be a service."

I watched him cross the room, scouting for Celine.

What a bullshitter. Joel Glazer had been on the phone with Broadus the day I talked to him. I wasn't out of his office door before the information was passed on. What Broadus had told me about their business troubles was almost word for word the story I'd heard from Joel.

*   *   *

When I got back to my apartment, the phone was ringing. Two rings. Three. I let myself in and snatched up the phone before the machine kicked in. Tommy Hevener. The moment I heard his voice, I realized I should have been screening my calls.

He said, "Hey, babe. It's me." His tone was both intimate and assured, like I'd been waiting all day in hopes of hearing from him. The sound of his voice gave me a jolt sufficient to make me salivate like a dog. I had to remind myself that while I didn't want to see him, I might need his help in getting Richard calmed down.

I ignored his seductive manner and said, "Hi. How are you?" All breezy and matter-of-fact.

"What'd you do to Richard? He's pissed as hell at you."

My stomach did a flip. "I know and I'm sorry. I feel terrible about that."

"What happened?"

"Ah. What happened. Well." *Think, think, think, think, think.* The lie lurched from my lips. "Lonnie wanted me to stay in the office, so he offered me a fifty percent discount on the rent."

"Why didn't you just say so? Richard would've understood that."

"I never had a chance. He was in such a rage I couldn't deal with him."

"Why didn't you tell me? We could have worked something out. Christ, and then on top of that he found out you went and put a stop on the check? You should have seen him. He was screaming at the top of his lungs. You don't know what he's capable of once he gets like this."

I thought I knew Richard's capabilities. "Can't you talk to him for me?"

"That's what I've been trying to do. I thought if I heard

your version of the story I could reason with him. You blew this one bad."

"You're right. I know that, but it's like I explained to him . . . I thought writing him a note would be less awkward than telling him in person."

"Big mistake. That's what set him off."

"I got that already. What do you think will happen next?"

"Hard to say with him. Maybe the whole thing will blow over. We can hope," he said. "Anyway, enough about him. When can we get together? I've missed you." His tone was playful, but it was all a front. I could either yield to him now or he'd go right on working on me until I did. I could feel a slow, stubborn anger begin to rise in my gut. I tried to keep my tone mild, but I knew the message wasn't one he'd accept. "Look, I don't think this relationship is going to work for me. It's time to let go."

There was dead silence. I could hear breathing on his end. I let the silence extend. Finally, he said, "This is your pattern, isn't it? Distancing yourself. You can't let anyone get close."

"Maybe so. Fair enough. I can see how you'd think that."

"I know you've been hurt and I'm sorry about that, but give me a chance. Don't shut me out. I deserve better than that."

"I agree. You do deserve better. Truly, I wish you well and I'm sorry things didn't work out."

"Can't we even talk about this?"

"I don't see the point."

"You don't see the *point*? What the hell is this?"

"I'm not going to argue. I'm sorry if I gave you the wrong impression—"

"Who the hell are you, thinking you can talk to me like this? You were the one came on to me."

"I'm hanging up now. Good-bye."

"Just a fuckin' minute. You stick it to my brother and I come to your defense and you think you can turn around and pull this kind of shit with me? You're out of your mind."

"Great. Perfect. Let's let it go at that." I set the phone down in the cradle. Belatedly, my heart began to bang like someone dribbling a basketball. I stood there waiting.

The phone rang and even though I was expecting it, I jumped. Two. Three. Four. The machine picked up. I heard my outgoing message and then he hung up. Thirty seconds passed. The phone rang again. I lifted the handset and depressed the plunger, terminating the call. I turned off the ringer and then, for good measure, I unplugged the phone.

I sat at my desk and took a few deep breaths. I was not going to let the guy get to me. If I had to, I'd talk to Lonnie about getting a restraining order. In the meantime, I had to find a way to get him out of my head.

I took out my index cards and scribbled down numerous new notes, filling in a few blanks. Like a Tarot reading, I laid out a spread of cards for review. Joel Glazer, Harvey Broadus, and Pacific Meadows formed an arc. Attached to those cards, there were two more: Penelope Delacorte, the associate administrator, and Tina Bart, the bookkeeper, who'd been fired. Joel Glazer and Harvey Broadus had gone to great lengths to suggest that Dow was at fault in the Medicare scandal brewing under the surface. The one item that didn't fit was the note I'd made about the liaison between Broadus and the frisky charge nurse who serviced him.

I returned to the card for Tina Bart. Where had she gone? No doubt Penelope Delacorte knew, but she wasn't about to tell me. On impulse, I leaned over and opened my bottom drawer. I hauled out the phone book and turned to the B's. When in doubt, says I, why not start with the obvious? Five *Barts* were listed, none of them *Tina* or *T*. There was a *C. Bart*, no address, conceivably short for *Christine* or

Christina. Single women do this abbreviation bit to avoid all the heavy breathers out there who dial numbers at random while pinching their pants. I plugged in the phone again and tried the number for C. Bart. After two rings, a machine cut in. The voice on the other end was one of those mechanical butlers, some computer-generated robot who talked like he was living in a tin can. "Please leave a message." Use of this proto-male was another device used by single women, who like to create the illusion of a guy on the scene. I reached for the Polk Directory and looked for the telephone number listed for C. Bart. The Polk Directory, also known as "the crisscross," lists addresses and phone numbers in two different ways. Unlike the usual phone book, which orders its information alphabetically by name, the crisscross arranges the listings by the street address in one section and by the telephone number in the second section. If you have only a phone number without a street address, you can look up the number in the Polk and find the corresponding street and house number, plus the name of the person living there. Similarly, if you have only an address, you can track down the name of the occupant, along with the phone number, providing the number's published. In this case, I found C. Bart at an address on Dave Levine Street, not far from Pacific Meadows. Penelope Delacorte had told me that Tina Bart was already working at Pacific Meadows when she arrived on the scene. Not too much of a leap to assume she was working nearby. Time to find out how much she knew.

Before I left the apartment, I searched out my old gun and tucked it in my shoulder bag. The gun is a Davis .32 semi-automatic with a five-and-a-quarter-inch barrel, loaded with Winchester Silvertips. During the past three years, I've taken a raft of shit about my use of this firearm, which I'm told is cheap and unreliable—a judgment that hasn't altered my lingering affection for the piece. It's small and tidy, weighing a nifty twenty-two ounces, and it feels good in my hand. I didn't believe Richard or Tommy would actually come after me, but I couldn't be sure. And that, of course, was the nature of the game they played.

22

IT WAS CLOSE to five o'clock as I traveled north on the 101. The afternoon light was already gone. Drizzle swirled through the moving traffic like a vapor and the action of the windshield wipers formed a fan-shaped smear where the mist settled on the glass and was waved away. Dave Levine is a one-way street heading toward town, so I was forced to take the Missile off-ramp and turn left onto Chapel. I swung up and around, catching the street at a higher point and following it down again. I passed Pacific Meadows on my right and began to scrutinize descending house numbers. The building I was looking for was only a block away. I found parking on the street and approached on foot, hunched against the misting rain.

The structure was a plain stucco box, four units in all, two up and two down, with an open stairwell up the middle leading to the second floor. Apartment 1 was on my right, with Apartment 2 just across from it. The name Bart had been written in black marker pen and attached to the mailbox for Apartment 3. I backed up ten steps and checked the second-story windows. Lights were on in several rooms on the front right-hand side. I climbed the stairs, knocked on the door, and waited. Behind me, through the open space between the halves of the building, I could see the rainfall like gauze swaddling the streetlights. A draft of air was being funneled through the gap and it was cold.

"Who is it?"

"Ms. Bart?"

I heard her secure the chain and then she opened the door a crack. "Yes?"

"Sorry to disturb you at home. I'm Kinsey Millhone. I'm a private investigator, working for Dr. Purcell's ex-wife. Could I talk to you?"

"I don't know anything. I haven't seen him in months."

"I'm assuming you heard his body was found up at Brunswick Lake?"

"I read that. What happened? The paper didn't really say."

"Would it make a difference to you?"

"Well, I don't believe he killed himself, if that's what they're trying to prove."

"I tend to agree, but we may never know. Meanwhile, I'm trying to reconstruct events that led up to his death. Can you remember when the two of you last spoke?"

She made no response, but there was information in her eyes.

A shift in the breeze blew a breath of fine rain against the side of my face. Impulsively, I said, "Could I come in? It's really getting chilly out here."

"How do I know you're who you say you are?"

I reached in my handbag and took out my wallet. I pulled my license from the windowed slot and pushed it through the crack to her. She studied it briefly and then handed it back. She closed the door long enough to undo the chain. She opened the door again.

As soon as I stepped inside, she went through the whole process in reverse. I removed my slicker and hung it on a hat

rack near the door. I paused to look around. The interior was a
curious mix of old charm and annoyances: arches and hardwood floors, narrow windows with yellowing wooden Ve-
netian blinds, a clunky-looking wall heater near the bedroom
door. The living room boasted a fireplace with a grate that
supported a partially charred log resting on an avalanche of
ash. The air in the apartment wasn't much warmer than the air
outside, but at least there wasn't any breeze. Through an arch
on the far wall, I caught a glimpse of the bathroom tile, a
retro maroon-and-beige mix, probably installed when the
place was built. Without even seeing it, I knew the kitchen
was bereft of modern conveniences: no dishwasher, no com-
pactor, no garbage disposal. The stove would be original, a
vintage O'Keefe and Merritt with two glass-fronted ovens
and a set of matching salt and pepper shakers in a box on top.
Rechromed and fully reconditioned, the stove would cost a
fortune, though one oven would never work right and the hip
young thing who bought it would unwittingly underbake her
bread.

Tina indicated that I could take a seat in a gray upholstered
chair while she returned to her place on the couch. She was
younger than I'd expected, in her forties and so lacking in animation I thought she might be tranquilized. Her hair was the
color of oak in old hardwood floors. She wore a sweat suit:
gray drawstring pants and a matching jacket with a white
T-shirt visible where the front was unzipped. She had her shoes
off. The shape of her foot was outlined in dust on the soles of
her white cotton crew socks. She seemed undecided what to do
with her hands. She finally crossed her arms and tucked her
fingers out of sight, as though protecting them from frostbite.
"Why come to me?"

"Last Monday, I went over to St. Terry's and talked with
Penelope Delacorte. Your name came up so I thought maybe
you could fill in some blanks. May I call you Tina?" I asked,
interrupting myself.

She lifted one shoulder in a careless shrug, which I took as assent. "I know you and Ms. Delacorte left Pacific Meadows at about the same time. She said the choices here were pretty limited in the health care field. Have you found another job?" I hoped to give the impression of a long, friendly chat between Ms. Delacorte and me instead of the one we'd actually had.

"I'm still looking. I'm collecting unemployment checks until my benefits run out." Her eyes were a pale gray, her manner flat.

"How long did you work for them?"

"Fifteen years."

"Doing what?"

"Front office. I was hired as a file clerk and worked my way up. Nights, I put myself through school and finally got my degree."

"In what?"

"Hospital Administration and Finance, which sounds more impressive than it is. I've always been more attracted to the accounting end of the business than to management, so I was happy where I was . . . more or less."

"Could I ask you some questions about Pacific Meadows?"

"Sure. I don't work there anymore and I have nothing to hide."

"Who owned the building before Glazer and Broadus?"

"A company called Silver Age Enterprises. I never knew the owner's name. There might have been more than one. Before that, there was another company called the Endeavor Group."

I reached into my handbag and took out a little spiral-bound notebook with a pencil tucked in the coil. I made a note of the two names. "With Silver Age, was the place owned and operated by the same people or were those two functions kept separate?"

"They were separate. The Medicare and Medicaid programs were enacted in the '60s and neither had much provision for fraud prevention. The regulations about arm's-length ownership and operations probably didn't come until the late '70s, when Congress passed legislation establishing fraud control units . . . for all the good that did. You have no idea how many different agencies go after these guys: the Office of Inspector General, the civil and criminal divisions of the U.S. Attorney's Office, the FBI, HHS, HCFA, and MFCU— the Medicare Fraud Control Units. Doesn't deter the fraudsters. Cheaters love rules and regulations. Every time you put up a barrier, they figure out a way around it. One of the many challenges of the entrepreneurial spirit," she added drily. "I saw Pacific Meadows change hands three times and the price came close to doubling with each of those transactions."

I made another note, thinking about ways to check out the dollar figures on those deals. "Did you work for Endeavor or Silver Age?"

"Actually, I think Silver Age was a subsidiary of Endeavor. The head of Endeavor was a woman named Peabody. She used to run all her personal expenses through our accounts payable. She'd renovate her house and write it off to Pacific Meadows as 'maintenance and repairs.' Or she'd put in new draperies at home and claim she'd had them installed in all the patients' rooms. Groceries, utility bills, travel and entertainment—she never missed a trick."

"Isn't that illegal?"

"Mostly. Some of it was probably legitimate, but a lot was fraudulent. I called a few items to the administrator's attention, but he told me, in effect, I'd better mind my own business. He said the company accountant routinely reviewed the books and everything was okay. I knew if I pressed the point, I'd have been out the door right then. It seemed easier to shut my mouth. When Silver Age came in, someone else handled the books for a while. Then he got fired and I took over again.

There was probably some tinkering going on at that point, but I never figured out what it was."

"Why didn't you quit and find another job?"

"I loved the work."

"You could have loved the same work somewhere else, couldn't you?"

"True, but I got stubborn. I figured one day they'd crash and burn and I'd be there to watch, maybe throw additional fuel on the fire."

"Did anything change when Dr. Purcell arrived on the scene?"

"Not the first couple of months. Then I noticed an increase in the number of charge slips for things like ambulance service and physical therapy, portable X-ray equipment, wheelchairs. I started keeping notes and then I wrote a memo to Mr. Harrington, the head of the billing department at Genesis. That was a mistake as it turned out, but I didn't care. He never said as much, but I'm sure he didn't appreciate the effort because it put him on the spot."

"You were a regular troublemaker."

"I sincerely hope so."

"So even before the audit, they were unhappy with you."

She nodded and said, "Very. They let some time pass and then they fired me. Dr. Purcell tried to intervene, but he had no power and he was overruled. Penelope got upset and she quit in a huff, which really worked in their favor. It made it look like we were guilty of wrongdoing and Genesis was cleaning house. That still gave them Dr. Purcell as a fire wall if the MFCU investigation proceeded . . ."

"Which it did."

"Oh, yes. They're not going to give up until they nail this one down."

"As I remember it, Joel told me Genesis was part of a group called Millennium Health Care."

"It is, but my guess is that some, if not all, of those

companies are shell corporations, set up to conceal the real ownership."

"As in what?"

"Company A, owned by Mr. Smith, buys a residential nursing home. Smith sets up a phony company with a slate of officers who appear to be unconnected to him. His company, A, sells the facility to this second company—also his—at a greatly inflated price, effectively converting the profits into capital gains . . ."

"Which are taxed at a lower rate," I said.

"Right. The second company can use the trumped-up value of the newly purchased facility as collateral for new loans. Meanwhile, bogus company C comes along and leases the building and grounds from the 'new' owner with a substantial boost in rents."

I held a hand up. "Hang on a minute." I ran the chronology back through my mind, trying to figure out what had caught my attention while she was laying it out to me. It wasn't anything she said; it was something I'd been wondering since I'd arrived at her door. "The night he disappeared, Dr. Purcell left Pacific Meadows at nine o'clock. Did he, by any chance, stop by to talk to you?"

She paused so long I didn't think she'd answer me. "Yes."

"About what?"

"He told me he had a meeting scheduled with the FBI. He thought he knew what was going on and who was behind it, namely Harvey and Joel."

"But those two wouldn't have been in any jeopardy, would they? I mean, from what I was told, they had nothing to do with the day-to-day running of Pacific Meadows. The real fiddle must have come from Genesis, since the Medicare checks were sent to them."

"There may be more of a connection than you think. Dr. Purcell must have gotten greedy because he began to sign off on charges he knew were fraudulent: X-ray and ambu-

lance services among them. He probably t̶o̶
those. The FBI put the squeeze on him an̶
agreed to help."

"But what would be the point of silenci̶n̶g̶
must be plenty of other people who know ab̶o̶u̶t̶ ̶t̶h̶i̶s̶.
You, for one."

"I never had any real authority. Now that he's gone, they can blame it all on him."

"Did he tell anyone else what he knew?"

"He never said so if he did."

"But why come to you? I gather you didn't even know him that well."

"He wanted my help. He figured I had nothing to lose."

"Do you think he told Joel and Harvey what he was up to?"

"Not if he was smart. I know he had lunch with Joel that day, but he didn't say anything else about it to me."

"I don't get it. With all these agencies at work, how come they haven't been caught?"

She shrugged. "Most of what they submit is legitimate and where the figures are false, everything else looks good. They use standard diagnoses and standard treatments. They're careful not to cross the line in any obvious way. It's like playing the float. They know how far they can push the system before the flags go up."

"But the flags did go up. Any idea why?"

"Someone must have phoned in a complaint because I talked to the fraud investigator last week and most of what I told him he already had in his files."

The phony bills for Klotilde had to be part of the scheme. "I've got some information that should be of help and I'd be happy to do a paper search early in the week if there's time."

"That'd be great. I'll be talking to him again and I can pass it on."

"Something else I'm unclear on. Why take the chance on billing items out to someone deceased?"

Listen, you're dealing with the local, state, and federal governments. You get caught, you say 'Oops' and give the money back. You think the government would prosecute for a couple hundred dollars' worth of 'errors'?"

"Yeah, right. What's the story on Harvey Broadus and nurse what's-her-name . . . Pepper Gray?"

"He left his wife, Celine, for her and then I heard he went back."

I studied her carefully, wondering if she'd answer the question that had just come to mind. "Were you the one who phoned in the complaint to Medicare?"

"Someone else did that."

"Who?"

"I'm not sure, but I suspect she did."

"Pepper?"

"Yes."

"Pepper was the one who dimed them out?"

"Well, think about it. When Harvey broke off their relationship, she was in the perfect position to blow the whistle on them. I noticed her name or initials showed up most frequently on charges for questionable goods or services. She probably dummied up the slips from the floor. Why should she go on protecting him once he dumped her?"

"Well, they're certainly tight now."

"Really. That surprises me. Imagine the bind that puts her in if he finds out what she's done . . ." She let the thought trail, punctuated by a nearly imperceptible smile.

On my way home, I stopped by the office to pick up some index cards. I had two fresh packs in my desk drawer and I wanted to transfer the notes I'd managed to scribble in my spiral-bound notebook. I drove down Dave Levine as far as Capillo, where I made a left. Passing State Street, I could see that downtown Santa Teresa was deserted in the rain. It was after six P.M. on a Saturday and most retail stores had closed.

Their windows were lighted, but the interiors were dim, sporting just enough wattage to foil the roving bands of burglars. I turned into the driveway running under Lonnie's building and parked in the narrow lot beyond.

I got out and locked my car door. Over the back wall, I could see lights coming from the cottage across the alleyway. I was unable to resist looking at the office space I'd leased one short week ago. The parking lot was empty: no sign of Tommy's pickup truck or his little red Porsche. The upper shutters along the right side of the one-story building were open, but the lowers had been closed. I saw a shadow intersect the light. Maybe Richard was showing the office to someone new.

I turned away from the sight, knowing I was well out of it. What was done was done and there was no point entertaining regrets. I counted myself lucky Mariah Talbot had showed up when she did. Otherwise, I'd be renting from a couple of stone-cold killers. I crossed Lonnie's lot and trotted up the stairs to the third floor. I let myself into the law offices, which were lighted but empty. I went down the silent inner corridor and unlocked my office door.

I crossed to my desk, opened the bottom drawer, and picked up the two packs of blank index cards still in their cellophane wrap. I opened one and began to make notes. For the next hour, I felt safe, absorbed in my work. At 7:15 I put a rubber band around my note cards and tucked them in my handbag along with the extra pack of blank cards.

I locked the office and let myself out again, trotting down the outside stairs. At the first turn, I glanced out through the opening in the stairwell. It's not a window in any true sense of the word, just a slot, one foot wide and maybe two feet high, intended to help with ventilation. From the second floor, I had a clear view across the alleyway to the rear of the Heveners' cottage. The back door now stood wide open. In the office to the right (which I still thought of as mine) the shutters stood open. The light was on, but the window now had the blank look of unoccupied space. Something seemed off, but I wasn't quite sure what it was. Maybe someone had gone out for a moment, leaving the backdoor open for convenience. Whatever it was, I had no intention of going over there to snoop around.

I continued down the stairs and crossed the small parking lot to my car. I drove home by way of the supermarket, stopping long enough to pick up toilet paper, wine, milk, bread, eggs, Kleenex, and a tall stack of frozen entrées. Once in my neighborhood, I was forced to park a block and a half away, which annoyed me to no end. With my bag and two loads of groceries, I had to struggle to let myself in the gate. Halfway across the patio, I caught a flash of movement to my right and someone stepped out of the dark. I jumped half a foot, barely managing to suppress a scream as I dropped one grocery bag and clutched at the other one. Tommy Hevener stood there, hands in his raincoat pockets. "Hey."

"Goddamn it! Don't do that! What are you doing here?"

"Let's talk."

"I don't want to talk. Now get out of my way." I hunkered to pick up my keys. One bag had ripped. I began to toss items back into the other bag. Half the carton of eggs were broken and the bread was mashed flat where I'd grabbed it in haste. I had no idea how I'd get into the apartment, lugging the few items that were still intact. "Oh, forget it," I said. I found my keys and crossed to my door, aware that Tommy had moved to intercept my path. He stretched out an arm, hand flat on the door, his body crowding against mine.

I turned my face to one side, trying to avoid contact. "Get away from me." I thought about my gun.

"Not until you tell me what's going on."

"If you don't get off me, I'm going to scream."

"You won't scream," he murmured.

"HENRY!"

"Shh!"

"HENRY!!"

Henry's back light went on. I saw his face appear in the door.

"HELP!"

"Bitch," Tommy said.

Henry came out the back door with a baseball bat. Tommy glanced at him, turned, and walked away at a leisurely pace, showing his contempt, showing he wasn't intimidated. Henry came across the patio at a quick clip, bat raised, looking as angry as I've ever seen him. I could hear Tommy's heels clatter down the sidewalk, sound diminishing. "What was that about? Should I call the police?"

"Don't bother. By the time they get here, he'll be gone."

"Did he hurt you?"

"No, but he scared the shit out of me."

"I think you should file a police report. That way they'll have something on record in case he does this again."

"I'll talk to Jonah on Monday."

"Do more than talk. That guy's dangerous. You need to get a restraining order out against him."

"For all the good it will do. Really, I'm fine. Would you help me get this stuff in?"

"Of course. Open the door and we'll get this picked up in no time."

Sunday was full of hard rain and gloom. I spent the day in my sweats, stretched out on the couch under a quilt in my sock feet. I went through one paperback novel and picked up the next. I had another two for backup, so I was in good shape. At five o'clock, the phone rang. I listened to the message, waiting to hear who it was before I picked up. Fiona. I felt such relief I almost warmed to her. She said, "Sorry I didn't have a chance to speak to you after the service yesterday. Blanche had her baby late in the afternoon."

"She did? Congratulations. What'd she have?"

"A little girl. Seven pounds, eight ounces. They named her

Chloe. Blanche was actually in labor at Dow's memorial. She and Andrew skipped the reception at the country club and went straight to St. Terry's. There wasn't even time to get her into the delivery room. She gave birth on a gurney in the corridor."

"Wow. That was close. How's she doing?"

"She's fine. The baby had to stay an extra day because of jaundice, but the doctor seems to think she's fine now. We'll bring her home this afternoon. I told Blanche I'd keep the children tomorrow so she can get some rest. I wish she'd have her tubes tied and put an end to this. She can't keep churning out infants. It's ridiculous."

"Well, I'm sure you're relieved everything's okay."

"Actually, I'm calling about something else. Last night when I went to the hospital to visit Blanche, I saw Crystal's white Volvo parked in the driveway of a house on Bay. You know that neighborhood. Parking's always at a premium. The hospital lot was full so I had to circle the block to find a space or I wouldn't have seen the car. Naturally, I was curious, so I went over again this morning and there it was. I'm assuming there's a way you can find out whose house it is."

"Sure, I can do that. Why don't you give me the address?" I made a note as she recited it and then said, "What's your concern?"

"I think she's finally showing her true colors. You know the rumor about Crystal's affair with that trainer of hers, Clint Augustine. I put it out of my mind until I spotted her car and then I began to wonder. Whatever she's up to, I think it's worth pursuing, don't you?"

"Assuming it was her."

"The license plate said 'Crystal,' big as life."

"How do you know she was driving? It could have been anyone."

"I doubt that. Like who?"

"I don't know, Rand or Nica, one of the household help."

"Melanie suggested that as well, though I don't know why either one of you would stoop to defending her. I called Detective Paglia and told him you'd be looking into it. As I said to him, this is exactly the sort of thing they should have been doing from day one."

I was certain Detective Paglia appreciated her input.

After we hung up, I dialed the gym and Keith answered the phone. I could hear weights clanging in the background. The Sunday faithful. "Hi, Keith. Kinsey Millhone. When I was in there last week, I asked you about Clint Augustine. Do you happen to have an address and home phone number for him? I've been thinking a personal trainer might be fun for a change."

"Let me see what I got. Hang on." I could hear him open the desk drawer and then flip through the tattered three-hole binder I'd seen on other occasions. "I know I got it somewhere. Here we go."

I jotted down the information, noting that the address he gave me was a match for the Glazer's house in Horton Ravine. "How recent is this? Someone told me he had a place near St. Terry's on Bay."

"Don't think so. Least it's the first I've heard."

"When did you last talk to him? He might have moved."

"It's been months. Might have been February, March, back around then. He used to come in here regular, maybe eight, ten times a week, although he might have moved his clients to another gym. Let me know if he's out of business and I'll take his name off the books. I got other good trainers if he can't help."

"Great. I appreciate that."

I pulled the crisscross from my bookcase and leafed through the pages until I found Bay Street. I ran a finger down the house numbers until I came to the relevant address. I'd hoped Fiona was wrong, but the listed occupant was *J. Augustine*, though the phone number was different from the one

Keith had given me. I dialed the number Keith had and got a disconnect; no surprise there. That must have been Clint's phone number while he was in the guest cottage on the Glazer property. Clearly, Keith's information was out of date. I returned the crisscross to my shelf. I couldn't believe Crystal had gone looking for Clint the very day of Dow's memorial service. I picked up the phone and dialed the house on Bay.

The man who answered had a phone manner that bordered on the rude. "Yes?" His voice was harsh and full of impatience.

"May I speak to Clint?"

"He can't come to the phone. Who's this?"

"Never mind. I'll try later."

The house on Bay Street was an old Victorian, probably built in the late 1800s: two stories of white frame with a wide porch that stretched across the front. This was a neighborhood where many of the single-family dwellings had been converted to medical offices servicing the hospital half a block away. There was no sign of Crystal's Volvo in the drive. A white picket fence surrounded the yard, which was small and bare of grass, thickly planted with rosebushes, pruned now to clusters of thorny stems. I could imagine, in full bloom, the blossoms would smell as dense and sweet as a potpourri. The soil was darkly saturated from the rain, which was falling now in a soft haze.

I cruised past the house, did a turnaround at the corner, and came back. I parked across the street and settled in to wait. Visiting hours at St. Terry's wouldn't begin in earnest for an hour so the streets were close to deserted. Even protected by a gauzy curtain of rain, I felt conspicuous sitting in the car by myself. This wasn't a surveillance—more like a sortie in the battle between Dow's wives. I didn't want to think about Crystal, whose history with men had been a series of disasters. She'd gotten pregnant by one guy and apparently been left to raise the child on her own. She'd had one husband who

abused her and another who looked oh-so respectable on the
surface, but, in fact, drank too much and had a peculiar bent
in bed. Clint was in his early forties, a good-looking guy, big
and well built. He didn't seem that bright, but he had enormous patience with his clients, whose struggles with fitness
were both diligent and short-lived. The last time I remembered seeing him was just after New Year's when a new batch
of converts arrived at the gym, whipped into a frenzy of re-
pentance after the holiday indulgences. His clientele was lit-
erally always heaviest around that time. Crystal had way too
much class to dally with the likes of him. On the other hand,
she was only one marriage away from life as a stripper, and as
slick as she seemed, she probably wasn't a whole lot smarter
than he. In love, as in other matters, people end up seeking
their own level. I adjusted my rearview mirror, ever mindful
of Tommy Hevener. Just because I didn't see him didn't mean
he wasn't there. I could feel my bowels squeeze down every
time I thought of him.

By 6:25 I decided Crystal wasn't going to show. I'd already
started my car when a white Volvo turned the corner off Missile and headed in my direction. She was at the wheel.

23

I KILLED THE engine and sat, watching as she slowed and pulled into the drive. I grabbed my umbrella and got out of my car as she was getting out of hers. This was one of those occasions where asking a direct question seemed the obvious route. I wasn't going to lurk in the bushes or peep over windowsills in search of the truth. "Crystal?"

She'd already let herself through the gate and she turned to look at me. She wore a rain-repellent parka, cowboy boots, tight jeans, a heavy white cableknit sweater. She clutched a neat stack of shirts against her body to protect them from the damp. Her makeup was light and her tousled blond hair was pulled into a knot. She stood with one hand on the latch and I could see her puzzlement.

"Can I talk to you for a minute?"

Her response time was ever so faintly slow. "About what?"

"Clint. We happen to be members of the same fitness gym."

"What do you want?"

I shook my head. "Someone saw your car here and thought you might show up again."

She closed her eyes and then opened them again. "Fiona."

I didn't cop to it outright, but I didn't see much reason to deny it, either. What was the point? She knew I'd been working for Fiona and who else, really, would be dogging her steps. "You should probably be aware she talked to Detective Paglia."

"Fuck. She just can't leave anything alone. What's she going to do, monitor my actions for the rest of my life? Have me followed around so she can point a finger at me? What I do with my time is none of her damn business."

"Hey, babe. It wasn't my idea. If you're pissed off, take it up with her."

"Oh, right." She paused while she struggled to get a grip on herself. When she spoke again, her tone was more resigned than angry. "Let's get out of the rain. It's ridiculous to stand here getting soaked."

I followed her through the gate. We went up the front steps and took shelter on the porch. I lowered my umbrella, pausing to shake off the water.

"I guess there's no point pretending you didn't see me today."

"I don't like it any more than you do."

"You know, the entire time I was married to Dow, she did everything she could to make life miserable for me. How much more shit am I supposed to take?"

"She's not the only one who heard the rumor about Clint."

"Who'd she get that from? Dana Glazer, no doubt. What an evil bitch she is."

"People talk about these things. Sooner or later, it was bound to come out."

"Oh, for pity's sake. You know what? There's no law that says I can't visit a friend, so why don't you go back and tell her to get fucked." She gestured dismissively, annoyed with herself. "Skip that," she said. "Why add fuel to the fire? Clint was my trainer. We did weights. End of sentence. There was never anything sexual between us. Ask him if you doubt me. I'll be happy to wait out here."

"What would that prove? I'm sure he's too much of a gentleman to kiss and tell."

"Don't you have any male friends? Does everything between a man and a woman have to be sexual?"

"I didn't say you were guilty of anything. I'm telling you how it looks. Tongues have been wagging. Fiona saw your car here yesterday and here you are again today."

She stared at me briefly and then seemed to make a decision. "Why don't you come in and I'll introduce you properly."

"Why would I do that?"

"Why not? As long as you've come this far. By the way, I found Dow's passport when I was going through his clothes. It was still in the breast pocket of the overcoat he wore when we went to Europe last fall."

"Well, that's one question down. Are those his?" I said, pointing to the shirts.

"Someone might as well get some use out of them."

She unlocked the front door, using a key, I noticed, from her own key chain. She pushed open the door and stepped aside, allowing me to pass in front of her and into the house. I don't know why I should have felt embarrassed, but I did.

The front room was done up as an old-fashioned parlor with a camelback sofa, occasional tables, and assorted Queen Anne chairs. Every item of furniture sported a hand-crocheted doily designed as protection from dirt and grease stains. There was a grandfather clock and lots of knickknacks; milk glass, cranberry glass, Steuben glass, Lladro, framed photographs of family members long since deceased. Crystal scarcely gave the room a glance as she proceeded down the hallway and through the kitchen to a glassed-in porch. Clint was seated in a La-Z-Boy looking out toward the yard. She put the stack of shirts on a small wooden table next to him. Crystal gave him a brief kiss on the top of his head. "I brought you some shirts and I also brought a friend. You remember Kinsey? She's a member of your gym."

At first, I thought: not Clint, mistake, has to be someone else. But it was him. Whatever his disability, he was considerably diminished. He was suffering contractures of his hands and a muscle weakness so pronounced that he could hardly move his head. He'd lost an enormous amount of weight. His eye sockets were puffy, a reddish-purple color, as though he'd been punched out. I could see skin lesions on his forehead and his arms. I tuned the rest of it out. Through the window, I could see a burly old guy working in the yard, tying up some vines; probably Clint's father, the man who answered the phone.

Crystal was saying, "We just ran into each other and she was asking about you."

"How're you doing?" I said, feeling like a fool. Clearly, he wasn't doing well and might never do well again.

"Clint has a systemic connective tissue disease called dermatomyositis. Severe in his case. It may be an autoimmune reaction, though nobody really knows. This has been going on since, what . . . the end of January, isn't it?" She addressed her remarks to him, as though for confirmation. "The doctors were hoping he'd go into remission so it seemed advisable for him to lay low."

"Is that why he rented the Glazers' cottage?"

"That's right. I wanted him close so I could keep an eye on him. After the lease ran out, it seemed best to have him move in with his parents for a while." She leaned closer to him. "Where'd your mom go, is she out?"

Clint's response was garbled, but she seemed to understand him, probably because she'd tracked his degenerating speech patterns for the past ten months.

"Why didn't you let people know what was going on?"

"Clint asked me not to and I honored his request. As long as you're prying, will there be anything else?"

"I'll have to tell Fiona."

"Of course," she said. "That's what she pays you for. I'm surprised you'd even mention it."

"It might go a long way to getting her off your back."

Crystal smiled at Clint, who was watching her with a dog-like devotion. "Cat's out of the bag," she said. "Remember Dow's ex-wife? She finally figured out we were having a torrid love affair. Kinsey's caught us in the act."

I could feel myself flush. Clint seemed to enjoy the joke and I could hardly protest. I said, "I probably ought to go."

"Good. He gets tired when we have visitors. I'll walk you to the door."

I could feel a brittle rage radiating from her as she accompanied me. I knew she resented the invasion of privacy, both his and hers. "Look, I'm sorry."

"Forget it."

"Did Dow know?"

"Someone else might have told him. I certainly didn't. People want to believe the worst. That's the hell of it," she said.

The freeway traffic was crawling, cars end to end, apparently slowed by an accident farther up the road. I drove home on surface streets to avoid the mess. All the streetlamps were on and the roads gleamed like patent leather in the falling rain. In my neighborhood, the houses glowed with light. I found parking right in front of Henry's. I was grateful for that as it saved me the half-block of splashing through puddles. I went through the squeaking gate and around the corner of my studio to the rear. Henry's kitchen lights were out. He was probably over at Rosie's where I'd catch up with him in a bit.

I unlocked my door and let myself in. As I closed the door behind me, someone slammed against it from the outside and sent me hurtling. My shoulder bag struck the floor with a *thunk* and I saw my key ring sail off and land on the rug.

went sprawling, hands flying out instinctively to catch my-self. I hit the floor and rolled as Tommy Hevener grabbed me by the hair, pulled me upright, and dragged me backward. I stumbled into him and he sat down abruptly, pinning me across his knees. I'd been flipped like a turtle and I was on my back, flailing for purchase. His raincoat was in a tangle but offered enough protection that I couldn't land a blow.

He choked me with one hand while he squeezed his fingers around my face, digging into my jaw so hard it forced my mouth open. He stuck his face against mine. I could feel his breath against my mouth. "Henry gave you the name of a jeweler in L.A. Turns out there isn't any such guy, so what the fuck was that about?"

The door swung back again and banged once against the wall. I shrieked, rolling my eyes in that direction. Richard was standing in the doorway in his black raincoat. He closed the door behind him, looking on with indifference as Tommy tightened his grip.

"Answer me."

"I don't know. I never dealt with him. Someone told Henry. He was just passing it on. You were there."

"No." He shook my head, using my hair for leverage.

I clawed at his hand, trying to pry his fingers off. The pain was excruciating. "Let go, let go. That's it. That's all. I never called the guy. I swear."

"Tell me you didn't find the safe and help yourself."

"What safe?"

"The fuckin' safe in the office. Don't play dumb. You know exactly what I mean. You broke in. You ripped us off and we want the stuff back."

"What stuff? I don't even know what you're talking about."

Richard said, "Get her up."

Tommy didn't move. His grip on my hair was so tight, I thought he'd tear out a hunk of my scalp. I couldn't move my head. I was nearly sick with fear. What had Mariah done? Had she set me up?

Richard said, "Tommy."

Grudgingly, Tommy loosened his grip. I turned on my side and rolled away from him. I lifted myself as far as my hands and knees, shaking my head while I gasped for breath. "I don't know anything about a safe. I never saw it." I put one hand against my throat, trying to suck down air. "I'd have to be an idiot to break in. I still have a key. It's on my key ring."

I fumbled across the rug for my keys and held them up to him. "Look at this. Think about it. If I'd done it, I'd have closed the place so you wouldn't know. Why would I leave it open and call attention to the break-in?"

"How'd you know the place was left open?" Richard asked. He seemed calmer than Tommy, but no less dangerous. He took the ring of keys and sorted through them until he found the office key, which he worked out of the bunch. He tossed the remaining keys to Tommy. I directed my response to both, looking from one to the other.

"Because my office is right there. Across the alleyway." Richard was silent and I felt myself babbling on. "I'm telling you the truth. Last night I stopped at the office. I looked across the alley and saw the door standing open."

"What time?"

"Seven, I think. Sometime around then."

Tommy said, "Why didn't you call the cops?"

"I thought it was Richard and he was showing the place."

Tommy was sitting with his knees drawn up, shaking his head. "Jesus. You don't know how much trouble we're in. Christ, everything is gone. Every goddamn . . ."

"Shut up, Tommy. She doesn't need to know. Let's get her out of here before someone shows up."

"I'm sorry your valuables were stolen, but it wasn't me. I swear."

"Yeah, well we're sunk, anyway. Wiped out. It's over."

"Knock it off," Richard said, and hauled me to my feet. "You take her. I'll drive."

"*I'll* drive. It's my truck."

"Right." Richard locked his arms around me, pinning my arms against my body. He lifted me off the floor and walked me to the door, half-dragging me, half-carrying.

I grabbed the doorframe long enough to get my feet down. I stiffened my knees, forcing him to halt. "Let me get my bag," I said, gesturing. I felt like a kid pleading for her teddy bear. Tommy leaned down and picked up my shoulder bag. He did a quick search, pawing through the contents. He found the Davis, checked the load, and tucked it in his pocket, tossing the bag aside. There went that hope. I glanced back, watching him turn the lights out and pull the door shut before he joined us on the patio.

His truck was parked around the corner. Richard held my left arm, his fingers digging into me so hard I knew I'd bruise. The two of them crowded against me, walking in a lockstep that forced me to trot along. What were they going to do with me, rape, maim, and kill? What would be the point of that? If they took me to the house, I could scream my bloody head off and no one would hear.

We reached the pickup truck. Richard opened the door on the passenger side. He flipped the seat forward and shoved me into the narrow space behind the seats, knocking my head against the frame in the process.

I said, "Hey!" This was pissing me off. I managed to rub my head while I squeezed into the well. Tommy got in on the driver's side. The two doors slammed in quick succession like rifle shots. Tommy jammed the key in the ignition and the engine fired to life. He pulled out with a chirp that probably left a little skid of rubber on the pavement. I clung to the seat back, trying to assess the situation.

For the moment, I was safe. Tommy was too busy driving to pay attention to me and Richard didn't have a sufficient angle to turn around and level more abuse. Rain was stinging against the windshield. Tommy flipped on the wipers.

I said, "Where'd you have the safe? The place always looked empty to me."

Tommy said, "In the closet floor, under the wall-to-wall carpeting."

"Don't play dumb." Richard was bored.

"How many people knew besides the two of you?"

Tommy said, "No one."

Richard snorted. "What's this, twenty questions? Would you give it a rest."

"Who opened it last?"

"Jesus, Tommy, this is bullshit. Are you buying this act?"

"He did. We had something we wanted to sell. He goes all the way down to Los Angeles on Friday and there isn't any such dude. He thought I pulled a fast one and he was pissed."

"When did he get back? Was it late?"

"No, it wasn't late," Richard snapped, exasperated. "It's five o'clock. I go over to the office and put the piece back in the safe."

"Everything else was still there?"

"Of course it was. Now would you shut the fuck up?"

"Maybe someone saw you with the stuff and followed you back. If they saw where the safe was hidden, they could have waited until you left and ripped you off."

"I said, shut your mouth!" He raised his left arm, torqued around in the seat, and bashed me in the face with a backhanded swing. The blow didn't have much force, but it hurt like a son of a bitch. I felt tears burn my eyes. I put my hands across my nose, hoping he hadn't broken it. Didn't feel like that.

Tommy said, "Hey! Cut it out."

"Who put you in charge?"

"Just leave her alone."

"Why, because you're fucking her?"

"He is not!" Who wants to be accused of screwing some

guy you can barely tolerate? There was a moment of silence. Then, I said, "Anyway, how'd they get the safe open? Was it drilled?"

"You are just not going to shut up, are you?"

I thought the question was a good one, but I shut my mouth and leaned away from the front seat, out of range. The space where I was sitting was small and cramped, scratchy with cheap carpeting. I groped around, hoping for a weapon—a wrench or a screwdriver—but found nothing. I felt along the circumference of the well and my fingers closed over a ball-point. I didn't think it'd be effective, but then again, why not? I clutched the pen in my fist, wondering what would happen if I jammed it in Richard's ear.

The drive to the house took seven minutes at top speed on the wet-slick roads that wound through Horton Ravine. I held on for dear life, the turns throwing me first this way and then that. As Tommy wheeled up the driveway, he picked up the remote control for the two doublewide garage doors and hit one of the buttons. The double door on the left began to roll open and a light came on. He pulled in, coasted to a stop, and set the hand brake. The adjacent bay was empty. Tommy's red Porsche sat in the next bay over and on the other side of that was a second Porsche, a shiny black one, presumably Richard's.

Richard opened the door and got out. He left the truck door ajar. I could see the two big garbage cans just outside the kitchen door where they tossed their trash. Above them, I could see a line of buttons on the wall. I thought he meant to hit one so the garage door would grind shut, but he peered into the truck bed. He opened the toolbox and fumbled among the contents. I measured the distance, but I wasn't going to have time enough to lean forward, pull the door shut, and lock it before he got to me. I turned to Tommy. "You were at my house last night. I saw someone in the office when I stopped off on my way home. You couldn't have stolen anything and then showed up at my place so soon afterward."

He turned to look at me. "What?"

"If it wasn't you, it was him. Who else knew the combination? Just the two of you, right?"

Richard came back with a coil of rope. "Nobody asked you. Now get out."

"Tommy, think about it. Please."

Tommy sat there for a moment. He got out of the truck and moved around the front to the passenger side. "Richard, what are we doing? This is dumb. We should have left her where she was. She doesn't know anything."

Richard scarcely looked at him. "Back off. I'll take care of it."

"Who put you in charge? What the hell is that for?"

"I'm going to tie her up and kick the shit out of her until she tells us where she hid the stuff."

"You're not thinking straight."

"Who asked you?" Richard said. "I told you not to fuck with her. This is all your fault."

"Oh, really. Now it's my fault," Tommy said. His annoyance had passed and there was something new in his face. He put his hand in his coat pocket; I knew he'd put the gun in one pocket, but I couldn't remember which. "You know, she's got a point. I know where I was last night and I can prove it because of her. How do I know you didn't clean out the safe yourself?"

Richard snorted. "Why would I do that? I don't have anyone to lay it off on, if you'll remember."

"You say that now. You could have taken everything to L.A when you went on Friday. You could have sold it all and kep' the money, then come back here and made it look like a bur glary. There's only your word you put it back where it was. never saw the jewelry after you came back."

"That's bullshit."

"I'll give you bullshit. The safe wasn't drilled. Somebody had the fuckin' combination. There are only two of us who knew. I know it wasn't me, so that leaves you."

"Stick it up your ass," Richard said. He put his hand on the seat back so he could reach for me. I leaned forward and swung the pen in an arc and brought it down hard on the back of his hand. Richard bellowed with rage. He tried to grab me, but I scooted back to the driver's side of the truck. Enraged, he flipped the seat forward, prepared to haul me out. I braced myself and kicked twice at his hand. I caught him smartly with the heel of my Saucony, jamming three of his fingers.

"Fuck!" He pulled his hand back, flashing a furious look at Tommy. "Jesus, Tommy. Help me out here."

"Answer my question."

"Don't be an idiot. I didn't take anything. Now let's get her out of here."

"You and I were the only ones who knew. Fuck this burglar shit. There wasn't any burglar."

Richard slammed the passenger side door. "All right, you shit. I'm telling you the truth. I didn't do it. You get that? I wouldn't do that to you, but you'd do that to me because you've done it before. So how do I know it wasn't you?"

"I didn't open the safe. You did that, Richard. You made a point of going down to L.A. alone. The jewelry's gone now, you—"

Richard flew forward and grabbed Tommy by the front of his coat. He pulled him forward and then shoved. Tommy stumbled but regained his footing and came back at him. I saw Richard's fist fly out, catching Tommy in the mouth. He went down, tumbling backward into the two plastic garbage cans that shot apart like bowling pins. I leaned down and reached around the side of the seat, fumbling for the lever that would release the seat back. I felt the lock give way. I opened the door on the driver's side. I slithered through the gap, crouched, and came up along the fender still in a crouch. I could hear the chilling sound of flesh on flesh, a grunt as someone took the brunt of a blow. I lifted my head. Tommy was dragging himself to his feet, trying to free the Davis from his raincoat pocket. His legs seemed to weaken under him and he went down. There was blood streaming from his nose. He moaned, looking up at his brother in a daze. Richard kicked him. He bent down and took the gun from Tommy's rubbery grip. He stepped back and leveled the Davis at his brother. Almost lazily, Tommy put a hand up and said, "Oh, Richie, don't."

Richard fired. The bullet tore into Tommy's chest, though the blood was slow to come.

Richard looked blankly at his brother's body and nudged him with his foot. "Serves you right, you little shit. Don't accuse me."

He tossed the gun aside. I heard it clatter across the garage floor and skitter under the truck. He hit the button that activated the other garage door. His manner was matter-of-fact as he moved around the red Porsche to the black one and got in. He started the car and put it in reverse. Engine whining, he backed out of the garage and down the drive.

I scrambled around the front of the truck on my hands and knees. I crawled over to Tommy to check his pulse, but he was dead. I spotted the gun. I was just about to pick it up when I caught myself. My hand veered off abruptly like an airplane pilot aborting a landing. No way would I mar the fingerprints that Richard'd left on the gun. I got up and went through the back door, turning the deadbolt behind me as I headed for the phone. I was feeling cold with dread, worried Richard would turn around and come back for me.

I dialed 911 and told the dispatcher about the shooting. I explained who the shooter was, gave her his name, a description of his Porsche, and his license number, H-E-V-N-E-R-1. I recited the address in Horton Ravine, repeating everything twice. She told me to remain at the scene until the officers arrived. I said, "Sure," and hung up. After that, I dialed Lonnie.

24

I FINALLY CRAWLED into bed at midnight. Detectives Paglia and Odessa arrived at the Heveners shortly after Lonnie showed up and they at least *pretended* to be sympathetic as they talked me through the events leading up to Tommy's death. They viewed me as a witness, not a suspect, which greatly affected their handling of me. Lonnie rode herd on them, nonetheless, protecting my rights any time he thought they were crossing the line in the course of the interview. The crime scene investigation seemed to take forever: finger-prints, sketches, and photographs; the endless narrative loop, in which I laid it all out again in excruciating detail. They bagged and tagged the Davis as evidence. It would probably be a year before I saw that gun again. Richard Hevener was picked up within the hour, driving south on the 101, on his way to Los Angeles. I figured it was still remotely possible he'd taken the jewelry, but I was not convinced. Lonnie was the one who drove me home.

Monday morning, I skipped the run and then I skipped the gym. I was feeling creaky and sore, my body a patchwork of

bruises. Emotionally, I was feeling battered as well. I drove to
the office and circled the block, finally finding a parking spot
about six blocks away. I hobbled the distance and took the
elevator up. When I walked into the firm, Jeniffer was sitting
at her desk, applying a final coat of polish to her fingernails.
For once, Ida Ruth and Jill didn't seem interested in perse-
cuting her. I found the two of them chatting in the corridor. At
the sight of me, they fell silent and fixed me with compas-
sionate looks. Jill said, "Coffee's on in back. Shall I bring you
a mug?"

"I'd appreciate that."

I went into my office and dialed Fiona's number. When she
answered the phone, we exchanged the obligatory chitchat. I
was guessing she hadn't heard about the shooting because
she never mentioned it. Or maybe she didn't care. That was
always a possibility with her.

In the background, I could hear metal banging, the scraping
of chairs, and assorted shrieks: Blanche's four rowdy kids
spending the day at Grandma's. With Fiona's bare cement
floors, it sounded like a roller rink or bumper cars. I said, "I
have the answer to your question about the person living in
that house on Bay. Turns out it's Clint Augustine's father and
Clint's living with him . . ."

"I told you they were having an affair."

"Well, not quite."

Jill appeared and set a mug of coffee on my desk. I blew
her a kiss and went on to describe Clint's medical condition,
which I gave Fiona by name. I'd read about dermatomyositis
in the *Merck Manual* I have sitting on my desk at home. Altogether not good, and his particular symptoms seemed severe.
"I'm guessing that in the last year, he's been in no shape to
engage in a sexual liaison or any other kind, for that matter." I
found it a relief to be talking about something other than the
night before.

Fiona's response was grudging. "Perhaps I've misjudged her."

"Hard to know," I said, not wanting to rub it in.

"What about the missing money?"

"The cops are looking into it so I'll leave that to them. I won't be charging for the time I put in."

She seemed to shake off her disappointment. "Well, I suppose that takes care of business. If you like, you can calculate what I owe you and deduct it from the balance of the retainer. No need for a final report. This call will suffice."

"Sure, I can do that. I'll put a check in the mail to you this afternoon."

There was a moment's hesitation. "I wonder if I could ask you to bring me that in cash?"

"Sure. No problem. I can have it up there this afternoon."

I was sitting at my desk, cleaning and organizing my files when Jeniffer came in and handed me a note.

Kinsey,
   Sorry I had to do that to you, but I didn't have a choice. Here's the difference between us: basically, you're decent and have a conscience. I don't.
                                                                                    Mariah

"Where'd you get this?"

"It was just sitting on my desk."

Feeling sick, I lifted the receiver and dialed 713 . . . the Houston, Texas, area code . . . and then 555-1212, for Directory Assistance. When the operator came on, I asked her for the sheriff's department in the county where Hatchet was located. She gave me the number and I made a note of it. I let it sit on my desk while I took out the file Mariah Talbot had given me. I glanced through the news clippings until I spotted the name of the sheriff who'd handled the Hevener murder case. I tried Mariah's number first and got the same recorded message I'd heard before. "Hello, this is Mariah Talbot. You've reached the offices of Guardian Casualty Insurance in Houston, Texas, . . ." I depressed the plunger. Anyone can leave a recorded announcement on an answering machine. Anyone can have a stack of business cards printed.

I dialed the Texas number and asked for Sheriff Hollis Cayo. I identified myself and told him where I was calling from. "I'm wondering about two murders you investigated in 1983. This was Jared and Brenda Hevener."

"I remember them," he said. "They were both fine people and deserved better than they got. How can I help?"

"I thought I should pass along some information. Tommy Hevener died last night. His brother shot him in the heat of an argument."

There was a moment of quiet while he took that in. "I can't say I'm surprised. I hope you're not telling me Richard's headed this way."

"No, no. The cops picked up him and put him in the county jail out here. I understand he's broke so the public defenders office will probably handle the case," I said. "One thing I was wondering. Was Casey Stonehart ever caught?"

"No, ma'am. He's gone, disappeared right after the murders, probably the work of them two boys as well. Our best guess is he's dead, but we may never know. Texas is a big state. Lot of acreage available for unmarked graves."

"I understand Brenda Hevener's sister and Guardian Casualty Insurance intend to file suit. Have you heard about that?"

"Yes, ma'am. I believe they're in the process of gathering information even as we speak. What's your interest?"

"I had an insurance investigator come into my office a week ago and I wondered if you knew her. This is a woman named Mariah Talbot."

I could hear the smile in his voice. "Yeah, we know her. 'Mariah the Pariah.' You're talking five foot nine, a hundred and forty pounds, twenty-six years old. Blue eyes and her hair's turned prematurely gray."

"Well, I'm glad to hear you say that. I was beginning to think she'd misrepresented herself. How long has she worked for Guardian Casualty?"

"I never said she did. Fact is, Talbot's the name of Casey's older brother. Got another one named Flynn. I think there's another couple brothers in there somewhere, but those are the two I dealt with. The fact is, that whole family's bad. In jail and out, a bunch of sociopaths."

I could feel myself squint. "And what's her connection?"

"The woman you're talking about is Casey's sister, Mariah Stonehart. The only girl."

I said, "Ah."

After we hung up, I laid my little head down on the desk. I should have known, I guess, but there was no doubt about it, she was slick.

At 10:30 I went over to the courthouse to do a records check for Tina Bart. I figured it would be a comfort to bury myself in endless mundane paperwork, where the chances of violence and betrayal were reduced to a minimum. Besides, I was genuinely curious about Glazer's business dealings, specifically his connection to Genesis Financial Management Services. The MFCU investigator was probably tracking the three larger corporations I'd heard mentioned—Millennium Health Care, Silver Age, and the Endeavor Group. Somehow I had the feeling things were beginning to snowball for Joel Glazer and his partner, Harvey Broadus.

I started with the Assessor's Office in the County Administration building, where I looked up the property tax records for Pacific Meadows. As expected, Glazer and Broadus were listed as the owners. Under their individual names, I checked for other properties they might own and made a list of those. I left the Assessor's Office and walked over to the courthouse to the County Recorder's Office. Files there were arranged

according to the Grantor and Grantee Indexes: those who sell
and those who receive. I spent an hour working my way
through real property sales, grant deeds, trust deeds, tax
liens, quit claims, and reconveyances. Tina Bart had been
right. The Pacific Meadows building and lot had changed
hands three times in the past ten years, and each sale had represented a substantial jump in price. The property was sold to
Maureen Peabody in 1970 for $485,000. She'd sold it, in turn,
to the Endeavor Group in 1974 for a tidy $775,000. The prop-
erty sold again in 1976 to Silver Age for $1.5 million, and
was finally purchased by Glazer and Broadus's company,
Century Comprehensive, in 1980 for a whopping $3 mil-
lion. By calculating the documentary transfer tax on the
grant deal, I could see that the current assessed value was
$2.7 million.

I crossed the street to the public library and started working my way back through the city directories, looking for
Maureen Peabody. Moving back and forth between the city
directory and the crisscross, I discovered she was the widow
of a man named Sanford Peabody, who'd been an officer
at the Santa Teresa City Bank from 1952 until his death in
the spring of 1969. Maureen had probably used the money
she inherited from his estate to buy the nursing home.

On a hunch, I returned to the courthouse and checked the
marriage records for 1976 and 1977. In February 1977, I
found a record of the marriage license issued to Maureen
Peabody and Fredrick Glazer, a second marriage for both.
She was fifty-seven at the time and he was sixty-two. It didn't
take much to figure out that Maureen was Joel Glazer's step-
mother. I was betting Maureen's name would appear again
among the corporate officers of both Endeavor and Silver
Age. The only question remaining was who owned Genesis,
the operating company for Pacific Meadows. I found the
company listed among the applications for registration of
a fictitious business name. The owner of record was Dana

Jaffe, Doing Business as Genesis Financial Management Services. The mailing address was in Santa Maria. For her home address, she'd used the house in Perdido, where she'd lived at the time I was looking for Wendell Jaffe. Joel Glazer had probably talked her into signing the DBA application before they married. She may or may not have understood the significance. On the surface, Genesis appeared to be separate and unrelated to Pacific Meadows. In truth, Glazer controlled both, which put him in the perfect position to reap the benefits of all the bogus Medicare claims. I was glad I wouldn't be around when Dana found out she was married to another crook. She was pissed when I helped to put her son in jail. Wait until she had to forfeit her life in Horton Ravine.

I left the courthouse, blinking at the hazy light as though emerging from a darkened theater. I glanced at my watch. It was now close to noon and I was curious what was going on with the police investigation. I deducted the two additional hours' work Fiona'd authorized. I then went by the bank and withdrew the $975 I owed her. I crossed Anaconda and walked along Floresta to the walkway where the Arcade sandwich shop was located. The take-out window was open but didn't seem to be doing much business. The picnic tables and benches were still way too wet for use. As I passed the plate glass window, I caught sight of Odessa sitting by himself at one of the small marble tables. The place was empty except for him, though the funky indoor coffee shop across the way was jammed. I waved and went in. I sat down in the bent-wire chair across the table from him.

"How're you doing?" he said.

"I've been through worse. I thought you'd be doing take-out and eating at your desk today."

"Too depressing. I need light. Fluorescent bulbs make me want to kill myself." He was working on another paper-wrapped burger in a red plastic basket surrounded by fries.

"At least you're eating well."

Odessa smiled. The damp air had added a halo of frizziness to his already unruly dark hair. Any woman in his position would be despairing, trying a succession of hair sprays, gels, mousses, and anti-frizz products. Paglia had it right: He'd shaved himself bald. Odessa gestured at the fries, fully expecting me to take one.

I shook my head. "I'm fine. I've just been nosing around in the public records. It looks like Dr. Purcell's business associates have been working a Medicare scam and trying to push the blame off on him."

"You're talking about Glazer?"

"And Harvey Broadus. Purcell had figured it out and had a meeting scheduled with the FBI. Who knows how far the two of them were willing to go to keep him quiet. What's the coroner have to say?"

"He found powder tattooing on his right temple. He didn't have much to work with, but he says it looks more like near-contact than a contact wound. Means the gun was held a short distance away instead of pressed right up against the skin. Purcell could have done it himself if his shooting arm was another eight inches long. They went back to scour the area near the reservoir, but so far no bullet. I think they're going to broaden their search. Could be he was shot somewhere else and then the car was moved."

"That'd be tricky, wouldn't it? With him sitting at the wheel?"

"That bugged Jonah, too. You know him. He got to thinking about that blanket Purcell had over him. Mohair, pale green? He asked Crystal and she said it was a gift from her. A year ago she put together this emergency road kit in case he ever got stuck: snacks, flashlight, bottled water, first-aid supplies— all of which he kept in the trunk of his car. Blanket was part of that. Jonah thinks the killer could have spread it over the body and then sat on his lap to drive him up to where we found the car. The blanket was used to keep the blood off his clothes."

"Well, that's pretty cold-blooded. Wouldn't the mohair leave fibers on the killer's pants?"

"Sure. Blood traces, too, but there's been plenty of time to dispose of the evidence."

I picked up a french fry, doused it in catsup, and put it down again. "I talked to Crystal last night. She came across his passport in an overcoat pocket from the last trip they took. What about Paulie? What's the story on her?"

"Jonah had me check on that after you talked to him. She got picked up the first time when she was thirteen. Grandmother thought somebody stole her car so she called the police. Turned out Paulie took it. She also got picked up once for loitering and once for malicious mischief. She's a kid with too much time on her hands and not enough supervision."

"She and Leila are sure trouble."

"We're still working on that. We sent someone down to the school to see if we can get a match on the dates she was off campus and the money being pulled from the ATM. Those girls go any place but home for the weekend, they have to get permission from a parent or guardian, plus an okay from the person they intend to visit. It's already looking like she managed to play both ends against the middle. Not easy to do. School officials have seen every trick in the book, but she's smart. We've subpoenaed the bank records and the records from the mailing service where he kept his post-office box. The D.A. and probation are talking to the judge this afternoon. We're hoping to wrap that up."

"Here's something else. The other day I stopped over at the Horton Ravine house. Leila had left school without permission. Crystal was having fits and gave me permission to search her room. She's got a locked metal box hidden under the mattress. It's probably dope, but it might be the missing money. She and Paulie may be planning to take off. You might be smart to keep an eye on them."

"We can do that," he said.

I got back to the office at 1:15. The rain was picking up again and I was tired of it. A curious depression had descended in the wake of the shooting with the adrenaline rush that accompanied it. The subsequent crash was accelerated by my conversation with Odessa. I envied them the hunt— Jonah Robb, Odessa, and Jim Paglia. Purcell had been murdered and though they might not be any closer to finding out who killed him, the process was under way.

I sat at my desk and I stared at the leaves on my fake ficus plant. From halfway across the room, the accumulated dust resembled a light layer of talcum powder. One day soon I'd really have to wipe that down. I swiveled in my chair and picked up a pencil. I drew a box on my blotter.

I spent the rest of the afternoon catching up on all the chores that I'd been putting off for the past week. I typed up the information I'd unearthed about Genesis and made photocopies of Klotilde's bills, adding as much of her chart as I thought reasonable. I was hoping no one would ask how I acquired the medical data. While I stood there at the machine, feeding in copies, watching the light on the copier go back and forth, I pondered Fiona's request for the $975 in cash. There was probably a simple explanation. I didn't think she was seriously concerned my check would bounce, so it had to be something else. The picture that kept coming to mind was her weedy hillside property. I visualized the front hall of her house with its decor of drop cloths and permanent scaffolding.

I was also brooding about that green mohair blanket Crystal had given Dow, about someone sitting in his lap after he'd been shot to death. You wouldn't want to drive far. Certainly not out on public roads where a pedestrian or a driver in the next lane might look over at just the wrong moment and spot you in the dead man's embrace. If you were the killer, you'd think about the reservoir—how nice it would be if both the dead man and the car disappeared from view. Jonah had been assuming the killer made an unfortunate mistake, miscalculating the position of the boulder, which prevented the car from being fully submerged. What if the reverse were true? Maybe the killer *intended* to have the car found. If Dow's death was meant to look like suicide, then maybe the casual error went the other way. The killer knew the boulder was there and thought the car would still be visible when daylight came. Instead, the vehicle veered slightly and sank too far down to be seen easily.

It wasn't until late afternoon that I opened my bottom drawer and hauled out the phone book, turning to the yellow pages under the section that listed painting contractors. There must have been a hundred, column after column, some of them with box ads, some with catchy sayings: DON'T PAINT YOURSELF INTO A CORNER WHEN YOU CAN LET US DO IT. CHARLIE CORNER & SONS, PAINTING. I had a quick vision of the Corner family sitting around the kitchen table, tossing back shots, coming up with log lines to stretch the advertising budget.

I started with the *A*'s and ran my finger down the names until I found the one I remembered from Fiona's sign out front. One line of print. RALPH TRIPLET, COLGATE. No street address. I made a note of the phone number. Fiona struck me as the sort who'd pick a lone operator, somebody too hungry for business to argue with her. She'd by-passed all the splashy half- and full-page ads.

I dialed Ralph Triplet's number. I was going to cook up a ruse, but I couldn't think of one.

The phone was picked up on the first ring. "Ralph Triplet Painting."

I said, "Hi, Mr. Triplet. My name is Kinsey Millhone. I

just finished doing some work for Fiona Purcell up on Old Reservoir . . ."

"I hope you got your money up front."

"That's why I'm calling. Is she a slow pay by any chance?"

"No pay is more like it. You seen that place of hers? White everywhere. You think that'd be simple enough, but we've gone through six shades so far. Everything from Frost to Alabaster, Eggshell to Oyster. Couldn't find anything to suit. I'd get half a wall up, and then she'd want something else. Too green, she'd say. Or get the pink out of it. Meantime, I haven't been paid in weeks. The architect filed a lien against the property and I'm threatening to do likewise. Meantime, I finally got around to checking her credit. Should have done that in the first place, but how was I to know. She puts on a good show, but she's busy using one credit card to pay off another. What'd you say your name was?"

"Doesn't matter," I said and hung up.

I pulled out the rubber-banded packet of index cards. This time I didn't add anything. I shuffled back through my cards, checking the information I'd picked up in the past week, particularly the details about Dow's last day. In passing, Mrs. Stegler had confided an item that caught my attention in light of everything I'd learned since then. She said while he was out at lunch, Fiona had stopped by. She'd waited in his office and had finally departed, leaving him a note. I'd sat in that office myself and I know how easily she could have opened his desk drawer and taken his gun.

Driving up Old Reservoir Road in the gathering dark, I could feel myself in a state of suspended animation. The only sign of agitation was that I was taking the curves a little too fast for the current road conditions, which were wet, wet, wet. I had an idea, an intuition to verify before I called Jonah Robb. I turned left on the road that angled up beside her property and pulled into the parking area behind the house.

I went around to the front door and rang the bell. She took her sweet time coming to the door. I stared off at Brunswick Lake. In the waning light, the surface was as silvery as mercury. It had been eleven days since I first stood in this spot, looking out at the same sweeping views. The steep sloping lot was now a fairyland of knee-high weeds: fox tails, wild oats, and rye bending in the passing breeze. With much more rain, the now-softened hillside would slide down into the road.

The door opened behind me. Even baby-sitting for her grandchildren, Fiona was decked out in a black wool suit with big shoulder pads and a pinched-in waist. The lapels and jacket cuffs were done in a faux leopard print. She had her hair concealed in a matching leopard print turban. Gloria Swanson had nothing on her. I held out the envelope. "I included an invoice for your records. I hope you don't mind signing for the cash."

"Of course not. Won't you come in?"

I stepped into the foyer. There was a tricycle in the hall and the floor was covered with the same sort of kiddie detritus I'd seen at Blanche's house: Tinkertoys, blocks, a sock, broken crackers, crayons. The kids had built an enormous tent with the painter's drop cloths, which were now draped over all the chairs in the living room. I could see them bumping around in there, erupting in the sort of harsh, artificial giggles that signal the prelude to a big stinking fight.

Fiona scribbled her signature on the receipt. Her fingernails were dark red. She wore the same shade on her lips. She had a smudge of lipstick on the surface of her two front teeth. The effect was odd, like a virulent attack of bleeding gums. I tore off the top copy and handed it back to her.

"How's Blanche doing?"

"She's fine. At least she's had peace and quiet for the afternoon. Andrew's picking the kids up after supper tonight . . . assuming we live that long."

"Mind if I use the bathroom?"

"There's one off the kitchen. You can help yourself."

"Be right back," I said.

Fiona returned to the living room and I could hear her issuing orders about the cleanup. The kids even seemed inclined to cooperate.

I walked through the kitchen and unlocked the door leading into the three-car garage. It was dark outside and the yawning space was gloomy. There was a BMW parked in the nearest space, but the other two were empty. She'd told me when Dow came to visit, she made him pull into the garage each time so the local tongues wouldn't wag. I flipped on the overhead light, which didn't help that much.

I took the flashlight from my shoulder bag and crossed to the far wall. I imagined myself sitting in Dow's silver Mercedes. I looked to my left and calculated the trajectory of a bullet fired from the front seat through the driver's head, through the car window, and into the wall. Right about there, I thought. I'd have bet money she never bothered to pry the bullet out of the dry wall. She'd had enough white paint on hand to cover any evidence of what she'd done. Who'd even think to look here? The cops with their metal detectors would be scanning down the hillside as far as the road.

In the light of the faulty overhead bulb, the wall appeared to be smooth. I ran a hand lightly over the finish, expecting to feel the faintly irregular patch of plaster fill. The wall was unblemished. Not a mark anywhere. I shone the light at an angle, hoping for the roughness in the surface to jump into bas-relief. There was nothing. I made a circuit of the space, but there was no indication whatsoever that Dow had been shot to death here before the car was moved. No fragments of glass, no oil patches on the floor where his car had sat. I stood there astonished. I wanted to wail with disappointment. This had to be right. I had been so sure.

The door to the kitchen opened and Fiona appeared. She stood and stared at me. "I wondered what happened to you."

I looked back at her, mouth suddenly dry, desperate for an explanation that would cover my behavior.

"Detective Paglia was up here earlier, doing exactly the same thing. He checked the walls for a buried bullet and found none."

"Fiona, I'm sorry."

"I'm sure you are." She paused a moment. "One question, please. If I'd actually killed Dowan, why in the world would I hire you?"

I could feel my cheeks grow warm, but I knew I owed her the truth. "I thought you needed to have the body found to collect on the insurance. If you hired me, you'd appear to be above reproach."

Her gaze bit into me, but she never raised her voice. "You're a very arrogant young woman. Now get out of my house."

She withdrew, closing the door behind her with a sharp report.

I let myself out. I got back in my car and started down the hill, reeling with shame and embarrassment. What defense did I have? I'd been wrong about her. I'd been wrong about Crystal and Clint Augustine. I'd been wrong about Mariah, who'd made a fool of me. I turned left at the intersection. I'd driven a block when I caught sight of a familiar figure walking backward along the side of the road. Paulie, with her thumb stuck out. Jeans, hiking boots, the same black leather jacket I'd seen her in before. Nice quality leather, too, and I wondered if she and Leila had paid for it with a portion of the stolen thirty grand.

I slowed and pulled over on the berm while she hurried to catch up. By the time she reached the car, I'd opened the door for her on the passenger side. "Hop in. Are you on your way to see Leila?"

"Yeah. She's staying down at the beach." She got in and slammed the door, smelling of dope and cigarettes. Her hair was brown and straight and might have been shiny if she'd kept it clean. I could see raindrops, like sequins, sprinkled among the strands. She had unconventional looks, but there was something haunting about her eyes, which were large and dark brown. "You can let me off in town. It's no problem finding a ride from there."

"I don't mind driving you. I could use the air," I said. I waited for passing traffic and then pulled onto the road. "You're lucky I came by. I'm usually not over in this area. Were you up at Lloyd's?"

"Yeah, but he was out and I couldn't find the key. I didn't want to wait for him in the cold. Aren't you sick of this fuckin' rain?"

I let that one pass. "The two of you are friends?"

"Kind of, because of Leila."

"How's she going to feel about it when he moves to Las Vegas. Think she'll miss him?"

"Big time. She was really bummed when she heard."

"Is she back at school?"

"Not until Wednesday. Her mom's driving her down."

"Well, maybe she'll get to visit Lloyd once he's settled," I said. "When's he taking off? He said a couple of days."

"Something like that. I'm trying to talk him into taking me along."

"You'd leave town?"

"Well, sure. I don't give a shit about this place."

"Don't you have a family here?"

"Just Gram is all and she wouldn't care. She lets me do anything I want."

I looked over at her. "Have you ever *been* to Las Vegas?"

"Once when I was six." A smile lit her face and her expression became animated. "We stayed at the Flamingo. Me and my sister swam in the pool and ate so much shrimp cocktail she barfed in a bush. After it got dark? We went around and finished all the drinks people left on the tables. What a blast. We were acting like nuts. We couldn't even walk straight."

"I didn't know you had a sister."

"I haven't seen her or my mom since."

I was curious about that, but I'd already asked a lot of questions and I didn't want her to think I was interrogating her . . . though I was, of course.

"I'd have a hard time with the heat."

"I like it. Even in summer, I bet it wouldn't bother me a bit. I could live there easy. What a hoot."

"Seems like money would be a problem."

"Not at all. I have lots." I could hear her hesitate, pondering the slip. Clearly, she'd told me more than she intended. "I could probably get a job parking cars at one of the big casinos. Something that paid good tips. This guy I know says a parking valet can make up to a hundred a day."

"I thought you were sixteen."

"Everybody says I look older. I got a fake driver's license says I'm over eighteen. Nobody checks. As long as you show up for work, what do they care?" She thought she had street smarts, but her notions of how the world worked were wishful thinking on her part. "You think I don't know how to take care of myself?"

"I'm sure you do."

"I'm fine on my own. I'm used to it by now. I'm living on the street half the time, anyway, so better there than here. Maybe Lloyd'll get a place and I can live with him."

"You think that's appropriate?"

She gave me an indignant look. "I'm not *banging* the guy. He's just a friend."

"What will Leila do if you leave? I thought the two of you were inseparable." What I was really thinking was how easy it would be for Lloyd to tuck the girls in the car with him before he left the state. I didn't believe Paulie would go anywhere without Leila. I glanced at her and watched her struggle with her response.

"That's her problem. She'll figure it out."

We reached Crystal's beach house. I pulled into the gravel parking area and Paulie got out. I didn't think Crystal would be glad to see her, but she'd probably be polite. I figured Leila and Paulie, inseparable as they were, would end up in jail together within the next few hours. So much for Vegas and her fabulous career as a valet car park.

I left the engine running, waiting while Paulie rang the bell. I noticed the house next door had a SALE PENDING banner now affixed to the FOR SALE sign. Crystal came to the door. If she objected to Paulie's presence, she seemed to keep it to herself. Maybe Leila was easier to get along with in Paulie's company. Crystal caught sight of my car and waved. I returned the wave and backed out of the drive, my headlights washing across the open carport where I could see the Volvo and the convertible. The slot on the extreme left was empty and I was guessing that was the space where Dow had kept his car. I felt a tiny jolt of electricity. I made the turn onto Paloma Lane, drove half a block, and then pulled the VW over to the side of the road. I got out and walked back to the house. As I moved into the drive, my footsteps crunched on the gravel like someone chomping on a mouthful of ice.

Crystal had closed the door and the area was dark. I could smell ocean. I could hear the pounding of the waves. The quiet was like nectar wafting through the still night air. The rain had left the heavy scent of seaweed, pine boughs, and solitude. I swear the very dark had an odor of its own. *Dare to be stupid,* I thought to myself. *Some people think you're stupid, anyway, so what difference does it make?*

As I had at Fiona's house, I placed myself in a spot that approximated the location of the Mercedes' front seat, picturing the car parked as it would have been had Dow pulled in that night. Maybe Crystal had promised him sexual treats, spelling out the possibilities in such succulent detail that he'd bypassed his scheduled visit with Fiona and come home to his wife. He must have pictured her coming out to meet him in a flimsy nightgown . . . something diaphanous . . . a thin, silky fabric that the ocean breezes would lift flirtatiously, exposing her legs. Crystal knew how to use her body to good effect. She could have retrieved the Colt Python .357 on an earlier occasion. She'd told the cops Dow kept it in his desk at work or in the glove compartment of his car. She had access to both, especially with Griffith's visits to the nursing home. Even if she appeared wearing sweats and running shoes, all she had to do was open the car door, lean across the seat, and kill him as sweetly as a kiss. Driving the body up to the reservoir was a nice piece of misdirection—the risk of being spotted on the highway apparently less important than this chance to put Fiona in the soup. Given the amount of money Fiona stood to gain, the police would naturally pursue the notion that she'd killed him herself.

I looked to my left and calculated the trajectory of a bullet speeding in that direction. After all, if a shot had been fired from a Colt Python across the space of the front seat and through the kindly doctor's head, one could only imagine the bullet traveling right on, smashing the car window, crossing ten feet of space, and plowing through the shingle siding of the house next door.

I crossed the patchy stretch of grass that lay between the carport and the structure next door. It might have once been a detached garage, joined to the house now and converted to a guest wing or family room. I took out my flashlight and turned it on. I moved the bushes aside and swept the beam across the rough-hewn shingles. The bullet hole was big, as black as a spider sitting on the side of the house.

I retraced my steps across the gravel parking pad to Crystal's front door. I rang the bell. She opened it a moment later, with an expression on her face as if I might be someone soliciting for charity or selling door-to-door. She said, "Oh. I didn't expect to see you. What's going on?"

"I'd like to use your phone."

She seemed puzzled but stepped back and let me pass in front of her. She was barefoot, wearing sweats, her hair pulled up on the top of her head. She peered out. "Where's your car?"

"It's parked on the road. The engine cut out and I need a way to get home."

"I can do that," she said. "Hang on a minute and I'll grab my keys."

"No, no. Please. I wouldn't want to trouble you. I have a good friend nearby and he's an experienced mechanic. I'll just ask him to take a look. Maybe he can fix it right there and send me on my way."

"Well, if that doesn't work out, I can always run you home."

From upstairs, I could hear the thunder of music being played at top volume. I pictured Paulie and Leila planning their escape. I really hoped the cops would show up before they made good on their "get-away." I wasn't sure where Rand was. Maybe off in the bathroom, getting Griffith ready for bed.

She showed me into the den and then stood in the doorway while I took a seat at the desk. I smiled at her briefly and said, "This won't take a minute," hoping she would leave. I picked up the receiver and dialed Jonah's home number. If Camilla answered, I was screwed. On other occasions, she'd left the receiver on the table and walked off, refusing to tell Jonah I was on the line for him. When the call was picked up, he said, "Jonah Robb."

"Oh, hi. It's me."

"Kinsey?" He sounded puzzled, as well he should have.

"Yes, it is."

"What's up?"

"I'm at Crystal's beach house. I've got a little problem and I'd love to have you take a look."

"All right," he said, cautiously. "I'm buying this. Like what?"

"No problem. I can wait. Is that convenient for you? Because if it's not, I can always try Vince."

"Well, you know, I'm right in the middle of something. Is this important?"

"Completely. You have the address?"

"I know the place. Are you in trouble?"

"Not yet, but I could be. I'll see you shortly and thanks. I appreciate this."

I replaced the receiver and when I looked up again, Anica had joined Crystal in the doorway. The two stood close together, Crystal in front, Anica slightly behind. Anica's hand was on her arm, and I suddenly understood what I'd been looking at all along. Anica said, "Is there a problem?"

"Not really. I'm waiting for a friend of mine to come give me some help. I had some trouble with my car. He'll be here in a bit."

"Oh. Well, why don't you join us for a glass of Chardonnay while you wait."

"I guess I could do that."

I followed them out onto the deck. We sat in the dark, just the three of us, sipping wine and chatting, listening to the surf rumble on the beach until Jonah arrived.